The God Particle

By Daniel Danser

Published By @ventura eBooks
207 Regent Street, London, W1B 3HH

Third Edition

Copyright © Daniel Danser

The Author asserts the moral right to be identified as the author of this work.

This novel is entirely a work of fiction. Names, characters, businesses, places, events and incidents are either the products of the author's imagination or used in a fictitious manner. Any resemblance to actual persons, living or dead, or actual events is purely coincidental.

All rights reserved. No part of this publication may be reproduced, stored in a retrieval system, or transmitted in any form or by any means, electronic, mechanical, photocopying, recording or otherwise, without prior permission of the author.

This book is sold subject to the condition that it shall not, by way of trade or otherwise, be lent, re-sold, hired out or otherwise circulated without the author's prior consent in any form of binding or cover other than that in which it is published and without a similar condition including this condition being imposed on the subsequent purchaser.

Cover design © Daniel Danser

ISBN 978-1-495-32992-0

For my wife, Paula.

'Lord, grant that my work increases knowledge and helps other men.

Failing that, Lord, grant that it will not lead to man's destruction.'

Percy Walker

PROLOGUE

The Vemork Heavy Water Plant, Nazi occupied Norway, 1942.

The Professor's anxiety manifested itself as a small, involuntary tic above his left eye as he waited in the anteroom to be summoned.

It had been much worse as a child. The constant eye-blinking, mouth twitches and facial grimaces had elicited derision from his classmates and frustration from his parents, who were referred to one physician after another in an attempt to cure his affliction. By the time he'd reached puberty, he was an introverted loner, preferring to study in the seclusion of his bedroom, avoiding any and all social interaction with his peers.

His disorder seemed to lessen by itself as he moved into adulthood, but the years of reclusiveness had taken its toll, making him feel awkward around people his own age. He was much more at ease with his teachers; they were only concerned with his academic ability, which was bordering on genius. He was always the top of his class in every subject, which compounded the alienation he received from his fellow pupils; however, it also gave him a sense of self-worth, an inner resolve to rise above the taunts and jibes, the mimicry and the mockery.

As a young man, he was able to control the twitches almost completely using the techniques taught to him by the psychologists he'd seen over the years. Whenever he felt an attack coming on, he would take a deep breath and think of something that was comforting, a secure place that he created in his mind.

As an adolescent, he would project his mind back to when he was a child and focus on the times his mother would wrap her arms around him. Nestled in the warmth of her bosom, she would gently rock him backwards and forwards, reassuring him that it would be alright. But, when she died, the memory became too painful, feeling only grief whenever he thought of her. It took years of uncontrollable tics before he was able to regain a mental image that worked as successfully. The contentedness he felt through the loving embrace of his wife was a strong enough panacea in all but the most extreme of situations. This was one of them.

He wasn't daunted by the individuals in the next room; he had dealt with their kind for most of his life. They were, quite simply, bullies. They had achieved their status through fear and intimidation, removing any individual that was a threat to their authority by whatever means was available to them. That meant, certainly for two of the people next door, having them arrested on trumped-up charges and shot.

No, his nervousness was for the lie he was about to deliver and whether they would swallow it. His life, the lives of the select number of people whom he had taken into his confidence, and those of millions of others, depended on it.

He had worked at the Vemork Heavy Water Facility since it was re-commissioned by the Nazis following the invasion of Norway in 1940. Prior to that, he'd been Director of the German nuclear energy project Uranprojekt, informally known as the Uranium Club, based in Leipzig, where he met his wife Clara, who was working as a research assistant there. She was the only woman, other than his mother, that had seen the person behind the affliction. She accepted his twitches for what they were. She hadn't reacted the way most people did on first meeting him, embarrassed to make eye contact, but had made light of his involuntary facial tics in a playful way.

'Are you winking at me, Professor?' she had teased. He'd reddened, and started to give her his practised formal explanation of the condition, when she laughed that mischievous laugh of hers, disarming him instantly. A brief courtship ensued and they were married in the following spring.

It had been over two years since he'd last heard that laugh and he missed it, and her, every waking moment. He wrote to her at least once a week but was never allowed to post the letters; such were the restrictions surrounding his top secret research. External contact was limited to fellow academics that could assist him in achieving his goal, and only then if they had been fully vetted by the Gestapo.

'They're ready to see you now, Professor Reinhardt,' the woman dressed in a khaki green knee-length skirt, beige shirt and black tie, said expectantly, holding the door open for him.

He promptly gathered his files together, brushed past her and entered the room. She followed him in, closing the door behind her and took up a seat in front of a typewriter in the far corner.

The room was brightly lit and dominated by a large, polished mahogany table, around which sat his audience dressed in their full ceremonial military regalia uniforms adorned with their medals. It was clearly a display of machismo. He felt decidedly underdressed – a peahen amongst competing peacocks. He recognised most of the faces – some he had met before, others he knew by reputation only. He had been given a list of attendees by his secretary that morning; it read like a who's who of the upper hierarchical tier of the Third Reich.

Reichsmarschall Göring was the most senior of the dignitaries and was, therefore, chairing the meeting at the head of the table. To his right sat Generalfeldmarschall Keitel, Supreme Commander of the Armed Forces and, to his left, was Heinrich Himmler. Reinhardt had never met the man before and wondered whether he was there in his capacity as Minister of the Interior or, more unsettlingly, in his other guise as Reichsführer of the Schutzstaffel, otherwise known as the SS. Sitting next to him was Albert Speer, Minister of Armaments and Munitions and, opposite him, was Philipp Bouhler, Chief of the Chancellery of the Führer.

The final two Reinhart knew well, having worked with both of them before the war. The first was Paul Harteck, director of the physical chemistry department at the University of Hamburg, but today acting as an advisor to the Heereswaffenamt, the Army Ordnance Office. The second was Abraham Esau, head of the physics section of the Reichsforschungsrat, the Reich Research Council. The latter two were obviously invited to verify what Reinhardt was about to deliver. The only person missing was the main man himself. However, as he made his way to the projector, the Professor noticed a hastily-hung picture of Mein Führer looking down at him from the normally bare grey wall.

'I trust we can dispense with the formalities, Professor Reinhardt?' Göring's voice boomed from the far side of the table, filling the room with a rich, baritone resonance.

'Er, yes, by all means,' the Professor replied, nervously pulling the steel-rimmed glasses to the edge of his nose and peering at the bull of a man over the top of them. The beads of perspiration had started to multiply on his forehead as though someone had just switched a shower on. He took out a handkerchief and mopped his brow and ran it over his balding pate. 'Does anybody mind if I open a window? I find it a little stifling in here.'

He was referring to the immense pressure he was under to convince the people around the table to abandon the project, but he knew they would take it as a benign comment about the stuffiness of the room. Nobody objected, so he went over and slid the window up. The cool breeze of a September morning wafted over him, giving him a slight respite and enabling him to clear his mind for the task in hand. He thought of his wife – her hair, her eyes, her mouth, her laugh, her embrace – and hoped he was doing the right thing. If he succeeded, he would feel her arms around him again soon; if he failed, they would probably execute her, along with the rest of his family.

He returned to the projector and faced his inquisitors. 'Gentleman, as you are all aware, this facility was set up with one purpose in mind – to establish the feasibility of using nuclear fission as a weapon against our enemies. I am here today to tell you that it is scientifically possible.'

Excited murmurs went around the table. This was the news they'd flown all the way from Germany to hear.

He ignored the rapacious looks on their faces and pressed on. 'However, the cost and resources required to produce a sufficient quantity of Uranium-235 may prove to be prohibitive. Having said that, my primary concern is for the theoretical proof that a bomb can be produced that has the capability of winning the war for Germany. I do not presume to evaluate the size of the nation's coffers or its willingness to divert those assets into a full-scale production facility, as I will leave that to the financial analysts.' He looked pointedly at Bouhler, who shifted uncomfortably in his seat. That was all he intended to say on the practicalities of manufacturing a device. He thought it would be enough to plant the seed and let the bean counters do what they did best, which was to save money.

Unfortunately for him, Speer had other ideas. 'What makes you think it wouldn't be viable?'

The Professor tried to control the tick above his left eye, which was more pronounced now than it had been for years. His lie was audacious in its simplicity. He had calculated the amount of the radioactive isotope it would take to make a bomb and simply multiplied the figure by a factor of a hundred. So, instead of 65 kilograms of Uranium-235, the conclusion in his research paper stated that it would require at least 6,500 kilograms for a bomb to be effective. He was aware that the newly-developed Heinkel He 177 bomber was capable of delivering such a large payload, but it would have to be modified to carry the ordnance under its fuselage.

The problem he had created wasn't with the logistics of the device, but in the manufacture of the raw materials.

He could feel the perspiration soaking into his shirt beneath his brown plaid waistcoat and jacket. 'As you may or may not be aware,' he continued, 'Uranium is an element that occurs naturally in low concentrations in certain rocks, predominantly pitchblende – or, to give it its geological name, uraninite.' He directed his comments to the non-scientists in the room. 'We currently have a mine in Joachimsthal, near the Czech border, that is capable of processing over ten thousand tonnes of ore each year, out of which we are able to harvest approximately ten thousand kilograms of pure Uranium. Unfortunately for us, the radioactive isotope that we require, Uranium-235, makes up less than one per cent of the chemical composition of Uranium. Therefore, with our current production capabilities, we are only able to produce approximately one hundred tonnes per annum of the radioactive isotope we need. It doesn't take a mathematician to work out that, at the current rate, it would take us sixty-five years to produce enough fissionable material to make a bomb, during which time we would have won the war by more conventional means.'

He paused to let the information sink in, before continuing. 'Our only option is to expand the facility at Joachimsthal to increase capacity, or source a new supply of Uranium from elsewhere.'

'And where do you suggest we source it from?' asked Himmler, his tone far from cordial.

'I understand the Russians have been stockpiling it as a by-product of their radium production, which they use in luminescent paint,' he responded, trying not to sound intimidated.

'I don't think they're just going to hand it over to us,' Himmler grumbled. He turned to face Keitel, who was sitting opposite him. 'And how is the war progressing on the Eastern Front, Generalfeldmarschall?'

He enunciated Keitel's official title with undisguised animosity. There was no love lost between these two senior officials. Himmler regarded Keitel as a spineless sycophant, nicknaming him 'Lakeitel', a pun on his name, meaning 'lackey'. Keitel had seen the atrocities that Himmler had ordered first-hand whilst in the field and regarded him as a monster. He would never admit to it, but he was actually terrified of the man.

He flushed at being put in the spotlight. 'We have launched an offensive on Stalingrad and are confident of a glorious victory for the Fatherland.'

'That just leaves the rest of Russia then,' Himmler said sarcastically under his breath, but loud enough for the rest of the table to hear. He turned his attention back to the Professor. 'Assuming we don't get the resources we require from our enemies, how long will it take to get Joachimsthal up to the capacity we need?'

'As I alluded to earlier,' replied the Professor, 'That is not in my remit. But what I will say is that, if we commit to producing an effective weapon, we would need to increase the output at Joachimsthal substantially. It would require a significant amount of manpower to build a large enough plant to produce the Uranium required, as well as a separate facility for the manufacture of the bombs.'

'We could always use the Jews,' Himmler sniggered. A few people around the table followed suit, but Reinhardt wasn't one of them.

'We could if you hadn't exterminated them all!' Keitel's impetuous remark brought the joviality to an abrupt halt, leaving a pregnant silence in the room as all eyes turned on him. His facial hue deepened further to a bright crimson colour as he realised he may have just overstepped the mark. 'What I meant was, er… we could use the Russian prisoners of war. They're in a much better physical condition than the Jews and are used to manual labour.'

His backtracking seemed to diffuse the awkwardness in the room and even elicited a nod from Göring.

'Okay, Gentlemen,' he said. 'I think I have all the information I need to take back to Mein Führer. From what I understand from Professor Reinhardt, it is theoretically possible to make a nuclear bomb, but we would have to expand our production facilities accordingly. We have the man-power to achieve this, but we would still need to reassign valuable resources away from the frontline in order to realise our objective. Am I missing anything?'

The question from Göring was thrown out to the table. A resolute shaking of heads was his reply. 'In that case, gentlemen, I'd like to thank you for your time and wish you all a good day.' He got up from his chair, stood to attention and saluted the picture on the far wall. 'Heil Hitler!' Everybody in the room followed his lead, but only one man was holding his breath.

CHAPTER 1

The alarm sounded in Reactor 5, as it had done dozens of times before. However, only one person heard it this time and he knew it wasn't a drill.

It had been over twenty-six hours since Katashi's shift had started and he had only managed to grab a thirty-minute nap during that time. He was exhausted but, fuelled by adrenalin and caffeine, he was still able to focus on the job in hand.

The initial shockwave had wiped out the power supply to the reactors, causing them to shut down immediately. Without power, the reactors would overheat, causing a meltdown. The backup diesel generators had kicked in, as they were programmed to do in such an event, pumping around thousands of gallons of water to cool the residual heat in the reactors. As long as the pumps maintained the flow, the fuel rods would cool down over several hours, making them safe.

Unfortunately, the tsunami had put paid to that idea. An hour after the initial seismic tremor, the twenty-foot wave had breached the compound's outer walls and flooded the diesel generators.

***

Katashi Negano was in charge of the Containment of Hazardous Materials Team (CHMT) based on-site at the Fukushima Daiichi power plant. His father had worked at the plant from when it had first been commissioned in 1971, but had to give up work through ill health. He now lived with his wife, Hikari, and their four-year-old daughter, Kimiko, in the coastal town of Soma. Katashi's mother had died when he was still a child, but he'd had an abundance of aunties to supplement his upbringing by his father.

He joined the Fukushima Power Corporation after graduating from Kyoto University with a master's degree in nuclear engineering. Because of his imperturbable, analytical nature, Katashi progressed rapidly through the company and joined the CHMT as second-in-command, being promoted to team leader three years later, when his superior retired. He was trained to deal with all conceivable man-made and natural disasters; unfortunately, the magnitude of the earthquake that hit the plant, and subsequent tsunami which followed, were outside the conceivable boundaries that the safety systems were designed for.

The initial earthquake siren instigated the deployment of the six-man CHMT, whose first task was to evacuate all nonessential personnel from the plant. Roll calls were taken and employees were loaded onto waiting coaches, to be ferried to the designated 'safe' town of Yonezawa, some thirty miles away, which was protected from the plant by the mountain range of Nishi Agatsuma.

Katashi had been through these measures several times before, but only as a training exercise. It wasn't exactly routine to him, but the constant enactments of 'what if' scenarios had ingrained the procedures into his, and his team's, psyche. He was regarded as a firm but fair taskmaster, practising emergency drills over and over again, until each member of his team knew their role and what was expected of them.

Whilst the evacuees were being boarded, Katashi and a three-man detail donned white, all-in-one protective suits with full head visors and breathing equipment, and went to ascertain what damage had been sustained to the three operational reactors. Luckily, only two days before, reactors 2, 4 and 6 had been closed down for routine maintenance. He would have had a communiqué from the control room if there had been a problem, but it was in his nature to check and double-check.

They arrived at the first reactor building, a forty-foot high, pre-fabricated construction made entirely of corrugated iron sheets.

The surprisingly flimsy structure was originally designed simply to keep the weather out and would offer no protection from anything generated during a nuclear reaction. Inside the building, the reactor core itself was encased in a thick steel vessel, capable of withstanding high pressures. This, in turn, was housed in a hermetically-sealed concrete and steel structure, known as the containment chamber.

After a thorough inspection of the outside of the building, Katashi was satisfied that there had been no external damage during the earthquake, probably due to the flexibility of the materials it was made from.

'All clear, we're going in!' Katashi gestured to the small door at the side of the building. Putting on his mask and breathing equipment, he led the team through the entrance.

The reactor building itself had no windows and was wholly lit by florescent tubes. The air smelt of diesel from the generators, which were producing the power to perform the crucial task of pumping water, through a series of pipes in the reactor core, to cool it down.

The noise generated by the massive turbines made communicating in such a confined area very difficult. In front of them was the containment chamber itself, a massive conical structure, with walls over six feet in depth, resembling a giant white beehive. The only way in was through a two-foot thick, lead-lined steel door.

Tamotsu, the youngest member of the CHMT, held a Geiger counter out in front of him. Katashi had a soft spot for Tamotsu; he reminded him of himself. He had only been with the company six months, but he was eager to learn. Qualified in Engineering Science, this was his first job since leaving university and he was keen to make an impression. Unlike Katashi, who had spent time in every department on the plant learning the ropes, Tamotsu had applied directly to fill the vacant position that became available when Katashi was promoted. His psychometric and aptitude tests weren't that outstanding, but it was down to Katashi to decide who he wanted in his team and, after interviewing Tamotsu for several hours, he had made up his mind. Tamotsu had the one crucial trait needed in this role: a cool head.

As Tamotsu surveyed the area around the outer building for radiation leaks, the others inspected the external surfaces of the containment chamber with flashlights for any damage.

'No sign of any radiation leaks, so far,' Tamotsu shouted to his superior.

The visibility in their masks was limited; not having full peripheral vision meant they had to turn their whole bodies in the direction they wanted to see, which slowed them down. Katashi was aware they had another two reactors to inspect after this one, but he wasn't prepared to cut corners; the slightest crack in any of the walls of the containment chamber could spell disaster, not just for the people in the plant, but for miles around.

With a series of hand gestures and nods, Katashi indicated that the inspection of the outer area was complete and that he and Tamotsu should go through the reinforced door to inspect the containment chamber, whilst the other two waited outside. He walked up the few steps to the entrance and placed his chin on the shelf, just below the retinal scanner. Staring down the lens he heard a hiss as the heavy door parted a fraction, breaking the seal between the purified air of the chamber and the polluted air outside.

Tamotsu, who had followed Katashi up the steps, was the first into the chamber. The door opened with surprising ease, given its size and weight. Inside, the chamber was brightly-lit and clinically white. A panel on the side wall indicated the status, temperature, pressure and output capacity of the reactor, through a series of green, amber and red lights. At that moment, it indicated that the core was in shut-down mode, but the temperature and pressure were still about half of its normal operating levels.

Tamotsu panned the room with his Geiger counter, but again it did not register any radiation, other than the small amount expected as a background reading, which was no more than an X-ray would deliver in a hospital. The steel-encased core had withstood one of the most violent earthquakes in Japan's history. Theoretically, the buildings were constructed to withstand twice the magnitude of the quake they had just experienced, a phenomena that, to date, had never occurred.

'All clear in reactor one. No signs of damage.' Katashi relayed the message to the control room via his walkie-talkie. 'Moving on to reactor three.' With that, he led Tamotsu out of the chamber, closing the heavy door behind them, to meet up with the other two members of the team who were waiting outside.

As Katashi stepped out into the open air, he was immediately struck by an eerie stillness. His first thought was that the loudness of the generators had dulled his hearing; however, as he strained, he could hear a low rumble in the distance, that grew louder and louder.

Thinking it was the aftershocks from the initial earthquake, he ordered his men out into the open, away from the building and any possible falling debris. As he turned, he could feel the air being sucked from around him; he had to brace himself against the unseen force for fear of it pulling him along, too.

And then he saw it. A huge wall of water came crashing into the compound, carrying with it remnants from its destructive path: uprooted trees and telegraph poles bobbed along like matchsticks down a storm drain; cars being driven remotely, turning, reversing and crashing into each other, like some macabre funfair ride; sections of houses, roofs, windows, doors and porches, all being swept along, incessantly, by millions of gallons of water. The perimeter of the compound offered no resistance to the sheer power of the wave, its walls dissolving instantly, like chalk, into the murky depths of the tsunami.

With no time to act, Takashi steeled himself for the inevitable. The second before the wave hit him, he sucked in a lungful of air from his respirator and held his breath. However, nothing could have prepared him for the solid mass of water that engulfed him, knocking him off his feet and tumbling him over and over. His only thought was to swim upwards, out of the maelstrom and ride with the wave; he knew it would be pointless to swim against the tide. He was so disoriented, and the visibility was so limited, that he couldn't work out which direction he was facing. As he was being carried along, at an incredible rate of knots, he could see shadows, but couldn't make out what objects they were.

For an instant, he thought he could see daylight and kicked as hard as he could towards the light, his protective suit giving him added buoyancy. He broke the surface, narrowly missing an upturned car which floated past just inches from his face, before being dragged back down by the undercurrent. He kicked out for the surface again, this time managing to grab hold of a thin branch which, fortunately, was still attached to a floating tree. He hauled himself up onto the trunk, exhausted. All he could do now was hope and pray.

CHAPTER 2

Over six thousand miles away, wearing an almost identical protective suit, Professor Erik Morantz finished inspecting the thermal shields in Atlas, one of four particle detectors equispaced around CERN's Large Hadron Collider (LHC).

This was the first time the collider had been fired up in over a year and everybody was, justifiably, on edge. During that occasion, a catastrophe was narrowly averted by the quick-thinking actions of one of the maintenance crew, who noticed a build-up of condensation around a pipe leading to one of the helium coolant tanks which supplied the heat shields. He quickly deduced that the only way this could happen would be if the supercooled helium was escaping. He raised the alarm and the collider was immediately shut down. If the leak had gone undetected, the gigantic magnetic coils at the heart of the collider would have overheated, endangering the lives of the two thousand people working there.

'The heat shields are working fine,' Professor Morantz spoke into the microphone in his helmet. 'Increase the power to seventy per cent capacity.'

Normally, Professor Erik Morantz would be directing operations from his office, in the control centre, but this time he was taking a personal interest. The publicity surrounding the numerous breakdowns of the collider was jeopardising his position as Director General and he couldn't afford to have another failure on his hands so soon after the last one.

'They're holding. Increase power to maximum.' He could tell by the computerised console on the side of Atlas that the thermal shields were functioning correctly. 'Okay, release the proton beams.'

The two beams were positioned in opposite directions around the 27-kilometre circular tunnel, which made up the particle accelerator. The theory was that the protons would increase speed as they passed through a series of superconducting radio frequency (RF) cavities, located around the tunnel. Just like pushing a child's swing, these RF cavities would give the particles a push each time they passed, steadily increasing the energy of the particles, until they reached the speed of light. The aftermath of the particles collision would be recorded by Atlas, or one of the other three detectors.

'How long do you want us to run the experiment for, Professor?' The voice of Deiter Weiss, Professor Morantz's second-in-command, came through his headset.

'Give it another fifteen minutes and then reduce power to fifty per cent,' Morantz responded. 'I'm on my way back to the control room now.'

He climbed into the white golf buggy, which was the preferred mode of transport in the tunnels, the alternatives being bicycles or walk. It would take him fifteen minutes to cover the three-mile journey back to the control room, through the service tunnels that ran parallel to the collider; enough time to contemplate his position at CERN.

He was one of the original founding members and had joined the project to identify the God particle when it was first conceived in 1984, at a symposium in Lausanne, Switzerland. It took a further ten years of lobbying to convince CERN that the Large Hadron Collider was a viable project; however, with the support of twenty countries, they finally gave their approval for the construction.

For the next fourteen years, Professor Morantz worked alongside architects, civil engineers, scientists, accountants and pen-pushers, to build the world's largest machine. Officially, he was employed by the Department of Quantum Physics at CERN, but he reported directly to the governing council. When it was time to choose a Director General to oversee all experiments associated with the LHC, there really was only one candidate. Morantz had lived and breathed what he referred to as 'The Creator' for practically a third of his life, shunning any and all social or family commitments, in the pursuit of knowledge. The knowledge consisted of one thing: the definitive proof that the God particle – or, to give it its scientific name, the Higgs boson – existed.

It wasn't that he hadn't had his fair share of female admirers when he was younger. Now in his early sixties, his portly stature had only developed over the last few years; prior to that, he'd had a lean and compact frame, which he was lucky enough not to have had to work at maintaining. The numerous times he had laboured through the night, on projects that had so engrossed him, that he'd lost all track of time, were now showing as deep furrows across his forehead. The copious hours of studying in dimly-lit rooms had etched lines around his eyes. His once full head of wavy black hair was now wispy, unkempt and silver-grey. But the one feature that hadn't changed over time, and was responsible for attracting so much female attention as a young man, was his piercing blue eyes. They were as bright and sparkly as they had ever been.

He arrived at the control room entrance, still debating as to whether he should step down from the project and let someone else take the helm. He wasn't getting any younger, and the amount of pressure he was under from the council, because of the negative publicity surrounding the previous breakdowns, was making him reconsider whether the role of Director General was right for him.

He was a scientist, not a politician, which invariably accounted for the abrasive relationship he had with the press. Whenever they asked him a direct question regarding the collider's lack of performance, he would tell them, honestly, that he didn't know why these failures were occurring, but he would look into it and report back to them when he had conclusive evidence.

Unfortunately, this never happened; the breakdowns seemed unrelated and random, isolated incidences of leaks, power surges and malfunctions.

If he were more politically-minded, like Deiter, he would have been able to put a more positive spin on the situation at the press conferences. 'Yes, everything's under control. These are minor setbacks, and we are making giant strides forward into new scientific frontiers.' But that just wasn't in his nature.

Deiter, on the other hand, was a totally different scientific animal. He was about ten years younger than Morantz. He hadn't really taken the time to get to know the man. In fact, he didn't actually care much for Deiter. He had been appointed at the same time as Morantz, by the council, and was everything that his boss wasn't. He was articulate and charismatic, self-assured to the point of arrogant, and meticulously groomed, from his tightly-cropped salt and pepper hair to his manicured fingernails. He wore silver-rimmed spectacles that gave him a scholarly look. He spoke English with a clipped German accent. He was very much the archetypal corporate scientist, the one seen espousing the virtues of a newly-formulated ingredient in a shampoo commercial.

Perhaps this is what the project needed, mused Morantz, somebody like Deiter to head it up. But, then again, Deiter lacked the passion, commitment and dedication that Morantz brought to the role. No, he concluded, Deiter was far too superficial and self-serving to carry the mantle of such a momentous chapter in scientific history forward to the next level. He would continue as Director General, but appoint Deiter as his spokesperson; that way, he could concentrate on what he considered to be the all-important task of finding the God particle and let Deiter deal with the minor distractions of the press.

He swiped his security card in the card reader on the wall and the door to the control room slid open.

'Any issues?' shouted Morantz, to nobody in particular, as he took off his protective suit.

'We're still checking the data from Atlas, but at the moment everything seems normal.' It was Serena Mayer that was the first to respond. Serena had been on the team for just over a year and was responsible for analysing the output from the four particle detectors.

'Great! Deiter, can you organise a press conference? It's about time we gave them some good news.'

'OK. Do you want to do it on-site or in town?' Deiter queried.

'Neither. I want you to take this one. I'm always delivering bad news, so I think it would be good for the project to have a new spokesperson.'

Deiter looked surprised, but pleased. 'Of course, I'll organise it immediately.' With that, he picked up the phone and dialled the switchboard.

'Put me through to the science desk at CNN.'

The operator keyed in the request on her computer and was instantly connected to the switchboard at CNN. However, instead of the polite American operative she usually spoke to, asking which extension she required, the operator received a busy signal. She tried again, with the same result.

'I'm sorry, but I'm getting an engaged tone. Do you want me to keep trying?'

'No. Try the BBC,' Deiter replied.

This time she got through to the main switchboard. 'Hi, I have a call from the research facility at CERN for the science editor. Can you put me through, please?'

'I'm afraid I have several calls holding. Can you phone back later?' came a clipped response from the BBC receptionist.

The operator disconnected the call without answering. 'The BBC seems to be very busy, also. Is there anybody else you would like me to try?'

Puzzled, Dieter asked to be put through to the local news station.

'Hello, I have a Dr Weiss, from CERN, on the line,' said the operator. 'Can you put me through to the producer, please?'

'Hold the line please. I'll try to connect you.' There was a short pause, and then a different voice spoke.

'Hello, Peter Lintz here. Thank you for returning my call.'

'I think there's been a misunderstanding,' Deiter replied. 'I'm not returning your call. I'm trying to organise a press conference.'

'Oh, I thought you were calling to give CERN's reaction to the earthquake?' Lintz responded.

'What earthquake?' Deiter queried.

'The one off the coast of Japan, measuring 8.9 on the Richter scale. Have you not seen the news?'

Deiter put the phone down.

'What's the problem?' Morantz asked.

'Apparently, there's been a massive earthquake off the coast of Japan,' Deiter replied. 'Can somebody switch the news on?'

The television screens around the control room blinked and then came to life. Helicopter images of the devastation caused by the tsunami were being commentated on by a news anchorman in the studio.

'We still don't have a clear picture of the devastation caused by either the earthquake or the tsunami. From what we gather, the earthquake, which measured almost nine on the Richter scale, set off a tsunami, which hit the northeast shoreline of Japan, at three o'clock in the afternoon, local time. Officials say six hundred and fifty people are dead and about fifteen hundred missing, but it is feared the final death toll will be much higher.'

Morantz shot Deiter an angry glance. 'Give the order to shut down immediately and then I want to see you in my office!'

Deiter joined Morantz in his office a few minutes later, closing the door behind him.

'It's just a coincidence,' Deiter was the first to speak.

'That's what you said the last time,' Morantz countered.

'It's Japan, they get earthquakes all the time.'

'Yes, but not on this scale,' Morantz said solemnly. 'I can't take the risk. What if it's not a coincidence? What if the collider is causing these disasters? I have to let the Council know immediately and let them decide what to do.'

Serena Mayer watched the television screen intently as the cameraman in the helicopter panned the devastated landscape. The news anchorman in the studio was now discussing the impact of the earthquake on the nuclear power plant at Fukushima, with a so-called 'expert on these matters'.

'What are the consequences if the nuclear reactors go into meltdown?' the anchorman asked the expert.

'Well, if we look at what happened at Chernobyl, for example,' replied the expert, 'an entire reactor exploded, sending up a massive fireball and radioactive plume that dispersed radiation over a wide area. People living near Chernobyl were killed instantly; but, as the radioactive cloud spread, several thousand more died within a few weeks from radiation poisoning. Over the long-term, tens of thousands more people were put at risk from cancer.'

'Are you saying that we could be witnessing a disaster of this magnitude?' the anchorman spoke slowly for dramatic effect.

'We can only base our conclusions on what has happened historically...'

Serena's attention switched from the television screen to Morantz's office, in the corner of the control room. She could see, through the window, the animated figure of Professor Morantz as he stood inches from Dr Weiss, waving his arms. She knew there was no love lost between these two, but they rarely argued and certainly never with this much ardour. Even though the door was closed and the voices muffled, if she strained her hearing she could make out snippets of the conversation between the two men.

'...I can't let you... responsibility... wait for another...' was all she managed to decipher from what Deiter was saying.

'...it's too late... can't stop me... this afternoon...' was what she picked out from Morantz's response.

'...never... you have no idea what... it's bigger than...' came Deiter's reply.

Suddenly, the office door flew open and out stormed Deiter. He strode across the control room, head down, hands buried in the pockets of his white lab coat, and stormed out.

Serena cautiously approached the open door of Morantz's office. The professor was now sitting behind his desk, his head in his hands, staring down at the phone.

'Can I help at all?' Serena timidly enquired.

Startled, Morantz looked up and then visibly relaxed as he recognised the stealth-like figure of his assistant, framed in the doorway.

'Thank you, Serena, but I must do this myself. Did you get any anomalies from the data you extracted from the detectors?'

'No, Professor. Everything seemed normal,' Serena replied.

'There is one thing you can do for me. Can you pull up the electromagnetic data readings before, during and after the experiment? I'm particularly interested in any surges or peaks that may have occurred, when the collider was at full operational capacity.'

'Certainly, Professor. I'll get onto it straight away.'

CHAPTER 3

Katashi's prayers were answered by way of an electricity pylon and a red Toyota Corolla. The pylon was at the far end of the compound; its three legs had buckled under the weight of the flotsam that had gathered around its base, but it was still holding its own. The tree, on which Katashi was clinging, snagged one of the legs. The Toyota, which was floating behind, hammered home the branches and the tree held firm against the rushing tide. Katashi shivered uncontrollably as he saw the lifeless, bloated face of an older man staring blankly at him through the windscreen. He looked away.

Now stationary, he relaxed enough to survey his surroundings. He took off his mask and breathing equipment to get a better view. The entire compound was flooded. Buildings were submerged up to their first floors and some of the flimsier structures had sustained considerable damage. The portacabins, which were being used as a temporary canteen whilst the main restaurant was being refurbished, had disappeared under the water altogether. One of the coaches ferrying personnel to safety was floating upside down, with only the air in its tyres stopping it from completely sinking.

Katashi could now make out the bodies of some of his colleagues, bobbing along with the rest of the debris. Selfishly, he scoured the area for any of his own team who may have perished, clearly identifiable by their white protective overalls; he didn't recognise anybody he knew and gave a sigh of relief, then instantly felt guilty for not mourning the loss of his other co-workers.

The tsunami hadn't destroyed the entire perimeter wall, at least not in this part of the compound, but it had washed away a section of about twenty feet, through which water gushed, carrying with it everything that the tidal surge had managed to scoop up, tear down or break apart. Occasionally, a large object would bridge the gap, creating a temporary dam, as smaller items built up behind; however, the force of the flow was too strong and a breach would inevitably occur, crushing the obstructions to pulp.

The Toyota, which had been so crucial in securing Katashi's vantage point, freed itself from the tree, spinning off in the direction of the waterfall. Katashi was relieved to be free from the horror of its grey-faced passenger. However, this relief was short-lived; he could feel the trunk beneath him shift, as the current tried to dislodge him from the pylon. One by one, the branches anchoring him to the steel structure bent, then snapped, until finally it was impossible for it to maintain its hold and it, too, broke free.

Katashi could see the roof of the Toyota some two hundred yards in front of him; somehow it was managing to stay afloat. As it neared the gap in the wall, it was joined by a small capsized boat, several trees and a slick of wooden planks, branches and household debris. The car slammed into the boat and they fused into one. Without faltering, they carried on their journey together.

The hole in the wall was now partially blocked by the thick branches of one of the larger trees. Smaller items were being washed through, unimpeded, but larger items were being sifted out, adding to what was fast becoming a mega-dam.

The car-boat careered into the wall, just to the left of the hole, with such force that Katashi was convinced it would punch its way through; but instead, the boat shattered, as if it were made of glass, breaking up into a thousand pieces, which were then dutifully carried through to the other side by the tidal flow.

As Katashi neared the blockade, he could hear the crushing of metal as the Toyota was being squeezed through an ever-decreasing gap between the wall and the branches of the tree. He searched frantically for somewhere to escape to, but there was nowhere. He knew, if he tried to swim for safety, the current would pull him back into the carnage. He closed his eyes and braced himself for the impact.

Several seconds passed, but there was no collision. Curious, he opened his eyes. The screeching noise, caused by the car scraping against the wall, had stopped abruptly. He expected to see the car to have either disappeared through the gap in the wall, or to have sunk; but as his eyes adjusted to the light, he could tell that neither had happened. The car, in fact, seemed to be coming towards him, the hideous apparition of the perished soul clearer than ever. Katashi looked around him and saw that all the wreckage had either slowed down, stopped or gone into reverse, depending on its momentum. The surge was receding.

He dived off his makeshift raft and swam, with astounding strength, towards the control room, which was located in the centre of the compound. By the time he reached the building, he was able to touch the floor on tiptoes. Brushing aside the branches and twigs that had collected around the door, he made his way inside and up the stairs.

'Katashi! You alright?' It was Masumi Makoto, head of operations and Katashi's boss. He looked up from the bank of monitors and gauges he was studying.

'I'm fine, but I'm not sure where the rest of my team is,' Katashi responded. 'Have you heard from any of them?'

'No, not since the tsunami hit.'

'What exactly happened?' Katashi queried.

'We're not a hundred per cent sure at the moment,' Masumi replied. 'But, what we can gather from news reports, is that the earthquake triggered a massive tsunami, which hit the northeast, deluging all towns along the coast and then sweeping inland.'

'Which towns were affected the most?' Katashi asked.

'As far as we can tell, Sendai and Soma took the brunt of the force. It's reported that most homes have been destroyed with estimated casualties...' Masumi checked himself, as he realised that Katashi's family lived in the area.

'I'm sorry,' said Masumi, resting his hand on Katashi's shoulder. 'You must be worried sick about your family. All landlines are down in the area, but you can try them on my satellite phone,' and he handed his phone over to Katashi.

Katashi sat down at one of the vacant desks and tapped in his wife's cell number. His heart skipped a beat as a fuzzy connection was made. Thankfully, he thought, they're safe. But his exhilaration turned to disappointment as the voicemail kicked in after the obligatory ten rings. He left a message for her to ring him back, trying to keep his voice as level as possible, but his anxiety was showing through.

He handed the phone back to Masumi.

'Let me know if my wife calls.'

'Of course,' Masumi replied.

'What's the situation here?' Katashi asked.

'Not good, I'm afraid,' replied Masumi, gravely. 'The surge knocked out the diesel generators and the core temperatures are rising. It's not critical at the moment, but if we don't get them back on-line quickly, it will be.'

'Ok. I'll round up the rest of my team and we'll see if we can get them started.' With that, Katashi left the control room and headed for Reactor 1, where he had last seen his team. By the time he had got back downstairs, the waterline had receded to waist height.

He thought it ironic that there was not a cloud in the sky, yet the place was flooded. He waded through the silt-laden water, but it was difficult to avoid the hidden rubble that had been deposited on the compound's floor. Twice he tripped on some unseen obstacle, falling face first, arms outstretched to break his fall.

He reached the reactor building to find two out of the three-man team waiting for him there.

'Where's Tamotsu?' Katashi enquired.

'We thought he was with you,' they replied, almost in unison.

Katashi recalled the last time he had seen Tamotsu. 'Have you checked inside?'

Katashi didn't wait for a reply, but instead headed for the closed door. With trepidation, he turned the handle and yanked as hard as he could, dislodging the sludge that had built up around the base of the door. It opened with some reluctance, revealing a pitch-black interior. The absence of noise from the diesel generators gave the room an empty presence.

Turning on his flashlight, Katashi entered and swept the beam around the building. Apart from the two feet of water he was standing in, there didn't appear to be much damage. He trained the light on what he first thought was a pile of rubble, halfway up the stairs; however, as he moved closer, he realised it was the crumpled body of Tamotsu. He knew straight away that he was dead; his head was turned at an impossible angle to his body, his eyes gazing, blankly, over his right shoulder. The force of the wave must have knocked him back into the building, breaking his neck instantly. It was a harrowing sight and, for a moment, Katashi felt the acid in the pit of his stomach lurch. He concentrated with all his might on not heaving.

The other two team members were now at Katashi's side, snapping him back to reality. They stood there a while in silence, staring down at their colleague's limp remains.

'At least he didn't suffer,' Katashi murmured in consolation, more to comfort himself than the others.

His body then stiffened. 'We've got a job to do, otherwise Tamotsu won't be the last casualty. We need to restore power to the cooling pumps before we have a total meltdown on our hands.' He looked around at his colleagues. 'You two, take Tamotsu's body into the containment chamber,' he ordered. 'We'll pay our respects later, when we have more time!' Then he turned and waded across the room to the generators.

The enormous Lister diesel engines, which were the powerhouse of the generated backup electricity supply, sat in twelve inches of water; however, Katashi could tell, by the distinct tidemark on the wall, that they must have been fully submersed at some point. He knew it would be futile, but he tried to restart the engines anyway, using the automatic ignition.

He pressed the red button and the turbines churned over, spluttered, and then died. He tried again, several times, but to no avail; saltwater had obviously got into the system. He knew he would have to strip the engines down, dry the individual parts, and reassemble them. But that would take time, and time was something the Fukushima power plant was fast running out of.

The only hope they had was to use the 'third-line' backup power, whilst Katashi worked to fix the diesel generators. The third-line backup supply was a bank of fifty batteries, in principle much the same as a standard car battery, except much larger and far more powerful. These were located in the containment chamber to protect them from the weather.

'Switch over to the battery backup!' Katashi shouted up to his two colleagues.

Within seconds, the huge pumps began to whir into action. It was now a race against time to get the diesel engines working, before the batteries exhausted themselves.

***

It had taken twelve hours to get the generators in Reactor 1 back on the grid, while those in Reactor 3 had only taken him just over eight; he'd worked quickly with knowledge gained from the previous one. Both reactors' cores were now cooling down as they were designed to do.

Unfortunately, this wasn't the case in Reactor 5; the core temperature was rising to a critical level. Unless power to the pumps was restored, the temperature of the fuel rods would continue to rise until they melted, pooling at the bottom of the reactor vessel. It would then just be a matter of time before the pressure built up to such an extent that the containment chamber would explode, creating an atomic shockwave, four hundred times more powerful than the bomb dropped on Hiroshima.

The backup batteries powering the pumps had run out two hours previously, at which point Katashi had ordered the rest of his team and the skeleton staff left behind to operate the plant, to evacuate. Nobody had argued.

The welfare of his family played heavily on Katashi's mind, despite his efforts to block everything out in order to concentrate on completing the task as quickly as possible. Just before he left the plant, Masumi had informed him that he still hadn't heard from his family. Images of his dead protégé, Tamotsu, mingled with pictures of his family, flooded into his subconscious. He knew Hikari had the commonsense to get to higher ground; it was just whether she had the time to pack his father in the car and collect his daughter from school, before the tsunami struck. There was nothing he could do about it while he was still in the power plant, so the sooner he could get the generators started the sooner he would be reunited with his family.

He had already managed to disassemble the generators, had dried each component and was in the process of reassembling them, when he heard the alarm. Meltdown was imminent. There was just no way of knowing exactly how long he had left. Theoretical scenarios could predict the system's anticipated breaking point but, in reality, there were too many factors that could affect the outcome.

His clothes under his protective overalls were wet through, his hair was matted to his scalp and beads of sweat formed on his top lip, but he reasoned that every second counted. As long as his protective suit didn't impede him, then he could put up with the discomfort rather than taking the time to strip off.

A loud bang, followed by a hiss of steam, made him jump and he dropped his wrench into the water, beneath the generators. Fumbling around on the floor, his hands sieved through the layers of silt, trying desperately to locate the tool. He adjusted his position so he could reach further under the generators. His fingertips nudged something hard. He stretched his hand out as far as he could and felt the cold steel of the spanner.

That was the last thing he ever felt. Katashi wouldn't have felt the shockwave of the nuclear blast as it ripped open the reactor. He wouldn't have felt his protective clothing evaporate in an instant, as the expanding fireball, three times hotter than the Sun's surface, burst through the containment chamber. He wouldn't have seen the flash of light, so intense that it melted his eyeballs. And he wouldn't have felt his blood boil and his body vaporise, leaving only his shadow etched on the wall, before it too disintegrated into shrapnel, as the shockwave continued its lethally destructive path.

CHAPTER 4

'Okay, who can tell me how we calculate the interaction between charged particles, in quantum electrodynamics?' Tom Halligan stared at each one of the twenty-two blank faces that stared back at him in turn. He may as well have just asked the question in Cantonese. The reaction would have been the same, he thought.

'Anybody?' he encouraged.

A pimply adolescent, who was wearing a cardigan that looked as though it had been knitted by his grandmother, raised his hand hesitantly. 'Is it Einstein's theory of relativity?'

Halligan exhaled slowly, looking down at his feet. He raised his head and addressed the class in general.

'Has anybody heard of Halligan's theory?' The same blank expressions. 'Halligan's theory states that, if you use that specific answer every time somebody asks you a question, one day it will be the right answer. Unfortunately, today isn't that day.'

Smirks appeared on all the blank faces, apart from the pimply adolescent's, who blushed with embarrassment.

'The answer this time, my friends, is Feynman Diagrams.' The bell rang signalling the end of class. Halligan had to shout over the top of it to make himself heard. 'Which is what I want you to write an essay on, as part of tonight's homework assignment. Two thousand words, on my desk, the day after tomorrow.'

With that, the class filtered out of the door, leaving Tom Halligan to pack his notes and stationery into his battered, brown, leather briefcase.

He looked up, expecting to see an empty classroom, but instead was rather surprised to see an elderly gentleman sitting on the back row.

'Hello, can I help you? I take it you're not one of my undergraduates?'

'No, Professor Halligan, and I'm sorry if I startled you,' replied the older man. 'My name is Frederick Volker. I am President of the CERN Council.'

Tom recognised the name, but had never met the man in person.

'And to what do I owe this honour?' Tom queried.

Frederick rose, rather slowly, from his seat at the back of the auditorium and made his way, cautiously, down the stairs to where Tom was standing.

'The honour is all mine, I assure you, Professor Halligan,' Frederick said warmly, grasping Tom's hand and shaking it effusively. 'I have been following your career rather closely.'

The man reminded Tom of his favourite grandfather. His hands were soft, but his grip was firm. His round face was framed by neatly-trimmed hair and beard that were alabaster white. When he smiled, his whole face lit up and his eyes changed colour from sea-green to azure blue. His tall, slender figure had a slight stoop, yet he looked the reverse of feeble. He was dressed immaculately, in a three-piece tweed suit that had obviously been designed by one of the leading fashion houses. His shoes were of the finest Italian leather, his shirt Savile Row. Frederick Volker certainly had expensive tastes when it came to couture, Tom mused.

'Is there somewhere a little more private we could go?' Frederick enquired.

'Of course,' Tom replied. 'If you'd like to follow me.' With that, Tom picked up his briefcase and led the elderly gentleman out of the room and down the corridor to his office.

As an Institute Professor, he was entitled to a corner office, which afforded windows on two sides and was larger than the normal faculty offices. The position of Institute Professor was the highest possible honour that could be awarded by the Massachusetts Institute of Technology (MIT) and it put Tom in a group of elite academics, who had 'Demonstrated exceptional distinction by a combination of leadership, accomplishment and service in the scholarly, educational and general intellectual life of the Institute or wider academic community,' according to MIT's policy manual. In reality, Tom had been rewarded for what he enjoyed doing the most, namely teaching and research.

'Please, take a seat,' said Tom gesturing to one of the high-backed leather Chesterfields.

'Thank you, Professor Halligan,' said Frederick, lowering himself into the sumptuous armchair.

'Please, call me Tom.'

'Thank you, and you must call me Frederick. By the way, Charles Brannigan sends his regards.'

'You know Charles?'

Charles had been Tom's mentor at the Brookhaven National Laboratory, on Long Island, New York when he was doing his dissertation there. At the time, it was the location of the world's largest collider before being superseded by the one at CERN.

'Yes, we bump into each other now and again, conferences, seminars, that sort of thing,' Frederick replied, vaguely.

Tom wondered what could have instigated a conversation between these two eminent figures that involved him, but decided not to say anything.

With the pleasantries out of the way, Tom was becoming anxious to know what had brought this distinguished gentleman all the way to New England, in person, to see him.

'So, what can I do for you, Frederick?'

'I'll get straight to the point,' Frederick replied, sensing Tom's anxiety. 'Are you aware that we recently lost our Director General?'

Tom had read in the newspapers about the death of Professor Morantz. 'Yes, I'm sorry. It must have been a shock. Suicide, wasn't it?'

Sadness clouded the older man's gaze. 'Yes, Professor Morantz had been under a great deal of pressure, for some time. There had been various setbacks with the collider which, I understand, he took personally.'

Tom could tell by the inflection in his voice that Frederick was finding it difficult to discuss the circumstances surrounding Professor Morantz's death.

'He has left a void that can only be filled by somebody with exceptional credentials,' continued Frederick. 'After much deliberation, the council would like to offer the position to you, Tom.'

'Me! Why me?' said Tom, astonished.

'As I said earlier,' Frederick replied, 'I've been following your career closely and I believe that you have everything we are looking for. Academically, you are regarded as the definitive authority on subatomic particles, by your peers. The research that you have done on quantum electrodynamics has advanced the way forward in terms of our own search for the God particle, while your published articles expound theories that go far beyond our current understanding of the origins of the universe. In short, you are a visionary with the passion and knowledge to support your hypotheses, and that's exactly what we need to drive the project to the next level at CERN.'

'I... I'm flattered, if not a little taken aback,' stuttered Tom.

'I know this is all very sudden,' replied Frederick, 'and I don't expect a decision straight away. But we are at a very critical point. It wouldn't be an exaggeration to say that we are on the verge of a breakthrough, the outcome of which could hold the key to how the universe and everything in it was created.' He rose from his chair and extended his hand to Tom. 'I'll leave you to your deliberations. I'm staying at the Ritz-Carlton in Boston if you have any questions. Otherwise, I'll phone you in two days for your decision.' He then shook Tom's hand, turned on his heels and left.

Tom stood there, speechless.

The day had started off as unremarkable as any other day. His alarm woke him just before 6 am. He poured himself a coffee and stared out of his window at the campus as it came to life. He was living in Ashdown House, one of the undergraduate apartment blocks, normally reserved for students with families.

He had been there for nearly six months, since leaving his marital home after discovering his wife was having an affair with one of his colleagues. There was no drama or culpability; he and Susan had just drifted apart. If anybody was to blame, Tom blamed himself; the number of nights spent in his research lab or at his computer, creating theoretical models or typing up a new paper, must have contributed to the act of driving his wife into the arms of another man.

He finished his coffee and donned his tracksuit. He was learning to take an intrinsic pride in his appearance. He had to admit that he had let himself go a little, especially around the midriff; this fact was pointed out by Susan in one of their 'heart to heart' discussions shortly after their breakup, along with the fact that his haircut and most of his clothes made him look older than his 36 years.

The hair was the easiest to resolve. He had gone to the on-campus hairdresser, sat down in one of the barber's chairs and said simply, 'Make me look younger!' It had worked. The stylist, used to giving the students the latest fashion haircut, had moderated her urge to replicate the most commonly requested 'messy bed-head' look and, instead, went for a more George Clooney meets Matt Damon, sophisticated but sporty, style. It had taken years off him and had even elicited the odd wolf-whistle from some of his female undergraduates.

The clothes were next; not such an easy fix. He had never been a follower of fashion per se; the latest trends were as alien to him as a sub-atomic particle would be to a football coach. Luckily, that wasn't the case with his brother, Matt, who would always buy him a designer shirt for Christmas or his birthday. It was to him he turned for advice as his fashion guru.

Growing up, the two brothers had always been like chalk and cheese. Tom's fascination for science stemmed from a chemistry set bought for him by one of his uncles. At school he would always get top grades in chemistry, physics and mathematics, so by the time he was eighteen it was inevitable that he would go to university.

Matt, on the other hand, was the archetypal athlete. At school, there wasn't a sport that he didn't excel in, but it was baseball where he really shone. Whilst captaining the local youth team, he was spotted by a New York Yankees' talent scout and signed up to a four-year apprenticeship. Leaving home at sixteen, he moved into dormitories on the outskirts of Manhattan, where he spent twelve hours a day practising and perfecting his swing until, finally, he was called up to play in the Major League.

Tom's hand-eye coordination was non-existent. He was always the last to be picked for any team sport at school. He did have a certain amount of kudos for having a brother who won every cup there was to win, but that didn't detract from his own humiliation of being left on the sidelines. Instead, he found solace in science.

'Matt. Hi, it's Tom. How do you fancy a shopping spree this weekend, just the two of us?'

Matt could never resist an invitation from his little brother and caught the next plane out of JFK to Boston.

The resulting transformation, from dour professor to stylish academic, was remarkable. Out went the cardigans, beige chinos and loafers, and in came merino wool sweaters, Armani trousers and designer shoes. His black, thick-framed glasses were replaced by rimless Gucci bifocals.

Tom had to admit that the makeover did give him a certain gravitas, as he caught his reflection in the mirror on the way out of his apartment to start his morning jog.

***

'How did it go?' The voice on the other end of the line came straight to the point.

'Good. I think he was taken a little aback by our offer, but I could tell he was definitely intrigued,' Frederick responded. He was now back in his hotel room, having spent the afternoon since leaving Tom at the Hayden Planetarium, a short walk from where he was staying.

'Did he ask about Professor Morantz?'

'No. He had read about his death in the papers, but I suspect, with his inquisitive mind, that that won't be enough to satisfy his curiosity,' Frederick replied.

'There is nothing that...'

'Just one moment, I've another call coming through,' Frederick interrupted, putting the call on hold.

'Hello, Frederick Volker here.'

'Frederick, it's Tom Halligan.'

'Tom! Nice to hear from you, although I have to admit I didn't expect you to call so soon.'

Tom gave a short laugh. 'When you left, it took me all of ten minutes to make up my mind. It would be a privilege and a pleasure to accept your offer. When do you want me to start?'

CHAPTER 5

The flight from Logan Airport in Boston to Geneva had taken a little over ten hours, with a scheduled stop at London Heathrow.

Tom was relieved to be finally on his way, as the endless goodbyes and parties were taking its toll. By nature he wasn't used to being the centre of attention; but, when he announced his departure to friends, family and colleagues, he had no choice and was thrust into the limelight. The university delivered a moving eulogy of the academic contribution he had made to his department, which was applauded by students and fellow lecturers alike; his brother professed his undying love for him in a bar downtown after far too many brandies, while his close circle of friends organised a French-themed party (he didn't have the heart to tell them that Geneva was actually in Switzerland), which involved a French maid kissogram, a meal in Brasserie Jo's and far too many brandies.

His parents invited the whole extended family around – including Susan, his ex, but not Jeff, her new partner – for a lavish Sunday roast dinner. His mother didn't have the greatest culinary skills, but she could certainly pull out all the stops when it came to a family gathering.

His anxiety about starting a new life in Switzerland was tempered by the university offering to keep his position open for as long as he needed it, and his brother promising to visit him at every opportunity, 'outside the baseball season, of course'.

Susan, on the other hand, was more apathetic. However, the fact that he didn't have to keep bumping into Jeff at work, who had once said to him, rather melodramatically, 'This University isn't big enough for the both of us', more than compensated for her lack of interest.

All in all, it had taken him a month to say his goodbyes and tie up any loose ends at work. CERN had provided him with an American Airlines First Class ticket to Geneva and told him that he would be greeted at the airport on his arrival. He had managed to get a night flight and was able to grab a few hours' sleep, in between the turbulence; as a result, when he landed in the morning, he was feeling relatively fresh.

He collected his suitcases from the carousel and headed for the 'nothing to declare' channel, dreading the solitary walk down the line of waiting relatives on the other side of the glass partition. He always felt like he was emerging onto a catwalk. As the glass doors slid open, he self-consciously scanned the apprehensive crowd, searching for his name on a plaque. It didn't take him long to spot the CERN logo on a laminated card being held aloft by a genial-looking man with a dark complexion, who smiled expectantly at each of the disembarking passengers as they approached him.

'Hi, I'm Professor Halligan. Are you here to meet me?' Tom, unsure of his new organisation's preferred salutation, reverted to his formal title.

'Yes, Professor, sahib,' beamed the man, using the Indian word as a mark of respect for his master.

'Please, call me Tom,' said the professor, putting his suitcases down and extending his hand.

'I am Anjit Gopal Bose,' said the man, shaking the proffered hand vigorously. 'But most people call me Ajay. Welcome to Geneva, Profess… er, Tom,' Ajay said, still holding onto Tom's hand. 'Please follow me.'

Tom recovered his hand and reached for his suitcases, but Ajay was there first. Picking the luggage up with surprising ease, given his diminutive stature, he set off towards the car park at a brisk pace.

Tom followed on behind carrying his flight bag over his shoulder. He couldn't help but notice that Ajay's dark blue suit was slightly too big for him and suspected that it may be his only one, or borrowed to wear on special occasions, such as collecting visitors from the airport. His boyish face was made to look prematurely older by the thick horseshoe moustache he was trying to grow, but this too looked too big for his slender features. His shock of thick black hair was neatly groomed and as shiny as his suit.

'Where are you from, Ajay?' Tom enquired, trying to keep pace with him.

'My family are originally from Kolkata, or Calcutta as you probably know it.'

'You're a long way from home. What brings you all the way to Switzerland?'

'My father was a scientist and so was my grandfather. You could say it runs in the family.'

'What did they specialise in?' Tom was now intrigued.

'Sub-atomic particles.'

'That's a coincidence, that's my…' Tom didn't finish his sentence. He stopped dead in his tracks, mouth open, in the middle of the airport concourse. Ajay carried on walking and had managed to cover thirty feet by the time Tom realised that he was being left behind and was attracting quizzical glances from his fellow travellers. He sprinted to catch up with Ajay.

'What did you say your surname was?' Tom asked, grabbing Ajay's arm to slow him down.

'Bose.'

'Have you heard of a man called Satyendra Bose?' Tom probed.

'Yes, he was my grandfather,' Ajay responded matter-of-factly.

Tom could hardly contain his excitement. Within his field, Satyendra Nath Bose was regarded, by many, as one of the founding fathers of particle physics. At the age of 30, Bose was instrumental in a key statistical discovery. He'd sent a paper to Albert Einstein describing a statistical model that led to the discovery of what would later be called the 'Bose-Einstein condensate phenomenon'. The paper described the two fundamental classes of sub-atomic particles – bosons, which he named after himself, and fermions, after the Italian physicist Enrico Fermi. Peter Higgs continued the research in the 1960s, using the theories set down by his predecessors, and purported the existence of a specific boson that would explain the very existence of the Universe. Simply put, without Bose there would be no Higgs, without Higgs there would be no God Particle, and without the God Particle there would be no Universe.

Bose never received the recognition that he deserved by his peers. Whilst several Nobel prizes were awarded to research relating to the concepts of the boson, Bose himself was never honoured. In 1954, some thirty years after his ground-breaking paper was published, the Indian government finally acquiesced by conferring Bose with the Padma Vibhushan, the highest possible civilian commendation.

Tom had studied Bose's model as an undergraduate and, to him, there was little doubt that the man was a genius. He idolised him, as a football fan would his favourite player. And here he was, in the middle of an airport, having his bags carried by his grandson.

'Did you know your grandfather well?' he asked Ajay, who had found a trolley and was loading the suitcases onto it.

'No, unfortunately he died before I was born,' replied Ajay. 'But my father used to tell me stories about him all the time.'

'Please Ajay, you must tell me all about him,' said Tom. 'What was he like?'

'But I have to get you back to CERN, or they will be worried about where you are,' Ajay said nervously.

Tom checked his watch. It was 8.15 am. 'Don't worry, I'll cover it off,' Tom said, trying to reassure him. 'I'll just tell them that I got delayed going through customs.'

'Okay, you're the boss,' Ajay responded, with a smile.

'Yes, I suppose I am.'

They found a coffee shop in the airport and, for the next two hours, Ajay recounted the stories his father had told him about his grandfather. Tom was enthralled, asking the odd question here and there to elicit more details about a particular incident. However, he was quite happy to sit back and listen to Ajay's monologue, whilst sipping his cappuccino.

'…and that was the second time my father had the pleasure of meeting Mr Einstein…' Ajay was in mid-flow when Tom's cell phone rang.

'Sorry, Ajay, I have to take this call,' Tom announced apologetically.

'Tom? It's Frederick Volker. Is everything alright? We were expecting you hours ago.' The paternal voice sounded concerned.

'Frederick! Good to hear from you. Yes, yes, everything's fine,' replied Tom. 'Just a spot of bother with some duty free purchases, but it's all sorted now and we're on our way.' He gave Ajay a conspiratorial wink.

'Okay, we'll see you shortly,' said Volker ending the call.

'I think I've played enough truant for one day,' Tom said, getting up from the table. 'But you must promise me that you'll finish your stories when we get back to CERN.'

***

It was a short drive from the airport to CERN, and Ajay had just enough time to finish the episode about when his father had met Albert Einstein for the second time. All too soon they arrived at the security entrance of the complex. Ajay showed his ID card to the man in the hut and the barrier rose to allow them through.

Tom had googled 'CERN' to gather as much information as he could about the organisation before his arrival, but what the websites failed to portray was the sheer size of the campus, sprawling off into the distance, where it seemed to meet the base of the Jura mountains. The buildings were mainly utilitarian in their design and reminded Tom of his own university's campus - function before form. He could see that the architects had at least tried to establish a pleasant environment to work in, by spreading the buildings out and creating 'green spaces' in between, which were laid mainly to lawn. Trees seemed to have been randomly planted in clumps or in rows around car parks in an effort to break up the concrete monotony.

He could see a giant dome in the distance, like a half-buried golf ball, which he recognised from his Internet research as the Globe of Science and Innovation, a visitor centre, frequented mainly by schools and visiting dignitaries. Next to that was a private runway with a single corrugated steel hangar built adjacent to it. He knew that everything above ground was only the tip of the iceberg. The real work went on three hundred feet below ground where the Collider was buried; this was not just for aesthetic and financial reasons (it would have been so much more costly to tear up the Franco-Swiss countryside and implant an ugly grey tunnel over its farms), but also because the Earth provides the greatest radioactive shielding.

They drove to the facility's main reception building, a six-storey-high concrete and glass structure, which housed the control centre and ancillary offices.

As they stepped out of the car, Tom noticed a bronze statue incongruously erected outside the entrance to the building. Its intricate detail and delicate features were at odds with its modern minimalist surroundings and would have been more at home in a museum or temple, rather than a research facility. The six-foot high statue depicted a semi-naked dancer of Asian origin, wearing an ornamental headdress and encircled by a ring of flames. He had four arms, two of which held objects, flames in one hand and an hourglass in the other. He posed with his left leg elegantly raised, balancing on what appeared to be a prostrate dwarf holding a cobra.

'That is Shiva Nataraja, Lord of the Dance,' Ajay volunteered, noticing Tom's frown.

The explanation did nothing to relieve Tom's expression.

Ajay tried again. 'It's a Hindu god.'

Tom's frown deepened. 'But why is it here?'

'It was a gift from my government.' Ajay hoped this would be enough to satisfy Tom's curiosity.

'Oh, I see,' said Tom, not really seeing at all, but sensing that he wouldn't get much more information out of Ajay. He therefore made a mental note to ask Frederick more about its significance as he walked past it and through the revolving doors into the building.

Frederick was waiting in reception to greet him; he had obviously been informed of Tom's arrival by the security guard.

'Tom, you made it at last! Welcome to CERN.' Frederick shook Tom's hand, warmly. 'I trust Ajay has been looking after you?'

'Yes, he's been quite entertaining,' replied Tom, directing his comments at Ajay with a smile.

'Good! Ajay, could you please take Professor Halligan's bags to his room in the accommodation block. Thank you,' Frederick said to Ajay, dismissing him. 'Come, let me introduce you to the rest of the team. They're dying to meet you.' Frederick put his arm around Tom's shoulders and guided him through the frosted glass doors at the end of the reception area.

'What's the story with Ajay?' Tom asked, as he was being escorted down a long, white, sterile corridor.

'You could say that Ajay is my ward,' Frederick explained. 'I promised his father, before he died, that I would look after him and make sure he would come to no harm. He's a simple soul, not academically bright, unlike his father and grandfather.'

'Yes, Ajay did mention that he was Satyendra Bose's grandson.'

Frederick laughed, but not unkindly.

'Yes, unfortunately, he didn't inherit his grandfather's scientific genes. Ajay's father was one of my closest friends; we worked together, for years, on a number of projects. One day, there was a tragic accident - Ajay must have been seven or eight at the time. The equipment we were working with malfunctioned, causing a massive radiation leak. I had just stepped out of the lab to get a coffee, otherwise we would both have received a fatal dose. By the time we had got our radiation suits on and were able to go back into the lab, it was too late for Ajay's father. We managed to get him into the decontamination chamber but he died on the way to hospital. Ajay's mother had died in childbirth and his father was an only child, so really I was the closest thing he had to a relative.'

By now they had reached the far end of the corridor. Frederick had paused to finish his story, before swiping his security card to open another set of frosted glass doors.

It was a hive of activity in the control room; technicians were monitoring a bank of 46-inch LED screens that covered an entire wall of the large, rectangular room. Each monitor displayed a different graph or scrolling set of figures highlighted in either green or red. It reminded Tom of the images he'd seen as a child of the NASA control centre during the lunar landings, except this was much more high-tech. The room itself was divided into four by semi-circular work stations or islets, each housing five consoles and each one being operated by an individual specialist.

'As you can see, we are in the middle of testing the alignment of the proton beams,' Frederick explained.

'How many people work at the facility?' Tom queried.

'We employ over two and a half thousand full-time and fifteen hundred part-time staff across the entire complex.'

Tom let out a low whistle.

'It may sound a lot, but you have to take into consideration that we are totally self-sufficient, we have our own hospital and fire brigade on site. We grow most of our own produce, farm our own meat and dairy products, purify our own water and even generate our own electricity. We are, for all intents and purposes, a small town unified by a single goal. And you, Tom, are its new Mayor.'

The gravity of his new position struck home.

'When you put it like that, it's quite...' Tom paused, searching for the right word.

'An honour?' Frederick offered.

'Daunting, I was going to say.'

Frederick gave a genial laugh. 'Let me introduce you to your deputy Mayor.'

They went over to a small syndicate of people huddled around a conference table in the centre of the room.

'Apologies if I'm interrupting, but I'd like to introduce you to Tom Halligan, our new Director General,' Frederick announced to the group, resting a hand on Tom's shoulder.

The gathering turned to face Tom in unison.

'And this is Dr Deiter Weiss,' Frederick pointed out the man in the middle of the huddle. 'If there's anything you need to know about the facility, Deiter's your man.'

Tom put out his hand to shake Deiter's. There was a brief pause and, for a split second, Tom had the uncomfortable feeling that Deiter was just going to leave Tom with his hand suspended in the air. But then he moved forward and grasped the outstretched hand in a vice-like grip.

'It's a pleasure to be working with you, Professor Halligan.' Deiter's face was impassive, but Tom could sense the insincerity in his voice.

'The *pleasure* is all mine,' Tom countered, emphasising the word 'pleasure'. Did he spot a flicker of annoyance cross Deiter's face? The two pugilists parted, retreating to the safety of their own corners.

'Now, if you'll excuse me,' continued Frederick, 'I'll leave you in Deiter's capable care to get you acquainted with the rest of the team. I shall pick you up at eight and I'll take you to my most favourite restaurant in Geneva.' With that, Frederick left the control room.

There was an awkward silence. Frederick had left a void in the room that Tom felt compelled to fill.

'So, how are the tests going?' Tom directed his question at Deiter. Again, a pregnant pause, a second too long, like a bad comedian misjudging his timing when delivering the punchline.

'We have initiated the alignment sequence and everything seems to be working perfectly.' The voice breaking the silence didn't come from Deiter, but from an attractive, auburn-haired woman standing just to the left of him.

Tom turned to face the person who had saved him from an embarrassing situation. 'And you are?'

'Serena Mayer.' This time, it was she who volunteered her hand first and Tom shook it gently. As he looked at her, he couldn't help but notice her brilliant green eyes, almost feline.

'And what is your speciality, Miss Mayer?'

'Please call me Serena. I am the Director of Statistical Analysis.' She spoke with an accent Tom had difficulty identifying.

The group started to disband and drift back to their workstations, leaving Deiter as her chaperone.

'Perhaps, when I've settled in, we could go over the figures from today's test?' Tom enquired.

She glanced furtively at Deiter.

'I can provide you with all the information you require,' Deiter interjected.

'I'd prefer to hear it straight from the horse's mouth,' Tom replied, emphatically.

'As you wish,' Deiter conceded.

'I'll catch up with you later then,' Tom said, turning his attention back to Serena. She nodded and left the two men to sort out their differences.

CHAPTER 6

By late afternoon, the jetlag had kicked in and Tom's head was pounding. He had taken a couple of paracetamol earlier, but they had done little to ease the pain behind his eyes. He excused himself from the meeting that he had been invited to attend and made his way to his accommodation.

The apartment was in keeping with the minimalist ethos that seemed to underlie the architect's vision of a research facility. The beige walls and fawn carpet reminded him of an inexpensive hotel room. The living room had been appointed with the bare minimum amount of furniture required to make its occupant feel comfortable, but not at home.

A large, square, orange sofa dominated the room, with a small, imitation wood table and chair tucked into one of the corners. A laptop computer sat on top of it, its screen open with the words, 'Welcome to CERN, Professor Halligan' scrolling across the monitor in luminous green writing. The opposite corner was filled by a TV, CD player and telephone on a matching imitation wood unit.

The kitchen, with its patio doors leading out onto a quadrangle, was functional and had been equipped with all the necessary appliances, cutlery and crockery. The 'theme' continued into the bedroom and consisted of a double bed, dressing table, wardrobe with full-length mirror and two bedside cabinets on which stood nightlights. The en-suite bathroom was just that.

Ajay had deposited his suitcases on the bed and had left a note on top of one of them, which read, *'I am in room 454, please come when you want me to finish the stories'*. Putting the note in his pocket, Tom moved the suitcases onto the floor and lay down on the bed. As much as he wanted to, he was far too tired to listen to Ajay's narrative.

***

The distant sound of buzzing seemed to grow louder and louder. At first, Tom couldn't work out what it was or where he was, as he groggily opened his eyes and saw the unfamiliar furniture. Then his brain caught up and he realised he must have fallen asleep. The buzzer rang again, longer this time. His brain told him it was the door bell and he must answer it in order to silence the noise, but his body was having difficulty actioning the request. It rang again. He managed to swing his legs off the bed and stand up, shakily. This time there was a knock followed by a familiar voice.

'Tom, are you in there?' It was Frederick.

'Coming!' Tom managed to reply, his brain and body finally working as one.

He opened the door to see a concerned face.

'This is the second time today that I thought I'd lost you,' Frederick smiled.

'Sorry, I must have dozed off. What time is it?'

'A quarter past eight. I've booked a table for us at nine, so you've got enough time to have a shower, if you want.'

'Thanks, I will.'

'Okay, I'll come back for you in half an hour. I need to have a word with Deiter, anyway.' Frederick closed the door behind him.

 Tom studied his face in the bathroom mirror; he was looking all of his 36 years. Despite his nap, and having slept on the plane, he was pale and dark circles had appeared under his eyes. He stripped off and let the steaming hot shower revive him.

Frederick, as punctual as ever, rang the doorbell just as Tom finished dressing. Noticing what Frederick had on earlier, Tom had chosen to wear dark trousers with a Dolce & Gabbana blazer and matching tie, mentally tipping his hat to his brother's impeccable dress sense.

'Much better, my dear boy,' said Frederick, and made a show of inspecting him.

'Thanks, I feel almost human again,' Tom replied.

'Good, because the restaurant I'm taking you to only caters for humans. Although there are other restaurants I know that are less particular, if you prefer?'

'It's your call,' replied Tom laughing. 'I'm in your hands.'

They were driven the short distance into the centre of Geneva in the back of Frederick's Mercedes. His driver, Louis, seemed to know all the short-cuts to avoid any traffic hold-ups and they arrived at the entrance to the Hotel d'Angleterre in less than fifteen minutes.

The hotel doorman, dressed in a dark green tailcoat and top hat, was standing by the side of the car before it had time to come to a full stop.

'Good evening, Herr Volker. It's very nice to see you again,' he said, opening the door on Frederick's side. Tom waited patiently while he did the same for him.

'And this is a colleague of mine, Professor Halligan. You'll probably be seeing a lot of him, as long as the food is up to standard,' Frederick chided the doorman, who was obviously used to the banter.

'I spoke with the head chef personally this morning, who told me that he was awaiting a delivery of the finest lobsters in the whole of Switzerland,' retorted the doorman.

'On your head be it! Lobster it is!' Frederick pressed some money into the doorman's hand as he held the door to the hotel open.

How did he do that with such fluidity? Tom mused to himself.

They made their way through the ornate reception, with its stuccoed ceilings and gilt detailing, and to the Windows restaurant, which was located at the front of the hotel overlooking Lake Geneva.

The Maître d' was waiting to greet them.

'Bonsoir, Herr Volker, it's a pleasure to see you again,' he beamed, as they approached him.

'Salut, Pierre,' Frederick used the informal greeting between friends.

'Your usual table, Sir?' He didn't wait for a reply, but led them to a table by the window.

'Thank you, Pierre. I'd like to introduce you to Professor Halligan, who's just joined us from America,' Frederick said, as they were being seated.

Pierre nodded cordially at Tom and handed him the menu.

'A little bird told me that you have some particularly fine lobster on the menu this evening,' Frederick said slyly.

'You are as well-informed, as usual, Herr Volker. If you'll just excuse me for a moment...'

Pierre backed away from their table, turned and marched through a door at the far end of the restaurant, returning seconds later with a large platter covered with a silver cloche. He removed the lid and presented them with two of the biggest lobsters Tom had ever seen. Their claws were tied with elastic bands but they were very much alive, obviously having just been lifted out of their holding tank in the kitchen.

'Maine lobster,' Pierre told them proudly. 'Flown in from America today.'

Frederick chuckled. 'I must say, Tom, they look a lot fresher than you did when I saw you earlier.'

'Okay, okay, I'll give you that one,' Tom replied, sheepishly.

Pierre was still holding the tray out to them, waiting for a decision.

'Not for me, thank you Pierre,' said Tom, making his mind up. 'It wouldn't be very patriotic of me to eat one of my fellow Americans.' He had never been very good with 'live' food at restaurants; he just didn't have the killer instinct, he supposed.

'I have no such qualms about eating one of your compatriots,' Frederick snorted. 'Tell Chef Michelle I'd like it grilled with beurre noire and lemon juice.'

'And for you, Sir?' Pierre cocked his head towards Tom.

He quickly scanned the menu and plumped for the filet mignon, served on a bed of truffle-oil mash and sautéed morel mushrooms. 'Medium-rare,' Tom added, before Pierre had time to ask.

'And could you tell the Sommelier that we'd like a bottle of ice-cold Sancerre and a bottle of his finest Châteauneuf-du-Pape,' Frederick concluded, without consulting the wine menu or Tom.

With that, Pierre discreetly left them to their deliberations, returning his prize catch to the kitchen to be despatched.

Tom took in his surroundings. The restaurant certainly lived up to its name - the vista was spectacular. The floor-to-ceiling windows along the front gave diners the best possible view of the imposing Jet d'Eau fountain, rising 450 feet into the air. Illuminated by spotlights on the shoreline, it resembled a magnificent Arabian stallion's white tail, rising majestically from the lake.

The restaurant's décor was no less impressive. Elegant crystal chandeliers reflected in mirrored walls above sumptuously studded charcoal leather seats, like stars above a pitch-black firmament, cleverly contrived to give diners the impression that they were eating outside.

'So, what do you think of our little operation so far?' Frederick asked, snapping Tom's focus back to the dignified gentleman seated opposite him, whom he couldn't help but like.

'Well, it's certainly bigger than the facility at Brookhaven and more... interesting,' said Tom, non-committedly.

'Interestingly good or interestingly bad?'

'Both, I think. You've certainly managed to gather together an influential group of eminent physicists, who are clearly at the peak of their individual specialities. But they don't seem to be working as a team.'

'In-ter-est-ing,' Frederick dragged the word out into its syllables.

Tom wondered if he'd said too much. 'Look, I'm sorry if I've overstepped the mark...'

'Not at all, in fact I think you've hit the nail right on the head,' Frederick cut in.

Tom smiled at Frederick's heavily accented colloquialisms.

'I've suspected as much since the death of Erik Morantz,' continued Frederick. 'Deiter's a very good scientist, but a very bad man-manager.'

'You could say that again!' Tom interjected, but then regretted his forwardness.

'It takes a very special person to take all the brain-power in one room and mould it into a unified intelligence. Morantz had the ability to do it, and that's what I see in you, Tom.'

'How did Professor Morantz die?' Tom asked, side-stepping the compliment. 'You can't always believe what you read in the papers.'

Frederick gave a heavy sigh. 'Of course, you have a right to know…' He paused as the wine waiter filled the glasses with a choice of the red or white wine Frederick had ordered. 'Erik was a brilliant scientist. It's really because of all his hard work that we have achieved as much as we have. But, towards the end, things were getting on top of him. As I told you when I first met you, there had been a few operational setbacks, which he took personally. We had a problem with one of the heat shields a few months back, which was luckily detected in time, otherwise we would have had a major catastrophe on our hands. There had been other minor breakdowns in the past, but not on the scale of the heat shield failure. They're all in the report I've asked Deiter to provide you with. You should have it on your desk in the morning.' He took a large gulp of the white wine he had chosen.

'Surely a few setbacks, even one as serious as the heat shield failure, wouldn't drive a man to take his own life?' Tom queried.

'I believe the balance of his mind was disturbed,' Frederick announced gravely. 'There is a fine line between genius and madness and I think, unfortunately, Erik crossed that line. The afternoon before he died, he came to see me. He was very agitated.

He was like a man possessed; ranting on about how we need to destroy the collider before it destroys the world, and that Deiter knew all about it and was letting it happen. He said that he had proof and was going to go to the media if we didn't stop the experiments immediately. The poor man - obviously some kind of breakdown.'

'So, what did you do about it?'

'I tried to placate him, of course. I told him that we'd shut down the collider immediately and look at the evidence to see if there was any truth in it. He seemed to calm down and we agreed to go through the data the next morning. That was the last time I saw him alive. He must have gone back to his apartment - your apartment - more disturbed than I realised, because they found him the next morning. He'd taken an overdose of sleeping pills washed down with a bottle of whisky.'

'And the evidence he said he had?'

'Nothing. The police searched everywhere – his apartment, office, computer – but they found nothing. Again, further proof of a deranged mind, I'm afraid. A tragic loss to us all.'

Frederick looked forlorn; he had obviously cared deeply about the man. A heavy silence fell between the two men, which was fortunately broken by the arrival of Pierre and their food.

He wished them 'bon appétit' whilst placing their respective dishes in front of them.

'I just hope that tastes as good as it looks,' Frederick said, smiling at Pierre.

Tom tried to lighten the mood by changing the topic of conversation. 'Why is there a statue of an Indian god at the entrance of the control centre?'

Frederick chortled. 'You mean Shiva the Destroyer?'

Tom frowned, which made Frederick laugh even more.

'I bet, at this stage, you're wondering what you've let yourself in for,' Fredrick mused.

Damn right, Tom thought, but didn't say anything.

Frederick continued. 'Don't worry, he's not all bad. He's also known as Shiva the Transformer. In Hinduism, he is regarded as the most powerful deity - his role is to destroy the illusions and imperfections of this world, paving the way for beneficial change. According to Hindu belief, this destruction is not arbitrary, but constructive. Shiva is, therefore, seen as the source of both good and evil and is regarded as the one who combines many contradictory elements.'

'But why is he here?'

'Shiva takes many forms,' Frederick explained. 'The one we have at CERN is Shiva Nataraja, or Lord of Dance. It is believed that he performs a cosmic dance to destroy a weary universe and make preparations for the god Brahma to start the process of creation. The symbolism of the dance is a metaphor for the cosmic dance of subatomic particles that we observe and analyse every time we operate the collider.'

'Okay, two out of three. I've got the "what" and the "why", but who put it there?'

'It was given to us by the Indian government in 2004, to celebrate the research centre's long association with their country. Don't forget that, if it wasn't for a certain Indian physicist, CERN would probably not exist and we wouldn't be here, enjoying this delicious meal. So, I'd like to propose a toast…' Frederick raised his glass. 'To Satyendra Bose.'

Tom clinked his glass against Frederick's. 'Satyendra Bose,' he repeated.

Frederick noticed that his plate was almost untouched, whilst Tom had nearly finished his meal. 'I've been doing all the talking and neglecting Chef Michelle's culinary masterpiece. I will be in trouble.'

They finished their meals in relative silence, but it didn't feel uncomfortable. They made small talk, but neither man felt obliged to fill the pauses between conversations. To Tom, it felt like he'd known Frederick for years; the stately man had a certain way of making him feel relaxed in his presence.

'And how do you like your accommodation?' Frederick asked, as he finished his last mouthful of lobster.

'I've lived in worse.' Tom thought about his student flat back at MIT.

'It's as temporary as you make it,' Frederick replied. 'Some people prefer to stay on campus because they are closer to their work. Erik was one of them. Others move out to the suburbs of Geneva, so they can have a distinct work-life balance. I am a strong advocate of the latter, and I'd recommend you do the same. I have a little place overlooking the lake. Why don't you come round for dinner? My wife makes a wonderful Schweinshaxe mit Sauerkraut. Mrs Volker is always scolding me for not bringing my work colleagues home.'

Mrs Volker. Up until now, Tom had regarded Frederick as either a widower or confirmed bachelor.

'Sounds delicious,' Tom said, not having a clue what the dish was. 'I'd love to.'

Pierre was hovering in the background and saw his opportunity to clear the table.

'Give Chef Michelle my compliments,' said Frederick. 'That certainly was the best lobster I've ever tasted.'

'And mine. The steak was superb,' Tom echoed the sentiment.

'Could I interest you in the dessert menu?' Pierre asked, looking from one diner to the other.

Tom was the first to answer. 'Not for me, thank you. I couldn't eat another morsel.'

'Could we just have the bill when you're ready, Pierre?' said Frederick. 'I would think my colleague is exhausted, it's been a long day for him.' He turned his attention back to Tom. 'I understand, from Deiter, that there will be a full operational trial tomorrow.'

'Yes, it should give me an insight into just what I've let myself in for.'

***

Louis was waiting for them, by the car, at the entrance to the hotel. He quickly extinguished his cigarette when he saw them coming.

'They'll be the death of you,' Frederick told him, reproachfully.

The return journey to CERN was even quicker, due to the lack of traffic. Louis pulled up outside the accommodation block; it was just after midnight. Frederick wished Tom goodnight and Tom thanked Frederick for a most enjoyable evening. Then he watched as the car left the compound.

CHAPTER 7

'I think we've found our man.' Frederick sat at the head of the large, polished mahogany table, addressing the five men and one woman that occupied the other seats to his right and left.

He had dropped Tom off at his quarters. However, instead of going directly home, he had instructed his driver to take him to an underground car park on the far side of the compound, where there were very few buildings and even fewer people to see him enter the lift, wait for the doors to close, insert a key into the control panel and press the 'alarm' button. Instead of the lift ascending to one of the three marked floors, the arrow indicated that he was going down.

After descending for almost a minute, the doors opened to reveal a brightly-lit, sterile, white corridor, at the end of which were two anonymous doors. The one on the right led into a windowless room where the meetings were convened; the one on the left, which could only be opened from this side, led into the underground maze of corridors and service tunnels that made up the bulk of the CERN complex. Volker had personally overseen the addition of this section to the architect's plans and referred to it as the Bunker. Apart from the people waiting for him in the room, the builders and the architect himself, nobody else was aware of its existence.

The others were already seated and chatting amongst themselves by the time he entered the room.

'What makes you so sure?' said the woman.

'He's intellectually capable of understanding our purpose and compassionate enough to support our motives,' replied Volker.

'But that's what you said about Professor Morantz,' the gentleman to his immediate left piped in.

Frederick sighed. 'I believe that, given time, I could have persuaded Erik round to our way of thinking. It was just unfortunate that we didn't get that opportunity.'

'And if your new recruit doesn't support our ideals, what do we do then?' the woman queried.

Frederick looked around the room at the blank computer screens on the walls before resting his gaze back on the woman. 'We'll have no option but to replace him,' he said with some finality.

'How sure are you that the experiment tomorrow will not be successful?' asked a man on his right, changing the subject.

Frederick looked to the man on his left for the answer. 'I have placed a small device on one of the coolant tanks, which is designed to cause a small leak when the Collider reaches maximum power. I have every confidence that the maintenance crew will discover the seepage and the operation will be closed down again, for a number of months, whilst they check that everything is in working order.'

The man who had asked the question nodded his approval.

'Now, if there are no more questions, I'd like to reconvene this meeting in two days' time.' Frederick looked at each one of the people sitting around the table in turn. He had known them for more years than he cared to recall and, as he looked at the age lines etched in their faces, it only served to remind him of his own mortality. Getting no response, he bid them all a goodnight and left the room.

CHAPTER 8

Tom was exhausted. He suspected it was a combination of disrupted sleep, jetlag, excellent food and nearly a full bottle of Châteauneuf-du-Pape. All he wanted to do was sleep until his body told him it was time to get up, but he had scheduled a meeting with Serena Mayer for 8 am the next morning to go through the previous day's data. Perhaps she'd understand if he didn't make it, but then again he didn't want to give the wrong impression.

He made his way to his apartment, past all the other nondescript doors, following the numbers printed on the walls to ensure he didn't get lost. The corridors were soulless and identical – one false turn and he would find himself walking around in circles in this concrete maze.

He opened the door with his key and surveyed his living room; it didn't look any more homely than he remembered. And then a shiver went down his spine as he recalled something that Frederick had said over dinner, which didn't really register at the time. *'He must have gone back to his apartment - your apartment - more disturbed than I realised because they found him the next morning. He'd taken an overdose of sleeping pills washed down with a bottle of whisky.'*

He was literally stepping into a dead man's shoes and probably sleeping in a dead man's bed, come to think of it. He closed the door behind him, wondering where they had found Erik's body. If he were to take his own life, where would he do it? The bedroom would be the most comfortable place, or maybe the sofa. But then again, the kitchen would be more practical.

The loud knock on the door nearly gave him a coronary, shocking him out of his reverie.

'Professor, sahib,' came the voice. 'It's Ajay. I picked you up from the airport this morning.'

Tom opened the door to see Ajay's smiling face. He was carrying what looked like a thick, black, leather-bound photo album under his arm.

'Professor, sahib, I have a scrapbook that I made of my grandfather, that I would like to show you.'

Tom groaned inwardly. He wanted to tell Ajay to leave it with him and he would look at it in the morning, but he could tell by the enthusiasm on his face that Ajay literally meant that he wanted to *show* it to him. Perhaps he regarded it as too valuable an item to let it out of his sight. Tom also recalled making Ajay a promise to finish the stories about his grandfather when they got back to CERN, so he only had himself to blame. So much for an early night.

'Come in, Ajay. I was just about to make a coffee,' Tom lied.

Ajay entered the apartment and stood awkwardly by the door.

'Please take a seat. The sofa would probably be best and then we can look at the scrapbook together.' Tom beckoned him further into the room.

Ajay eyed the orange sofa as though it was a wild animal.

'Is something wrong?' Tom asked, catching his expression.

'I haven't been into this apartment since Professor Morantz, since Professor Morantz…' Ajay was having difficulty finishing his sentence. 'Since I found Professor Morantz on the couch.'

Well, that certainly answers that question, Tom thought.

'Okay, if you're uncomfortable in here, why don't we look at the scrapbook in your room?'

The suggestion seemed to pacify Ajay and the savage look on his face was replaced by a genteel smile. 'Follow me, sahib,' he said to Tom, making a hasty retreat through the door.

Ajay's apartment was the size of Tom's living room, not what he'd expected for the grandson of the great physicist. A single bed took up the whole of one wall. Along the wall opposite was a kitchen sink and worktop with a microwave and a two-ring hob on it. Underneath was housed a small fridge. The single window that provided all the natural light was centrally positioned between the two walls, and the 'designers' had managed to squeeze a small table and chair underneath it. To the right was a narrow bookcase stacked from top to bottom with books. A door to the left of the kitchen sink was obviously where the bathroom was, Tom surmised. The décor and carpets were the proverbial beige and fawn, although Tom had difficulty in determining the colour of most of the walls as they were plastered with newspaper cuttings.

Tom scanned the articles' headlines:

'Massive quake kills thousands in China'

'Wenchuan earthquake leaves 5 million homeless'

'Earthquake rocks Port-au-Prince, Haiti, thousands feared dead'

'Magnitude 7.1 earthquake strikes Chile's Maule Region'

'Tsunami triggered by Chilean earthquake leaves thousands homeless'

'Pacific coast of Tōhoku, Japan, hit by massive earthquake and tsunami'

'Earthquake off the coast of Sumatra measures 8.6'

'Fukushima Nuclear Power Plant in melt-down after quake hits'

'500,000 dead or missing after worst nuclear disaster ever'

'Are you, by any chance, interested in natural disasters, Ajay?'

'Not all, only earthquakes.' Ajay was making the coffee and had his back to Tom.

'It's an interesting subject. Would you like to be a seismologist?' Tom ventured.

'As you can see, I read a lot of books on the subject…' Ajay turned around and pointed to the bookcase beside the window. 'But I don't think I'm smart enough.'

Tom was getting a bit too tired for small talk. He looked around for a suitable place to sit and chose the edge of the bed. Ajay joined him, carrying two steaming mugs, which he placed on the floor in front of him. He grabbed his scrapbook and sat next to Tom.

***

Tom had finally managed to get back to his bed just after two in the morning. Ajay had gone through his scrapbook, meticulously explaining the contents of each page, in detail. It mainly consisted of press cuttings from the time Satyendra Bose's historic paper was published in conjunction with Albert Einstein, as well as personal letters from him to his son, Ajay's father, and postcards to Ajay from the places his grandfather had visited. The last few pages were dedicated to when his grandfather was honoured by the Indian government and ended with his obituary, with eulogies from people who had known him personally through either work or his private life.

Tom had grown very fond of Ajay in the short time that he'd known him. However, fatigue had finally got the better of him and he made his excuses to leave with as much bonhomie as he could muster.

CHAPTER 9

Tom had hit his snooze button three times before he finally gave in and forced himself out of bed. Half asleep, he made his way to the bathroom mirror; the dark lines under his eyes were still there. He decided that a shower was the only antidote to his tiredness; but, no sooner had he turned on the faucet, than the phone rang.

'Good morning, Professor. I hope I didn't wake you?' It was Deiter. *Why did he always sound as though he was being sarcastic?*

'Not at all, I've been up for hours.' Tom didn't want to give Deiter the impression that he was somehow the weaker man for being exhausted – it was childish, but he couldn't help himself.

'Good! Then you wouldn't mind coming into the office to go through one or two things before we set up the initialisation sequence for today's experiment?'

'Of course not. I'll be there straight away,' Tom said, trying his best to sound wide awake. He hastily put the phone down before he was caught out.

He checked his watch; it was just after 6.30 am. *They certainly want their pound of flesh,* he mused as he forsook his shower and quickly got dressed. He was out of his apartment within ten minutes and made his way to the main reception building, where he had been dropped off the previous day. It seemed like a week ago.

The complex was as deserted as it had been when he'd left Ajay in the early hours of the morning. As he approached the statue of Shiva, adorning the entrance to the building, he couldn't help but recall Frederick's conversation the previous evening. *Shiva the Destroyer, he had called it. Surely Brahma the Creator would have been a more fitting donation from the Indian government?*

He headed for the doorway but, as he walked past the sculpture, something colourful caught his eye. He looked down at the feet of the statue, where somebody had placed a bouquet of white and red flowers. He stepped closer to inspect them and noticed that there was a card nestled between the stems. He picked it up and read the sentiment. *'Om Sarva Mangal Manglaye Shivay Sarvaarth Sadhike Sharanye Trayambake Gauri Narayaani Namostu Te.'*

Puzzled, he made a mental note to ask Ajay its significance when he next saw him, and returned the card to the flowers before making his way into the building.

Deiter was already discussing the contents of a computer screen with two other people, whom Tom recognised as junior technicians from his previous day's introductions. There had been too many names to remember and it certainly wasn't one of Tom's fortes. He just hoped that he'd be able to pick up their names from Deiter before he was put in an embarrassing position. Deiter obliged almost immediately.

'Ah Professor, there you are. You're just in time,' Deiter said, almost cordially. 'You remember Max and Peter? We're just tweaking the Collider's alignment based on yesterday's test results.'

He was grateful to Deiter, but he still didn't know which one was Max and which one was Peter. He played it safe and acknowledged both of them with a single nod.

Tom knew from his research that the alignment of the proton beam was critical to the success of the Collider. The positively charged protons that made up the beam must be aligned and made to bend so as to go round in a circle. This was done by 9,000 magnets strategically placed throughout the 27-kilometre tunnel.

The 'dipole' magnets caused the protons to bend consistently in one direction to get round the circle. The 'quadrupole' magnets focused each beam so that it stayed compact, to increase the probability of a collision when the beams were brought together. Having just one of the thousands of magnets a nanometre out of sync could mean the difference between identifying the God particle and the proton particles missing each other altogether.

'We've fed in the data from yesterday's tests, made the necessary adjustments to the magnets and now we're ready to run a computer simulation,' Deiter informed Tom without taking his eyes off the screen. 'If you watch the monitors on the wall over there, you'll see the results.'

Tom turned in the direction of Deiter's gesture to see five of the computer displays flick to life. The centre console showed a 3D schematic drawing of the LHC. The two on either side displayed the now familiar sets of scrolling green figures.

'The monitors showing data each represents one of the four detectors placed around the Collider where the two beams intersect,' Max or Peter told him.

'And the centre one will show the beams' trajectories based on our computations,' Peter or Max added.

'Okay, run the simulation,' Deiter instructed.

The centre screen zoomed in on a computer image of the particle accelerator. It was so lifelike, Tom had to remind himself that it was all being generated by a small box under the desk where Deiter was sitting and not hundreds of feet below ground.

To achieve the maximum collision velocity, Tom was aware that it was necessary to give the protons a 'push start', using a series of smaller particle accelerators to increase their energy before being released into the tunnel as a beam. Once there, the RF cavities would take over and increase the velocity of the protons until they reached the speed of light.

'Protons reaching maximum containment velocity,' one of the technicians announced.

'Release the first beam in three… two… one… now!'

The computer-generated image panned out to show a bright yellow beam circulating through the tunnel.

'Release the second beam in three… two… one… now!'

A blue beam emerged, travelling in the opposite direction to the yellow one. The beams intersected at four points on the diagram, indicated by a faint glowing green ball, which seemed to get brighter the longer programme was allowed to run.

'Why are the intersection points intensifying?' Tom asked, hoping it wasn't a stupid question.

'The green balls represent the number of collisions the protons make,' Deiter responded, his eyes still firmly glued to the monitor. 'As the beams speed up, the number of collisions increases, which is why they glow brighter. The figures on the screens give us a prediction of the actual number of hits we're achieving per second.'

Tom turned his attention to the screens to see the figures steadily increasing.

'And how long before the beams reach maximum velocity?'

'Twenty minutes, but we'll run the simulation for an hour to see if there are any fluctuations in the collision rate,' one of the technicians replied.

'You boys having fun?' Serena Mayer had walked into the office unobserved. 'Men and their computer games,' she mockingly chided.

Tom turned to face her. Her green eyes sparkled mischievously, making his pulse race a little faster. He tried to play it cool.

'Serena, I'd almost forgotten about our eight o'clock meeting. Shall we go to my office?' Without waiting for a response, he led the way across the room.

'I've left the file Herr Volker asked me to compile for you, on your desk,' Deiter shouted after him.

It was the first time the two technicians had been distracted enough to take their eyes off their computer screens. Their gaze followed Serena, intently, as she strolled after Tom, only returning to the task in hand after her shapely body had completely disappeared from view.

'When you two have quite finished,' Deiter said irritably.

***

Tom sat behind his desk and waited for her to come through the door. He picked up the thick manila folder that Deiter had left for him and started to thumb through the pages without taking much notice of its contents.

'Please, take a seat,' he gestured to the chair opposite him. 'Can I get you a coffee, tea or anything?'

'No, thank you.'

'Good, because I have no idea where the coffee machine is.' Tom smirked at his own remark, but Serena's face remained impassive.

She sat down, put her briefcase on the floor beside her and crossed her legs. Her skirt rode up to just above her knee, an action that didn't go unnoticed by Tom. There was an awkward silence as he absently flicked through the pages of the dossier. He was struggling to come up with an opening gambit that would impress her without sounding too arrogant.

'So, how did it go yesterday?' he blurted out. *Safe, if not a little too generic.*

'Well,' she replied.

'Good, good.' He returned his attention to the file in an attempt to buy himself enough time to formulate his next 'killer' question.

'And how do you like it here?' was the best that he could come up with.

'The hours are long, but the work is very interesting.'

'Good, good.' More page turning. Then he put the folder down on his desk and leant back in his chair. 'I hope you don't mind me asking, but where is your accent from?'

'I grew up in Israel, but my parents moved to America when I was fourteen. I continued my studies there and graduated from university five years ago.'

'And which university was that?' Tom enquired, to be polite.

'MIT,' she said, smiling at him.

'That's a coincidence. I was a professor at MIT.'

'I know,' she laughed, the mischievous glint returning in her eyes. 'You taught me.'

'I don't remember you,' Tom exclaimed, rather tactlessly.

She feigned a hurt expression.

'Sorry, I didn't mean I don't remember you,' he bumbled. 'I meant I didn't recognise you. Sorry, I mean I don't remember teaching you.'

She laughed again. 'I don't blame you. It was only for one semester, when you first arrived at the university, and it was my last term. So I hardly had any classes to attend,' she said, letting him off the hook. 'But you did give me a "C" for one of my papers.'

This time it was Tom's turn to laugh. 'You probably deserved it. I hope it didn't affect your career too much?'

'No, but I did think you were quite mean at the time.'

***

They spent the next hour laughing at the merits and foibles of the various lecturers they had both known at the university, him from a colleague's perspective and her from a student's perspective. Deiter, meanwhile, paced backwards and forwards between his work station and Tom's office. Finally, when he couldn't stand the joviality any more, he knocked on the door.

'I'm sorry to disturb this important meeting, but we need Ms Mayer to be able set the parameters for today's experiment.' His face had definitely gone a few shades redder.

'My fault, Deiter,' Tom said apologetically. 'We were just discussing mutual acquaintances.'

Deiter stormed back to his desk.

Serena got up to leave. 'Do you want me to leave the results of yesterday's tests with you?' she asked Tom, retrieving her briefcase.

'Why don't we go through them over dinner tonight? My treat for being so mean to you at university.' The words were out of his mouth before he had a chance to think about it. He wasn't accustomed to asking attractive women out on dates, but they were getting on so well, it seemed the natural thing to do.

'I'd like that. Where and when?'

'I only know one restaurant in Switzerland, but I know for a fact they do a very good fillet mignon, and the lobster's not bad either. Shall we say the Hotel d'Angleterre at eight o'clock?'

'I'll look forward to it.'

Tom watched her as she went over to speak to Deiter. By his body language it was obvious that he didn't appear best pleased that she was getting on so well with the new Director General. *Well, that's something you'll just have to live with, Dr Weiss!*

CHAPTER 10

'Release the first beam in three... two... one... now!' Deiter was instructing the same two technicians as earlier that morning, only this time it wasn't a computer game.

All the workstations in the room were manned and all the computer screens were being observed by at least one operative. The tension in the room was palpable. Unlike the previous day's test, the room was deathly silent.

'What's the status of the heat shields?' Deiter barked across the room.

'Heat shields fully operational, temperature stabilised,' came the response.

'Okay, release the second beam in three... two... one... now!'

Tom stood behind Deiter. He knew he wasn't expected to be an active participant in today's experiment, but that didn't stop him feeling like a spare part. He turned to the computer screens on the wall he had observed that morning. This time, the schematics were showing a computer-generated image of the actual beams that were circulating some hundred metres below them, while the data screens were recording the actual number of times the protons smashed into each other. As with the earlier simulation, the figures were steadily increasing, and were updated on a scrolling roll every second.

The other screens around the room were now showing CCTV footage of various parts of the Collider. With 27 kilometres to cover, it was obvious to Tom that they could only focus on the vital components; even so, they flicked from one image to another every ten seconds.

Tom was surprised to see that there were still workers underground. The tunnel itself would have been cleared and sealed long before the experiment was initiated, so what were they doing down there? He looked around to see if he could find somebody who wouldn't be too distracted by a question and decided to approach a group of three technicians monitoring the proton collisions.

'Why are there still people underground when the experiment is running?' He directed his question to the most senior-looking individual out of the group - or, at least, he was the oldest.

'That's the maintenance crew,' replied the technician. 'They're checking for any coolant leaks around heat shields while the Collider is running.'

Tom frowned. 'Isn't that dangerous?'

'Only if there's a leak,' the technician replied with a smirk.

Tom didn't see the funny side of it. 'Who instructed them to do that?'

'Professor Morantz. We had an incident about eighteen months ago, but luckily it was detected in time, otherwise the whole place could have gone up. Since then, he ordered the maintenance crew to check for leaks whenever the Collider is operational. I suppose he thought that it would be better to risk the lives of a few men than a few hundred.'

Tom didn't like the sound of that one bit. He couldn't disagree with Professor Morantz's logic, but endangering a single life was unacceptable. He had just discovered his first task: to identify any threat from leaking coolant without the need for human intervention.

'Check heat shields!' Deiter was still shouting orders across the room.

'Satisfactory.'

'Increase power to seventy-five per cent.'

A technician tapped in the figure on his keyboard. 'Power at seventy per cent.'

Tom checked the data screens again. The numbers were still increasing. He checked the CCTV images of the tunnel. He could see a group of four workers, dressed in protective suits, inspecting a pipe leading to one of the helium coolant tanks, with flashlights. He was trying to work out what they were doing when the camera flicked onto another part of the tunnel. He stood there, his eyes transfixed on the screen, waiting for the image to return. It took a full sixty seconds for it to come around again. This time, he could see the men slowly walking away from the pipe, obviously satisfied with their inspection.

'Heat shields effective.' This time the technician didn't wait to be asked before volunteering the information.

'Increase power to maximum.'

'Power at maximum.'

'Heat shields holding.'

Tom was still watching the group of men. They had just walked off the screen when the monitor flashed white and then went blank. He checked the other monitors, which were all working normally. He turned his attention to the data screens. He noticed that the figures on the far left monitor were descending whilst the others were still increasing.

And then the alarm sounded.

'Code red! Code red!' Deiter tried to make himself heard above the blaring siren.

Everybody, apart from Tom, seemed to know what to do. He managed to catch hold of a young woman's arm as she scurried past him. 'What is code red?'

'Emergency shutdown and evacuate the complex.' She didn't wait around to be asked any more questions and hurried out of the room.

Tom surveyed the room. Some technicians were tapping frantically on keyboards, whilst others were collecting their belongings and disappearing through the doors at a brisk pace. Deiter was flitting from one workstation to another, issuing instructions. Everything appeared controlled but he could see the anxiety on people's faces.

'We'd better go.' It was Serena who had sidled up beside him.

'Shouldn't I be the last man out or something?'

'Like the captain going down with his ship?' she teased. 'That's very noble of you, but not necessary. We've got a strict protocol for this type of emergency. "All extraneous members of staff should evacuate the complex immediately and report to the assembly point." You should have read your emergency manual, Professor, tut, tut. I think that deserves a "D" minus. Come on, I'll show you where we have to go.'

***

It was over four hours before they were allowed back into the complex, during which time four fire engines, three ambulances, one federal and two local police cars had arrived. The ambulances were the first to leave, two of them carrying the bodies of the two workers who had been pronounced dead at the scene of the explosion, the third carrying the other two badly-burnt workers. The fire engines had left after putting the fires out, but only when they were confident that there wouldn't be a risk of the fires re-igniting by using their thermal imaging cameras. The police cars were still there.

A whole section of the complex where the explosion had taken place was cordoned off by police tape, not just from a structural safety standpoint but also because it was officially a crime scene.

'…until they had conducted their enquiries and were satisfied that there was no criminal intent involved,' as Tom was told by Inspector Gervaux, the senior officer in charge of the investigation, who had an air of aloofness about him.

'We will need to interview everybody that was involved in today's *experiment*,' the Inspector added. It was obvious to Tom by the way he sarcastically emphasised the word 'experiment' that he wasn't a huge fan of the organisation's objectives. 'Could you please arrange six interview rooms where my colleagues can conduct their questioning and identify the staff that we will need to speak to.' Without waiting for a response, he left Tom to rejoin the other officers.

'Something tells me this is going to be a long day,' Tom muttered to himself.

CHAPTER 11

The sun was just rising over the Bosphorus on a cold, grey, November morning, when Hamil Sadik arrived at his 'office'. Unlike the modern chrome and glass skyscrapers that could be found in the business quarter, his office was a sixth-century masterpiece of Byzantine architecture. With its golden mosaics, marble pillars and rich wall coverings, not to mention the impressive Grand Dome, the Hagia Sophia had long been considered by most art historians as the eighth wonder of the world, and Hamil Sadik tended to agree.

Hamil was a family man who often joked that his spreading girth was as a result of his wife trying to kill him with kindness by feeding him too much. His two children had flown the nest years ago, only to return most weekends with their own fledglings. He doted on his grandchildren, of which he had six, and always maintained that the prerogative of a grandparent was to spoil them rotten without having the guilt of parental responsibility.

But, at the age of 60, he was finding it more and more difficult to keep up with their energetic antics. His eyesight had deteriorated over the last few years to the extent that he now wore glasses all the time as opposed to just for reading. His hair had faired a little better. Unlike most of his contemporaries, who were either going grey or thin on top, his was still as full and dark as when he was a teenager, which he wore military style – short back and sides. Although he wouldn't admit it, he often found the odd rogue silver hairs, which were dispensed of as soon as they were discovered. His bushy moustache was subjected to the same treatment, borrowing his wife's tweezers to perform the operation.

He checked his watch. It was just before 7 am, two hours before the museum was due to open to the public and three hours before the dignitaries arrived. He had made good time from his home on the outskirts of Istanbul, despite having to take a detour over the Galata Bridge to avoid a traffic jam that had been announced on the radio.

As he let himself in through the Judas gate, set in the magnificent Imperial entrance at the front of the building, he reflected, as he had done so many times before, on how lucky he was to have been given the position as Curator - or 'Guardian', as he liked to think of himself - of this historic symbol of Turkey's heritage. That was almost three years ago to the day and, ever since then, he'd been awed by the sheer size of the temple built by the Emperor Justinian nearly fifteen centuries ago.

He walked through the highly-decorated portal, stopping at the entrance to the nave to switch on the resplendent wrought iron chandeliers so he could survey his domain in all its glory. His thick-rimmed glasses had steamed up; he polished them on the lapel of his overcoat, before returning them to his ruddy face. So vast was the structure that he had to look at one section at a time to take in the whole shape of its interior. His eyes led from the monolithic blue, green, and blood-red columns of marble and stone brought from every corner of the empire, to the soaring vaults, then to the smaller domes, finally coming to rest on the great mosaic figure of Christ in the central dome that had taken almost two years to restore.

It had been a controversial decision at the time to allow the layers of the calligraphic medallion quoting the Light Verse from the Qur'an, which had adorned the prime position of the Grand Dome for over five hundred years, to be peeled back to reveal the Christian Messiah as judge and ruler of all, looking down as though from heaven itself. Heated discussions had taken place in parliament between the various religious sects, but it was the historians that had won the day led by an impassioned speech by Hamil, lambasting the Ottoman Turks for plastering over such important religious artefacts when they converted the temple into a mosque in the fifteenth century.

He always looked forward to arriving at his place of work and would always see something new to pique his interest. But today, he didn't have time to indulge in this passion, he reminded himself, because today they were unveiling several large mosaics as well as the new face of the Grand Dome. Today, he had to get ready for the President, the Prime Minister and the Minister of Culture and Tourism along with their entourages and the world's press. He hated these public showcases, but he was astute enough to realise that they generated the interest necessary to attract the funds from the country's coiffeurs to enable him to continue his restoration work. So today he would press the flesh, smile at the cameras and answer all the questions the journalists put to him, because tomorrow he could stand here again and marvel at the exquisite craftsmanship of true artisans from an era long forgotten by most people.

***

As Hamil Sadik was arriving at his office, Giyas Macar was already halfway through his working day. He had been woken by his father at 2 am, as he had been every morning since leaving school the previous year. At the age of 16, and without any qualifications to his name, it was inevitable that he would be joining his father on the small fishing boat that had been passed down to him by his father. When his father eventually retired, through ill-health rather than choice, Giyas would become the proud owner of a rather dilapidated trawler.

A great deal had changed since his grandfather's time: over-fishing, increase in maritime traffic, light pollution from the city, global warming and water pollution. Whatever the cause, tuna and swordfish were now extinct from these waters.

Giyas could still remember the stories his grandfather used to tell him as a boy, about how they'd caught gigantic tuna and swordfish and how the best restaurants in the city would fight to get the freshest catch, as soon as they'd docked, to serve to their European clientele. He recalled his grandfather telling him about the time he'd caught an enormous swordfish in his nets; so big was this monster of a fish, that the boat nearly capsized when he started to drag it in and he had to cut it loose. Fishermen's stories maybe, but that's all they had to remind themselves of the prosperous times.

All they could hope to catch these days were lüfer, a popular fish amongst the locals, but even their numbers were dwindling year by year. A lot of the other fishermen had given up altogether, turning their boats into private fishing vessels for the tourists. However, his father had told him on numerous occasions that it would be a cold day in hell before he hung up his nets and pampered to the spoilt, rich tourists. He had used a lot more expletives to convey his views, but the sentiment was the same.

Giyas's scrawny muscles ached from the sea-sodden weight of the nets as he threw them over the side, whilst the weather-beaten figure of his father stooped over the wheel, trying to steer a straight course through the pounding waves. He was distracted by the sound of a helicopter above him and looked up just as a wave came crashing over the side, knocking his puny frame off-balance and showering him in icy water. He regained his foothold and continued to let out the nets, ignoring the sound of the rotor blades as they passed by; he had to concentrate on getting the lines out straight, as their meagre catch so far today wouldn't even pay for the fuel they had used, let alone be enough to support the family. He prayed for a bountiful catch.

***

Traffic Dawn's day had started as unremarkably as any other. That wasn't her real name, of course, but it hadn't stopped some bright spark in the office giving her a nickname the first day she started her new job as Airborne Dawn Traffic Correspondent for the only English-speaking radio station in Istanbul – Radyo KO. The executives picked up on it and created a natty little jingle which Dawn - or Maria Spencer, which was her real name - hated, 'Traffic Dawn, your eye in the sky'.

One advantage of working for a radio station as opposed to a TV channel was that she could quite easily leave the Traffic Dawn persona at the station and slip back into her true identity once she had finished for the day and nobody, apart from her friends, would be any the wiser. But that was all the advantages she could think of.

From as far back as she could remember, she had wanted to be a TV presenter. Growing up in the UK, she had always been fascinated by children's programmes - not for their content, but the way the presenters interacted with their audiences, captivating impressionable little minds with stories and poems, or making useful things out of everyday household items. She had applied to as many TV channels as she could, once she'd finished her degree in Communication Studies, but nobody was hiring without experience. One helpful rejection letter suggested that she should try radio work and, once she'd served her apprenticeship there, then they may consider her for a role in TV.

Her Turkish mother and English father split up the day she graduated from university; they later told her that they hadn't been getting on for years and were 'Just waiting for the right time' before going their separate ways - she back to Ankara in Turkey and he back to his alter ego, namely a transvestite called Monica. It was whilst visiting her mother that she met one of the sound engineers from the radio station, in a local bar, who told her about a vacancy for a 'roving reporter' based in Istanbul. He went into far too much detail about how the station he worked for was part of a network of phantom stations scattered throughout the country, all sharing the one resource in Ankara to save on costs. And, with modern technology the way it was, as long as you had 'Eyes on the ground', as he described it, the unsuspecting listener was none the wiser that their 'local' radio station was actually being broadcast from a modern office building in the country's capital.

The next morning, she phoned the number he had given her and was ecstatic when they asked her to come in for an interview. Her euphoria dissipated somewhat when they told her that the position for the 'eyes on the ground' reporter for Istanbul had already been filled, but there was still a vacancy for 'eyes in the air', which would entail reporting on the state of the city's traffic from a helicopter. Her enthusiasm was dampened even more by the fact that she would be expected to be on air from 6 am to 6 pm, six days a week. But, with little else going on in her life, and at the tender age of 24 with nothing to lose, she accepted the role when it was offered to her.

She was now sitting next to Devrim, a rather rotund agency pilot with a wandering eye and a penchant for *Top Gun*. Unfortunately for him, the mirrored Ray Bans and slick-backed black hair made him look more like a Sicilian gangster than Tom Cruise. He'd asked her out on a date, the first time they'd flown together, which she politely declined, stating that she just wasn't ready for a relationship. She didn't consider herself unattractive, with her long wavy blonde hair and slim figure that she'd inherited from her mother (or was it Monica?), and she could certainly do better than the letch beside her, but for the time being she was concentrating on her career. There were worse jobs than hers, she consoled herself, spotting a small fishing boat being buffeted by the waves some 500 feet below them.

'There, to your left. I can see a line of brake lights,' she said into her mike, as she scanned the main arterial roads in and out of Istanbul for any signs of congestion.

'No, just traffic signals,' came the reply through her headset, in heavily-accented English.

'Dawn, you're on air in thirty seconds. Anything to report? Over.' The voice of Seb, her producer, broke into the conversation.

'Nothing, apart from the earlier accident which closed the Unkapani Bridge, but that seems to have re-opened now and the traffic's moving freely. Just in time for the morning rush. Over,' Dawn replied.

'Okay, just tell the nice listeners that and then hand back over to the studio. Fifteen seconds, we'll run the jingle and then you're on. Over.'

She could hear the radio station as it was being broadcast through her headset. 'That was Survivor with Eye of the Tiger. Talking of which, let's go to our eye in the sky, Traffic Dawn, with the latest update on the roads. Traffic Dawn, your eye in the sky. Hi Dawn, how are the roads looking this morning?'

***

Hamil was just covering the mosaics with dust sheets ready for the grand unveiling, a piece of theatre that always seemed to please the TV cameras, when he heard a low rumble. His first thought was that they must have diverted the traffic down the normally quiet side streets because of the earlier accident; but, as the noise intensified, his second guess was that it was a helicopter. He was right. He could distinctly pick out the rhythmic beat of the blades as it passed overhead.

He was standing on a platform of wooden planks, forty feet in the air, supported at either end by scaffolding, which his protégés, all final year Archaeology students from the nearby Koç University, had used to painstakingly remove the metal masks and white plaster from the intricate glass and gilt mosaics. If the Ottoman Turks had been able to see how masterfully the mosaics had been restored they would have realised, to their chagrin, far from destroying these works of art, as they had intended, they had actually helped preserve them for future generations.

The sound of the helicopter returned, only this time it was much louder. It made the perch he was standing on shake and the ladder, which was propped against the scaffolding, clatter to the ground. He was annoyed with himself because he had told his students, on numerous occasions, that they should always ensure it was fixed securely with ties before climbing up. He would have to wait for his cleaners to arrive in half an hour before he could get down, which was fine because he still hadn't finished his preparations.

He couldn't imagine the size of the helicopter that was capable of causing such vibrations, and then suddenly a distant memory came flooding back to him, which made his heart beat faster and his mouth become instantly dry. He had only ever experienced this sensation once before in his life, when he was a young boy on holiday in Fethiye with his parents, but that was enough to leave an indelible impression on his mind.

They had been staying at his great aunt's house by the coast, when she burst into his room in the middle of the night, shouting for him and his sisters to get outside and stand away from any buildings. He must have slept through the initial tremors but, by the time he'd reached the top of the stairs, the whole house was shaking. He froze, not knowing what was going on, but his mother appeared behind him, picked him up and carried him outside to join the rest of the family on the beach. Several other households had already congregated on the sands and were being joined by people running from every direction, some crying, some screaming; but the majority just huddled in groups, staring silently in the moonlight, as they watched the houses in front of them crumble to a pile of rubble.

***

'What's that over there?' Dawn was pointing to what looked like a plume of smoke rising from a street just in front of them.

Devrim pushed the joystick forward and the helicopter descended to get a better view.

'It looks like a house has collapsed onto those cars,' she said, as the downdraft from the helicopter swirled the cloud around them. She could see the half-demolished building, in the middle of a row of houses, and just make out figures running into the street covered from head to foot in dust.

'Gas explosion? You'd better let the station know. That road is going to be blocked all day,' Devrim told her, hovering just above the commotion.

'Seb, it's Dawn. Over,' she spoke into her microphone and waited for a response from the station.

'Go ahead, Dawn. Over.'

'We've got an incident on…' She checked the map on her lap for the street name.

She was trying to work out where they were, when Devrim's alarmed voice came over her headset.

'Dawn, look!'

She looked down to see the whole terrace collapsing in on itself, like a house of cards. The explosion took them both by surprise. The shockwave hit their undercarriage a full second before they heard the boom, propelling them higher into the air. Devrim gritted his teeth as he tried to regain control, pulling back the joystick as far as it would go. The nose rose sharply, but the turbos failed to deliver the thrust and they didn't gain any more height. Instinctively, he pushed the stick to the left and the helicopter banked, just in time to avoid the huge fireball that had erupted. He pulled back on the controls again and this time he was relieved to hear the pitch of the engines change as they started to ascend.

***

Giyas was cold, tired and soaked through to the skin, despite wearing an all-in-one weather-proof suit with several layers of clothes underneath. He was just hauling in his third catch of the day when he heard the sound of the explosion in the distance. His father must have heard it, too, because he turned around to ask him what it was.

'Another bomb, maybe?' Giyas suggested.

They were constantly living under the threat of bomb attacks from one or other of the extremist groups, so it came as no surprise to either of them. Only the day before, a Kurdish terrorist had killed himself, a policeman and injured several others, in an apparent suicide attack on a local police station.

His father didn't say a word; his thoughts were with the innocent victims and their families. He shook his head and returned to the wheelhouse to navigate the boat. Giyas was well aware of his father's views on the subject and would no doubt be hearing more of them over the dinner table that evening. Being of Hungarian descent, he had had his history lessons from his father from a very early age. He knew all about the Ottoman Turk invasion of his country in 1541, and the subsequent deportations and massacres throughout their 150-year rule before the Prince of Transylvania rescued them from their subjugation. His father would always talk fondly of the 'old country', of the traditions and cultural values of its people, despite never having set foot on Hungarian soil himself.

Another meagre haul, Giyas thought to himself as he pulled in the last of the nets. His father turned around and Giyas could see the disappointment in his sunken, aging eyes.

'We'll try the other side of the bridge. Maybe our luck will change,' his father shouted over his shoulder as he turned back to steer the boat on a new course.

***

Hamil knew that he had to get outside and into open space, which meant the Sultan Ahmet Park, located next to the museum, but first he had to get down from the dais, which was starting to sway wildly backwards and forwards as the tremors increased. He realised that there was no point in trying to retrieve the fallen ladder; his only two options were to either jump or try to scramble down the scaffolding. With time and fitness not on his side, he chose the former.

He took off his overcoat and fell to his knees to eye the drop; he reckoned that he could increase his chances of not sustaining an injury by hanging onto the wooden planks by his fingertips and then letting himself fall. He manoeuvred into position by turning his back on the nave and lowering himself slowly over the side. He held onto the edge of the platform, his knuckles white from the weight of his own body, his legs dangling in open space. He could hear the sound of his own heart pumping blood through his veins as his arms took the strain.

He was just about to let go, when he heard an ominous creaking sound above him. He managed to turn his head and look up to see all the wrought iron chandeliers swaying in unison, like some bizarre metronome. He could see that the plaster around where they were fixed to the ceiling had cracked and large pieces were starting to fall onto the marble floor below him.

He held his breath, closed his eyes and let himself drop. The first chandelier smashed to the floor at exactly the same time he did and with similar consequential damage. It had landed just three feet from where he now lay, spraying him with shards of glass as it disintegrated. It was such a loud crash that he almost hadn't heard his own leg snapping. The pain shot through his body instantly, causing him to let out an involuntary animalistic shriek that echoed around the vast hall. His body shivered uncontrollably and he started to perspire despite the wintry temperature.

***

They had passed under the First Bosphorus Bridge, which spanned the continents of Europe and Asia, by the time Giyas had secured the nets and joined his father in the cramped wheelhouse. The spray from the waves lashed at the windows and the small windscreen wipers were struggling to clear them sufficiently enough for them to see where they were going.

'If it gets much rougher, we'll have to call it a day,' his father said, peering through the smeared glass.

Giyas pulled on the green woollen hat his grandmother had knitted him and went out on deck to see if he could get a better view, but he couldn't. Looking back at the suspension bridge, he could see the headlights of the commuters on their way to work. A distant rumbling could be heard over the boat's engines as they strained to cope with the pitching sea. *Thunder*, he thought. They would definitely be returning to port early.

Another wave smashed over the side, drenching him again. He was past caring now, as he didn't think he could get any wetter. He wiped the salt water out of his eyes and stared back at the cars. The bridge appeared to wobble, almost imperceptibly; Giyas knew from experience that the sea could play tricks on your eyes. He watched intently, another wobble, this time more pronounced. The sound of the thunder grew louder. Vehicles were slowing down; a lorry at the front braked, which concertinaed through the line of traffic causing a jam in the middle. He could see motorists switching their hazard lights on as they joined the orderly queue.

Then, suddenly, a shudder travelled from one side of the bridge to the other, like a concrete Mexican wave. The bridge started to oscillate up and down, slowly at first, but then seemed to gain momentum. The majority of the cars on the bridge were now stationary; some motorists had abandoned their vehicles and were running to the relative safety of the shores.

Giyas wanted to run to tell his father, but his feet were rooted firmly to the spot, his eyes transfixed on the bridge as the undulations grew more and more violent, throwing cars, buses and trucks high into the air as though they were toys, and landing on the terrified pedestrians as they tried to flee. Then, one of the central suspension cables snapped, like an overstretched rubber band, followed by another, then another and another, in quick succession. The oscillations turned into a violent torsional twisting motion, like a demonic skipping rope, hurling vehicles and their passengers off the side of the bridge.

As the cables failed, one by one, two gaping fissures appeared at either end of the structure, which spread rapidly along the full width of the road; Giyas could see slabs of concrete falling from underneath the bridge in their wake. And then, with an almighty crack, which could be heard well above the sound of the raging sea and the rumbling of the earthquake, the whole middle section fractured, plummeting some two hundred feet into the Bosphorus, creating a thirty-foot wave as it disappeared into the murky depths, taking with it the remaining vehicles, their contents and anyone unfortunate enough not to have made it to the sides.

The wall of water came crashing towards the small fishing vessel releasing Giyas from his spell. He turned to warn his father but, as he did so, the first wave knocked him off his feet and slammed him hard onto the deck, winding him. As he lay there, trying to catch his breath, he could see his father in the wheelhouse struggling to retain control. The second, larger wave engulfed the boat, capsizing it. Giyas tried desperately to cling onto the nets, but the force of the water ripped them out of his grip and tossed him into the freezing sea.

Giyas struggled to the surface but there was no sign of the boat or his father. He trod water as the waves pounded down on him, hoping that his father had somehow managed to survive, but he knew in his heart of hearts that it was unlikely. He would only be able to last, himself, a few minutes in these conditions, a combination of the exertion he had to put in just to stay afloat and the extreme cold that would soon deplete his energy reserves.

Then, bobbing up and down in the swell, he spotted one of the fishing buoys that had been hanging over the side of the boat. He swam over to it and managed to reach out and grasp the rope it was tethered to before being swamped by another wave. This time, he was determined not to let go. As the water receded, he quickly pulled the float towards him and wrapped his arms tightly around it. The relief was instant; his newfound buoyancy meant that he could save his energy as he didn't have to fight against the troughs and peaks.

He knew his chances of being rescued were slim; some of his best friends had perished in milder weather conditions than these, but as long as he could stay afloat he still had a fighting chance. His toes were the first to go numb, then his fingers, then his legs. He recognised the symptoms immediately and clung tighter to the buoy. He was so tired and couldn't keep his eyes open.

He wasn't afraid to die, he just felt sorry for his mother. He could picture her being told by the harbourmaster. She would get a knock on the door in the early evening after the boat had failed to return to port. She would have a headscarf on and be wearing an apron, having spent the afternoon preparing a steaming hot stew, ready for when her men returned. She would open the door and be surprised to see the portly frame of Mr Levent standing there, head bowed, cap in hand. He'd look up at her with sad, bloodshot eyes and she'd know that he'd been crying. She would ask him in… that was the last thought Giyas Macar had before he succumbed to hypothermia, slipping gently below the waves to join his father.

***

Hamil had managed to avoid most of the falling debris as he made his way across the marble floor towards the nearest side entrance. A large piece of masonry had landed on his damaged leg, which must have made him black out because he woke up covered in rubble. Not knowing how long he'd been out for, he shook his head to clear the fuzziness and a cloud of dust from his hair made him cough.

He raised himself onto his good knee, then transferred all his weight onto his outstretched arms before pulling himself forward, whilst dragging his broken leg behind him. He'd invented the technique after twice trying to stand on his good leg and hop, but both attempts had ended after just one jump, the ground shaking so much that it was impossible for him to keep his balance, and both times he'd landed awkwardly on his fracture, making him cry out. So, while the hand-pull method was excruciatingly painful (his palms and knees were encrusted with blood and dirt from cuts he'd sustained from the shattered glass of the chandeliers that now littered the floor) and exhausting, it was the lesser of the two evils.

He knew that nobody was coming to rescue him - his cleaners would have their own problems to deal with, if the earthquake was as bad as he suspected. Therefore, the only hope he had was to make it outside and put his trust in a passing Samaritan to take him to safety.

He focused on his goal, an elaborately carved wooden door set in an arch of golden mosaics depicting the Virgin Mary guarded by two seraphim. He had tried to steer a path away from any walls and pillars, the plaster and brickwork crumbling so much so that daylight streamed in through holes and cracks. He wondered how much longer it would be before one came tumbling in on him.

His progress was slow and made even more arduous by having to go around larger objects that had fallen in his way. But he had reached his halfway point – directly beneath the Grand Dome - and allowed himself a moment's rest to look up at the compassionate face of Christ, gazing benevolently down on him. He lay on his back, his chest heaving from his exertions, to study his greatest achievement to date. The incandescence radiating from the gold aura surrounding the figure illuminated the entire cupola. The vibrancy of the colours that made up the central figure was now on show for the first time in half a millennium.

However, as he studied the face of Jesus, his emotions turned from pride to incredulity, then to terror as the Lord's expression changed; the altruistic smile morphed into a hideous, toothless grin. As the crack widened, it distorted the features even more, making the image appear as though it was laughing at him. He tried to crawl away, but he was too slow and the recently restored figure of the Christian Messiah, as judge and ruler of all, came crashing down on him, burying him under a mound of plaster and gilt mosaics.

***

'Dawn, are you alright?' Seb's voice came over her headset as the helicopter climbed to a safe height, above the cloud cover.

'Yeh, we're both fine,' she replied shakily. 'But that was a close call.'

'What happened?'

'Not sure, some kind of explosion?' Dawn looked at Devrim for inspiration. The pilot just shrugged.

'Well, leave that for the time being. We've had a hysterical listener on the phone, reporting a major traffic incident on the First Bosphorus Bridge. Can you make your way over there and see what all the fuss is about?'

'Will do. I'll come back to you when we're there. Over and out.'

It took them less than ten minutes to get to the bridge from where they were, using the helicopter's GPS. As they descended out of the cloud, Dawn could not find the words to describe the panorama that unfolded in front of her, but would later tell her mother that the only word she could come up with, in hindsight, was 'apocalyptic'.
They both sat there in stunned silence, mouths agape, surveying the devastation all around them.

'You there yet, Dawn? Over,' Seb broke their trance.

'I... I... er... I can't believe what I'm seeing,' Dawn managed to say with some effort.

'Well, try! You're the wordsmith and our sponsors don't pay us to guess what you're seeing. It's not TV, you know!' Seb said angrily.

'I... I... can't describe it.'

Seb moderated his tone, sensing that it was something serious. 'Sorry, Dawn. What is it? A multiple-car pile-up? Is the bridge closed?'

'No, it's gone.'

'Gone? What do you mean, gone?' The irritation was back in Seb's voice.

'I mean, the whole middle section of the bridge… isn't there. Just the supporting pillars are left at either end. It must have collapsed into the sea.'

'What else can you see?'

Dawn looked around and below her. 'The whole city's gone and there are fires everywhere,' she replied in a monotone voice, still trying to comprehend what her eyes were registering.

She couldn't see a building standing that was over one floor in height. Streets were buried under a mass of debris and cars were crushed into unrecognisable lumps of metal. It was reminiscent of the images of Nagasaki and Hiroshima after the Americans had dropped their atomic bombs. A thick layer of smog had started to form over the conurbation.

'Okay, Dawn, listen to me,' replied Seb, his voice agitated. 'There must have been an earthquake. We've had some tremors here, but nothing on the scale of what you've experienced. I'm going to put you on air across the whole network. I'll get one of the presenters to talk you through what you can see. Are you ready, Dawn? This could be your big break.'

The words seemed to snap her back into reality. She heard her lead-in, via the headset. 'We interrupt our scheduled programme to bring you some breaking news of an earthquake that has devastated Istanbul, from our reporter on the scene.'

'Hi, this is Pete. I understand you have some breaking news?' It was obvious that was all Pete had been told.

She recognised his voice as one of the presenters on Radyo Ankara. 'Hi Pete, this is Dawn,' she replied in far too jolly a voice.

'More serious!' Devrim hissed under his breath, as he manoeuvred the helicopter closer to the ground to get a better view.

She lowered her voice a couple of octaves. 'I am witnessing what can only be described as devastation on a biblical scale.'

She could see Devrim nodding his approval out of the corner of her eye.

'Can you describe to our listeners what you can see?' Pete prompted.

'Yes. We're flying over what's left of Istanbul. Most of the buildings have been levelled by an earthquake and I can see thick smoke rising into the air from fires that have broken out across the city.'

'And what about survivors?'

Devrim pushed the controls forward and they descended. He pulled the stick back, levelling the helicopter at just a hundred feet above the ground, the downdraft from the rotor blades fanning the conflagration.

'I can see a few people caked in soot and dust, just sitting in the middle of the carnage, dazed. Others appear to be digging frantically, trying to rescue loved ones trapped under piles of rubble. But the majority are clambering over the debris, still dressed in their night clothes, trying to get away from the fires.'

'And how many casualties do you think there are?'

'It's difficult to tell,' Dawn looked down at the ground below her, but she couldn't determine if what she could see were just heaps of clothes or bodies. 'I suspect that most people were still in their beds when the earthquake struck, so we can expect a significant loss of life.'

She signalled to Devrim to take them higher to get an aerial view of the holocaust.

'There are very few buildings still standing,' she went on, 'and I can see the Hagia Sophia. However, it appears to have sustained considerable damage.' She pointed at the building rising incongruously above the smoke.

Devrim accelerated in that direction.

'I can see that one of the exterior walls has fallen down, the minarets have gone and the Grand Dome has caved in. But, apart from that, it seems to have withstood the brunt of the earthquake fairly well. Wait! I can see the ground shuddering in front of us. It must be an aftershock… it's shaking the building... part of the roof's just fallen in… now the walls are crumbling… What's that, over there?' Dawn was pointing to a prone figure inside the ruins. 'I can see somebody inside the building… he's waving up at us. We're going in to get a closer look.'

Devrim steered the helicopter until it was hovering just above the building. Dawn had a clear view of the interior through a large hole in the roof.

'I can see the person now, it looks like a man. He's crawling towards the door at the side of the building. The ground's still shaking quite badly and the roof's disintegrating, slabs of plaster are missing him by inches, but he's nearly made it. If he can just get outside we'd be able to land in the park and pick him up. He's made it to the door, but he's struggling to stand up to open it. He's up! He's leaning against… Oh my God!'

'What is it, Dawn?'

Silence.

'Dawn, are you still there?'

Still no reply.

'Dawn, can you still here me?'

'Yes, we're still here…' Dawn sounded deflated.

'What happened?'

'There was another massive shudder and the walls just collapsed in on themselves. There's nothing left of the building.'

'What about the person inside?'

'Buried! There's no way he could have survived.'

'Okay. Stay on air, Dawn. We'll be right back to you after a word from our sponsors,' Pete informed her as they went to an ad break.

Dawn felt sick.

'That was great, Dawn. Keep focusing on the human tragedy perspective,' Seb encouraged her through her headset. 'We've had NBC, CBS, Sky and the BBC, not to mention all the local TV stations wanting to interview you when you get back to base.'

Great! She was finally going to get to fulfil her lifelong dream of being on TV. But, somehow, she didn't think she'd have the stomach for it anymore.

CHAPTER 12

'Bonsoir, Professor Halligan.' Pierre held out his hand to take Tom's coat from him. 'And, may I say, it's a pleasure to see you again so soon.'

'Thank you, Pierre,' Tom said, as he handed his coat over.

'Will you be joining Herr Volker and Dr Weiss this evening?'

Tom was a little taken aback by the question. 'Er… no, I didn't realise they were dining here. I'm actually meeting a young lady, but I'm a few minutes early.'

'I see. Then let me show you to one of our booths, they're a little more… intimate.'

Tom caught the insinuation and blushed. 'Oh… no… that won't be necessary. She's a colleague from work.'

'Of course she is, Sir.'

Did he detect a hint of sarcasm in Pierre's voice? Or was he just being a bit paranoid?

He followed Pierre across the restaurant to a table in the corner. He spotted Deiter in the seat he had occupied the previous evening. He was deep in conversation with Fredrick, which was probably why neither of them had noticed him. He thought about going over to their table to say hello, but their discussion seemed so intense that he decided it would be impolite to interrupt them. He sat down on the chair proffered by Pierre with his back to them.

'Can I get you an aperitif, while you are waiting for your guest?'

'Thank you, Pierre. I'll have a scotch on the rocks, a large one. On second thoughts, make it a triple.'

Tom's nerves were getting to him. He still couldn't believe he'd had the gall to ask Serena out, on only the second day of his new job. It was under the pretence of work, he reminded himself. But, after the day he'd just had, that was the last thing he wanted to talk about.

Pierre returned with his drink and a menu. 'Perhaps you'd like to browse the menu. I'm afraid we've sold out of the lobster, but we do have some excellent pan-fried sea bass fillets, served on a bed of celeriac mash, accompanied by a cream of saffron sauce.'

'Sounds delicious,' replied Tom. 'But it would have to go a long way to beat the fillet mignon I had last night.'

Pierre smiled and left the menu with him.

Tom checked his watch. Five to eight. He glanced over his left shoulder to the entrance. No sign of her. He glanced over his right shoulder and could only see Frederick's face reflected in the window. He didn't look as jovial as he had the previous evening; in fact, he looked tired and drawn. He was shaking his head at something Deiter was saying to him, his expression stern.

Tom felt a little guilty about spying on a man he admired so much, but this was a different side of Frederick that he hadn't seen before. Besides, who wouldn't practise a little voyeurism if they knew they could get away with it?

'I'm not interrupting anything, am I?'

Tom jumped around with a start to see his date standing next to him. Pierre was shadowing her. They were both peering at the same reflection of Frederick he had been studying.

'No. I was just… er… I was just…'

'Snooping?'

Tom laughed. 'Busted! You caught me red-handed.'

She slipped onto the leather banquette opposite him and put her tan-coloured briefcase on the floor.

She was wearing a black, off-the-shoulder cocktail dress with high heels and carried a matching clutch bag. Her hair was tied back in a loose, messy bun with long, angular bangs at the front which showcased the diamond and pearl dangle earrings and matching drop pendant necklace. She wore just enough make-up to accentuate her green eyes and high cheek bones, with a hint of cinnamon-coloured lipstick to complement her olive skin. The overall effect? Tom thought she looked stunning, confident in her own skin, unlike he, who was feeling rather self-conscious about the fact that he hadn't had time to change out of his work clothes.

The investigation by the police had gone on all day and Tom felt obliged to oversee the proceedings. They had only managed to get through about a tenth of the workforce by the time he'd left the office at seven that evening. Inspector Gervaux had assigned six of his men to conduct the interviews allocating thirty minutes per employee. They had started with the maintenance team and then moved on to those present in the control room when the explosion happened. Tom realised that he would be seeing quite a lot of Inspector Gervaux over the next few weeks, which he didn't relish the thought of.

'Aperitif, Madam?' Pierre handed Serena a menu.

'Yes, I'll have what he's having.'

'And will that also be a triple, Madam?'

Serena gave Tom a knowing smile. 'Why not?'

'Busted again!' Tom said with mock guilt written all over his face.

***

The evening went better than Tom had hoped. The food was excellent, the wine was flowing and so was the conversation. He found they had much more in common than attending the same university; keep-fit, theatre, food, travel, families and friends were just a few of the topics they covered. They both managed to avoid mentioning 'the elephant in the room', until after they'd enjoyed their dessert, when Serena brought up the subject.

'So, any news on the two injured maintenance workers?'

'I phoned the hospital, just before I came out,' replied Tom. 'One's still in intensive care and the other one they said was stable. That's all the information they were prepared to give me because I wasn't family.'

'Talking of which, did you have to inform the relatives of the deceased?'

'Thankfully not. I was dreading it all day. I really wouldn't have known what to say. But when I spoke to Frederick about it, he kindly offered to take over that responsibility, as he said he knew them.'

'It really is terrible. Did the police give you any indication what caused the explosion?'

Tom gave a derisory snort. 'I don't think Inspector Gervaux likes me very much. The last thing he'd do is confide in me. Did they mention anything to you during questioning?'

'Nothing. They just seemed to be gathering information - what I did, how long I'd worked for CERN, where I was at the time of the explosion, if I'd seen anything, that sort of thing.'

'I was talking to one of the technicians during the experiment, who told me that there'd been an incident about two years ago when a disaster was narrowly averted. Do you know anything about that?'

'It happened just before I started working there,' said Serena. 'Apparently, there was a leak in one of the helium coolant tanks. The whole operation was closed down for over a year and every part of the collider was checked over with a fine-tooth comb. I can't believe it's happened again.'

'We're not sure that it has, not until we get the final police report,' Tom reminded her. 'Have there been any other incidences that you're aware of?'

'You're beginning to sound like the investigation team,' she said, flashing a smile at Tom. 'We've had minor breakdowns, but nothing more than you'd expect from such a complex piece of technology.'

'And what about the data readings during the test and the experiment?'

She reached down and retrieved a file from her briefcase.

'I've summarised the output from both days,' she said, handing a single sheet of paper from the file, across the table, to Tom.

He studied the data in silence, until he'd reached the end of the document.

'Temperature readings normal. Detectors registering intensified activity as power increases, which is what you'd expect. Kinetic energy levels normal. Direct correlation between electromagnetic radiation and power output. All seems to be in order,' Tom concluded, passing the paper back to Serena. 'So, what do we put these malfunctions down to? Coincidence?'

'It certainly looks that way,' replied Serena.

'Coffee or digestif?' Pierre appeared at their table with his usual discretion.

Tom looked around the restaurant to see that they were the last ones there. He hadn't even noticed Frederick or Deiter leaving.

'I think we'd better be going,' he said. 'We wouldn't want to outstay our welcome.'

'As you wish, Sir. I'll bring you your bill.'

Tom turned his attention back to his date. 'Are you staying on the complex, or do you have an apartment in town?'

'That's a bit forward of you, Professor Halligan,' she teased.

Tom blushed again. 'I only meant that we could share a taxi if you were going back to the complex.'

'That would be appropriate,' she said, continuing the pretence of being straight-laced.

'Well, we wouldn't want to do anything inappropriate, now, would we?'

Tom paid the bill and they left the restaurant, giggling like teenagers.

***

'Thank you for a very pleasant evening.' They were standing outside Tom's door. 'Are you sure I can't offer you a nightcap?'

'Professor, sahib! Professor, sahib!' They both turned in unison to see Ajay running at full pelt towards them down the corridor. He just managed to stop short of them in time. 'Have you… seen the… TV? It's… it's Shiva,' he gasped, bent over with his hands on his knees, trying to catch his breath.

'Ajay, slow down and tell us what's wrong,' Tom said, trying to calm him down.

'…the earthquake.'

Tom let them into his apartment, switched on the television and flicked through the channels to find an English-speaking news programme. Tom stood to one side of the TV, whilst Serena and Ajay positioned themselves on the couch, his earlier phobia almost forgotten as he focused on the images of the holocaust being broadcast.

All eyes were glued to the set as a young woman, who looked tired and drawn, was being interviewed by an ABC News reporter. 'We have with us Dawn Spencer, a local radio station presenter, who witnessed the devastation first hand. Tell us what it was like, Dawn.'

'It's Maria.'

'Sorry?'

'My name is Maria.'

'Sorry. Tell us what it was like, Maria.' The runner was going to get it in the neck for that cock-up.

Maria had lost count of the number of interviews she'd done over the last twelve hours; the questions were always the same. She had formulated the answers in her head and could almost deliver them verbatim, like a script. She could also anticipate the next question before it was asked.

'We were reporting on the early morning traffic, in our helicopter, when the first of the tremors shook the city. Initially, we thought it was a localised gas explosion, but then we soon realised it was an earthquake. We were just above the clouds when the whole city got flattened. As we descended, we could see the full extent of the devastation. The quake must have shaken the buildings to their foundations, because all that was left were piles of rubble.'

Ask me about the casualties.

'And did you see many casualties?'

'Because it was so early in the morning, a lot of people must have been trapped in their houses as they collapsed. I could see men and women digging in the ruins, dragging individuals out by their arms and legs. But it became obvious, quite quickly, that the majority weren't so lucky, as bodies littered the streets. Makeshift bandages were being tied around the injured, but as there were no hospitals and no medical treatment available, they were left to suffer in agony.'

'Did you see any emergency services on the streets?'

'Most of the roads were inaccessible. Even if there had been any ambulances or fire engines still running, they wouldn't have been able to get through. Fires were burning out of control. Some survivors did try to douse the flames with buckets of water, but it was futile.'

'And how long was it before you saw any assistance from outside the city?'

'Military helicopters were the first on the scene. They managed to land on some of the parks that hadn't been affected by the quake. They were carrying medical personnel and supplies, which they administered to whoever they thought needed it the most. The helicopters took off, evacuating the most seriously injured, whilst the walking wounded were being treated on the ground.'

'Thank you, Maria.' The reporter turned back to face the camera. 'There you have it, a harrowing account from an eye-witness to what is being described by experts as a mega-quake. It's difficult to say, at this early stage, what the final death toll will be, but it is likely to run into the millions. This is Celia Burrows, ABC News, reporting from a city that has been wiped off the face of the earth. Over to you in the studio, Bryan.'

'Thank you, Celia,' Bryan spoke into the camera, his voice grave. He turned his focus to the screen behind him where his guest, a professor of seismology from Harvard University, was waiting patiently for his cue.

'Professor, we've just heard from our correspondent in Istanbul. She is describing this as a mega-quake. Would you agree?'

'The scientific name for it is actually a megathrust earthquake,' replied the professor. 'It is the most powerful kind of earthquake on the planet. The magnitude of the one that hit Turkey measured

10.5 on the Richter scale, the largest earthquake since records began.'

'What could have caused such a quake?'

'The surface of the earth is divided into giant plates of rock - and most earthquakes occur at faults where two of the plates meet. Where the plates are colliding, one of the plates usually gets pushed down under the other. Not surprisingly, this process can be very violent. The two plates can get stuck together and the result is that the area around gets compressed. Eventually, the strain on the fault becomes too much. The plates suddenly slip past each other and the result is a megathrust earthquake.'

'Could we have predicted this happening?'

'Earthquakes, by their nature, are very unpredictable. You never know for sure where the next one will occur. But we have been aware for some time of the possibility of one occurring again in Istanbul. The city is situated near the North Anatolian Fault, close to the boundary between the African and Eurasian Plates. This fault zone, which runs from northern Anatolia to the Sea of Marmara, has been responsible for several deadly earthquakes throughout the city's history. Among the most devastating of these was the 1509 earthquake, which caused a tsunami that broke over the walls of the city and killed more than 10,000 people. More recently, in 1999, an earthquake, with its epicentre in nearby Izmit, left 18,000 people dead, including 1,000 people in Istanbul's suburbs...'

Tom switched off the TV, but the three continued to stare at the blank screen without saying a word.

It was Ajay who broke the silence. 'Om Sarva Mangal Manglaye Shivay Sarvaarth Sadhike Sharanye Trayambake Gauri Narayaani Namostu Te.'

Tom and Serena both turned to look at Ajay.

'What does that mean, Ajay?' Tom recognised the words from the card that was in the flowers on the statue.

'It's a prayer to Lord Shiva,' replied Ajay. 'It means, O! the divine couple Shiva Parvati! Thee, the protectors of this universe, along with Lords Brahma and Vishnu. We pray to you for our well-being, prosperity and the enlightenment of our souls.'

'Did you place the flowers on Shiva's statue?' Tom asked.

'Yes,' Ajay said bashfully, looking down at his feet.

'But why?'

Ajay didn't answer, but kept his gaze firmly on the floor.

'Why, Ajay?' Tom said, a little more forcefully than he'd intended.

When Ajay looked up, Tom could see tears welling in his eyes. 'I pray to Shiva, to show compassion and restraint.'

'And you think that Shiva is responsible for this earthquake?' Serena said gently, putting her hand on Ajay's arm to soothe him.

'I know he is,' Ajay protested vociferously, taking them both a little aback. 'I'll prove it to you.' Ajay stood up and walked out without saying another word.

CHAPTER 13

Frederick had reconvened the meeting in the Bunker a day earlier than anticipated. He wanted to make sure that, in the unlikely event they were questioned by the police, they all knew what to say.

He had already found out what had gone wrong with the device which caused the explosion. But he wanted the person responsible to explain to the others the circumstances which led to the deaths of two maintenance workers and left another two in hospital.

He opened the meeting by thanking everybody for making it at such short notice, before turning to the man on his left to take the floor.

The man played anxiously with his silver-rimmed spectacles. Beads of perspiration formed on his forehead despite the air conditioning regulating the temperature of the room at a steady 23°C. He cleared his throat nervously.

'I would firstly like to apologise for attracting the unwanted attention of the authorities, which could potentially put us all in jeopardy. Secondly, I would like to reassure you that I will do everything in my power to ensure that the investigation is brought to a swift, innocuous conclusion. Thirdly, I would like to give you my personal undertaking that nothing like this will ever happen again.' Suitably humbled, he took off his glasses, wiped his brow with a handkerchief, and sat back in his chair.

'But how did it happen, exactly?' the only woman in the group spoke up. She clearly wasn't going to let him off the hook with just a grovelling apology.

He returned his glasses to his face and cleared his throat again. 'I underestimated the amount of charge required to cause the pipe to fracture. Luckily, the escaping helium dampened the explosion somewhat, causing minimal damage.'

'Apart from the two casualties,' somebody at the far end of the table interjected.

'Yes, the loss of life is very regrettable,' the bespectacled man replied. 'But I don't need to remind you of what would happen if the Collider was allowed to discover the God particle.'

'We are all well aware of the consequences,' interjected Frederick. 'But our code does not permit the loss of life in order to prevent the God particle from being discovered.'

The man shrank back in his chair, accepting the admonishment.

'I think the main purpose of this meeting,' said Frederick, trying to steer the discussion back on track, 'is to discuss how our exposure, following this tragic incident, can be minimised. Our forefathers were forced to go underground, and it is our legacy to maintain that anonymity until we achieve our objectives. Having the police crawling all over the facility puts that at risk.'

'We need a scapegoat,' the woman proffered.

Frederick frowned. The idea of implicating an innocent person didn't appeal to him, but he knew, deep down, that it made sense.

'Any other suggestions?' he looked around the room at the blank faces staring back at him. No other proposals were forthcoming. 'Okay, who do you have in mind?' he said resignedly.

'One of the maintenance team,' a man on his right proposed.

'No. We need somebody in authority,' the man with the spectacles stated. 'Somebody with access to the plant twenty-four seven.

Somebody who could enter the tunnels without raising suspicion. Somebody who has a scientific knowledge of how the Collider works but, more importantly, how it could be stopped.' He could see the others round the table nodding their agreement - everyone, apart from Frederick.

Frederick could see where this was going, and he didn't like it. 'You mean, somebody like Tom Halligan? But he's only been with us two days.'

'Exactly why he would be the perfect candidate. He arrives, and the very next day there's an explosion,' the man with the glasses countered.

'But what about motive? Surely, that would be the first thing the police would look for?' Frederick raised the objection, but he knew he'd already lost the debate. The others round the table could sense they'd found their sacrificial lamb.

'Leave that to me,' the man replied, taking off his glasses and wiping his brow again. 'The fate of one human is inconsequential compared to the fate of the entire world.'

'I guess so,' Frederick conceded, diffidently. He closed the meeting by thanking everybody again. As they rose to leave, he turned to the person on his left. 'I'd like you to stay behind. There are a few things we need to discuss.'

The others filed out of the room, leaving Frederick alone with Deiter.

***

'What do you think that was all about?' Tom joined Serena on the couch.

'I have no idea. I've never seen Ajay that agitated before.'

'I know he's interested in seismology. Perhaps seeing the aftermath of that quake in Turkey has brought the reality home to him.'

'We were all upset by the images, Tom,' she replied. 'But it doesn't account for his belief that some Indian deity is responsible for causing it.'

'True. Perhaps we should…'

The door to Tom's apartment flew open and Ajay rushed back into the room. He was carrying a red leather-bound folder with the initials E.J.M. embossed in gilt on the front. He handed it to Tom.

'Where did you get this from?' Tom asked, noticing the gold letters.

'It was Professor Morantz's. I found it over there, when I discovered his body, so I took it for safekeeping.' Ajay pointed to the small table in the corner of the room.

Tom opened the binder to read its contents. The document was divided into five sections, each marked with a different date. Within each section were pages and pages of statistics, all time-coded by hour, minute and second.

'What do these figures mean?' Tom shared the file across his and Serena's laps.

'They appear to be data readings from the Collider, going back to when it was first operational,' Serena replied, staring quizzically at the pages.

Tom thumbed through the file.

'Look, he's circled some of the readings in red. What do they signify?'

'Those are the electromagnetic radiation readings,' replied Serena. 'It looks like he's highlighted the times when they reached a peak.'

'He's also scribbled some notes in the margin next to them,' Tom observed. He read the first one aloud. 'Sichuan, China, twelfth of May, 2008. Richter scale, eight. Eighty-three thousand, five hundred dead and three hundred and seventy-five thousand injured.' He turned to the next section and found a similar notation by the peak readings. 'Do you have a pen?' he asked Serena, who scrabbled around in her briefcase and managed to find one. He started to transfer Morantz's observations onto the last page in the dossier, which was blank.

Sichuan, China: 12th May 2008. Richter scale – 8.0 / 83,500 dead, 375,000 injured.

Viti Levu, Fiji: 9th November 2009. Richter scale – 7.7 / 58,000 dead, 170,000 injured.

Haiti, Caribbean: 12th January 2010. Richter scale – 7.0 / 316,000 dead, 300,000 injured.

Maule, Chile: 27th February 2010. Richter scale – 8.8 / 44,800 dead, 111,000 injured.

Fukushima, Japan: 11th March 2011. Richter scale – 9.0 / 550,000 dead, 1.2 million injured.

When he finished writing, he gave a long, low whistle.

'The dates of these earthquakes match exactly the dates when the Collider was operational. When did you say the Collider was last out of action following the leakage incident?'

'It happened just before I arrived,' said Serena. 'So it would be about February 2010.'

'And you said that it wasn't operational for just over a year, as a result?'

'Yes, we fired it up again in March 2011.'

'That tallies.'

'Are you saying what I think you're saying?' Serena turned to Tom, searching his face for the answer.

'I'm not sure what I'm saying. But what I *do* know, is that Morantz thought that the Collider was responsible for causing the deaths of…' Tom quickly did the sums in his head. 'Over a million people, not to mention whatever the death toll in Istanbul will eventually be.'

'Shiva is using the Collider as a tool to destroy the world,' said Ajay, standing behind them, looking over their shoulders. They had almost forgotten he was there.

'Why would Shiva do that?' Tom asked, trying not to sound condescending.

'Because it is written in the scriptures, that when Shiva performs the Tandav, the cosmic dance of death, at the end of an age, the world will be destroyed and a new one will be reborn.'

'And you think that time is now?'

Ajay nodded, solemnly.

'Do you think Morantz took his own life because he felt guilty about the earthquakes?' Serena asked Tom.

'It doesn't make sense. Why the hell didn't he tell somebody about it?'

'He was going to,' Ajay answered. 'I saw Professor Morantz the night he died. He came to my room because he wanted to read the cuttings on my wall. He said he was compiling a file that would prove the Collider was responsible for causing these earthquakes and he would show it to the newspapers.'

'That makes even less sense,' said Tom. 'If he was going to expose the Collider, why would he commit suicide before he'd had a chance to speak to the press?'

'Perhaps it wasn't suicide,' Serena ventured.

Tom was silent for a while, trying to remember something that Frederick had told him over dinner. And then it came to him. He repeated his thoughts out loud.

'Frederick said that Morantz came to see him the afternoon he died. He'd told him that they needed to destroy the Collider before it destroyed the world, and that Deiter knew all about it and was letting it happen.'

'So, Deiter could have killed Morantz to stop him going public?'

'I don't like the guy, but I wouldn't have put him down as a genocidal manic,' Tom scoffed.

'You're right,' said Selena closing the file. 'I think we're getting a little carried away with our suppositions, or we've drunk too much red wine. But what do we do now?'

Tom checked his watch. It was two-thirty in the morning. 'Let's sleep on it, and in the morning I'll speak to Frederick. Do you mind if I hang onto this, Ajay? Incidentally, why haven't you shown it to anybody else?'

'I trust only you, Professor, sahib.'

'What about your father?'

'I trust only you, Professor, sahib,' Ajay repeated.

CHAPTER 14

Ajay returned to his room, feeling relieved that he had given the file to the Professor and was confident the sahib would do the right thing. He knew, as soon as he'd met him at the airport, that he could trust him. His assured demeanour, considerate attitude and gracious mannerisms all indicated that he was a man of integrity.

He regarded himself as a good judge of character, despite being betrayed by the only other person he'd respected and loved.

Ajay was eight when Frederick applied to the courts in India to act as guardian for his best friend's child. With no living relatives and the only other alternative being an orphanage, it was just a matter of formality that he was awarded custody. Ajay couldn't remember much about his father, but he did keep a photo of him, which Frederick had given him, by his bedside. The picture was of Ajay, as a boy, sitting on his father's knee, both smiling at the camera for posterity. He had mental pictures of his mother from what Frederick had told him about her, but they were fuzzy and didn't hold any sentimental value.

He had grown up in Dusseldorf, where his father had worked before the accident, moving in with Mr and Mrs Volker following the tragedy. They were kind to him and eventually he came to accept them as his parents. Frederick and Irma were unable to conceive a child themselves, so for their part they treated Ajay like the son they could never have.

Being in a minority of one at school, he was often picked on and bullied by the other pupils. He found solace in religion, preferring to learn from the Pandit at the local Hindu temple than his teachers at school. Frederick had always encouraged him to follow his ancestral creed, in order to preserve a sense of heritage and cultural roots.

He was fascinated by the folk stories and traditions that had been passed down through the generations and would often spend any spare time he had helping out at the temple with the menial chores, just so he could hear the priest recount some more fables. And that was how he spent his adolescence; whilst his peers were discovering the vices of drink, drugs and girls, Ajay would be learning the Vedic Texts, the most ancient religious teachings which define 'truth' for Hindus.

At the age of 16, he had given up on school altogether and spent his days shadowing the priest, whom he had become close to over the years. He even considered devoting his life to the faith and becoming a Brahmin or teacher of scriptures, like his mentor, until it was explained to him that he didn't come from the right caste and, therefore, would never be accepted as a priest. This rocked his conviction somewhat and he began to spend less and less time at the temple and more and more time moping in his bedroom, which led to the inevitable clashes with his parents.

Without any job prospects, he fell in with the wrong crowd and discovered the vices that he'd missed out on while growing up, namely drink and drugs. Unable to afford either habit, he reverted to stealing, firstly from his parents and then, as the habits took hold, from houses. He was arrested for burglary, after someone recognised him whilst leaving a house by the window, and he was sentenced to two years in prison suspended for a year on the condition that he sought professional help for his addictions.

That was when Fredrick thought that a change of scenery would do them all a world of good and accepted a position on the CERN council, which meant moving to Switzerland. Ajay's initial experience of his new country was from the inside of the Geneva Rehabilitation Centre, where he spent the first six months getting clean. He left the clinic looking healthier than he had done in a long while, with a determination to get his life back on track.

Frederick found him a job at CERN, after pulling a few strings, and set him up in the accommodation block to give him a sense of autonomy; however, in reality, he had asked the night porter to keep an eye on him and inform him if Ajay received any guests or was seen going out late at night. To Frederick's relief, over the next four years there had been nothing to report.

Ajay enjoyed his newfound independence but would always visit his parents at the weekend, when they would spend their time together on trips into the countryside, visiting the surrounding villages or boating on the lake. Ajay felt that he was now closer to his parents than he'd ever been and, with a regular wage coming in, he could afford to treat them to the odd meal or present.

He loved his job. He didn't have an official title, but everybody knew that he was the general dogsbody. Ajay didn't mind his lowly position, however, because it gave him the opportunity to meet so many different people. He would load boxes, deliver mail, organise refreshments for meetings, ferry people to and from the airport, deputise for reception staff – every day was different and every day would bring him into contact with a new set of employees who were always friendly towards him.

He did have his favourite; the girls in the canteen would always tease him, making him blush, but there was one girl in particular that had caught his eye. She was quieter than the others and didn't join in the banter, but would always give him a radiant smile whenever she saw him.

On one occasion, when he was helping to unload a delivery to the kitchens, she came out for a cigarette by herself and asked him for a light. He fumbled around in his pocket, despite knowing that he didn't have a lighter on him because he didn't smoke. When he'd made enough of a show of trying to find one, he apologised and went back to stacking the boxes. The next day, armed with two lighters and a carton of cigarettes, he made certain that he was in the right place when another delivery turned up. And, sure enough, whilst he was carrying the goods into the kitchen, she came out. Before she'd had a chance to take a cigarette from her packet, he'd already dropped the two cases of fish packed in ice and offered her one of his cigarettes.

She smiled coyly at him. 'Thank you. I didn't know you smoked.'

He lit hers and one for himself, suppressing a cough as he took in the smoke. 'Yes,' he replied, 'but I'm trying to give them up.'

This was, in fact, only the second cigarette he'd tried in his life. The first one was loaded with skunk, given to him by one of his depraved 'friends' when he'd gone off the rails. On that occasion, he coughed so much that he thought he would pass out and vowed never to try another, preferring the simpler-to-ingest cocaine to get his highs.

'Me too,' the girl said. 'It's a disgusting habit, when you think about it. My name's Jasmine, by the way.'

'Ajay, pleased to meet you.' He held out his hand for a formal greeting.

She smiled again and shook his hand gently, feeling a little embarrassed by the gesture.

'Have you been here long, Jasmine?' He liked the sound of her name when he said it; it suited her delicate features, petite figure and dark, chocolate-coloured eyes. She wore a none-too-flattering catering hairnet, but he could tell from her fringe that her hair was black and silky. Her complexion was lighter than his own, suggesting that her family came from one of the more northern regions of India.

'This is only my second month in Geneva,' she said. 'My father got a transfer at work, so our family came with him.'

'Who does he work for?'

'The Hinduja Bank in the city.'

'It must have been difficult for you to leave your home,' Ajay said, remembering his own immigration. 'Where did you live before?'

'My family are originally from Kashmir, but we've moved around a lot with Dad's work.'

'Do you like it here?'

'The country or the canteen?' Jasmine asked, smiling.

'Both.'

'I like working here because the people are so friendly,' she replied. 'But I haven't seen much of Geneva. We spent the last few weeks in a hotel while my mother looked for a place for us to live. All our stuff is being shipped over, so I'm living out of a suitcase at the moment.'

'I could show you around Geneva, if you like?' said Ajay seizing the opportunity to spend more time with this pretty girl.

'I'd like that,' she flashed him another smile.

'Tonight? I could pick you up when you finish work.'

'Okay, I'll see you tonight. I must get back to work, otherwise I'll be in trouble,' she said stubbing out her cigarette before scurrying back inside, leaving Ajay standing there with a big grin on his face.

It was several minutes before he saw the puddle of water starting to form around his feet from the defrosting ice seeping out of the boxes he'd discarded earlier. The supplier had finished unloading the rest of the goods and had driven off without Ajay even noticing. He picked up the fish and took it into the kitchen, oblivious to the trail of water he was leaving behind him. His mind was on more important things; he had to ask his father if he could borrow one of the pool cars for his date that evening.

Frederick was usually to be found somewhere on site. Although he was President of the Council and could have spent his days pushing pieces of paper backwards and forwards across a desk, he preferred to take a hands-on approach by involving himself in the day-to-day running of the facility. Ajay knew his best bet of tracking him down quickly was to ask one of the security team that patrolled the premises.

'Have you seen Herr Volker?' he asked the first uniformed guard he saw.

'I saw him when he arrived this morning,' replied the man. 'He went into the main building, but I haven't seen him since.'

Ajay went to the main reception to ask and was told that Frederick had left the building about ten minutes ago.

'Which direction was he heading?'

'He took one of the golf buggies and drove off left.'

Ajay ran down the stairs and jumped into one of the buggies parked at the front of the building and set off after him. He had to ask another two security guards on the way before he was able to spot the white cart turning into an underground car park in the distance. Ajay had never been to this area of the compound before; he hadn't had any need to.

He followed his father through the entrance. As his eyes became accustomed to the gloom, he could see that the car park was almost deserted apart from five black Mercedes, the same model as his father's, parked side by side along one wall, and two white buggies which were abandoned in front of the lift. He parked next to the cars and walked back, peering through the darkness to determine any form of life. It was desolate. As he waited for the lift to arrive, he wondered what his father could be doing in such a remote part of the complex and who the other cars belonged to.

He could hear the gentle hum of the electric motors as the lift made its way to him, but it seemed to take an inordinately long time. Finally, the doors opened and he stepped in. Not knowing which floor his father was on, he decided to go through them one at a time and pressed the first floor button. The journey took a couple of seconds and the doors slid open again to reveal an empty rectangular office space. The walls had been painted and the floor tiled, but it was evident from the musty smell that it had never been a functioning work environment.

He stepped back in the lift and tried the second floor, only to find it identical to the level below. He got out on the third, which was the same as the other two, and walked across to one of the windows to look out. He could see the compound buildings to his right and, to his left, the perimeter, beyond which were green pastures stretching across the landscape towards the horizon.

But what struck him as odd was the road that dissected the fields ending at a barrier in the fence. To the side of it was a small sentry hut. He cupped his hands around his eyes and pressed his forehead against the glass to get a better view. He could just make out a figure sitting in the box. He was dressed in a uniform, but it didn't look as though it was the same as the ones the guards wore on the compound.

As he watched, the door to the hut opened and the man stepped out, stretching his legs. He was clean-shaven, dark-skinned with tightly-cropped black hair. Ajay could see clearly now his navy blue jacket and trousers, light blue shirt and matching tie, as opposed to the grey/green apparel of the CERN security force. But the biggest difference he could see was what he was carrying over his shoulder; it looked like a machine gun, whereas the compound's patrolmen carried hip-holstered hand guns.

Puzzled, he returned to the lift. *If his father wasn't here, then where was he?* He did a cursory check of each floor on the way back to the basement, just in case he'd missed him, although he thought it unlikely as there were no hidden corners or partitions.

He made his way back to the buggy and was just about to return to the main building when he heard the electric motors of the lift start up again. Instinctively, he bolted for one of the dark recesses by the side of the shaft. He couldn't work out what had spooked him; perhaps it was the heavily-armed security presence, or the derelict building itself. But either way, he got the distinct impression that he was trespassing.

He heard the doors open, followed by the voices of several people. From his vantage point, he could see them getting into their cars, their breath condensing in the chilled air as they said their goodbyes. Four men and one woman started their engines, demisted their windscreens and drove out in an orderly fashion. He was about to run across to his buggy, when the lift doors opened again; this time, he recognised the voices of his father and Deiter Weiss. He wanted to emerge from his hiding place and speak to them, but he thought they might think he was spying on them. No, he would remain where he was until they'd gone and choose his moment to ask his father about the building later.

He could hear them clearly but, as the conversation between the two men progressed, he regretted his decision not to make himself known. What he was listening to made the hairs on the back of his neck stand on end.

Suddenly, the exchange stopped mid-sentence.

'How did you get here?' Frederick asked Deiter.

'By golf buggy, of course. It's parked next to yours.'

'Then whose is that one over there?'

Ajay looked over to his own buggy, sitting there as prominent as a single milk tooth in a baby's smile.

'We know you're there,' Deiter shouted. 'Come out and we won't have to call the guards.'

He thought of the machine gun, but stayed put.

'You've got until the count of three to show yourself,' continued Deiter. 'Otherwise we'll call in the dogs.'

Ajay had seen what those dogs could do to a man's padded arm, when he'd watched them practising their training on campus.

'One... two... three...'

He stepped out of the shadows behind them. Frederick and Deiter spun round to face the interloper.

'Ajay! What are you doing here?' Ajay could see the mixture of bewilderment and anger on his father's face.

'I... I... came to find you,' he began. 'I wanted to borrow a car for this evening. I have a date.' Even Ajay thought it sounded weak, especially after everything he'd seen and heard.

'What?' shouted Frederick. The bewilderment gave way to pure anger. 'How long have you been skulking there?'

'Not long,' Ajay said feebly.

'Certainly long enough to eavesdrop on our conversation,' Deiter retorted.

'Leave this to me, Deiter,' replied Frederick. 'You go back to the facility, otherwise people will be wondering where you are.'

'But he could jeopardise everything.'

'I said, leave this to me. It's my problem and I will sort it out,' Frederick shouted, his face bright red. Ajay had never seen him that angry before.

Deiter reluctantly left them to it.

Frederick paced backwards and forwards, trying to control his temper so that he could think clearer about what to do next. He churned over in his mind the context of the conversation that Ajay must have overheard, to ascertain what damage had been done. He'd heard them discussing Shiva, but he wouldn't be aware of its significance. He had seen the members, but probably wouldn't be able to recognise any of their faces again, so he couldn't expose them. He would obviously have picked up there was a hidden agenda, when it came to the Collider. *Damn*, he thought to himself, *how could we have become so careless, breaking the golden rule of never discussing anything about our mission outside the Bunker?*

Frederick walked calmly back to where he'd left Ajay. He hadn't moved from the spot; his face was ashen, head bowed, staring at his feet.

'This is a very serious situation,' Frederick began. 'What you've heard and seen here today is part of a grander scheme, which I'm not at liberty to confide in you. It's not that I don't trust you; it's that I am bound by a code that has been passed down to me. The consequences of going against those protocols could put billions of lives at risk. Do you understand?'

Ajay nodded meekly, not really comprehending the enormity of the situation.

'Okay. What I need you to do is agree to a pact. A vow never to divulge anything that you've heard or seen here today to another living soul. Are you prepared to do that?'

Ajay nodded his assent, still staring at the floor.

'I need you to say the words,' his father replied, sternly.

Ajay looked up and met Frederick's gaze. 'I swear that I will never tell another living soul,' he said quietly.

'On everything that you hold dear?'

'Yes.' Ajay put his hand on his heart. 'I swear, on everything that I hold dear, that I will never tell another living soul.'

Frederick let out a heavy sigh, releasing most of his pent-up anger. He knew that that should be enough to guarantee his son's compliance, but he wasn't prepared to take any chances.

'You said you had a date this evening,' he said. 'Is it anybody I know?' His voice was calm now, almost congenial.

'Just somebody I met in the canteen. Her name's Jasmine,' Ajay told him, bashfully.

'Pretty name,' replied his father. 'I'm sure she's a nice girl, but I think under the circumstances you should keep a low profile for a couple of days. I still need to convince Deiter and the others that you will keep your word and that you're not a threat.'

Ajay looked crestfallen. 'But I gave you my word.'

'And I believe you, but they don't know you like I do. Why don't you tell her you'll take her out at the weekend, instead? That should give me enough time to sort things out?'

Ajay reluctantly agreed and left to tell Jasmine that he wouldn't be able to make it that night. He just hoped that he hadn't blown his chances and she would agree to see him at the weekend.

Frederick watched his son get into the buggy and drive out of the car park. He reached inside his jacket pocket and retrieved his mobile phone. Scrolling through his address book, he found the number and pressed the quick dial button.

'Bernard? Hi, it's Frederick. I have a favour to ask.'

***

Jasmine had been very understanding. He told her that he had to do some work for his father and it couldn't wait. Not so much a lie as a half-truth; his father *was* the reason he wouldn't be able to see her. When he asked her out on Saturday instead, she had initially played hard to get, accusing him of standing her up and telling him that she didn't know if she would be available; but, seeing the hurt look on his face, she quickly changed her tune and told him that she didn't have to work weekends so they could spend the whole day together.

They had arranged to meet at 10 am at a café on the Rue du Rhône, one of the main shopping streets in the city. Ajay was there twenty minutes ahead of schedule to make sure he got a table in the window so he could see her when she arrived; he covered his bases, as he wasn't sure if they were supposed to be meeting inside the premises or outside.

Café Le Monde was a small, bustling, art deco style coffee shop serving light lunches and exorbitantly priced coffees to the affluent shoppers who frequented the street's luxury goods stores. It smelt of its wares; the aroma of richly-roasted dark coffee beans and sweet pastries permeated the air. Ajay had never been to the place before, but he had chosen it for its location; it was directly opposite the Jardin Anglais, where he planned to start his tour. His itinerary was meticulously planned to take in most of the sights worth seeing in Geneva, ending the day at the Hôtel d'Angleterre, on the other side of the lake. On several occasions, he had heard his father talk about how good the restaurant was and it sounded like the ideal place to impress his date.

He wore his best designer jeans, white shirt and a black puffer jacket to protect against the bitter cold of a grey November morning. He sat in the window warming his hands on the skinny latte with an extra shot and caramel flavouring. Daunted by the extensive menu, he had ordered the first coffee on the list; the extras were up-sold by an eager, commission-hungry, pre-pubescent sales assistant. He watched the people through the window as they tried to carry their oversized carrier bags stuffed with haute couture to waiting cars. He checked his watch; it was half past ten. She was running late.

She wouldn't be so vindictive as to stand him up in retaliation for the other night, surely? he reasoned. No, she was far too kind-hearted a person to do that! But he couldn't wait for her all day.

Why hadn't he asked her for her mobile number? But then, why would he have needed it? They'd already arranged to meet. If she wasn't able to make it, she could always phone the café.

Give her another thirty minutes, he thought to himself.

He ordered a second latte, this time without the trimmings, at the counter and took it back to his perch by the window, to continue his people-watching. Another thirty minutes passed. Just as he was about to leave, he thought he spotted Jasmine in the milling crowd. His pulse raced and his mouth went instantly dry as he tried to peer through the throng of people, but as the scarf-swathed individual drew closer he realised that the woman was too old to be her.

Disappointed, he left the café and drove back to the facility.

***

Ajay parked up and made his way to the canteen. He had worked out on the drive back that she'd probably been asked to work. It wasn't unusual for the catering staff to get a call at the last minute to cover a colleague who was off sick, especially if there was a function on or a visiting dignitary. He'd also come to the conclusion that the reason she hadn't been able to let him know was because she wouldn't have had time to look up the café's phone number if they were that short-staffed.

He pushed open the frosted-glass double doors expecting to see a hive of activity. However, he was taken aback when he saw that there was just one person wiping down the tables and refilling the salt and pepper pots.

'We don't open until twelve,' the woman shouted across the room when she saw Ajay standing in the doorway, staring at her.

'I'm looking for Jasmine. Is she working today?'

The woman put down her cloth and walked over to him. He recognised her as the ringleader of the group who teased him. He read the name on her lapel badge: *Mary*. She was in her mid-forties with a face that looked older due to too many package holidays and cigarettes. Her teeth were crooked and yellowing from the effects of the nicotine. Ajay could smell the smoke on her breath as she stood in front of him.

'You not heard?'

'Heard what?' Ajay replied.

'She's been deported.'

'Deported?' Ajay repeated. 'But why? How?'

'Something to do with her dad's visa,' the woman replied. 'The police said it wasn't legal. They came yesterday and arrested her. Apparently, they took her and her family to the airport and put them on the next plane to India. Can't say I'm surprised.'

Ajay was speechless. Only two people knew that the real reason Jasmine's family had to leave the country was to prevent him forming a friendship with somebody he could confide in. But Ajay couldn't work out how his father had the power or authority to deport people at will.

***

As he sat in his room, the thought crossed his mind again. It had been over a month since the incident and he was still no nearer to finding out. He had confronted his father about the extradition, but he had denied all knowledge or involvement in it. That was the first time in Ajay's life that he knew his father wasn't telling him the whole truth, and the fragile bond between father and son, that was so dependent on trust, broke.

He had kept his side of the bargain by not telling anybody about what he'd seen or heard and would continue to do so, not out of any respect or duty to his father, but because he owed it to himself. However, his vow didn't prevent him from passing documents onto somebody else who *could* discover the truth.

A sharp rap on the door interrupted his reverie. He opened it to find Deiter standing there, a black leather holdall slung over his shoulder.

'Mind if I come in?' Without waiting for a reply, Deiter barged past him and entered the room. Ajay could smell the alcohol on him. 'Close the door. I think you and I need to have a little chat. We wouldn't want anyone to overhear us, would we?'

Ajay reluctantly complied. He was fearful of Deiter and went out of his way to avoid him at all costs.

Deiter stood in the centre of the small room and put his bag down on the table underneath the window. 'I see you've been taking a keen interest in my handiwork,' he said noticing the newspaper cuttings on the wall. 'I didn't realise I had such a big fan.'

Ajay shot him a quizzical look and was about to ask him what he meant, when he was silenced by a dismissive wave.

'We can talk more about that later,' continued Deiter. 'But at the moment there are more pressing things we need to discuss. Please take a seat.' He gestured to the single bed.

Ajay perched on the edge of the mattress, his hands folded in his lap. Deiter pulled the chair from under the table and positioned it directly in front of Ajay. He sat down and crossed his legs, as if they were old friends discussing the latest sports results.

'It has been brought to my attention that you've been spending rather a lot of time in the company of our new Director General. Can I ask why?' Deiter's tone was level, but Ajay could detect a menacing undercurrent.

'He was... he was... erm... interested in my grandfather,' Ajay replied, thinking back to the first time he'd met the professor.

Disbelief showed on Deiter's face. 'Satyendra Bose? Why would he be interested in *him*?'

'He said that he was inspirational and had a big influence on his career.'

Deiter didn't look convinced.

'And I showed him my scrapbook,' Ajay added, retrieving it from the side of his bed.

He handed the book to Deiter, who gave it a cursory inspection then tossed it irreverently back onto the bed. 'What else did you talk about?'

'Nothing.' Ajay had no compunction in lying to this man.

'I don't believe you.' The menace in Deiter's voice began to surface.

'It's the truth,' Ajay replied, staring defiantly at him.

Deiter returned his gaze, trying to detect any hint of dishonesty in his eyes. Ajay was the first to look away.

'I know about your promise to your father,' said Deiter, keeping his voice level. 'He's convinced you'll keep your mouth shut. I, on the other hand, am not so gullible. If I find out that you've been speaking to *anybody* about what you know, then I would have no option but to…'

'Kill me? Like you killed Professor Morantz?' Ajay blurted out, his courage driven by anger. But he realised his error as soon as the words left his mouth.

Deiter lunged. His reflexes were as fast as a coiled cobra's, grabbing Ajay around the neck with one hand and pushing him back against the wall, knocking the wind out of him.

'What do you know about that?' Deiter demanded, his face flushed, inches away from Ajay's. The stench of alcohol on his breath would have made Ajay gag if he wasn't already struggling to inhale. Seeing he was in distress and not wanting to kill him just yet, Deiter released his grip and sat back in his chair. Ajay slumped on the bed, gulped in a lungful of air and started to cough.

'It's of no consequence,' Deiter said, regaining his composure. 'It just saves me the time and effort of impressing on you what I'm capable of. You see, Morantz was a very weak man. I tried to persuade him to join our cause, but he was insistent on going to the media. He left me no option, really.'

Ajay managed to regulate his breathing. He looked up at Deiter, who was inspecting his fingernails. His placid demeanour was betrayed by the wildness in his eyes. *Was he really trying to justify what he'd done?*

'So you killed him?' Ajay croaked.

'Let's just say I assisted him in reaching a conclusion to our conflict.'

'And now you're going to kill me,' Ajay sat up, nursing the bruises on his neck.

'Kill you? Kill you? What do you take me for? I'm not a monster,' Deiter replied indignantly. 'I'm here to help you.'

'Like you helped Professor Morantz?'

'Now *that* is entirely your choice.' Deiter reached over to the desk to retrieve his bag. 'I have here ten thousand Euros and a one-way ticket to India.' He unzipped the holdall and showed Ajay its contents. 'You can either take the money and disappear for good, or suffer the consequences. It's up to you; I have no preference either way. Do I make myself clear?'

Ajay understood completely the implications of Deiter's concealed threat and decided his best course of action would be to remain silent. He was wrong.

'Do… I… make… myself… clear?' Deiter enunciated each word separately with increasing intensity.

'Yes,' Ajay replied in a hoarse whisper.

'Good. I'll leave this with you then.' Deiter stood up abruptly and threw the case on the bed. 'If you're still here in the morning, then I'll have to assume that you'd like another one of our little chats, only I won't be able to guarantee it will be as friendly next time.' With that, he walked over to the door to let himself out. 'I do hope you make the right decision, for your sake,' were his parting words, as he disappeared into the corridor.

Lying back on the bed and breathing deeply, Ajay began to contemplate his options.

He could speak to his father, but then he already knew the two men were accomplices. Perhaps his father had even sanctioned Deiter's actions? Had his father also been involved in Professor Morantz's murder?

He could go to the police, but would they believe him over an eminent physicist like Deiter? Probably not. Besides, what could he tell them? That Professor Morantz didn't really commit suicide and that he'd been given ten thousand Euros to keep quiet about a non-existent murder? If he had a problem trying to comprehend what had just taken place, the police would have no chance.

He could tell Professor sahib. At least *he* would believe him, but it would also put him in danger. He already knew Deiter had killed once, but by the look in his eyes earlier Ajay knew he was capable of much more.

Or he could just carry on as normal and 'suffer the consequences' as Deiter had put it. He was under no illusion what that meant.

No, he didn't really have any options.

He dragged his blue canvas suitcase out from under the bed and started to pack.

CHAPTER 15

Tom awoke alone, much to his disappointment. He contemplated whether that still would have been the case had the night gone differently. Ajay's appearance had certainly altered the course of any possible romance. He looked at his alarm clock. It was seven-thirty.

Serena had fallen asleep on his couch after they'd exhausted the discussions on the evening's events. Tom was unsure whether the gentlemanly thing to do was to let her sleep there with a throw over her, or wake her up and offer her his bed while he slept on the couch. He had chosen the former.

He got out of bed, slipped on a pair of trousers and tip-toed into the lounge, not wanting to wake her. He needn't have bothered; she was in the kitchen making coffee, wearing the cocktail dress that she'd had on the night before, only it was slightly more crumpled than the last time Tom had seen it.

'Morning. Jeez, you look as rough as I feel,' she said, taking a bite out of a heavily-buttered slice of toast. 'I hope you don't mind, but I helped myself to your bread, although I couldn't find anything to put on it.'

'Yes, sorry,' replied Tom. 'Funnily enough, I just haven't had the time to go to the grocery store. I'll make a note to go at the weekend for you.'

Serena smiled over at him and took another bite of her toast.

'By the way,' he continued, 'you're the second person to have commented on how rough I look since I've been here. It must be catching.' He folded his arms across his chest, self-conscious of his naked top half.

'Oh! And who else have you managed to lure back to your apartment in such a short space of time?' she said in mock indignation.

'It was Frederick,' he replied solemnly.

'Oh! I see. I didn't know you were that way inclined,' she replied, unsure whether or not he was being serious.

'I'm not. He came to collect me after I'd had an afternoon nap.'

'Or that's the story you'd *like* everybody to believe,' she said. 'I'm fairly broad-minded about these things. You can confide in me.'

This time it was Tom's turn to wonder whether she was joking or not. She could read the expression on his face and laughed. 'I'm joking, of course… I'm not broad-minded at all.'

'I think we'll call that a draw,' replied Tom. 'Any chance of a coffee?'

'Sure, I've just made a pot. Help yourself.'

'So, what are your plans for today?' he asked, pouring himself a cup.

'Well, firstly I've got to get back to my apartment without anybody seeing me. I look like something the cat dragged in,' she said finishing her toast.

She looked absolutely perfect to Tom. She had let her hair down and wiped off her make-up, but that didn't detract, in the slightest, from her natural beauty.

'And then after I've had a shower and made myself look presentable,' she continued, 'I'll make my way into the office. See if I can dig up any more information on the Collider's electromagnetic radiation readings. What about you?'

'More interviews, I'm afraid. I need to be around in case the police need to ask me anything. But at some stage I need to catch up with Frederick to discuss Professor Morantz's folder. Let me try him now, to see if we can set up an appointment.'

He reached for his mobile phone, which was charging on the kitchen worktop, and dialled the number from memory. The phone connected but it went straight through to voicemail. He left a message.

'Hi Frederick, this is Tom. I was hoping we could meet up today to discuss a rather interesting file that I have in my possession. Without giving too much away over the phone, I believe it could be the missing evidence that we discussed over dinner the other night, or I may just be the butt of a rather elaborate practical joke. Either way, let me know when you're available. Thanks. Bye.'

Tom pressed the end button and set the phone back in its charger. He didn't know why he felt the need to be cautious, but he did. He just hoped his message wasn't too cryptic for Frederick to understand what he was talking about.

'You don't think it could be fake, do you?' Serena asked.

'I don't know. Perhaps you could verify the readings against your data, and then we could meet up for lunch to discuss your findings? I'll make sure I see Frederick after we've spoken. Why don't you take the file with you and make a copy of it? I'm not sure why, but I think we should keep this between ourselves for the time being, or at least until I've had a chance to discuss it with Frederick. He'll know what to do.'

'You know, you don't always have to use work as an excuse to see me.' Serena crossed the living room and retrieved her shoes from where she'd kicked them off the night before. Carrying them in one hand, her clutch bag in the other and the folder under her arm, she presented herself to Tom. 'How do I look?'

'Put it this way,' he replied, grinning. 'That cat that dragged you in had great taste.'

'You old smoothie,' she walked back to him and kissed him on the cheek. 'Wish me luck. I wouldn't want to give the office gossips something to talk about.'

'Where is your apartment, by the way?'

'Next door.' She left him standing in the kitchen, the heady scent of the perfume she'd worn the night before lingering after her.

CHAPTER 16

Tom arrived at the main office an hour later. The police were already there, ticking the names of the workers off a list as they entered. He noticed that fresh flowers lay at the feet of the statue as he made his way up the stairs.

His passage into the building was blocked by an unsmiling uniformed officer. 'Nom, m'sieur?'

'Pardon?'

'Your name please?' the officer repeated in heavily accented English.

'Professor Tom Halligan.'

The official scanned down the first page of his manifest with his pen, then the second page, the third, fourth and fifth, by which time Tom was feeling the cold wintry morning nip at his fingers and toes. He hadn't bothered to put on a jacket because he had no reason to think he'd need one. He was only going from the accommodation block to his office, or so he thought.

'Is this going to take long? Only I'm freezing my nuts off.'

There was no reaction from the officer until he finished checking the last page. 'Non,' he said looking up at Tom.

'What do you mean, "non"? I work here.' Tom was stamping his feet, trying to regain the circulation he'd lost in his extremities.

'Il n'est pas possible.'

'Sorry?'

'It is not possible,' the officer said with a sigh, the translation obviously an effort for him.

'It's very bloody possible! I am the Director General,' Tom snapped, losing his patience more with the bureaucracy than the individual. 'Let me speak to Inspector Gervaux.'

The policeman turned his back on Tom and spoke into his walkie-talkie. Tom couldn't quite hear the exchange and, even if he could, he wouldn't have been able to understand it. After several minutes, the young officer half-turned to face Tom and looked him up and down, before turning away again to resumed his conversation with his superior. It was another five minutes before the officer finished talking. He turned his focus back to Tom, who was rubbing his hands together frantically in an effort to keep warm.

'You may go in, but Inspector Gervaux would like to see you immediately. He is waiting in your office.'

I bet he is, thought Tom. *And he won't be as bloody freezing as I am.*

Without a word, he went through the revolving doors and into the building, the warmth of the reception making his fingers tingle immediately. He hadn't felt that sensation for a long time and it evoked childhood memories of snowball fights and sledging, and then warming frozen hands and feet in front of an open fire.

***

'Ah, Professor Halligan, apologies for delaying you outside. Your name wasn't on the payroll list we obtained from your wages clerk. I understand that you have only recently joined CERN?'

Inspector Gervaux peered over the top of his glasses, which were perched on the end of a large, aquiline nose. He was clean-shaven apart from a pencil-thin moustache, which seemed to underline his beak, making it more conspicuous. His hair was mousy-brown and had started to recede, which he compensated for by growing it slightly longer than fashionable and combing forward.

He wasn't quite in the same class as Donald Trump, but Tom suspected that it wouldn't be much longer before he could give him a run for his money. Tom guessed that they were probably about the same age. He had his jacket off with the sleeves of his crisp, white shirt rolled up and his tie thrown over one shoulder. But what bothered Tom the most about him was that he was sitting in Tom's chair.

'Yes, I've only been here a couple of days,' he replied. 'And thanks for letting me know I'm not on the payroll. That may affect how much work I do around here.' The pun went straight over the inspector's head. 'May I?' Tom said pointing to his own seat.

It took the inspector a few seconds before he realised what Tom was referring to and apologised, moving himself and his papers to the other side of the desk.

'Your man on the door said you wanted to see me,' said Tom, sitting in the warm seat recently vacated by the inspector.

'Yes, I have the initial report from our forensic team.' The inspector looked through his glasses at a sheet of paper on the desk. 'It appears they have found traces of an explosive device.'

'A bomb?' Tom said incredulously. 'I don't believe it. Who would want to sabotage the project?'

'The motives for planting such a device could range from a disgruntled employee to an extremist group and anything in between,' Inspector Gervaux informed him, leaning back in his chair and taking his glasses off. 'We are now treating this…' he paused for dramatic effect, '…as a murder investigation.'

Tom surmised the inspector had been reading too many Agatha Christie novels. 'Do you have any suspects?' he asked, knowing that was the customary response.

'Do you know a man called…' said the inspector, referring back to his paper, '…Anjit Gopal Bose?'

'Ajay, yes. Why?'

'We received an anonymous tip-off suggesting he could be involved.'

'Ajay? No way. He wouldn't hurt a fly.'

'Do you know this man well?'

'I know him, but I wouldn't say I know him well.'

'Then how do you know what he's capable of?'

'Well, I don't,' replied Tom, baffled. 'But he's just a messenger boy.'

'Professor, some of the most notorious murderers in history had menial jobs. The Yorkshire Ripper in the UK was *just* a delivery driver, Harold Fritzl in Belgium was *just* an electrician, Jeffrey Dahmer in your own country killed at least seventeen people and he *just* worked in a chocolate factory. I could go on.'

'Okay, okay. I get the point. But Ajay's not a serial killer.'

'We will follow up any leads we have,' replied the inspector. 'Most of the time they turn out to be nothing more than an over-zealous do-gooder playing detective, or a vindictive colleague trying to exact revenge on a workmate. But we have to take them all seriously.'

'But Ajay was liked by everybody,' Tom protested.

'Obviously not, otherwise we wouldn't have had the tip-off. Do you know where we can find Anjit? Only he hasn't shown up for work yet, and the officer I sent to his room reported there was no answer.'

CHAPTER 17

Frederick had returned his call and they arranged to meet just after lunch. He didn't know if he was getting paranoid or not, but he thought he could detect a note of tension in Frederick's voice. *Perhaps the police have already spoken to him about Ajay's disappearance?* he wondered.

Tom spent the rest of the morning trying to avoid the inspector. It wasn't that he didn't want to help the police with their enquiries; he just wanted a chance to speak with Ajay first. He wasn't prepared to accept that he was such a bad judge of character.

Just before lunch, he decided to check on Ajay's apartment for himself, in case he was hiding there and too frightened to answer the door to the police. He may be holed up, ready to make his last stand, as Inspector Gervaux would have it. He thought it prudent to grab his jacket on the way past his own apartment, just in case he had any more problems getting back into the office.

As Tom made his way down the corridor, he noticed that the door to his apartment was slightly ajar. He could have sworn he'd pulled it to and heard the lock click before he'd left in the morning. He wasn't a citizen's arrest type of person, so figured his best course of action would be to make as much noise as possible to give any intruder a chance of running away, then leave it to the police to track him down later.

He stood a few feet away from the door to allow safe passage for any fleeing criminals and started up an imaginary conversation on his phone. 'No, I'm not in my office. I'm just going back to my apartment to pick my jacket up. Yes, I'm there now. No, I won't be too long. I'll see you shortly.'

He held his breath and inched closer, trying to hear any movement coming from inside his apartment. *Nothing.* He knocked on the door.

'Hello, is there anybody in there?' He didn't know what he'd do if somebody answered him. 'Yes, I'm just robbing your apartment. I won't be too much longer.' As it happened, there was no reply. Tom breathed a sigh of relief and pushed the door open with his foot. *Still nothing.* He peered cautiously into the room.

There was no sign of a burglar, but there was evidence that somebody had been there. The apartment had been ransacked. He stood in the entrance, surveying the carnage. The large orange sofa was tipped over; its fabric had been slashed and stuffing spilled out onto the floor, like entrails. The unit housing the TV and CD player lay on top of it, its contents smashed beyond recognition, their constituent parts scattered across the floor. The small table, upon which the laptop computer was placed, had been tossed across the other side of the room, but Tom couldn't see the laptop anywhere.

He made his way into the kitchen, picking his way around the debris. He could feel a cold breeze on his cheek – the patio doors leading to the quadrangle were wide open. He thought perhaps he had disturbed them, after all. The kitchen was in a similar state as the lounge. All the cupboards had been unceremoniously emptied onto the floor, which was now covered by a carpet of glass and china. Drawers had been pulled out, their contents tipped onto the kitchen work surface before being discarded. He didn't need to go into the bedroom to know that it would have received the same treatment.

He dialled the main CERN number from the mobile he was still clenching in his hand and asked to be put through to Inspector Gervaux. He had to wait several minutes before he heard the heavy French accent on the other end.

'Hello, Inspector Gervaux. How may I help you?'

'Inspector? Hi, it's Tom Halligan. I think I've been burgled.'

***

'And you say the only thing missing is your laptop?'

Inspector Gervaux was jotting down everything that Tom was telling him in his notebook. It had taken him less than ten minutes to get to the apartment. He had with him a short, broad-shouldered gentleman with a squat neck and a heavy mono-brow arranged in a constant frown over close-set eyes. He had a round face with black, short-cropped hair. A badly-stitched scar ran from one side of his mouth to just below his cheek. If Tom hadn't known better, he would have sworn he was looking at somebody who came from the wrong side of the law. He was introduced as Sergeant Lavelle.

'As far as I can tell,' replied Tom. 'But, as you can see, it's difficult to work out what's here, let alone what's gone.'

The three men were standing in what was left of Tom's bedroom. His mattress and duvet had been shredded, covering everything in a layer of snowy-white downy feathers. His clothes were strewn across the floor, the pockets of his jackets and trousers ripped open.

'Do you have any idea who could be responsible for this?' the inspector asked.

'No, I don't. Perhaps it was an opportunist thief,' Tom suggested.

'It doesn't look like a regular burglary. It appears more like they were looking for something.' It was the first time Sergeant Lavelle had spoken. Even when he was first introduced to Tom, he had simply nodded a greeting. His voice was gravelly, with a mix of French and German accents.

'But what?' Tom tried to rack his brains. 'I don't have anything of value.'

'What was on the laptop?' Inspector Gervaux enquired.

'Nothing of mine. I haven't even had time to log on since I arrived.'

'Was it a new laptop?' Sergeant Lavelle interjected.

'As I said, I hadn't really had a chance to use it,' replied Tom. 'But, going by everything else, it was probably a hand-me-down.'

'Pardon?' the two men said in unison.

'It probably belonged to my predecessor,' Tom explained.

'Ah yes, Professor Morantz.' Inspector Gervaux closed his notebook and pocketed it. 'I will send our forensics team in to see if they can find any fingerprints or DNA. But, I must advise you, if they were professionals it's very unlikely that we will find anything. If you remember something that could help us, please give me a call.' He handed his card to Tom.

He watched the two men leave, then turned his focus back to his bedroom. It was clearly uninhabitable. He gathered a pile of underwear, socks, T-shirts and a pair of trainers from the floor, grabbed the American Airlines complimentary wash bag from his bathroom and stuffed them into his flight bag, which he located in the living room; there really wasn't anything else worth salvaging. He put on a sweater, gave one last perfunctory glance around and left the apartment without locking it, then made his way to the canteen.

Serena was already there, sitting on a small table by the window picking at a tuna Niçoise salad. She saw him as soon as he came in and waved him over.

'Going somewhere?' Serena asked, motioning to the bag over Tom's shoulder.

'Long story,' Tom replied taking the seat opposite her. 'My apartment was broken into and this,' he indicated to the flight bag, 'is the sum total of all my worldly possessions.'

'Oh my God! Did they take much?'

'I don't think so, but they trashed the place and my clothes with it. Apart from what I'm wearing and the few essential items I managed to recover, everything else was either ripped to shreds or smashed.'

'Who would do such a thing?'

'I'm not sure, but the police seem to think they were looking for something.'

Serena automatically reached for the tan-coloured briefcase in front of her. 'You don't think they were after this, do you?'

Tom looked bemused. 'What, your briefcase?'

'No, dummy. Morantz's file.' She tried to say the words without moving her lips, but would have failed spectacularly to get a job as a ventriloquist.

Tom was a little taken aback by the insult, but warmed to the way familiarity had crept into their relationship.

Up to that point, it hadn't crossed his mind that the file could have been what they were looking for.

'But nobody knew I had it…' Then he remembered the voice message he had left earlier that morning. 'Except, of course, Frederick.'

'What would Frederick want with the file?'

'I don't know, but I'm seeing him this afternoon. Why don't I just ask him?'

'Do you think that's wise? After all, somebody *did* break into your apartment and he was the only person who knew you had it.'

'Frederick's not the breaking and entering type.'

'Who else could it be?'

Tom thought for a moment. That was the second time in one day that his character judgement had been brought into question. 'Alright, perhaps I won't ask him directly,' he replied. 'But I should be able to determine how desperate or not he is to get his hands on the file, by his reaction when I show it to him. Did you manage to confirm the figures, by the way?'

'Yes and they stack up. The earthquakes all happened when the Collider was producing its maximum electromagnetic output.'

'And the one in Istanbul?'

'The timings match, but I haven't been able to extrapolate all the figures yet.'

Tom studied the half-eaten meal in front of Serena.

'Aren't you going to get anything to eat?' she said, noticing him eyeing her plate.

'No, I seem to have lost my appetite.'

'Do you want me to come with you?' Serena offered.

Tom knew the chivalrous thing to do would be to exclude Serena in case he had totally misinterpreted Frederick's intentions. 'Do you mind?' he said. 'I think it would help if you were there to verify the figures.'

CHAPTER 18

Tom had arranged to meet Frederick in his office, which was in a different part of the complex to the main building. At the time, he decided it would be a more discreet location than his own office, which was swarming with police. As he sat next to Serena in the golf buggy, he was wishing he could have reversed that decision.

'Did you manage to make a copy of the data?' he asked, pulling into a parking spot in front of a two-storey, anonymous grey building.

'Yes, why? Do you think he's going to steal it from us at gunpoint?' Serena joked.

Tom didn't know what to think or say, so he remained silent. He was feeling a little apprehensive as he made his way into the building.

'We have an appointment with Frederick Volker,' he told the receptionist. Serena was by his side; she reached out and gave his hand a quick squeeze, out of sight of the woman behind the counter. She had heard the nervousness in his voice.

'I'll just let him know you're here. Can I have your names, please?'

'It's Professor Halligan and Serena Mayer.'

The receptionist punched Frederick's extension number into the computerised switchboard. When he answered, she informed him that his visitors had arrived.

'He said he'll be right down. If you'd like to take a seat,' she said pointing to the row of black plastic chairs behind them.

They sat in the two furthest away from the reception counter.

'I feel like I'm waiting to see the dentist,' whispered Tom, leaning conspiratorially towards Serena.

'I quite liked my dentist, actually. He once asked me out on a date,' she replied chattily.

'Is that allowed? Doctor-patient relationships, I mean?'

'Well, strictly speaking, he wasn't a doctor,' Serena replied. 'So I suppose so. But I turned him down, anyway.'

'Why?'

'I didn't want to have to find a new dentist if it didn't work out. Where I grew up, good dentists were hard to find. Boyfriends, on the other hand, were plentiful.' She chuckled at her own witticism.

'I bet they were,' he retorted, with a hint of jealousy.

Just then, Frederick burst through the door with all the ardour of a teenager.

'Tom! Welcome to my lair. And I see you've brought the delectable Miss Mayer with you. What a pleasure!' His enthusiastic welcome dispelled any doubts that Tom had about Frederick's disposition. 'Come! Come! Let me show you to my office.' He put his arm around Tom's shoulder and shepherded him through the door, holding it open for Serena to follow. 'Up the stairs, first on the left,' he shouted after them.

They reached the landing and stood back to let Frederick lead them in.

His office was much bigger than Tom's but, despite its size, it felt more homely, more lived in. Photos of family and friends adorned the walls. Tom recognised Ajay in a few of them and wondered, again, if Frederick had been told of his disappearance. The ubiquitous florescent strip lights were turned off and, instead, a softer illumination was provided by a tall standard lamp in one corner.

Thick, dark green curtains dressed a large window that overlooked the car park Tom had used earlier. A mahogany bookcase stretched the full length of one wall and was stocked with rows and rows of ancient books bound in vellum, the aroma of which filled the office with a sweet, camphorous scent.

His work station was an antique leather-topped pedestal desk and a matching green, high-backed chesterfield chair. Two plain green leather chairs occupied the other side of the desk. Pot plants filled corners and niches. It reminded Tom more of a gentleman's study than a place of work.

'As you can see, I do like my home comforts,' Frederick commented, closing the door behind him and taking up position behind his desk.

Tom left Serena to join Frederick and wandered over to the bookcase. He scanned the books' bindings for titles or authors he would recognise, the musty smell of the parchment almost overpowering him. He was familiar with the names of a few of the authors – Galilei, Kepler, Copernicus, Pflaum – but he was embarrassed to admit that, apart from Einstein and Newton, he hadn't read any of their works.

'Are all these originals?' he asked, tilting his head to read the vertical writing of one book spine.

'I'm afraid so,' replied Frederick. 'It's more of a compulsion of mine rather than a hobby. If my wife were to discover how much I'd spent on my cosmic collection, I can guarantee you I'd be a single man the very next day.'

'Are they all about astronomy?' Serena asked, studying the titles.

'Astronomy, science, physics, they're all linked together, really.'

'Do you have a favourite?' She could tell by the light shining in his eyes that he was bursting with pride.

'Far too many, my dear,' said Frederick. 'But, if I had to choose one, it would be Galileo's *Sidereus Nuncius,* printed in 1610, in which he first announced his use of a telescope and his subsequent discoveries that there were craters on the Moon, that the Milky Way was made up of stars, and that Jupiter had moons. Quite remarkable for his day.'

Tom was only half listening to the conversation going on behind him; astronomy had never been his forte. But then his excitement grew as he spotted a book he knew well. He stretched to his full height and managed to pull it out with his fingertips – *QED: The Strange Theory of Light and Matter* by Richard P. Feynman. He opened the cover and noticed that there was an inscription: '*To my dear friend Freddy, without your inspirational guidance, I would still be in the dark.*' It was signed *Dick.*

'Did you know Richard Feynman well?' Tom asked.

'Ah, I see you've found his book. We worked together on a number of projects and became quite close. But don't take too much notice of that dedication, he always was a bit over-generous with his praises,' Frederick replied modestly. 'I could bore you all day with my library, but I'm sure that's not the reason you wanted to see me.'

'As fascinating as it is, unfortunately not.' Tom returned the book and went to sit next to Serena. 'As I said in the message I left you, I believe we have the evidence that Professor Morantz was going to take to the newspapers.'

'Evidence of what?' Frederick sat forward in his chair and clasped his hands together on the desk.

'I'll let Serena explain,' replied Tom. 'She's better at figures than I am.'

As Serena went through the data in detail, Frederick listened intently to her, interrupting only once to ask if she'd checked the figures for herself. As the briefing progressed, Tom observed the blood draining from Frederick's face. He looked visibly shaken. His vitality had been replaced by a dark, life-draining weariness. At one point, Tom was convinced he was going to faint.

Serena finished by rounding off with her conclusions. There was a reverential silence, the three individuals absorbed in their own thoughts.

Frederick was the first to fill the void. 'What have we done?' The sentiment was almost inaudible. 'What *have* we done?' he whispered again. His eyes were glazed over, staring into space.

'Frederick?' Tom was concerned for the man's health, if not his physical, then certainly his mental. He didn't respond. 'Frederick?' he repeated louder. This time he managed to get through. Frederick looked at the two people opposite him as though they were strangers. 'What do you think we should do?' Tom urged.

'I... I don't know,' came back the feeble response.

Tom turned to Serena, who was mesmerised by the transformation in the man. Cupping a hand over his mouth he said in a low voice, 'I think we need to take this file to the authorities and let them sort it out.'

'No!' The single word was delivered with such force that it made them both jump. The spell was broken. Blood rushed back into Frederick's face and his eyes regained their clarity. 'No,' he repeated, softer now, but with as much conviction. 'Involving the police would only entail a lengthy investigation, at the end of which they will indubitably find that no individual is culpable. Science created this abomination and it is up to us to sort it out. We will have to stop all experiments involving the Collider, immediately, with a view to closing down the facility permanently. And pray to God with thanks that this came to light when it did.'

Tom couldn't question his reasoning, but he wasn't accustomed to taking the law into his own hands. 'Surely somebody has to be held accountable for these atrocities?'

'We all are,' Frederick said mournfully. 'Scientists by their very nature are driven to explore the unknown, discover new worlds, push the boundaries to the edge of man's knowledge, and then push further. The intangible desire to explore and challenge the boundaries of what we know and where we have been has provided benefits to our society for centuries, but not without a cost, the currency of which is usually the lives of innocent victims.'

'But somebody *should* be made to pay,' Tom argued.

Frederick's eyes saddened. 'It's a burden we must all shoulder. It's the price we have to pay for the advancement of civilisation. Take Rutherford, for example. He was one of the founding fathers of nuclear physics and considered by many to be one of the greatest experimental scientists that ever lived. Should he have been made to pay for the deaths of over two hundred thousand people when the Americans dropped their atomic bombs on Nagasaki and Hiroshima, some twenty-five years after he split the atom?'

'Perhaps,' Tom speculated.

'Perhaps,' Frederick conceded. 'But perhaps we have lost our way. Perhaps, in our quest to achieve the ultimate goals for the collective good, we have forgotten about what's really important – the individuals.' Tears pooled in his eyes. 'I don't have all the answers, Tom,' he said earnestly. 'But I do know that going to the police won't bring back those poor souls who have perished as a result of our arrogance. We must learn from this. We need to inspire future generations of scientists to be ethically motivated and morally responsible. If we can accomplish *that*, then the loss of those lives will not be in vain.'

'But the scientific profession already has a high standard of integrity,' Tom said, indignantly.

'That's what I like about you, Tom,' Frederick replied. 'You're an idealist. But history has shown us that scientists are capable of morally abhorrent behaviour. Look at the heinous experiments Mengele performed on the inmates of Auschwitz in the name of scientific research.'

'You could argue that we have learnt from our mistakes, developed codes of conduct to prevent those sorts of atrocities ever happening again,' Tom reasoned.

'You would like to think so, but even today scientists serve as apologists for the tobacco and pesticide industries, and cosmetics are routinely tested on animals. Is that morally acceptable? What I'm saying is that beneath the white lab coat is a human being, who is vulnerable to all the usual temptations of the real world.'

'One thing's puzzling me,' Serena said. 'Why don't we just go to the press with the information we've got, as Professor Morantz wanted to do?'

'When Erik came to me,' replied Frederick, 'the afternoon before he died, and told me that he was going to the media with proof that the Collider was going to destroy the world, I was naturally very sceptical. I thought he'd lost his mind. But it made me think about what would happen if the story was true. How would the world react? At first, there would be a media frenzy; we would be inundated by an army of reporters and camera crews seeking an exclusive. And it wouldn't just be our facility in the spotlight; every research establishment in the world would come under the scrutiny of the press. Newspapers, in particular, are notoriously indiscriminate when it comes to apportioning blame.'
Frederick paused for a moment, sighed, then continued.
'Secondly, the hype would generate mass hysteria. At best, we're talking about the demand for the immediate closure of all research facilities, at worst – lynch mobs. Next, once the furore had died down, there would be a period of reconciliation. Debates would go on between eminent scientists on the one side and lawmakers on the other; naturally, the lawmakers would win, as they would have to be seen to take action. More governing bodies would be set up and more legislation passed.'

Selena made as if to say something, but Frederick continued without giving her the chance to speak.

'The long-term consequences for science as a doctrine would be devastating,' he went on. 'It would set scientific research back hundreds of years and it wouldn't just be physicists that would be affected. Every disciple in the science arena, from astronomy to oceanography, would be regulated to such an extent that we wouldn't even be able to produce a new formula of dandruff shampoo without getting it approved first. Medical research, I fear, would be affected the most. It's already a race against time to come up with new drugs and procedures to prevent and treat chronic diseases. Can you imagine how many more people would die as a result of slowing down the pace of that development with bureaucratic red tape – a hundred, a thousand, a million times more than have been killed in the Earthquakes? So, when we make our decision, it isn't just the loss of life we need to consider, but also the potential loss.'

'So what do we do now?' Serena asked, anxiously.

'I have some... er, colleagues,' he replied. 'I'd like to run it past them to get their perspective. Do you mind if I take the file with me?'

Tom and Serena exchanged glances. 'I've made a copy for you,' Serena said quickly, rummaging in her briefcase. She took it out and slid it across the desk to Frederick. Tom picked up their file from the desk and secreted it in his flight bag.

'Thanks, I'll come back to you as soon as I've had a chance to speak with them,' he said absently, flicking through the pages.

'Did you, by any chance, tell these colleagues about the message I left on your voicemail this morning?' Tom enquired, trying to sound nonchalant.

'No, I've been busy all morning trying to locate Ajay,' Frederick lied. He had, in fact, phoned each one of them as soon as he'd heard the message to arrange a rendezvous in the Bunker to discuss the document.

'Any luck?'

'No,' said Frederick. 'It's very unlike Ajay to go missing. We had some problems with him when he was a teenager, but what parent doesn't?' Frederick hoped that that wasn't the reason he'd gone missing this time. 'I'm sure he'll turn up sooner rather than later. There's probably a girl involved somewhere.' Frederick stood up from behind his desk, indicating the meeting had concluded.

Tom and Serena followed suit. Tom was debating whether to shake the man's hand or kiss him on the cheeks; he was still unsure what the local custom was. However, the decision was taken away from him as Frederick lumbered around the desk and caught hold of him in a man-hug, Tom responding with the obligatory patting on the back. They released and Frederick turned to Serena, arms still outstretched. She obliged – the embrace much gentler and briefer.

'Thank you for entrusting me with this information,' Frederick held the door open for them. 'As I said, I'll be in touch.'

Tom and Serena said their goodbyes and made their way back down the stairs to the golf buggy.

It was late afternoon and the sun was low in the sky, casting long shadows on the ground. The cold breeze had upgraded itself to a squall and had picked up some snowflakes along the way, which it deposited in their faces as they drove away. Tom's cashmere jumper offered little protection against the biting wind. They didn't say a word to each other until they were in sight of the main office building.

'So, what do you make of all that?' Tom parked the buggy and got out.

'It's a lot to take in,' Serena got out the other side and followed him up the steps.

'I know. But do you think we can trust him?'

'We don't appear to have much option,' Serena replied, thinking back to Frederick's elicitations.

CHAPTER 19

There was a tense atmosphere in the Bunker that evening. Everybody, apart from the woman, had been able to make it at short notice, CERN's two private jets having been dispatched immediately to collect them from various locations across Europe.

The lights were dimmed and the wall-mounted monitors, which Frederick had switched on prior to their arrival, were showing news reports of the devastation caused by the earthquake in Istanbul. The volume had been turned down, but that didn't lessen the impact of the programme on the people seated around the table. In fact, it had the opposite effect; taking away one of their sensory faculties made them concentrate even more on the detail of the images being broadcast.

Frederick watched their faces as they reacted to the scene of a body being discovered by rescue dogs. It had been over twenty-four hours since the initial quake and the incidences of survivors being found had diminished exponentially.

The International community had reacted swiftly. Donation centres had been set up in most countries overnight, with initial requests for food, blankets and fresh drinking water. An appeal for money would come later, but currently it wouldn't be of much use to the hundreds of thousands of homeless people trying to survive the harsh conditions of a Turkish winter. Teams from the Red Cross and Blue Crescent had flown in and were facilitating the construction of tent cities by the army, outside the affected zone. Médecins Sans Frontières were in the thick of it, dispensing minor medical treatment where necessary and setting up field hospitals for the more seriously injured. The dead weren't a priority. Bodies were being unceremoniously stockpiled in the streets as there was nowhere left to put them.

The enormity of the aftermath pervaded everybody's mood, as they stared at the unfolding drama.

Frederick flicked a switch and the fluorescent strip lights came on. Everybody blinked, adjusting their eyes to the sudden glare.

'*We* are responsible for that,' Frederick said gravely. They turned to him, bewilderment etched on their faces. 'I have here a document,' he held up the copy that Serena had given him earlier, 'which was compiled by Professor Morantz, just before his death. It clearly shows a pattern of earthquakes that took place at exactly the same time the Collider was operating at maximum capacity.'

'Where did you get that?' Deiter asked, sharply.

'That's not important. What is important is that the figures have been independently verified. Based on this information, we have no option but to conclude that the Collider is responsible for causing these earthquakes.' Shock replaced bewilderment on the faces in front of him.

'But how?' the man on his far right asked.

'We know that the Earth's molten iron core produces a magnetic field which envelopes the planet,' explained Frederick, 'entering at the South Pole and exiting at the North Pole. The outer core of the Earth is, in effect, a giant molten magnet. What we have inadvertently created in the Collider is the world's second largest magnet. I believe that, when the Collider reaches maximum capacity, the resultant electro-magnetic waves interact with the Earth's geomagnetic field causing instability. This imbalance is then transferred through the Earth's mantle to the tectonic plates, which realign, causing an earthquake.'

'Science 101,' the man who had asked the question said, nodding his head. 'Magnets attract. How could we have missed such a fundamental flaw?'

'Because we were so preoccupied discovering new science that we forgot about the old,' Frederick said despondently.

'Are you seriously asking us to believe that the Collider produces enough electromagnetic force to pull the Earth's core towards it?' the man opposite him asked sceptically.

'No, that's not what I'm saying at all,' Frederick replied patiently. 'The Collider causes a butterfly effect. The Earth exists in a state of fragile polar equilibrium; the tiniest influence on one part of the system can have a huge effect on another part. The magnetic waves the Collider generates upset the natural balance of the Earth, which leads to a chain of events, the outcome of which can clearly be seen on those screens.'

They switched their attention back to the monitors. There was a red banner running along the bottom of the bulletin with the words, '*Warning! Viewers of a nervous disposition may find some scenes disturbing*' scrolling across it. The images showed a bulldozer laden with corpses, its giant steel caterpillar tracks trundling towards a deep trench. It stopped just short of the hole, raised its bucket and tipped the bodies into the mass grave before turning around to collect another load.

'Can you prove it?' Deiter cut in.

'Our primary objective is to prevent anything like this happening again,' Frederick replied resolutely. 'This document empirically proves that the earthquakes are linked to the Collider, which is enough for me to recommend to the Council that we close down the facility immediately. The hows and whys can wait.'

He paused to gather his thoughts before addressing the group again. 'Gentlemen, we have to face the stark realisation that we have failed in our mission to protect civilisation from itself. Our organisation was founded by our forefathers with the sole edict of preventing such a catastrophe taking place. Our myopic resolve to undermine the discovery of the God particle, by whatever means necessary, has resulted in bringing about the very disaster we were trying to avert. I take full responsibility for the part I played in allowing the Collider to be built in the first place, my only defence being that I truly believed that we would have been able to control it long enough to misdirect those dogmatists, determined to split open the smallest known particles with scant regard to the consequences.'

He paused again, letting out a brief sigh. 'I will, naturally, be stepping down as head of this cell, but first I must convince the CERN Council to cease all future activity without alerting the media to our intentions. I couldn't desert my post without at least trying to rectify some of the damage we have done.'

There were a few objectors around the table to Frederick's announced resignation. Deiter wasn't one of them.

Frederick ignored the protests. 'None of us are getting any younger,' he continued. 'And, whilst maturity brings with it a degree of wisdom, technology is moving at such a rapid pace that it takes a younger mind to keep up with all the developments. It is to this end that I propose we approach Tom Halligan to join us.'

There were a few proponents around the table. Again, Deiter wasn't one of them.

'Look!' one of the men facing the screens shouted. 'If the Collider was responsible for causing the earthquakes and it is currently inoperative, how is *this* possible?' He was pointing to the broadcast, which had replaced the earlier warning with a newsflash banner reading *'Reports are coming in of a major earthquake in San Francisco'.*

Everybody was perplexed – everyone, that was, apart from Deiter. If Frederick and the others hadn't been so absorbed in watching the TV report, they would have been disturbed at the sight of Deiter, a triumphant glint in his eyes, mouthing the words 'It's started, it's started' over and over like some demonic chant.

CHAPTER 20

Tom and Serena had parted on the steps of the main building but had arranged to meet up later that evening, more for companionship than anything else. Tom said he needed to catch up on some emails, whilst Serena called it a day and went back to her apartment.

He made his way to his office through the control room. There were a handful of technicians still there, but very little work was being done – they were all watching CNN World News. Tom glanced at the screen; a wave of guilt and remorse swept over him as he saw the homeless survivors, their tear-stained faces, a portrait of shock and incredulity.

Then the images were gone, replaced by a helicopter's perspective of what was once an extensive bridge over a vast body of water, with only the two supporting concrete and steel structures left at either end of the span. Tom assumed it was the First Bosphorus Bridge, but then couldn't help thinking how similar it looked to the Golden Gate Bridge before rationalising that all suspension bridges would look the same if subjected to a massive earthquake.

Inspector Gervaux was sitting behind his desk again, much to Tom's annoyance. This time, however, he didn't wait to be asked to vacate his seat, as he saw Tom coming.

'Ah, there you are. My officers have been looking for you,' he said as Tom stepped into his office. 'There have been some developments and we would like you to clarify a few points down at the station.'

'Is that really necessary?' Tom replied, a little bemused by the request.

'I'm afraid so,' the inspector said firmly. 'I have a car waiting, if you would like to follow me. Do you want to get your jacket? It's rather chilly outside.'

'I don't have one,' replied Tom. 'My clothes were vandalised, if you remember.' His annoyance at having to accompany the inspector was showing through.

'Ah yes, the break-in...' The inspector left the words floating ambiguously mid-sentence. 'This way, please.'

He led Tom out of the building and around the corner. A black Peugeot was waiting, the engine ticking over to enable its occupant to keep the heater on.

'You two already know each other,' Inspector Gervaux said, opening the rear door for Tom.

Sergeant Lavelle found it difficult to turn his bulky frame in the driver's seat, so acknowledged Tom with a grunt as he got in the car.

'Nice to see you again, too,' Tom responded, but the sarcasm fell into the cultural divide.

Inspector Gervaux got in the back, beside Tom, who wondered whether this was hierarchical protocol or just in case Tom tried to make a break for it. *I really will have to stop watching those crime thrillers*, he told himself.

The short journey to the police station took place in complete silence. Tom watched out of the window as the landscape changed from countryside to suburbia. The wind had died down but there was a lot more snow in the air. A thin, white blanket covered the trees and rooftops, though it hadn't managed to pitch on the ground yet. Tom hoped he'd be able to get back to the complex before it did.

They pulled up in front of an elegant four-storey building in the heart of Geneva's old district. Its brown stone façade and wrought iron balconies were more befitting an upmarket hotel than a place where the city's lowlifes were guests. The only architectural features belying its image as a luxury lodge were the bars on the ground floor windows.

As Sergeant Lavelle switched off the engine, Tom heard a distinctive click indicating that the rear doors were unlocked. If he *was* indeed a criminal and had wanted to make a run for it, now would be his chance. Instead, he waited patiently until the others had sorted out their paperwork and personal belongings before opening his car door and stepping out into the freezing night.

They made their way into the building in single file, Inspect Gervaux at the front, Tom in the middle and the sergeant bringing up the rear. Only the absence of handcuffs would affirm to a sharp-eyed onlooker that he wasn't being arrested. They walked past the duty sergeant dealing with an early evening drunk, who had difficulty standing on his own two feet without the assistance of the other two officers flanking him, and up a flight of stairs to a suite of interview rooms.

Inspector Gervaux chose the nearest empty one, switched on the fluorescent lights and ushered Tom in. The room was large, about the size of Frederick's office, but without the homeliness. Cream walls smelt of new paint. Tom wondered what had happened to prompt the make-over. A single white metal table sat in the centre of the room, its tubular legs bolted to the shiny tiled floor. Three uncomfortable-looking plastic chairs were haphazardly dotted around it. There wasn't a two-way mirror covering one wall, as he had envisaged there would be; instead, two CCTV cameras hung from the ceiling at either end of the room to record both the interviewer's and interviewee's audiovisual responses.

They took up their respective seats, Tom on one side of the table, the two inquisitors on the other. He tucked the flight bag he was still carrying out of sight, under his chair. Inspector Gervaux checked his watch and said, in a louder than normal voice, that the time was eighteen thirty-three. It took Tom a second to realise that the recording device must be voice-activated.

The palms of his hands were damp. He hadn't felt nervous on the way to the station, but now he was in this formal environment it was clear that he was there for more than just a friendly chat. And, despite having done nothing wrong, he felt the onus was on him to prove his innocence.

Sergeant Lavelle read him his rights.

'Am I being arrested?' Tom's voice cracked.

'Not at the moment. We have brought you in for questioning,' the inspector informed him.

'Could you please tell us your name and date of birth for the record?' the sergeant said in a monotone voice, clearly bored with having to ask the menial questions. Tom could sense that he was desperate to be lead interrogator, but that duty went to Inspector Gervaux.

'Do you recognise this man?' the inspector showed Tom a picture of Ajay that had obviously been taken a few years earlier. It took him a moment to identify what was different about him, before he realised he was moustache-less.

'Yes, that's Ajay.'

'Do you mean Anjit Bose?'

'Yes, that's his name, but I call him Ajay.' Tom tried not to sound pedantic. He didn't want to antagonise these two so early on in the interview.

'And how do you know Anjit?'

'I met him for the first time when he picked me up at the airport when I arrived here.'

The inspector searched through his papers and retrieved a slightly blurred photograph of an Asian talking to Tom; the MIT administration building could clearly be seen in the background. He slid it across the desk.

'And who are you with in this picture?'

It could have been one of a number of his undergraduates. MIT had strong links with several South Asian countries. The first Indian student had entered MIT just fifteen years after the Institute opened its doors at the end of America's Civil War. Tom usually had two or three students from that region in each academic year. The only similarities between the individual in the photo and Ajay were the dark skin, black hair and slight build.

'I couldn't tell you, off hand,' replied Tom. 'It's probably one of my undergraduates.'

'Is it Anjit Bose?' Sergeant Lavelle piped in, desperate to get in on the action.

'No. I told you, the first time I met Ajay was when I got here. I taught a number of South Asian students during my time at MIT. It could be any one of them.'

Inspector Gervaux put the photo back, then tried a different tack. 'How well do you know Anjit?'

'I wouldn't say I know him that well at all,' replied Tom, 'as I told you when you asked me the same question in my office.'

'Can you tell us what you did, on the first day you arrived at CERN?'

Tom couldn't work out where this was leading. He thought back – it had only been two days ago, but it felt like months.

'I arrived and was met at the airport by Ajay. He took me to the complex, where I met Herr Volker, who introduced me to the team. I was feeling a little jetlagged in the afternoon, so I had a nap before going out to dinner with Herr Volker in the evening.'

'And then what did you do?'

'I went back to my apartment.'

'Did you go straight to sleep?'

Tom suddenly realised where the line of questions were leading. 'No... I... er... I went to Ajay's room.'

'And why did you go there?' the inspector asked evenly.

'To look at his scrapbook,' Tom replied meekly. He knew it would sound implausible, even before he'd said it. Why hadn't he made something up? Why hadn't he just told them they were discussing the merits of nuclear thermodynamics in developing countries or something? They wouldn't have known the difference. But then again, if they had managed to arrest Ajay and he was being interviewed in one of the adjacent rooms, their stories wouldn't have matched, which would make it look more suspicious than it was. No, as ridiculous as it sounded, he had to stick with the truth.

'Pardon?'

'I went to look at his scrapbook. He is the grandson of Satyendra Bose, who I'm a great admirer of.' Tom tried desperately to make it sound credible.

'*Scrapbook?* What is *scrapbook?*' the sergeant asked Inspector Gervaux. There was a brief exchange in French between the two detectives, followed by a peel of laughter.

'What's so funny?' Tom asked irritably.

'I explained to Sergeant Lavelle what a scrapbook was, and he said that his four-year-old niece has one which she sticks pictures of princesses in.' The inspector's smile faded as he asked his next question. 'Professor Halligan, are you attracted to Anjit?'

The insinuation took Tom completely by surprise and knocked his composure. He raised his voice. 'I don't know what you're suggesting, but my sexuality has got nothing to do with you. But, just for the record, no, I'm not gay.'

The gloves were off. It was Sergeant Lavelle's opportunity to impress his boss. He slammed his palms down on the tabletop.

'What do you take us for?' he shouted. 'Do you think we are bumbling fools, like your Inspector Clouseau in the Pink Panther movies? Do you honestly expect us to believe that, after travelling all the way from America, working a full day in the office and then going out for dinner in the evening, you still had the capacity to visit a young man's room? A man whom you say you didn't know very well, in the early hours of the morning, just to look at his childish hobby?'

Putting it that way, Tom could see it from their perspective and it didn't look good for him. 'I agree, it may sound far-fetched,' he replied, 'but it's the truth. I have no reason to lie to you. You must believe me.'

'Why did Anjit visit your room last night?' asked Inspector Gervaux. 'I understand that you were in the company of...' He took out the notebook from his breast pocket and thumbed through the pages. 'A Miss Mayer.'

'What are you suggesting now? A ménage a trios?' Despite his predicament, Tom couldn't help the gibe.

'Professor, we are not suggesting anything. We are only trying to establish the facts,' the inspector replied calmly.

'Okay,' said Tom, letting out a heavy sigh. 'Ajay came to tell us about the earthquake in Istanbul. It's a hobby of his.'

'Like the scrapbook?' the sergeant quipped, snidely.

Tom ignored the comment. 'He thought we should know about it.' He considered his words carefully. He didn't want to alert them to the fact that he thought the Collider was responsible, at least not yet.

'And why would you be so interested in the earthquake?' Inspector Gervaux probed.

'Because it's such a monumental natural disaster,' replied Tom earnestly. 'I should think everybody who's seen the images has been moved by the tragedy.'

'Oui, c'est terrible,' the inspector agreed. He rifled through a few more pages in his notebook until he found the relevant entry.

'Moving on to the break-in you had. You said that you had no idea who was responsible, or what they could be looking for. Now that you've had a chance to think about it, do you still maintain that to be the case?'

'Yes, I'm still at a loss.'

'Do you mind if we look in your bag?'

'My what?' Tom had forgotten all about the flight bag he'd tried to conceal under his chair.

'The bag you brought in with you,' Sergeant Lavelle spoke slowly as if he were speaking to a child.

'Do you have a warrant?' Tom thought about the implications of them discovering the folder. To them, it would be a meaningless set of figures with some scribbled notes of when a few earthquakes occurred. He should be able to bluff his way around it.

'Professor,' said Inspector Gervaux, 'as I said earlier, you are not under arrest. You are merely helping us with our enquiries. Our forensics team did a thorough search of your apartment and, whilst they couldn't find anything specific that would be of interest to an intruder, they did find traces of an unusual chemical on your kitchen worktops, which we've sent off to the lab to be analysed. We're not sure, at this stage, whether or not it is related to the explosion, but refusing to allow us to look in your bag would only add to our suspicions that you are hiding something from us.'

Tom reluctantly reached under his seat and put the bag on the table between them. Sergeant Lavelle stood up and rifled through its contents. The clothes were of no interest to him, but he smiled as his fingers brushed the leather folder. He extracted the file and passed it to his superior, the expression on his face reminiscent of a Rottweiler retrieving a stick for his master.

Inspector Gervaux smoothed the red leather cover with the tips of his fingers, coming to rest on the indentation in the bottom right hand corner, where the initials had been embossed. 'Where did you get this?'

'I… I'd rather not say.'

'Of course, you have the right to remain silent,' the inspector replied. 'But, at this stage in our enquiries, it could be an indication of your involvement.'

Tom could see the logic in that and didn't think it would be detrimental to his position to tell them who'd given it to him. 'Ajay gave it to me. He found it in Professor Morantz's room, when he discovered his body.'

'So he stole it,' the Rottweiler barked.

'He took it for safekeeping.'

'Safekeeping from whom?' Sergeant Lavelle had found his voice and his bone and he wasn't about to let it go.

'I don't know,' replied Tom. 'You'd have to ask him.'

'Why did he give it to you?'

'Because he trusts me.'

'Why didn't he hand it in to the police?'

'You'll have to ask him that.'

'What did he expect you to do with it?'

'The right thing, I assume.'

'What is the right thing?' The man was relentless.

'I don't know,' Tom said truthfully.

Inspector Gervaux had been scanning the pages whilst his colleague practised his interviewing technique.

'Professor,' he said, 'do you know what these figures represent?'

'Yes,' Tom said abjectly. He knew when he'd been beaten. He rested his chin on his chest and stared at his hands spread out on the table. 'They're output readings from the Collider showing the levels of electromagnetic radiation.'

'And the notes scribbled in the margins?'

'They indicate the dates and locations of earthquakes which occurred when the Collider was operating at maximum capacity.'

Inspector Gervaux closed the file and set it down on the table in front of him. 'Interview terminated at nineteen thirty,' he shouted up to the CCTV cameras. 'We really must get a more voice-sensitive system,' he said turning to Sergeant Lavelle.

'So, what happens now?' Tom raised his head and met the inspector's gaze.

'You're free to go. But I must insist that you don't leave the country until we have concluded our enquiries.'

'But what about the earthquakes? Don't you understand the implications of the figures in that file? The Collider is responsible for causing them!' Tom was beside himself. It wasn't the reaction from the authorities he'd anticipated.

'It's an interesting conspiracy theory,' replied the inspector. 'One that I may have taken a little more seriously if it hadn't been for today's events.'

'I don't understand?' Tom said, shaking his head.

'The earthquake that hit San Francisco, earlier today. Reports indicate that it measured 11.3 on the Richter scale, the largest in recorded history. Are you saying the Collider is responsible for that as well?' The inspector gave Tom a second to answer, but he just sat there, dumfounded, shocked by the news he had just been given. The inspector continued. 'Perhaps it's also responsible for global warming, or the alien landing at Roswell, or even J F Kennedy's shooting?' Sergeant Lavelle sniggered at his boss's attempt at humour. 'I'm not a big fan of these types of hoaxes, Professor, and if I find that you're involved in instigating one, I'll have you arrested for wasting police time.'

Inspector Gervaux began shuffling papers back into his folder.

'My priority,' he continued, 'is to apprehend the person or persons responsible for planting the device that killed the two maintenance technicians. Now, at the moment, my number one suspect is missing. I'm uncertain what your involvement is, at this time, but if the lab results indicate a connection with the chemical found in your apartment and the explosion, then you will be charged. In the meantime, if you do hear from Anjit at all, it would be in your best interest to let us know immediately. Now, if you don't mind making your own way back to the facility, it will give us an opportunity to continue our investigations. Good evening, Professor.'

Tom picked up his bag and the folder from the table and left the interview room, dazed and confused.

CHAPTER 21

It had taken Tom fifteen minutes to pick up a taxi outside the police station. Several had passed him by, even though they had their lights on to indicate they were available. His lack of attire in such a heavy snowstorm, coupled with the fact that he was surrounded by drunks and reprobates, must have sent out the wrong signals. Eventually, he managed to slip into the back of a cab that had been dropping somebody off at the station.

'Where to?' the driver shouted into his rear-view mirror as he viewed Tom suspiciously. He was of oriental origin and wore brown trousers, a beige tie and a navy blue body warmer over a khaki shirt.

Tom didn't know whether to reply to the back of the man's head or the dark brown hooded eyes peering at him through the mirror. He chose the latter.

'CERN, please.'

He hoped the taxi driver wasn't the chatty type so he could brood on the outcome of what had just taken place. He wasn't in luck.

'Terrible news about the earthquake. Where you from?' He had obviously picked up from Tom's accent that he wasn't a local, a skill all taxi drivers must acquire as part of their training. The man's shoulders relaxed, his concerns about being attacked by some crazed psychopath who had just escaped from the police station abated.

'America.'

'Where 'bouts in America?'

'Boston.'

'You been San Francisco?'

'Once.'

'At least you seen it. Nothing left now. Bridge gone, cable cars gone, skyscrapers gone, even Alcatraz gone, and that was one sturdy prison.' The man's eyes spent more time looking at Tom through the mirror than they did on the road, which made Tom nervous. 'I have a cousin in China Town, in the city, but my mum's sister hasn't heard from her, since the earthquake.'

'Were there many casualties?' Tom's ruse of supplying single word answers, to deter him from asking any more questions, obviously wasn't working, so he decided to give up and join in the conversation.

'Millions,' the driver said enthusiastically.

Tom knew the total population of the city was less than one million, but he wasn't going to correct him.

'First Turkey, then America,' continued the driver. 'Where next?'

The same question had crossed Tom's mind when he'd been told about the quake in the interview room. *There had to be a connection somehow.*

'Did the news reports give any indication of what caused the quake?' he asked.

'Yeh, bloody big fault – Saint Andrews.'

'San Andreas?' He couldn't let that one slip.

'Yeh, that's what I said, Saint Andrews. Apparently, it was long overdue. Why do they build cities if they know there's going to be an earthquake? Don't make sense.'

He has a point, Tom thought. 'Because it's human nature to think that it will never happen to them,' he replied.

Driving conditions were visibly deteriorating. They passed several lorries spreading grit on the roads, but they were fighting a losing battle. The taxi's windscreen wipers were having difficulty clearing the snow from the screen and visibility was down to less than a hundred metres. None of this seemed to bother the cabbie, who was in full flow, espousing the probable causes of the disaster.

'I blame scientists, myself,' he went on. 'They always meddling with nature – genetically modified crops, global warming. We don't know half of what they get up to.'

Tom moved in his seat to escape the man's eyes reflected in the mirror. He hoped it wouldn't take too much longer before they arrived at the facility.

'What you do at CERN?' the driver asked cautiously, suspecting that he may have put his foot in it.

'Er... I'm the Catering Manager,' Tom lied to save the other man's embarrassment.

'Phew! I thought for a minute you were going to say a scientist.' He laughed nervously. 'Anyways, as I was saying...'

The driver was quite content to listen to the sound of his own voice, so Tom switched off and watched, out of his window, as the residents of Geneva trying to cope with the blizzard. Most people had taken the sensible approach of staying indoors. There were hardly any pedestrians on the streets. The ones that had braved the elements, through necessity rather than choice, had their full winter garb on – woolly hats, gloves, scarves, overcoats and boots. Tom looked down at his own clothes – jumper, trousers and brogues. He wouldn't be venturing out anywhere in this weather.

They finally arrived at the main entrance of the facility and stopped at the barrier. The man in the security hut slid back the window and shone a torch into the back of the taxi. Tom had seen him around the complex but didn't know him by name. He wound down his window and handed his ID card over.

'Have a good evening, Professor Halligan,' the guard said, handing it back and pressing the button to raise the barrier.

The driver caught sight of Tom's sheepish expression in the mirror. 'What you Professor of then? Soup?' he said chuckling to himself.

Tom sunk lower in his seat.

They pulled up outside the accommodation block where Tom got out. He fished in his wallet and handed several notes over; he felt obliged to give the cabbie an extraordinarily generous tip to ease his own conscience. The driver thanked him profusely and set off back the way he had come, with a big smile on his face, leaving Tom standing ankle-deep in the snow, a few Euros lighter. *The price you pay for dishonesty,* he thought to himself. He shrugged it off and made his way to Serena's apartment.

CHAPTER 22

'Where've you been? I was getting worried about you,' Serena said, standing back from the door to let Tom in.

'It's nice to know you care,' he replied, kissing her on the cheek as he brushed past her. 'I've been down at the police station helping Inspector Gervaux with his enquiries.'

'Did they arrest you?'

'No – well, not yet, at least. Did you see the news about the San Francisco earthquake?'

'Yes, I've just switched it off. It's very disturbing. So, tell me what happened.'

It took Tom over an hour to recount the details of his brush with the law, aided by an ample supply of malt whisky courtesy of his hostess.

'Have you had anything to eat?' she asked, filling his glass for the third time.

'Not since this morning.' The effects of the alcohol on his empty stomach expedited his tipsiness. 'Are you trying to get me drunk, Miss Mayer?'

'No,' she said putting the bottle on the table. 'But I think you should eat something.' His vulnerability was bringing out her maternal instincts.

'Well, I'm not exactly dressed for going out,' he replied. 'And, with the state of the roads, you can forget about pizza deliveries.'

'I'm sure I can rustle something up for you,' she said, leaving him on the couch and going into the kitchen.

The layout of the apartment was the mirror opposite of his, but it was what she'd done with the furniture that made it look more spacious. The large orange sofa, which she had covered with a rust-coloured faux fur throw, had been pushed up against the wall, leaving space in the middle of the room for a round shag-pile chocolate-brown rug. A large parlour palm sat on the small imitation wood table, which had also been concealed by a throw, but this one was covered with geometric patterns of African origin. The unit housing the TV was in the same position but, as well as the appliances, it housed photographs and ornaments. She had managed to find a painting, the hues of which complemented the colour scheme of the apartment perfectly. A large picture of a sunset over the Serengeti, featuring the silhouette of a solitary elephant, hung on the wall above the sofa.

'I like what you've done to the place,' Tom shouted into the kitchen.

'Thanks. Is there anything you can't or won't eat?' Tom could hear her rummaging through cupboards.

'I'll eat pretty much anything, as long as it's not moving.' He thought back to the dinner he'd had with Frederick and shuddered at the thought of the lobster.

He got up, taking his whisky with him, and stood in the doorway of the kitchen. She was wearing a pair of pink cut-off jeans and a simple vest T-shirt. She would have looked good in a bin liner, he thought, as he watched her from afar. He'd learnt from bitter experience not to cross the threshold into a woman's domain when she was preparing a meal. That occasion had ended in a huge row, with him taking the blame for the burnt offering that was presented on the table. Words like *interfering* and *distracting* came to mind.

He had to admit to himself, that he had been partially responsible; after all, it was he who made the first move that culminated in them making love on the kitchen work surface.

'How does chicken foo yung grab you?' she said taking a half-eaten roast chicken out of the fridge.

'I can't wait. What is it?'

'Mashed-up chicken, mushroom and onion omelette.'

'Since you put it so eloquently, it sounds very appetising. My taste buds are already tingling.'

'Okay, you take the meat off the carcass and I'll prepare the other ingredients.'

'What, eggs, mushrooms and onions?'

'There's an art to chopping onions, I'll have you know,' she said scornfully.

They worked side by side, him hacking the meat off the bones with a knife, and she wiping the tears away as she sliced the onion.

'So the police didn't believe there was a connection between the earthquakes and the Collider?' she managed to say between sniffs.

'No, they thought I was a crank – or, at the very least, a fool for taking the figures seriously.'

'But I verified those figures and they did coincide.'

'I know, but how do you explain the San Francisco earthquake?'

'Perhaps it's a coincidence? Maybe it was going to happen anyway? It's about sixty years overdue, according to seismologists.' She blew her nose on some kitchen roll.

'Hell of a coincidence, wouldn't you say?'

'What if it was due to happen and the Istanbul quake somehow triggered it off?' Serena put the eggs, mushrooms, onions and seasoning into a wok, which was heating on the cooker. 'Looks like you've massacred it,' she said, scooping the morsels of meat up with two hands and adding them to the pan.

'That would make more sense. But how could we prove it?' he continued, ignoring her last comment.

'Isn't there anybody we could ask as to whether it's at least a feasible hypothesis?'

'The only person I know that has any understanding of earthquakes is Ajay,' said Tom, washing the smell of poultry off his hands. 'And he's gone AWOL. But even if he was here, I wouldn't think he's got the in-depth knowledge required to make a judgement.'

'Frederick?'

'I'll ask him in the morning.'

'What about the chemical they say they found in your apartment?'

'I'm hoping it's something innocuous, like cleaning fluid,' Tom said trying to draw a close on the topic. He'd just about had enough of earthquakes and conspiracy theories for one day. 'Now, if my services are no longer required, I will take my leave and await your delectable supper in the lounge area.' He picked up his whisky and headed out of the kitchen.

'Yes, Your Majesty,' she curtsied as he passed her by.

It took her less than ten minutes to follow him into the lounge with two hot steaming plates. Tom hadn't realised how hungry he was until he'd smelt the onions cooking. Now he was ravenous.

'I'm afraid His Highness will have to make do with one's lap on account we ain't got a table.' Serena put on her best British accent, which was reminiscent of Eliza Doolittle in *My Fair Lady*.

'Atrocious! I didn't realise how sparsely the other half lived,' he responded, lording it up.

'Could you ever forgive a poor peasant girl?' She sat next to him, fluttering her eyelashes.

'That depends on the fayre, wench.' He took a mouthful of the food. It was delicious. 'Uh, mmmm.'

'Is it to Sire's satisfaction?'

'If this is anything to go by, I'll promote you to head scullery maid.'

'Gee, thanks,' she said sarcastically.

They finished their meals, managing to avoid all mention of the disasters that had taken place over the past couple of days, although it was never far from Tom's mind. Serena dutifully cleared the plates into the kitchen, whilst Tom scoured her CD collection.

'You certainly have an eclectic taste in music,' he said when she rejoined him in the room. Her catalogue ranged from eighties pop to classical, with a selection of everything in between. 'Aren't you a bit young for Kajagoogoo?' he asked, holding up their 1983 debut album.

'That's what happens when you have two older brothers!' She made her way back to the couch and sat with her legs tucked underneath her.

'Funny, I'd have put you down as an only child,' he replied, putting on a smooth jazz compilation.

'Why, because I'm spoilt?' she pouted.

'Definitely!' He made himself comfortable beside her.

'I'll have you know, when I was growing up my mother used to tell people that she'd had three sons because I'd always prefer to play boys' games.'

'You, a Tomboy? Now that really is stretching the imagination.'

'It's true! I didn't even own a dress until I got to America.'

Tom noticed a flash of sadness cross her eyes. 'Did you miss Israel much?' he asked, his voice serious.

'At first. I had to leave all my friends behind in Haifa. As a young teenager, I found that very difficult. We didn't have access to the mobile phone technology the kids use today. I couldn't just text them, and Skype wasn't even invented, so it was hard to keep in touch. Eventually, I made new friends and lost contact altogether.'

'Why did you move to America?'

She told him how their father had returned home one evening, tears running down his face, his hands and clothes covered in blood. After he'd showered, changed and composed himself, he'd sat them all down at the kitchen table and explained how he'd been on his way home from work, when there'd been an explosion on a bus on the opposite side of the road. He'd parked up and made his way across the debris-strewn carriageway with several other motorists who had stopped. They were first on the scene and were confronted with the aftermath of a suicide bomb. As they fought their way through the twisted metal and shattered glass at the front of the bus, it was evident that the passengers towards the rear, where the terrorist had detonated the device, hadn't survived.

Selena described how her father had broken down as he described how he'd helped to get the injured off the bus and comfort those passengers still trapped in the wreckage, until the emergency services arrived. He hadn't gone into too much detail, but it was evident from his face that he'd seen a lot more than he was telling them. It wasn't until the next day that the final death toll of fifteen was reported by the papers.

Serena's own tears began to fall when she described how she'd gone to school expecting to see her best friend, Ellie, waiting for her at the entrance, as they did for each other every morning. She'd hung around for her as long as possible, hoping she was just running late, before having to go into assembly. It was there that the school was informed by the headmaster that Ellie, along with another three pupils, had died in the explosion.

Serena's father had then decided to safeguard his family by moving to America to join his brother.

Tom put his arm around her to comfort her and she buried her face deep into his chest. He could feel the violent sobs rack her body as he held her tightly. Tom suspected that she wasn't just grieving for a long lost friend; the tension that had built up over the past couple of days was being released. He stroked her hair, which seemed to soothe her, as the convulsions soon subsided.

'I'm sorry,' she said looking up at him, her eyes brimming with unshed tears.

'I didn't realise my choice of music would have such a profound effect,' he replied, smiling.

She managed a laugh, but her eyes never left his. He bent his head to kiss her and she met him half way. Their lips touched, tenderly at first, and then with more eagerness. She reached up and gently caressed his cheek with the tips of her fingers. He moved his body around so he could kiss her shoulders, pulling the thin straps of her vest down over her arms. She let out a moan as his lips brushed the nape of her neck. She turned towards him, her hands finding the buttons on his shirt and deftly undid them, one by one.

He broke away from their embrace, pulling her down onto the rug. Tom had imagined this moment from the very first time he'd seen her and wondered whether she would be a passionate lover. He wasn't disappointed. They made love all night, time and time again, until finally, exhausted, they fell asleep in each other's arms.

CHAPTER 23

They were awoken the next morning by the sound of a mobile phone ringing. It took Tom a couple of seconds to realise it was his. He checked his watch; it was just after eight. He scrambled from under the throw they had used as a blanket and tried to identify where the sound was coming from. It was the loudest from his trousers, which had been thrown over the back of the sofa. He reached into the pocket and retrieved his phone.

'Hello?' Tom said sleepily.

'Tom, good morning. It's Frederick.'

'Morning, Frederick. How are you?'

'I'm fine. Would you be able to come to my office this morning? There's something rather urgent I would like to discuss with you.'

'And Serena?'

'No, just you, Tom. And I'd appreciate it if you didn't mention to Miss Mayer that you were meeting me.' Frederick put the phone down.

He turned to Serena, who had stirred at the sound of her own name being mentioned. 'What was that all about?' she said, stretching her arms above her head.

'Frederick wants to see me in his office… alone.'

'Is that wise?' She threw the cover off, unabashed at her own nakedness. Tom realised he, too, was naked. She sidled up to him, draped an arm around his neck and pressed her body up to his.

Tom could feel himself stirring again as he felt the warmth of her against his skin.

'Probably not,' Tom replied, wrapping his arms around her.

'Do you have to go straight away?'

'Definitely not.' He swept her up into his arms and carried her into the bedroom.

***

An hour later, Tom was on his way to Frederick's office in one of the golf buggies, with Serena beside him. She had dressed quickly after their lovemaking and slipped out of her apartment, returning a few minutes later with a plastic carrier bag, which she presented to him. He'd looked inside to see a security guard's jacket. When he'd asked her where she had got it from, she just smiled and tapped her nose with her index finger. Not wanting to look a gift horse in the mouth, he didn't press the point and slipped it on. It was a tight fit, but would certainly do the job until he'd had a chance to go into town to purchase a replacement.

They had agreed that she would drop him off and then discreetly wait for him away from the building to avoid being spotted by Frederick, should he look out of his window.

***

It was still bitterly cold. Tom zipped up the front of his newly acquired jacket and pulled the collar up to protect his face. The snow had stopped falling and the sun was trying to make an appearance from behind grey, patchy clouds. The crispness of the snow crunched beneath the small wheels of the cart as they drove down the central boulevard.

Serena was directed to stop about a hundred metres short of the office and reverse the buggy in between two buildings. She had a clear sight of the entrance and would be able to see Tom as he came out.

'Is this cloak and dagger stuff really necessary?' she whinged, putting the fur-trimmed hood up on her padded jacket.

'If it was up to me, then I would have you in the meeting with us,' replied Tom. 'But Frederick was insistent that I didn't tell you about it. I don't know what he's up to, but I get the distinct impression that I'm about to find out.' He jumped out of the buggy. 'If I'm not out in an hour, call Inspector Gervaux.'

Serena still didn't know when to take him seriously. The expression on her face must have mirrored her feelings, because Tom laughed and told her that he was only joking and would text her if there was a problem. He made his way across the street.

She watched him all the way into the building, then sat back and prepared herself for a long wait. She smiled to herself as she began to reminisce about the previous evening's lovemaking. However, in her reverie, she failed to notice the two figures in the golf buggy that had pulled up further down the street, who were also watching Tom as he entered the building.

***

'Thanks for coming, Tom. Please take a seat.' Frederick was back to his usual warm and vibrant self.

'You left me little choice,' replied Tom. 'You sounded so mysterious on the phone, I just had to come and find out what it was all about.'

Frederick gave a short laugh. 'Yes, sorry about that, but it will all become clear when I explain to you why I wanted to see you.' He played with the pen on his desk for a few minutes; he seemed to be finding it difficult to know where to start. He took in a deep breath and exhaled slowly, deciding his only option was to lay all his cards on the table at once.

'When I last saw you,' he began, 'I mentioned that I would like to run the document you showed me past a few colleagues. Well, those colleagues are in fact an esoteric group of eminent scientists, whose sole purpose is to steer mankind away from any paths that could potentially lead to an apocalypse.'

He looked earnestly at Tom, whose expression had turned to a mixture of incredulity and scepticism. He paused, waiting for the inevitable questions, but when none were forthcoming he pressed on.

'Ever since the Ancient Greeks turned science into a vocation, man has been experimenting with his natural environment, the outcome of which has not always been certain. Until fairly recently, the consequential damage that could be inflicted on the population as a whole, as a result of those experiments, was negligible. Gunpowder, TNT, gelignite, semtex – the most powerful explosives of their time could, at worse, cause only localised damage. But the splitting of the atom changed all that. It was a turning point in the history of scientific experimentation. The energy released when one neutron is cleaved from a single uranium nucleus is fifty million times greater than when a carbon atom combines with oxygen in the burning of coal. Can you imagine the cataclysmic damage that could have ensued if scientists had been allowed to conduct experiments on those materials without the proper guidance?'

His eyes never left Tom's face, trying to gauge his reaction like a player in a poker game. But Frederick knew it was too late to stop now; he had already played his hand. 'It became evident shortly after the discovery of X-rays that radiation was not only a source of energy and medicine, but it could also be a potential threat to human health if not handled properly. When Thomas Edison's assistant died from a radiation-induced tumour as a result of too much X-ray exposure, he vowed the same fate would not fall on his fellow scientists. He therefore banded together with the early pioneers of nuclear experimentation to ensure not only their safety but, more importantly, the safety of mankind.'

Tom was listening intently. He made no attempt to interject or ask any questions.

'They formed a group that would meet on a regular basis to share ideas and philosophies,' continued Frederick. 'They exchanged views on potential risks which, eventually, they developed into a code of practice and ethical standard. The group grew in popularity and became respected as the ultimate authority on radiation. By 1914, it had over a hundred members worldwide, all dedicated to the pursuit of atomic knowledge through a strict and disciplined set of rules and regulations...'

CHAPTER 24

Inspector Gervaux had arrived at the facility just after nine in the morning. He had prepared himself to oversee another round of employee questioning by his officers, which was laborious but necessary. He knew from experience that criminals weren't caught by dramatic breakthroughs, as portrayed in the cinema, but by the detail often found in the most innocuous of places: an email, a wastepaper bin, a passer-by who initially couldn't recall the crime.

That axiom was shattered five minutes after his arrival at the complex by a phone call from the lab telling him they'd had a dramatic breakthrough on the substance found in Tom Halligan's apartment. It was potassium chlorate, the same grade as the residual compound collected at the scene of the explosion.

He'd met his sergeant on the steps of the main building and told him about the results from the lab. Lavelle's expression didn't change, but inside he was pleased that he would get another opportunity to break the arrogant American. They made their way over to the accommodation block after establishing from the receptionist that Tom hadn't yet turned up for work.

They arrived at the apartment to find the door ajar. A cursory look inside was all it took to confirm that no attempt had been made to tidy it up after the burglary. They went through to the bedroom, which was in a similar state; the duvet and mattress were still spewing their feathery contents onto the floor. *There's no way he could have slept in this bed last night,* the inspector thought to himself. They left the apartment and returned to the main building.

He had asked Lavelle to assemble his men in Tom's office, where he told them that a thorough search of the facility was required. As soon as the suspect was apprehended, they were to radio in and Lavelle would call off the search. In the meantime, they would speak to the Chief Security Officer to ascertain whether Tom had left the compound.

***

Frederick rose from his seat and made his way to the window, perching on the sill. Tom's gaze followed him, but the bright sunshine streaming into the room made it difficult for him to discern Frederick's features clearly, as he continued his monologue.

'And then came the war. Initially, these physicists were unaffected, as both the Germans and Allies each developed their own alternatives to conventional weapons – mustard gas was the German's choice, whilst the Allies preferred biological warfare, predominantly smallpox. But, as the war progressed, both sides looked for a more *permanent* solution and the spotlight shone on the work being done in the field of radioactive elements. The side that could harness the destructive components in radium or uranium would have a war-winning advantage. The Germans were the first to realise this and set about rounding-up as many scientists in this field as they could find in the occupied territories. Fifty-four men and women were initially asked, then coerced, then tortured and, finally, killed for their knowledge, but not one of them broke the sacred code to which they had sworn allegiance, to protect mankind from itself. If they had cooperated, the outcome of the war would have been very different.

'The Allies got wind of what the Germans were up to and tried to respond by approaching their own scientists, but came up against a similar brick wall. Most were incarcerated as conscientious objectors and their research grants taken away from them. After the war, they found it very difficult to get any kind of work...'

***

The first hour had drawn a blank. An inspection of the security log had established that Professor Halligan had left the previous evening with the two policemen and returned by himself, some two and a half hours later. The absence of any other records meant that he was either still on the base or he had managed to by-pass the security systems protecting the perimeter walls and scaled the nine-foot high fence without detection. That was a highly unlikely scenario, Inspector Gervaux was informed by the Chief Security Officer, whilst sitting in his rather small office, surrounded by TV monitors flickering from one image to the next, as the entire base was being watched by electronic eyes.

***

As Tom squinted up at the silhouette in front of the window, he could tell that Frederick was getting emotional. Frederick cleared his throat and continued.

'The few remaining physicists that were still in a position of influence took the decision to form a clandestine organisation, not only to protect themselves, but society as a whole. They realised that the attention shown by the militia in their chosen field would make it difficult for them to operate in the best interests of humanity. They could see the writing on the wall – if the powers that be wanted to exploit their discoveries for use in weapons of mass destruction, they would be incapable of stopping them through rational debate. The only option open to them was to infiltrate all nuclear programmes in an effort to hamper the development of atomic bombs from within. They successfully achieved their objective for over twenty years, until midway through the Second World War, when the American government discovered it had dissidents in its ranks. A witch hunt was conducted, which led to several of our key members being arrested and shot as spies. That initiated the formation of the Manhattan Project, an ultra-secretive research programme specifically designed to develop an atomic bomb for use against the Axis powers.

'Under the control of the military and funded to the tune of $26 billion in today's money, our members found it impossible to influence the inevitable progression towards unleashing the power of the atom for use on the battlefield. The rest, as they say, is history. Over 350,000 civilians were killed when the Americans dropped their atomic bombs on Nagasaki and Hiroshima. The images sickened the scientists working on the project so much that some refused to do any further work and left immediately. Others stayed on, but wrestled with their conscience about the moralistic virtues of their science, many feeling remorse and guilt for their part in creating what amounted to the cruellest and most inhumane technological instrument ever used against another human being. Our membership went from less than a hundred to over a thousand overnight, many looking to atone for their misguided ambitions.'

***

The next hour had been spent in the Chief Security Officer's cramped office studying the CCTV camera footage of the complex, starting with the accommodation block the previous evening, which clearly showed Tom exiting from a taxi and going inside. Fast forwarding through the tape revealed several people coming and going during the night, but none could be identified as their suspect.

The morning images were much clearer because of the daylight, but the volume of people increased substantially, making the identification process slower as they had to freeze the recording on each individual in order to eliminate them. They reached real-time recording with no sign of their suspect having left the accommodation block.

***

Frederick returned to his seat, which gave Tom the opportunity to ask about the German effort to produce a nuclear bomb.

'Professor Reinhardt,' explained Frederick, 'who was head of our organisation at the time, was also responsible for the atomic research team for the German military. He managed to dissuade the Nazis from building a bomb on the grounds that it was too expensive and uncertain, and had no hope of success before the end of the war.'

'And Oppenheimer? Wasn't he a member of the organisation?' Tom knew all about the Manhattan Project. Every undergraduate in atomic physics had learnt how Oppenheimer had been given the onerous task of bringing together the greatest scientific minds of his day to work on a project that had the sole purpose of killing thousands of people. He was noted for his mastery of all scientific aspects of the project and for his efforts to control the inevitable cultural conflicts between scientists and the military. He was an iconic figure to his fellow scientists, as much a symbol of what they were working toward, as a scientific director.

But it wasn't so much Oppenheimer's scientific or administrative achievements that were to be debated in the lecture halls around the world to this day, but more the ethical values of science as a tool to advance the human race. The question asked was how could the development of the atomic bomb be justified for the good of mankind?

Proponents argued that it shortened the war, saving the lives of many more soldiers and civilians that would have been killed had the war been allowed to continue to its natural conclusion using conventional weapons. The opponents, however, cited not only the indiscriminate way the bomb decimated everything in its path, but also the lasting effects of radiation on future generations of families fortunate or unfortunate enough to have survived the initial blast. This usually leads onto the wider implications of having such a weapon in the arsenal of a select number of countries who use it as a threat to make lesser nations capitulate, as opposed to being the ultimate deterrent and an essential instrument in maintaining world peace.

'Robert?' Frederick said fondly. 'You could say he is responsible for making the organisation what it is today.'

Tom looked confused, but let Frederick continue. 'What most people don't know about Robert Oppenheimer is that, not only was he a brilliant scientist, but he was also a deeply religious man. The two aren't mutually exclusive, you know,' he added, seeing Tom's frown deepen. 'He was a devout follower of Hinduism. When he was a young man, he memorised the entire seven hundred verses of the Bhagavad Gita, or The Song of the Bhagavan, in its original Sanskrit form, after learning the language. Years later, on seeing the flash the first time he tested the atomic bomb in the desert in New Mexico, he was heard to say, *"If the radiance of a thousand suns were to burst into the sky, that would be like the splendour of the Mighty One"*. And when the huge, sinister, mushroom-shaped cloud rose into the sky, he quoted another line from the poem, *"I have become death, the shatterer of Worlds"*.'

Tom gave an involuntary shudder, as though somebody had walked over his grave.

***

When there was still no sighting of the Professor, next came known associates. An officer was dispatched to check on the apartments of Serena Mayer and Anjit Bose, whilst the inspector and his associate re-ran the tapes looking to see if Serena had left the accommodation block. They found her on three separate occasions on the morning tapes. One was at exactly 8.55 am when she was seen leaving. The next was six minutes later when she was returning with a bag, and the third was seven minutes after that when she was spotted leaving again, but this time in the presence of a security guard.

When questioned about the identity of the man she was with, the Chief Security Officer wasn't able to offer any assistance as he couldn't recognise him because his face was obscured by the collar on his jacket. But he did inform the inspector that it was against company policy for a member of his staff to fraternise with a CERN employee and, when he was able to establish who it was, he would be disciplining them.

It was of no concern to Gervaux, who brushed off the comment and asked to see the camera footage that would track Serena's movements. She was seen getting into one of the buggies at the front of reception with the security guard and driving off. Another camera picked her up driving down the main boulevard, which then switched to another camera as she drove out of its range. She was last seen reversing into an alley between two buildings by a fourth camera.

All eyes were on the screen, waiting for her to emerge, but several seconds passed without an appearance. And then the security guard walked out, crossed the road and entered a building on the opposite side. They watched the footage for several more minutes, but there was no sign of her.

***

'But how could his conscience permit him to be involved in such a project that was clearly against his faith?' Tom challenged.

'Robert was given a job to do, which you could argue went against all religious ethicalities. He could have turned it down, of course, but he believed that, in creating the ultimate weapon, a weapon so powerful that it could destroy entire nations, the enemy would recognise the futility in continuing the conflict and lay down their arms, thus saving countless lives. What he didn't know about at the time was the huge chasm that existed between the two sides' attitudes to captivity. It was driven into the psyche of every Japanese soldier and citizen that death must be preferred to surrender. It took two physical demonstrations of the bomb's capabilities for the Japanese to acquiesce, an act that Robert had no part in, but the consequences of which plagued him for the rest of his life. The fact that only eight countries in the world today have nuclear weapons capability, and Hiroshima and Nagasaki were the only times the bomb has ever been deployed against an enemy, is testament to the achievements of Robert and the organisation over the years.'

'So how does one man prevent nuclear arms proliferation?' Tom queried.

'Not one man, but one organisation,' Frederick corrected. 'After the war, Robert became head of the organisation. He gave it an identity and a purpose. The skills he had used in coordinating an interdisciplinary project that involved not just physics, but chemistry, metallurgy, ordnance and engineering to build the world's first atomic bomb, he channelled into ensuring that the world would never have to witness the aftermath of another one being detonated in an act of aggression. He realised that scientists by themselves wouldn't have the authority to prevent such a catastrophe happening, so he surreptitiously recruited influential figures from the world of politics, the militia and the private sector. He managed to get himself into the position of chief advisor to the newly created United States Atomic Energy Commission and used his influence to lobby for international control of nuclear power to avert an arms race.'

Frederick paused for a moment. Gazing out of the window, then continued.

'Whilst working publicly on President Eisenhower's Atoms for Peace campaign, which sought to encourage countries to use nuclear technology for energy purposes, his real influence was as a cohesive force in a clandestine organisation committed to the prevention of the development of nuclear armaments. The two roles went hand in hand. Whilst the former gave him legitimate access to countries aspiring to develop their own nuclear programmes, the latter enabled our organisation to infiltrate the facilities to ensure that the technology was being used appropriately. Ironically, the first nuclear reactors in Iran and Pakistan were built under the programme. SHIVA managed to impede the transition of Pakistan's nuclear energy to missile capability until the mid-1980s, as we are still doing in Iran, although I fear we are losing control in that particular facility.'

'Shiva? As in the statue at the entrance of the main building?' An image of Ajay suddenly flashed through Tom's mind.

Frederick gave a wry smile. 'I thought you may have guessed by now. I mentioned earlier that Robert had given our organisation an identity. He chose SHIVA from his Hindu teachings – the transformer or destroyer. He thought it appropriate at the time, because of the mission we were embarking on. If successful, we would transform the world into a better place by producing cheap nuclear fuel that would benefit the whole of mankind. If we failed, then…'

'But why are you telling me all this?' asked Tom.

Frederick was just about to answer when the phone on his desk rang again. He held up his hand in an apology to Tom and took the call. 'Volker here.'

There was a pause as the person on the other end of the line asked a question.

'A security guard?' Frederick repeated, looking puzzled. Then he glanced up at Tom and realised what the inspector was alluding to. 'Er… yes, I asked him to come to see me because I wanted to know if there had been any news on Ajay.'

Another pause.

'Over an hour ago. Why?'

A longer pause this time. 'I see,' said Frederick. 'Well, if I spot him on the base, I will let you know immediately.'

Frederick replaced the handset in the receiver and turned his attention to Tom. 'I think we should get you out of here. That was Inspector Gervaux. They're looking for you in connection with the bombing.'

'That's ridiculous!' Tom replied indignantly. 'I'll go and speak to him straight away.'

'That wouldn't be advisable. They seem to think that they have enough evidence to arrest you for murder.'

'What evidence?'

Frederick didn't answer.

'What evidence, Frederick?' Tom repeated more slowly.

'It's possible that you've been framed.' Frederick held up the palms of both hands to stop Tom asking any more questions. 'What's important now is to get you to a safe place until we can sort this out with the authorities. If they arrest you now, there's no guarantee they will listen to reason.'

Tom was bewildered. 'But I don't understand…'

'I'll explain later,' replied Frederick. 'But at the moment, I'm not sure the Inspector believed my story about the security guard, so we really should get out of here.'

***

'Nothing.' Sergeant Lavelle had just finished reviewing the tapes, which focussed on the entrance to the building the security guard had entered.

'Is there a back way out?' Inspector Gervaux asked the Chief Security Officer without taking his eyes off the screen.

'Not to my knowledge.'

'Then he must still be in there.' Inspector Gervaux's usually Germanic composure was giving way to his French temperament, which Sergeant Lavelle had witnessed only on a handful of occasions and knew to stay out of his way until balance was restored. Unfortunately, this time he had no option but to ride it out.

'Not any more.' Sergeant Lavelle was pointing to the screen, which was showing Herr Volker leaving the building accompanied by the security guard.

All three men watched intently as the two people got into a black car and drove off down the main boulevard.

'Can you track them?' It was more of a demand from Gervaux than a question.

'Of course. We have one hundred per cent coverage of the entire complex,' the Chief Security Officer said with pride. He was a little uncomfortable sitting in front of the large monitor with two policemen hunched over either side of him. He was used to the confines of his office but, with three fully-grown adults occupying the space, it was feeling decidedly claustrophobic. To make matters worse, somebody had been eating garlic and he knew it wasn't him. He moved the mouse over the vehicle's number plate and right-clicked. A red box appeared which stated that LPR (licence plate recognition) was activated.

'We should be able to monitor the car wherever it goes now,' he said. 'The cameras will automatically pick it up when it passes by.'

The car was driving off into the distance and it was just a speck now. Lavelle looked over the shoulders of the seated man at his superior and rolled his eyes.

'Any second now another camera should pick it up…' continued the Chief Security Officer, his top lip beginning to sweat. 'Wait… wait… wait.' The car had disappeared entirely from view. Just as he was starting to lose faith in the technology, the monitor flickered to show the vehicle filling up the whole screen again. 'There!' he said with a sigh of relief.

'Wait. Go back,' Gervaux demanded. He had seen a white object appear in the bottom right-hand corner, just before the image changed.

The security officer pressed some buttons on the keyboard and the picture reverted to the previous scene. The white golf buggy being driven by Serena had immerged from the alley and was following the black Mercedes.

'Can we track both vehicles at the same time?' asked the inspector.

'Yes, I can toggle between the two.' The Chief Security Officer demonstrated by pressing the forwards and backwards keys with his forefinger – the Mercedes, golf buggy, Mercedes, golf buggy.

'Okay, keep the camera on the buggy,' Gervaux instructed.

The vehicle was moving much slower than the Mercedes but, because the boulevard was straight, the inspector assumed Serena was able to maintain line-of-sight contact. As the cart approached the top of the screen it was joined by yet another from the bottom.

'Looks like we got ourselves a convoy,' Lavelle said in the worst American accent Gervaux had ever heard.

'Can we track that one as well?' the inspector asked.

'Sorry. We can only alternate between two cameras at the same time,' the security officer replied, apologetically.

'Okay, go to the lead vehicle.'

He pressed the back button to see the Mercedes disappearing into an underground car park. The two policemen waited patiently for the cameras to pick it up again. The seconds ticked by and the security officer shifted uncomfortably in his seat.

'Why have we lost sight of the vehicle?' demanded Gervaux. 'Can we switch to inside the building?'

'We don't have any cameras in there,' the security guard mumbled sheepishly.

'I thought you said you had a hundred per cent coverage of the complex?' Gervaux retorted angrily.

'We did have, but Herr Volker ordered us to remove the CCTV from the car park shortly after the site was commissioned.'

'Why would he do that?' Lavelle chipped in.

'I… I'm not sure,' came the stuttered response.

'Didn't you think to ask, at the time?' the sergeant pressed.

'But Herr Volker is head of CERN Council. It wasn't our position to question his authority,' the security officer protested indignantly.

'How can you secure the complex if you can't see what's going on?' Lavelle countered.

'What's that building being used for?' Gervaux asked calmly, trying to diffuse the spat.

'It's not,' replied the security officer. 'I mean, it's vacant. From what I understand, it was sub-let to another company because it was surplus to requirements, but they have never occupied the building. They even have their own security check-point on the far side of the compound.'

'So you'll be able to tell us if anybody's been coming and going over the last few weeks?'

The security officer shook his head. 'We don't operate that gate. They have their own people.'

'Isn't that a little odd?' the inspector queried.

'It's not unusual for sub-contractors to be used in the security business. Besides, Herr Volker authorised it.'

Inspector Gervaux fell silent, trying to make some sense out of it all. Their prime suspect, Anjit Bose, had gone missing, but he was a known associate of Halligan, whom they had subsequently discovered was implicated in the bombing. Herr Volker, who just happened to be their prime suspect's parental guardian and the person responsible for recruiting Halligan, was, from what they had seen today, capable of harbouring a fugitive. Ergo: Volker *had* to be the ringleader. *But why would he want to destroy the Collider?* He didn't have all the answers, but the one thing he was certain about was that they needed to have a serious conversation with Herr Volker about his involvement.

'Can you go back to the buggies?' Gevaux requested.

One cart had stopped just outside the entrance to the car park and was now abandoned. There was no sign of the other.

'I think it's time we joined the party,' the inspector gestured to his sergeant, who followed him out of the door.

CHAPTER 25

Tom had been filled in on the way to the Bunker as to why Volker suspected he had been framed by Deiter to act as scapegoat for the bombing.

'But why me?' he asked as they turned into the underground car park.

'Nothing personal, but you were the ideal candidate.'

'Thanks,' Tom replied sarcastically and then had a thought. 'Is that why you recruited me in the first place?'

Frederick looked hurt. 'Not at all. None of this was planned. The idea was simply to disable the Collider as we had done in the past. It was supposed to look like an accident and nobody was supposed to get hurt. Unfortunately, Deiter miscalculated the amount of explosive required, which resulted in the deaths of those poor maintenance workers and brought the police to our doorstep. The last thing SHIVA needs is this kind of attention.'

Frederick's explanation made sense, but Tom still wasn't fully able to trust him. He understood the motives behind the organisation, but didn't necessarily agree with the way they set about achieving their objectives. Two men had died and he could go to prison for a very long time as a result.

That was why he hadn't told Volker that Serena was following them. He had seen her pull out of the alley in his wing mirror and was concerned that she wouldn't be able to keep up. He had every intention of slowing Frederick down if she dropped too far back, but he hadn't needed to. As they turned into the car park, he looked to his left and could just make out the outline of the white buggy in the distance.

They got out of the car and Frederick led them to the lift. He pressed the button and the doors slid open immediately, reassuring Frederick that nobody else was in the building. If he'd have had to wait for the lift to arrive, it would mean that either somebody was in the offices above them or, worse still, in the Bunker. They stepped in and Frederick retrieved the key from his pocket and inserted it into the control panel. He pressed the alarm button and the lift started to descend.

'What is this place?' Tom felt a little uneasy about losing his backup. *There's no way Serena would be able to follow me down here.*

'We call it the Bunker,' replied Frederick. 'It's the operational headquarters of our unit. SHIVA has developed a matrix of autonomous cells scattered throughout the world. Each group is led by a head, often working in isolation, making all the decisions based on the fixed fundamental principles of our founding fathers. Each cell has an objective and functions independently, making the main organisation virtually immune to detection or penetration by our adversaries. The identity, location, or actions of other cells is restricted to the upper echelons to prevent a total network collapse in the event of an individual unit being compromised.'

'Sounds very sophisticated,' Tom observed as the doors opened again. Frederick preceded Tom out of the lift and made his way down the corridor.

'It has to be. We've learnt over the years, from bitter experience, that we are seen as a threat to man's quest to develop the ultimate weapon. Our members are relentlessly pursued and, once exposed, ruthlessly expunged.'

'But why is SHIVA here? CERN is dedicated to the peaceful pursuit of the discovery of the God particle.'

Frederick stopped and turned to Tom. 'Given the downturn in the global economy, CERN is one of only a few government-funded organisations in the world never to have had its budgets cut. The Collider itself cost nearly $5 billion to construct and we spend a little over that each year in running costs. To date, the project has cost over $25 billion. Putting that into perspective, America's space shuttle programme was axed to save the US economy a tenth of what we spend each year in search of the God particle. So, ask yourself one question – *cui bono?* Who benefits?'

Tom shrugged.

'Are you aware of the expression, "whoever pays the piper, calls the tune"?' Frederick waited for Tom to acknowledge before continuing. 'The research to discover the God particle is being conducted in the name of science; but, once we have proven its existence and can replicate it at will, then the implications are that it could be used for military applications.'

'The ultimate deterrent – a doomsday weapon?' Tom suggested, expounding on Frederick's inference.

'It's possible,' Frederick concurred. 'SHIVA's mission here was to prevent it ever getting to that stage. It was to forestall the discovery of the God particle to such an extent that its monetary backers would lose faith in the project and move onto something else.'

'So, you weren't aware that the Collider could affect the Earth's electromagnetic field?'

'Not until you showed me the document. In hindsight, I should have listened to Professor Morantz. But at the time it sounded preposterous.' He opened the door to the Bunker and switched on the lights. 'We should be safe down here. Only SHIVA is aware of its existence.'

'But I can't stay down here forever,' Tom protested.

'The reason I've told you all this is that I want you to become part of SHIVA,' replied Frederick. 'I want you to take over my role as head of this cell. What we need now, more than any other time in SHIVA's history, are visionaries, leaders that can inspire the next generation of scientists to follow a moralistic code. I'm not getting any younger and my usefulness to the organisation is almost at an end; but what I can do is speak to Inspector Gervaux and tell him that I planted the device and implicated you. That way, you'll be in the clear to continue the work we started here.'

Both men were startled by the slow clapping of hands. They spun round to see Deiter framed in the doorway and, behind him, Serena struggling against the grip of a security guard in a navy blue uniform, holding a semi-automatic weapon out in front of him.

'Very commendable, Herr Volker,' he said. 'But I suggest that nobody is going anywhere for the time being.'

CHAPTER 26

Gervaux and Lavelle reached the underground car park in less than five minutes, where they found the two abandoned golf buggies and the black BMW.

'You go interview the security guard on the gate, I'll search the building,' Gervaux ordered.

The inspector scanned the car park for any signs of life before approaching the lift. He pressed the button and heard the muffled whir of the winch mechanism behind the double stainless steel doors. It took several seconds for the sound to stop and the doors to hiss open. He stepped in. Deciding to work from the top down, he pressed the third floor button.

Seconds later, he was standing in an empty office, which clearly hadn't been commissioned since it was built. Electric cables protruded out of bare walls, waiting for the new occupants to decide where they were going to position the sockets. The floor tiles were covered in a thick layer of dust, in which Gervaux could make out the impression of a single set of footprints leading off to the far side of the room. He followed the trail to a large, panoramic window and looked out. He could see his sergeant talking to the security guard at the perimeter of the compound. They were standing outside what looked like a sentry hut. Lavelle had his notebook out and was jotting something in it.

The inspector turned away from the window and followed the tread marks back to the lift. From the shape and style of the imprints, Gervaux's guess was that they were made by some kind of trainer or sneaker and, by the sharpness of the ridges, they were fairly new. He would leave the identification of the exact make, model and size to his forensics team, who he would ring once he'd checked the rest of the building.

He took the lift down and stepped out onto the second floor, but could tell immediately that it was empty; the footprints had ventured into the office space for about ten feet and then doubled back. He walked over to the window, which afforded the same view as the one on the floor above, only at a shallower elevation. He could see Lavelle putting his notebook away as the security guard disappeared into the hut.

After checking the first floor and coming up empty-handed, he made his way back to the car park, where Lavelle was waiting for him.

'How did you get on with the security guard?' Gervaux enquired.

'He was a bit reluctant to start with,' his sergeant replied. 'But when I told him he could be implicated in a murder case, he was more forthcoming.'

'And?' the inspector prompted impatiently.

Lavelle quickly retrieved his notebook from his breast pocket and found the appropriate pages. 'His name is Ahmed Singh Lalli. He's only been working in the job for less than a month. He's employed by a company called Shiva and has strict instructions not to let anybody through the gate unless they carry a company identification card. He didn't see anybody for the first two weeks, but he said that recently there has been a lot of activity; people coming and going, maybe two or three times a week.'

'What about Volker and Halligan?' asked Gervaux. 'Did they leave through the gate just now?'

'He didn't recognise the names, but he said that nobody has left during his shift, which started at eight this morning.'

'Do you believe him?'

Lavelle shrugged. 'Put it this way, after the talk I had with him, he values his freedom more than he does his job.'

'Then they must still be here,' replied Gervaux. 'I want this place sealed off. Nobody leaves the compound unless we can verify their identity, and only then if we get a note from their mothers. Call in reinforcements if you have to. I want the entire complex searched from top to bottom with a fine-tooth comb. And call the forensics team; there are some footprints on the third floor I want analysed.' Gervaux scanned the car park again, expecting his quarry to suddenly materialise. 'Where are you, Halligan?' he muttered to himself.

CHAPTER 27

'Your arrogance is responsible for that.'

Deiter stopped in front of the television screen and pointed to the images of the devastation caused by the latest earthquake. He had been pacing back and forth in front of his captives like a caged animal. He flicked a switch on the remote control and the screen went blank. He turned round to face the three people seated in front of him, their hands and feet tied with PlastiCuffs, nylon rope binding them to their chairs. The security guard had taken up a position behind them, the muzzle of his automatic pistol resting in the crook of his arm.

'Did you really think you could control the Collider?' he was directing his question at Frederick.

'We had to. We believed we could prevent the discovery of the God particle...'

'And stop man destroying himself,' Deiter finished his sentence for him. 'Yes, yes, I'm fully aware of your *beliefs*,' he added sarcastically. 'But you failed to consider the consequences of your actions.'

'Which were?' Volker asked defiantly.

'This,' Deiter gestured to the newsreel. 'You were right about the butterfly effect. The electro-magnetic waves generated by the Collider *do* have an effect on the Earth's geomagnetic field, causing it to become unstable. But what you failed to realise is that it's self-sustaining. By disturbing the polar equilibrium, you have set in motion a chain reaction, the balance of which cannot be restored until it has completed its inexorable march towards the final solution.'

'Meaning?' this from Serena.

'Total polar reversal,' interjected Tom. 'What we are witnessing is a phenomenon that has taken place several times over the millennia. North becomes south and vice versa. The last one took place about eight hundred thousand years ago, but as none of us were around to see it reports on how it affected the human population are a bit sketchy. The difference between this one and all the previous ones is that this is man-made.'

'I don't understand. Why are you doing this?' Volker shook his head, trying to rationalise Deiter's motives.

'I didn't – *you* did!' Deiter raised his voice, pointing an accusatory finger at Volker.

'But YOU could have stopped it,' Volker spat back.

Deiter nodded sagely, as if contemplating the suggestion for the first time. 'Yes, I *could* have stopped it. I *could* have allowed Morantz to go to the media with his findings. But, then again, so could have you. Moranz told me before he died that he'd spoken to you and told you that he thought the Collider was responsible for the earthquakes.' Deiter shrugged. 'You did nothing about it.'

'I didn't believe it was true at the time.' Volker's response was almost inaudible, sadness clouding his eyes.

'Didn't believe, or didn't *want* to believe?'

Volker was silent.

'So, why didn't you put a stop to it? It would have been the right thing to do,' Serena asked indignantly.

Deiter resumed his frantic pacing. He seemed to be struggling with his internal demons. 'It would have been the right thing to do,' he repeated over and over, mimicking Serena's words.

His actions were becoming more animated now, his ruddy complexion deepening to an unhealthy crimson. Serena thought he was going to have a heart attack. He stopped abruptly in front of her, turned on his heels and lurched towards her, his face stopping inches away from hers. She recoiled instinctively, but her bindings held her so she couldn't turn from the manic eyes that were now boring into hers.

'Let me tell you what happens when you *do the right thing.*' His last words were delivered with a mocking sneer.

Serena could see spittle accumulating at the corners of his mouth and she could smell his putrid breath. She tried to look away from the insanity evident behind his dilated pupils, but she was transfixed, like a rabbit caught in the headlights.

After what felt like an eternity, he released her from the spell, turning his attention to Volker. 'Professor, I believe you knew my father?'

Frederick stared back at him blankly.

'Let me re-phase that,' continued Deiter. 'I believe you knew *of* my father?'

The vacant expression remained on Frederick's face.

Deiter took a few steps back, positioning himself centrally to his captive audience and prepared himself as if he was an actor delivering a soliloquy. He took several deep breaths and trained his eyes just above his spectators' heads.

'My father was one of the greatest scientists that ever lived,' he bellowed as if to a packed auditorium. Sensing he had grabbed everybody's attention, he continued. 'My father *did the right thing* and was castigated by his peers, the American Government and the very people whose lives he saved. It's time the world knew the truth of what *really* happened during the war.'

For the next hour, Deiter delivered a monologue on the life of his father, starting with how he had grown up in abject poverty on his parents' farm in a small village in Bavaria. What little money they had spare was spent on doctors' fees in an attempt to cure his affliction, which manifested itself as a severe facial tic.

As a child he was expected to help out with the daily chores once he finished school, working long into the night when the crops needed harvesting. Exhausted, he would climb into his bed, which he shared with his four younger brothers and sisters, and read by candlelight until he fell asleep.

His appetite for literature was insatiable. At the age of 10 he had read an entire library of books, mainly donated to him by his teachers, who recognised the latent genius in him. He passed the necessary exams to be selected for higher education with flying colours. Unfortunately, the nearest high school – or Gymnasium, as they were then called – was in Bremen, which meant a four-hour round trip on the local bus. It suited his education as he was able to read uninterrupted for the entire journey, shunned by his fellow pupils because of his facial twitches. As a consequence of his imposed absence, the farm suffered and, eventually, his father had to sell the land that had been in the family for generations, moving closer to the city in rented accommodation so their son could be nearer to his school and have access to the necessary doctors for his treatment.

For the next nine years, he studied classical literature. The Gymnasiums placed a heavy emphasis on Greek and Latin. This classical education aimed to produce not only educated scholars but also useful contributors to German culture, combining rationality with high cultural scholarship.

At the conclusion of his Gymnasium studies, he received his 'leaving certificate', or Abiturzeugnis, which entitled him to admission to university for his professional training. He chose Berlin University because of its scientific credentials, where he was tutored by the great theoretical physicists of the time, Planck and Born.

Having published a paper in a professional journal, which he was required to do to gain his doctorate, his next step to realising his goal of becoming a teaching professor was to attain a further degree called the Habilitation. This initially involved obtaining a temporary assistantship in an institute of his chosen field.

The paper he published for his doctorate, entitled 'Do atoms have sex?' which was initially published in a locally distributed science journal, was picked up by *Popular Science Monthly* and reprinted in its entirety.

With a circulation of over one hundred thousand copies, it was read and discussed by every eminent scientist on the planet, including the Director of the Kaiser Willhelm Institute for Physics in Schöneberg, who sent him a telegram stating:

'I was intrigued by your article in Popular Science Monthly – stop – It would be an honour to discuss your theories further – stop – please contact me at your earliest convenience – stop – Albert Einstein – stop'

The excitement of receiving his first telegram was surpassed only by the fact that the celebrated Director of one of the most respected institutes in Germany wanted to discuss his thesis with him.

Within a day of their meeting, he had received an offer for an internship, which required him to teach a minimum of one seminar, with the rest of his time devoted to research. After six years, it would lead him to a major publication that he could submit for his Habilitation.

More importantly for him, however, was that he would be getting paid – admittedly not a huge amount, but enough to be able to live on and send some money home to help his parents, who had been so supportive.

Regrettably, he didn't get a chance to tell his mother the good news. Not wanting to worry him whilst he was taking his exams, his father hadn't informed him that she had fallen ill and, despite the doctor's best efforts, she died two weeks later from typhoid. The effect on him was devastating. His tic, which he had managed to keep more or less under control, returned with a vengeance.

On turning up at the Kaiser Willhelm Institute for his first day, nobody recognised the disheveled, embarrassingly shy individual as the confident and enthusiastic person he'd been only days before.

For the next six years he literally kept his head down and concentrated on his chosen field of research – *'Nuclear fusion as a source of stellar radiation'* - surfacing only occasionally to deliver the lectures that were stipulated in his contract. Over that period, he made very few friends, self-conscious that he was unable to control the blinks and twitches that made him stand out as a freak. Since his mother's death, he and his father had grown apart. He secretly despised him for not speaking out when his mother was ill. He had reconciled the fact that he probably wouldn't have been able to save her, but the choice of being there or not, when she needed him the most, had been taken away from him. He understood that his father had done it for what he thought were the right reasons at the time, which only added to the guilt he felt for his absence.

His life changed drastically the day he published his Habitation thesis. If his doctorate thesis had made the science community's tongues wag, this one had them thrashing back and forth. It didn't harm his credibility, either, that his tutor was none other than the Nobel Prize-winning physics laureate responsible for defining the laws of relativity. Using his mentor's rather simplistic equation $E=mc^2$, he was able to demonstrate that the Sun's energy is derived from a thermonuclear reaction of hydrogen fusion into helium.

His article was published across the globe, not just in the scientific press but also in the popular newspapers, although somewhat 'dumbed down' for its readers. He was an overnight sensation, despite having taken six years to get there. Job offers came flooding in. From an early age, all he ever wanted to do was teach. The kindness of his tutors at school had had a deep impact on his psyche. But now, opportunities were opening up in areas he had never considered before, both at home and abroad.

The year was 1933 and a charismatic orator by the name of Adolf Hitler had just been appointed as chancellor to the ruling National Socialist German Workers Party. He was gaining popular support by attacking the Treaty of Versailles and promoting Pan-Germanism, anti-Semitism, and anti-Communism. Einstein could see the writing on the wall; born to Jewish parents, his time as a respected theoretical physicist was ebbing away. He chose to emigrate to America but, before he left, he begged his young protégé to go with him. He had secured a position at the Institute for Advanced Study in Princeton, New Jersey. As tempting as it was, the newly-qualified professor wasn't yet ready to give up on his beloved country; instead, he accepted a position at the German nuclear energy project in Leipzig, where he worked his way up to become Herr Direktor.

During the war, he was transferred to a top secret facility in Norway, where he developed his theoretical postulations of nuclear fission into a practical application. It was a device so lethal that it was capable of turning the tide in favour of Germany, overnight.

But he was a man of conscience. He had seen the atrocities that his compatriots were capable of. Some of his closest friends had been incarcerated for no other reason than their parents followed a certain doctrine. Many of his learned colleagues had been forced into exile rather than renounce their religious beliefs. He had been on his way home from work when he'd witnessed the rampaging mobs smashing the shop windows of anyone suspected of being Jewish, dragging the owners out into the street and beating them to a bloodied pulp, whilst the authorities looked on without intervening. It sickened him to his core; he could no longer say that he was proud to be a German.

His conscience would not allow him to contemplate the heinous acts that could be carried out if he gave the principles of how to make an atomic bomb to the Nazis. But it wasn't just a matter of telling his masters that he didn't know how to make one; they would just coerce another scientist, and another, and another until finally they achieved their objective. No, he had to convince them that it *could* be done, but would take far more resources than was currently available and let them decide that it wouldn't be worth it. It was a gamble. They could still decide to pursue the project to its ultimate conclusion but, with rumours that the German forces were being stretched to capacity, especially on the Eastern Front, he didn't think they would.

So, on that fateful day in September 1942, he did the right thing and changed the world forever. In front of some of the most powerful men of the Third Reich, he put on his best poker face and played his hand. And they fell for the bluff, hook, line and sinker. The project was abandoned within weeks as being too costly. Facilities were closed down and resources re-directed to more conventional weapons. He was re-assigned to the Reich Air Ministry and stationed at Peenemünde Airfield on the Baltic Coast, where he worked on the V-1 flying bomb until the end of the war.

Not satisfied with having averted a holocaust, the likes of which the world had never witnessed before, he had one last heroic act to perform. He believed that he could foreshorten the war, saving thousands of lives, if he could pass his findings to the Allies, on the proviso that they would never detonate the bomb but use the device as a deterrent to force Germany into an armistice. Having received the assurances via a highly-respected neutral intermediary, he handed over his entire research.

'…and the rest, as they say, ladies and gentlemen, is history.' Deiter stood his ground, waiting for the audience to burst into rapturous applause. Instead, he was greeted by three blank faces and a rather bored-looking security guard.

'Your father was Reinhardt?' Volker asked incredulously, breaking the silence.

'Yes, Professor Viktor Reinhardt,' Deiter corrected. 'A brilliant scientist who saved the world, but couldn't even get a job teaching physics in high school when the war ended. He was ridiculed by his so-called peers, who insisted that the errors he made when calculating the amount of radioactive material required to make a bomb weren't deliberate, but were the actions of an incompetent fool. He took his own life – a broken man, destitute and riddled with guilt for passing his research to the Americans. And all because of some misguided loyalty to the human race.

'And that's why you're doing this?' Serena's face was a mask of contempt. 'Out of some kind of twisted revenge for you father not having received the recognition you think he deserved?'

Deiter's face flushed. 'My father was a weak, pathetic man,' he barked. 'I was ashamed to carry his name through life, so I changed it to my mother's maiden name. He should have stuck to his principles as a physicist and developed the bomb for the Nazis. As scientists, it is not in our remit to be morally judgemental. We push back the frontiers of knowledge and let others decide what they do with the results... *that's* what we do.'

'Even if it means hundreds of thousands of innocent people could die?' Serena interjected.

'Yes, and that's exactly what happened as a result of my father *doing the right thing.* The only difference is that the innocent victims, in his case, changed from Western to Asian. Does that make it easier for you to digest?' Deiter sneered back at her.

'I'd love to know what Freud would have made of this guy's father complex,' Tom whispered to Serena as Deiter turned away from them.

He must have caught the gesture out of the corner of his eye, because he suddenly snapped his head round to face Tom. 'If you've got something to say, Professor Halligan, why don't you share it with the rest of us?'

Tom hadn't felt this admonished since he was a schoolboy. Furthermore, he could feel his face colouring with embarrassment. 'Er... I was just saying to Serena that you can't keep us down here forever. Sooner or later, we'll be missed.'

'I have no intention of keeping you here for long,' Deiter replied, icily.

'Then what do you intend doing with us?' A nervous edge had crept into Serena's voice.

'I'm glad you asked, Miss Mayer,' Deiter smiled benignly, picking up on her anxiety. 'The Collider is due to be tested tomorrow to ascertain what damage was done during the explosion. You three will have front row seats. Only, I fear you may be a little too close for comfort.'

'You're insane,' Serena blurted out.

'In a mad world, only the mad are sane,' Deiter quoted. 'The human race's voraciousness to destroy itself is matched only by its ingenuity in achieving it. Well, this time they may have just realised their goal and scientists will not be there to put a stop to it. In fact, the experiment will be brought to the doorstep of millions – literally. Unfortunately for them, they won't be around to share the results with the rest of us who are left.'

'Is that all this is to you? Just an *experiment*?' Serena asked, provokingly.

'Not *just* an experiment, my dear,' replied Deiter. '*The greatest* experiment the world has ever seen.'

'And what makes you so certain you will be one of the survivors?' Volker queried.

'There's an element of uncertainty in every experiment we do,' replied Deiter. 'That's what makes it interesting – but what we do is balance those risks against the probable outcome. Take where we are, for example. Switzerland is a land-locked country, so there is little danger from tsunamis. If there were a mega-quake in the Mediterranean, then we have some of the highest mountains in the world where we can take refuge until the flood waters subside. There have been no reports of earthquake activity here since the fourteenth century, so it's a fairly safe assumption that there are no active fault lines in the region.'

'You'll never get away with it,' Tom ventured.

Deiter ignored his protestation, gesturing to the security guard to leave the room.

'It's been a very…' Deiter searched his mind for the right adjective. '*Cathartic* experience, and I would have liked to discuss my hypotheses further. Unfortunately, time is not on my side. In the meanwhile, I'll leave you with your handiwork, Professor Volker.'

He pressed a button on the remote control and the TV flicked to life, showing the havoc caused by the San Francisco quake, before following the guard out. They all flinched in unison as they heard the metallic clang of the tumblers clicking into place as the door locked with some finality.

CHAPTER 28

The warm waters lapped at his bare feet as Chad lay prone on the surfboard, waiting for the right time to paddle. Timing was everything. The difference between catching the wave and a total wipeout… or, on this occasion, death.

In his short career, he had never been daunted by the size of the swells and had competed at most of the big wave locations around the world – California, Hawaii, Tahiti, even the UK. The opportunity to travel whilst doing something he really enjoyed was the reason he turned pro in the first place.

He wasn't academically bright; even so, it hadn't been easy for him to tell his father that he was dropping out of his final year at High School. He'd expected some resistance, but not on the scale that ensued after he'd told him that he'd got a sponsor and wanted to become a professional surfer. During the blazing row, his father had called him a moron – or, at least, that's what he thought he'd said. It wasn't until much later, after he'd stormed out of the house and met up with his buddies, that they'd explained to him the definition of an oxymoron and he realised his old man was referring to the words 'professional' and 'surfer' being contradictory as opposed to him being one. It didn't matter by then, however. They had both said things in the heat of the moment they couldn't go back on. *Besides, anybody who dissed his passion, dissed him.*

Growing up in San Diego meant that he was never far from the love of his life.

He started surfing at the age of 6 when he was given his first board – a five-foot Liquid Shredder soft board – by his parents as a present after writing a letter to Santa. He quickly outgrew it (and the need for Father Christmas) and traded it in for a seven-foot hardboard, which had the ability to turn more easily.

By the time he'd reached High School he was spending more time on the beach than he was in classes. On more than one occasion he found himself grounded and his board confiscated by his parents after receiving a visit from the truancy officer.

It was around this time that he started to notice the groups of bikini-clad girls hanging around the beach, particularly whenever there was a surfing competition on. The guys referred to them as 'groupies' or 'babes' and bragged about how many they'd had. He never really considered himself as good-looking, but the attention he was attracting from the younger girls seemed to contradict that opinion.

He had studied his naked form in the full-length mirror in his bedroom to work out whether there was something he was missing. His shaggy, sun-bleached blond hair was parted at the side, with a long fringe over his aquamarine blue eyes. It fell in layers to just above his shoulders. He had noticed his muscles starting to develop, particularly the ones he used for surfing – his triceps and chest muscles he used to quickly push himself to his feet, while his upper back and neck muscles helped him keep his chest up off the nose of the board, so he could paddle more efficiently, and his leg muscles were essentially the powerhouse – calves for balance and control, thighs for speed and direction. They were the ones that particularly ached after surfing all day.

He was of average height, compared to the other guys he hung out with. And his nose certainly wasn't as big as the Cohen brothers – if anything, it tipped up slightly at the end. His teeth were straight and white and his lips full. All-in-all, he couldn't understand the interest he was getting; but, as his father always said, 'There's no accounting for taste.'

Surfing is an art form, an expression of one's creative and athletic impulses, slashed across the fluid, unpredictable canvas of the ocean surface. Over the next three years he'd honed his skills and his body to become one of the foremost virtuoso surfers in the area. By the time he was seventeen, he had surfed the entire San Diego coastline and had even competed in some events, winning trophies for his speed, control and power. That's when he got spotted by a local surfboard shack and was offered a sponsorship deal. It didn't provide him with much of an income, but it did pay for travel expenses and equipment costs – as long as he was doing well and wore the T-shirt.

He'd left home shortly after the bust-up with his old man to join the circus, which was the professional surfer's circuit. Having passed his driving test the previous year, he used the money that his family had given him towards his first car to buy a 1999 Four Winds motor home for a dollar short of fifteen thousand from a local dealer. He hadn't haggled with the salesman about the price because he was told that another three people were interested in it and he didn't want to lose it. It slept five at a push, but most of the time it was just him and his two surfboards. He did have the occasional overnight guest; but, because of the transient nature of his chosen career, he was never in one place long enough to forge a lasting relationship.

His goal was to get on the Association of Surfing Professionals' (ASP) World tour. However, for that he needed a more generous sponsor. His big break came when he was competing in the American Pro Surfing Series at Huntington Beach, California. It was a sixty-four man knock-out competition, based over five heats, with a fifty per cent elimination rate after each round. He'd managed to get down to the last eight and was up against some old pros. He knew that wave selection was the single most important factor for winning the heat, as did the other seven competitors.

The wave he selected would determine the manoeuvres he was able to perform; marks were awarded by the panel of judges on how radical and controlled those movements were over the functional distance of the wave. In short, the bigger the wave, the better chance he had to impress the judges with his speed and power. His technique for selecting a good wave started on the shoreline, where he would watch the swells come in, getting a feel for their breaking patterns and gauging their size. After a short time, he was able to predict how big an oncoming wave would be and where it would begin to break. He'd paddle out to the site and wait for the next big swell.

Catching the wave was the easy bit – it was what you did after that that would determine whether you received a high score or not. You can't read the characteristics of a wave in advance; you have to be able to adapt your movement to suit the idiosyncrasies of your chosen ride. On this particular occasion, that ride turned out to be a real bitch. It started off okay – breaking to the right, the tip peeling back in a continuous line to form a twenty-foot glassy canvas on which to paint his turns.

He was about halfway to the beach when the centre of the wave collapsed; he narrowly avoided a wipeout with a power turn that took him away from the crashing surf. He had just completed this manoeuvre when the same thing happened in front of him. With no room to turn this time, he angled the board at the crest of the wave and popped over the top into the calmer waters behind the surf, knowing that he'd blown his chances of a decent score. Dejected, he paddled back to the beach and made his way to his motor home to brood, without even bothering to hear his scores. The consolatory pats on the back and sympathetic looks he received confirmed what he knew already.

He was halfway through his third bottle of Bud, when somebody wrapped on his door. He was in two minds as to whether to ignore it, when the door opened and the interloper stepped in.

'Hey dude, don't you wait to be invited in?' Chad said grumpily.

'Not usually,' the man countered. 'Name's Hogan. I represent a clothing manufacturer. You may have heard of us.' He handed his business card over.

Chad took it and read the details. 'Steve Hogan, Sponsorship Manager, North America.' That caught his attention, but what piqued his interest more was the logo on the top of the card. Rip Curl.

'You did well out there, kid.' There wasn't a hint of pity in his voice.

'I was totally walled off,' Chad replied despondently.

'Yeah, but before that, you did well. It was just bad luck – you did the best you could with the hand you were dealt. I've been in this business long enough to spot real talent when I see it. Let's say you offer me a Bud and we'll discuss what I have in mind?'

Two days later, Chad had a contract in his hand entitling him to a full sponsorship deal including a remuneration package of $250,000 per year. *Who's the moron now?* he thought to himself as he signed his name at the bottom of the document.

***

That same thought crossed his mind again now as he waited for the biggest wave of his life. It was, of course, one of those urban legends that went around the surfing community – everybody had heard of somebody doing it, but nobody knew their name or had met the person who had done it. It was always, 'Some dude in Thailand…' or 'This Aussie guy…'

There was always enough information to make it sound convincing, but never enough detail to prove it either way. Well, he was about to find out first-hand whether it was a fallacy or not. *Could a pro surfer ride out a tsunami wave?*

***

It had been just over three years ago that he'd signed up as one of Rip Curl's rising stars. They had appointed him a Personal Assistant, who was responsible for organising his calendar, booking him into the tournaments, making the travel arrangements, setting up the photo shoots and interviews – everything, really, apart from wiping his arse. All he had to do was be at the designated pick-up point at the allotted time and he would be whisked off to the relevant beach via a plane, train, boat or automobile.

He had traded in his old motor home for the four and five-star hotels that the company were putting him up in. He wasn't complaining – he got to do what he loved doing the most without the hassle of organising it. And the chicks! Those had increased exponentially. And it was a lot more comfortable screwing on a king-size Marriott bed than it was in the back of his old motor home. There had been a couple of girls that had wanted more than a casual relationship, but either he hadn't found the right one or he just wasn't ready to settle down. Either way, they were given the cold shoulder if they got too pushy.

After two years of mastering his craft in the minor tournaments, netting himself a cabinet-full of trophies and a healthy bank account of prize money, he had got to realise his dream of competing in the ASP World Championships. The tour had taken in Brazil, Fiji, French Polynesia, France, Portugal, Hawaii, America and his final destination – the Gold Coast, Queensland, Australia.

It was here, after a particular late night and an even later morning, that he switched on the TV in his hotel room to discover that an alert had been put out by the Joint Australian Tsunami Warning Centre (JATWC) of an earthquake off the west coast of Vanuatu. Although the islands themselves had received little damage from the tremors, the displacement of the sea floor had generated a huge tsunami, which was heading for the east coast of Australia. A clock on the bottom left-hand corner of the screen indicated the estimated time of impact – 48 minutes and 10 seconds… 9 seconds… 8 seconds… 7 seconds…

He'd looked out of his bedroom window to see a slow-moving, almost stationary, line of traffic heading inland, away from the coast. His first thought was to join them, then he considered moving to the top floor of the hotel. Finally, he decided on his current course of action. If he was going to die, he wanted to do so doing something he loved, not trapped in a car like a rat in a box, or crushed to death by falling masonry.

He'd raised the comatose form that had slept beside him with a gentle shake of the shoulders before telling her the good news. It had taken the images on the TV and a trip to the window before she finally believed what he was telling her. Her first reaction was to panic; she ran around the room, screaming and gathering the clothes she had discarded on the floor the night before. Chad had to physically restrain her before she calmed down enough to take in her option. Being a non-surfer, her best bet would be to get to the roof of the hotel and tie herself onto something stable. She dutifully agreed and left the room in a state of shock, having only managed to put on half her clothes.

Chad had donned his wet suit and made his way to the underground car park, where his rented Subaru Outback was parked, his surfboard having been secured to the roof rack with bungee cords. It was a relatively easy journey to the beach – his side of the road being devoid of all vehicles. He was amazed at the variety of hand gestures, facial expressions and signals that people used to try to tell him he was going the wrong way. Only once, at a police checkpoint, did they try to physically turn him back; but, when he explained that he'd left his younger sister playing on the beach, they let him through.

All that was left for him to do was choose any one of the deserted parking slots by the beach, unclip his board from the roof, paddle out to sea, and wait.

***

If the countdown on the TV was accurate, he figured he wouldn't have much longer to wait. He ran through his strategy in his mind one last time. If the urban myths were to be believed, the first indication of the wave approaching would be the 'drawback', where the shoreline recedes dramatically, exposing the normally submerged seabed for hundreds of feet. To counter being stranded, like so many fish would be, he had paddled far out to sea.

He looked back over his shoulder at the beach and could see the sun glinting off the roof of the solitary vehicle, some half a mile away in the distance. He would be carried along with the retreating tide, taking him further out to sea, towards the horizon, powerless to fight against the currents sucking him towards the unstoppable wall of water.

He had heard that, as the wave approaches shallower water, the leading edge slows down, but the trailing part is still moving rapidly in the deeper water behind, causing it to compress. This piling up – or *shoaling* – results in the growth of the wave; the height it finally achieves is determined by the depth of water near the shoreline. Chad would always make a point of knowing the underwater topography before any competition. A big wave wipeout can push surfers down twenty to fifty feet below the surface. Strong currents and water action at those depths can slam a surfer into a reef or the ocean floor. The notice boards on surfing websites were always full of condolences for the latest casualties, with an estimated fifty surfers dying each year, professionals as well as amateurs.

He had done his homework. He knew that the Gold Coast had a steep underwater shelf that ran to a depth of two hundred feet before plunging vertically down, three miles, to the ocean floor. Even with his limited education, he could work out that that meant he was going to encounter the mother of all waves.

But the enormity wasn't his only concern. He was proficient enough to be able to ride any size wave – as long as it had a clean face. That meant that, when the wave broke, it did so from the crest down, leaving a carpet of blue sea rolling towards the shore on which to surf. Unfortunately, tsunamis differed significantly from wind-generated waves in a number of ways. Not only were they bigger and faster, but, contrary to popular belief, they come ashore as a large, cresting wave. When a tsunami hits shallower waters, the shoaling effect breaks up the leading edge of the wave, turning into a wall of mushy white water that rolls towards the coastline like a gigantic surge.

Because there would be nothing for the bottom of the surfboard to grip on to, he'd essentially get bounced around in the foamy mess until he fell off, and that's something he needed to avoid at all costs. His strategy was to wait until the very last moment and then 'duck dive' under the surge. A difficult manoeuvre at the best of times but, given the speed of the approaching wave, he'd have to time it to perfection. Essentially, he would paddle as fast as he could towards the wave to build up momentum; then, before getting caught in the maelstrom, he would hold down the front of the board so that it submerged. Taking a deep breath, he would kick as hard as he could and follow the board under the surface, pushing down on the back of it with his foot to gain extra depth.

The deeper he could go, the better chance he had at surviving the initial onslaught.

Next, he would have to judge when the front edge of the wave had passed over him, before pulling up the nose of the board and allowing himself to float to the surface.

And this is where an idiosyncrasy of a tsunami may work in his favour; in fact, he was counting on it. All waves are made up of a series of peaks and troughs – the high point being the peak or crest, and the low point the trough behind it before another wave starts. The distance between these two points in a normal oceanic wave can be measured in terms of feet; but, with a tsunami, it's measured in miles. If he could time it so that he missed the turbulent water at the front and surfaced just after the peak on the back side of the wave, he should be in a position to ride it all the way inland until it burnt itself out. He would then have enough time to get to higher ground before the next one came in.

He had been through his strategy what seemed like a thousand times in his mind but there were too many 'ifs', 'buts', or 'maybes' for him to feel confident. He would have to wing it, react to the conditions as they happened, relying on his experience and instinct. He didn't mind admitting to himself that he was the most scared he'd ever been in his life.

To top it all, he knew that tsunami waves were a lot longer than the ones he was used to, sometimes stretching for hundreds of miles. So, once he was committed to riding it, there was no turning back. He couldn't simply pull away to the side to avoid a wipeout, as there were no sides.

He sensed it coming, long before he saw it. The sea went as still as a mill pond and the ubiquitous cawing of seagulls ceased abruptly. He looked up at the cloudless blue sky, which was eerily deserted. It was as though he'd stepped into a photograph – there wasn't a trace of movement anywhere. And then came a rumble. Not in the air, but through the sea, as the sound waves travelled four times faster in the water than their airborne counterparts. It started as a low resonance in his solar plexus, increasing in intensity, until the surfboard beneath him began to vibrate.

The previously calm surface became choppy, forming small peaks, which buffeted him from side to side as they rose and fell. He started to paddle towards the horizon, anxious to meet his opponent on his own terms. His hands powered through the surf, feeling the tension on his palms as he pulled back, driving the board forward.

He was into a steady rhythm and making good speed when, suddenly, the water resistance increased and it felt like he was pushing through treacle. The force of the current was so strong that his biceps burnt after just a couple of strokes and he decided to conserve his energy for the main event. But, instead of slowing down, he seemed to be going faster. He looked behind him to see the coastline receding in the distance – *the drawback.*

Bring it on! His fear had morphed into anxiety driven by a determination to succeed. He recognised the feeling from the way he felt before every major competition – the fear of failure. Anybody who said they didn't get nervous were either supremely confident (and were often the ones the condolences were for) or they were liars.

He gripped the sides of his board firmly and raised himself to his knees to get a better view. It was almost imperceptible at first; but, as he stared, he could just make out a thin white line on the horizon. And then he heard it. If he hadn't known any better he would have mistaken it for the boom of distant thunder. The blue space above the sea narrowed as the wave started to rear up in the distance. The reverberations increased, enveloping him in a wall of sound as it echoed off the beach.

His momentum had picked up; he must have been doing at least thirty knots, equivalent to the speeds he'd reach surfing in a big wave competition. The sea continued to rise in front of him and he could now clearly distinguish the frothing, destructive water as it barrelled towards him at over five hundred miles per hour. He felt his heart beat rapidly against his ribcage as adrenalin coursed through his veins. He tried to calm himself by taking in a deep breath and exhaling slowly; it seemed to work. His mind focussed on what he had to do. *Timing* he reminded himself. Too soon and he may not be able to wait long enough for the turbulent water to pass overhead; too late, and he would be caught up in it. He tried to anticipate how long it would take to reach him, but it was travelling at such a pace it was impossible to judge.

The sound now was almost deafening. The skyline was totally obliterated by the towering wall of water that stretched the full length of the horizon. At the last moment he decided on the lesser of the two evils. He would dive early – at least he would have a chance then. He knew his lungs were in peak condition; he had never smoked in his life – apart from the odd obligatory spliff, of course. He felt the spray off the advancing wave on his face and decided to go for it. He inhaled, held his breath and then put all of his weight on the front of the board, which dutifully sank below the surface. He instantly shifted his weight to his right leg to push the back of the board down before going under himself.

The whole procedure had taken less than two seconds to complete but, at the speed the wave was travelling, it was still probably a split second too late. As he sank towards the seabed, he was hit by the force of the surge which tumbled him over and over like a rag doll. He managed to hold onto his board and kicked out, hoping to release himself from its grip. He was so disoriented he didn't know if he was surfacing or going deeper.

The spinning stopped abruptly as the front of the board struck something solid; only his physical fitness prevented him from being catapulted forward, his biceps taking the brunt of the jolt. He peered into the murky water to see what had happened, but visibility was down to zero. He dragged himself along the length of the board and felt for the tip. It was buried in the silt of the seabed. He gripped the sides and pulled, but it didn't budge – the force of the impact had driven it deep. He tried to get a purchase on the silky floor with his legs, but it was too slippery. *Should he leave it and risk surfacing without it? No – he would be a sitting duck. His board wasn't just a floatation device; it was his ticket to ride.*

He tried again, conscious he was using up precious seconds of air. His bare feet slid along the bottom as he heaved to dislodge it. His left foot brushed against something hard. He adjusted his position, his toes searching out the object and felt it again – a smooth rock. Whether the tsunami had deposited it there or it was a natural part of the underwater topography, he didn't care. He tested his weight against it – it was stable. With both heals dug into the sand and the balls of his feet leveraging off the boulder, he tugged with all his might.

He felt the board give slightly and strained harder. Suddenly, he was back-peddling. It was so unexpected that his brain switched to self-preservation mode, automatically releasing his grip on the board, freeing up his hands to break his fall. But, instead of crashing to the ground, his buoyancy forced him towards the surface. He made a mental note to have a word with his brain, if he survived, that that instinctive reaction wasn't necessary in water.

He twisted his body around and swam back to retrieve his board, feeling along the bottom to where he thought it should be. All his exertions were taking its toll on his oxygen reserves. His muscles ached and he had a burning sensation in his chest. If he didn't head for the surface soon he would definitely run out of air. His hands searched the bed whilst his legs kicked to keep him down –

nothing. Then he felt the rock. In his mind's eye, he pictured the location; the board couldn't be more than two feet away from it. He did a quick sweep of the area, but drew a blank. *Perhaps it was a different rock?*

It didn't matter. His time was up. His lungs were telling him that he needed to take a breath. He had to fight against the reflex; the pain in his chest was almost unbearable. He did a quick mental calculation. If the depth of the sea was a hundred feet before the wave arrived and the height of the wave was a hundred feet, that meant he had to swim up two hundred feet before he broke the surface. He wasn't worried about the bends, as that didn't affect free divers; it was the nitrogen absorption from the tanks that caused the problems for scuba divers. What he was worried about was how long it would take him – a minute and a half, maybe two minutes. *On second thoughts – he didn't have time to worry.* Whatever fate awaited him up there without his surf board was put to the back of his mind.

He pushed off the seabed with as much force as his legs could muster, keeping his arms by his side to make himself more streamline. He counted the seconds off to take his mind away from wanting to gulp in a lungful of sea water. Ten seconds… he had read somewhere that the frog kick was the most efficient way to propel yourself under water – more forward thrust with less effort. He wasn't in a position to argue and gave it a go.

Thirty seconds… he looked up to see if he could see the surface, but the visibility was still as bad. He could feel the force of the wave carrying him along with it. Forty-five seconds… his lungs were screaming for him to take a breath and the pain was excruciating. He prayed he'd make it before he blacked out. One minute… abandoning the streamline approach, he used his arms to push the water past him, hoping it would increase his speed, more through desperation than any kind of logic. One minute twenty seconds… it seemed to be getting lighter – either daylight was filtering through or he was suffering from the effects of hypoxia. He remembered something about how people hallucinate when their brains get starved of oxygen.

One minute forty seconds… he couldn't fight against the urge to breathe any longer. His whole body was racked with severe shooting pains as his muscles demanded a fresh supply of oxygen. His willpower was losing the battle to prevent his body from doing what it did naturally. He inhaled, feeling the cool, salty water enter his larynx. But there was no relief from the pain. His bronchi, unable to recognise the fluid as something it could process, rejected it, making him cough. But, as he spluttered, he breathed in more water. *So this is what it feels like to drown*, the thought flashed through his mind.

One minute forty-five seconds… his cognitive function was unimpaired; he knew exactly what was happening to him, but was unable to control the convulsions. He gasped one last time and felt a rush of air enter his respiratory tract. He thrashed around, trying desperately to keep his head above the waterline, frantically gulping in the life-saving sustenance in-between retches. After a few more breaths, his lungs resumed their normal rhythm and the spasms subsided, but he was exhausted.

He looked around to get his bearings. He was being carried along by the wave; it took all his effort to stay afloat by treading water. He had surfaced a good distance behind the leading edge and was elevated enough to see that it had already made landfall; the beach and the line of cars beyond were totally submerged. He knew his chances of surviving were slim unless he could find a buoyancy aid. He craned his neck to see over the tons of seaweed that lay in a carpet of green around him and spotted something white bobbing up and down a hundred yards away to his left. He summoned the last reserves of his energy and swam over to it.

CHAPTER 29

Tom was unsure at first what had woken him, and then he realised it was the urgency in the voice on the TV.

They had spent what seemed like hours wrestling with their handcuffs in an effort to free themselves, but to no avail. It was only when their wrists became too bloodied and painful to continue that they had to admit defeat. Even if they had managed to get out of their constraints, there was still the locked door to deal with and possibly an armed guard on the other side.

Resigned to the fact that they would have to look for another opportunity to escape, either when they were being transported to the Collider or when they were in it, they started to theorise on how best they could thwart Deiter's plans. They had managed to keep a track of time using the digital clock on the TV, so Tom knew it was some time after four in the morning before they had formulated the outline of a strategy that could, theoretically, work. Not being an exact science, there were no guarantees as to the effectiveness of their postulations. The best they could hope for would be to slow the polar reversal down enough to give people time to react, either by mass evacuation of the potentially dangerous areas like coastlines and fault lines, or preparing themselves for the inevitable. At least they would have a choice and, possibly, a chance.

To put their theory to the test obviously involved at least one of them escaping, and that person was nominated as Tom. Frederick had the most knowledge and Serena was the fittest, but Tom had enough of both to make him the ideal candidate. The other two said they were prepared to sacrifice themselves if necessary to ensure that he got away. Tom's remonstrations at the thought of this were only half-hearted; he knew, deep down, that it may be the only way to save millions of lives. He also knew, without question, that if he were in their position, he would do the same.

He couldn't remember dozing off, but the sleep he did manage to get was restless and fitful, not aided by the fact that the nylon cord binding him to the chair dug into his arms every time he tried to move. He looked across at his fellow captives, who were reposing in a similar, uncomfortable position, before turning his attention back to the now almost hysterical voice on the TV that had woken him up.

The image on the screen was grainy and kept going in and out of focus; it was evident that the person taking the footage was doing so on their mobile phone, high up in a building. Regardless of the lack of visual clarity, Tom could make out a lone figure clambering onto a surfboard. If it hadn't been for the tickertape words running along the bottom of the newscast, he would have sworn he was watching some holidaymaker getting out of his depths in rough seas. But he did read it: *'Newsflash – mega tsunami hits Gold Coast of Australia, thousands presumed dead.'*

The running commentary from the person taking the film, despite being heavily censored for expletives, helped define what the viewers were watching.

'*Bleep* me, this guy's *bleep*-ing nuts. He's on the board, he's on the board, he's lying on the board, now he's trying to get up. *Bleep* me, have you seen the size of that *bleep*-ing wave! That's one mother *bleep* of a wave. He's up, he's up on the board. No, he's down again, he's kneeling down. He's trying to steady himself. He's back on his feet… steady… steady… he's up. He's riding it, he's riding the mother *bleep*. *Bleep* me, I've never seen anything like it! This guy must have *bleeps* of steel.

'He's turning, he's coming back the other way, he's trying to keep his speed steady. Go man! You can do it! He's turning again, he's about two hundred yards out, but he's moving too fast. If he comes in at that speed he'll be smashed against the buildings like a squashed *bleep*-ing tomato. Hundred and fifty yards. He's turning again. Slow the *bleep* down, man! A hundred yards. He's kneeling down again, now he's lying down, he's dragging his feet in the water. Fifty yards… he's gonna do it! He's slowing down. He's past where the beach was. He's level with the buildings. Grab the tree, grab the *bleep*-ing tree. He's got it. The tree's snagged him. *Bleep* that's got to *bleep*-ing hurt. He's lost his board, but he's alright. I can see him climbing up the branches to the top of the tree. He's safe. That's more than I can say for us. *Bleep* me, the water's up to the third floor. We need to get on the *bleep*-ing roof!'

'I see you've been keeping up to date with how our little experiment is going.' Deiter had entered the room whilst Tom had been preoccupied with the drama unfolding on TV.

Damn, that's the second time he's sneaked up on me. Tom made a mental note to keep looking over his shoulder whenever Deiter was in the vicinity. Not that he was planning to be around him for much longer. But his heart sank when he saw the two goons who had followed him through the door. Both sported crew cuts, a thickset jaw and a physique Arnold Schwarzenegger would be jealous of. They were killing machines and their weapons of choice appeared to be Kalashnikovs, which hung loosely over their shoulders.

So much for making a run for it on the way to the Collider, Tom thought despondently. He glanced over at Serena, who was stirring from her sleep. Her expression changed from placid to consternation as she became aware of her situation.

'Morning, darling. Coffee?' Tom whispered.

She managed a weak smile, which vanished the minute she saw Deiter. Frederick was also awake and eyeing his captor warily.

'I trust you all slept well?' Deiter enquired. When nobody answered he continued. 'As you can see, the experiment is progressing as planned.' He turned to the TV, which was showing the devastation caused by the floodwaters along the Gold Coast. 'It's a pity that none of you will be around to see the final conclusion.'

He watched the scenes intensely, enraptured by the catastrophic damage caused by the tsunami. He forced himself to turn away. 'Still, look on the bright side. At least you won't have to spend years in a maximum security prison for a crime you didn't commit. Inspector Gervaux is convinced that the three of you, along with Ajay, are some sort of scientific terrorist cell. He suspects you are on the run and has set up road blocks, closed the airports and train stations and has hundreds of men combing the countryside looking for you. You're quite famous, really. All the news stations are running the story, along with the pictures of you that I kindly provided Inspector Gervaux with. So, when your bodies are discovered in the Collider, it can all be explained away as a tragic accident. Unbeknown to anybody, you must have *holed up* there, waiting for the *heat to die down* before you *made your getaway* – all very dramatic stuff. The media are going to lap it up.'

'Leaving you in the clear to wreak havoc on the world,' Tom concluded.

'Precisely,' Deiter beamed.

'And what if we don't go along with your plan?' Serena asked.

'Then I'll shoot you here and drag your bodies into one of the service tunnels.'

'Won't that look a bit suspicious?' she countered.

'Not really. The public have already been warned not to approach any of you as you are armed and extremely dangerous. So, all we have to do is tell the authorities that we discovered you whilst doing a routine inspection of the tunnels and tried to apprehend you. You resisted, shots were fired, but thankfully you were the only casualties. I don't think there's going to be much sympathy from the general public about your demise. In fact, I can see myself as being a bit of a hero.' Deiter seemed to thrive on this idea. 'Your choice. Shall we go?'

Tom couldn't see much of a choice. He had never really considered how he would die. He had always assumed that it was far enough in the future not to worry about it. But, at the moment, that future was beginning to look decidedly close. He certainly didn't want to be shot where he sat, like a rat in a trap. And, whilst he was still alive, there was always the possibility that he could escape. No, he *had* to escape. Perhaps there would still be an opportunity for the three of them to overpower the guards on the way down to the Collider. It had to be worth a risk.

'Okay, let's get on with it,' Tom instructed, with as much courage in his voice as he could muster.

'Good, I'm glad you've seen sense. Who wants to go down first?'

Fuck! So much for plan A.

CHAPTER 30

Inspector Gervaux had commandeered the whole floor above his office and turned it into an incident room, much to the chagrin of the filing clerks who had previously occupied it. He had direct communication with all points of exit from the country. Roadblocks had been set up on all major and minor roads. Photos of the four terrorists had been widely circulated, the media doing their bit for once. He had requested and been granted additional personnel from the Swiss army to strengthen the border crossings. He had over a hundred officers on the ground conducting door-to-door enquiries. Helicopters had been deployed to carry out wide-sweeping aerial searches. This was the biggest manhunt that Switzerland had ever seen. *So why wasn't there so much as a single sighting of the fugitives?*

'Are you certain you covered off every single inch of the complex?' Gervaux must have asked this question of Sergeant Lavelle over a dozen times during the last twenty-four hours.

'Yes, I told you. I supervised the search personally,' Lavelle replied exasperated.

'Then where are they? Not a single sighting, not even a hoax call.' Gervaux turned back to the whiteboard on which the four individuals' photographs were pinned at the top, the rest of the board being completely blank.

'How are we getting on tracking their mobile phone signals?' He was staring searchingly at the photos in the hope they would give up their owners' whereabouts.

Lavelle shifted uncomfortably. 'Nothing. There hasn't been a signal transmitted since around midday yesterday, which was when we saw them last.'

'How many officers did you leave at CERN?'

'Two at each entrance and a four-man dog team patrolling the perimeter.'

'Something doesn't stack up. We follow them into a disused building and they just vanish off the face of the earth. We're missing something.' Gervaux ran a hand through his receding hair, then seemed to make up his mind. 'Get your coat, Lavelle. You and I are going to have another look at that building.'

CHAPTER 31

As Gervaux and Lavelle were leaving the office for the short drive to CERN, Serena's hands were being re-tied above her head to TIM – or Train Inspection Monorail, to give it its full title. The 'train' itself consisted of three stainless steel wagons, each about the size of four microwave ovens laid end to end: control, motor and battery. A pan-tilt zoom surveillance camera, spotlight, anti-collision detector and emergency stop button were fitted to each end of the train. The rail, which was anchored to the roof of the tunnel, ran around the entire length of the Collider. The train was piloted remotely from the safety of the control centre and had a top speed of 10km/hour. TIM could send back crucial data on environmental conditions within the tunnel, a task that would otherwise be impossible to achieve manually due to the extremely high levels of radiation whilst in operation.

Serena's bodyweight was being supported by the platform she was standing on, some ten metres above the floor of the tunnel. Her arms were stretched to capacity and secured to the control section of the small train by PlastiCuffs, forcing her onto tip-toes to relieve the burning sensation in her shoulders.

She glanced back and could see Frederick about four feet behind her; he was bound to the motor carriage and was also finding it difficult to alleviate the discomfort. A further four feet beyond him and, hitched to the final wagon, was Tom. Being that much taller than both of them, he didn't appear to be having the same issues. He nodded a reassurance to her, but she could tell from the fear in his eyes that the gesture lacked sincerity and did little to console her.

'As you've probably worked out, you'll be going on a little ride,' continued Deiter. 'Unfortunately, I could only get you one-way tickets.' He stepped back from the passengers, admiring his efforts.

The two armed guards were already making their way down the metal ladder to the safety of the control room, having performed their duties impeccably.

It had taken nearly thirty minutes to get to where they were now. They had avoided the most direct route from the Bunker, which would have taken them less than half that time, through the main tunnel; instead, they had traversed through a warren of deserted corridors and service shafts, in order to elude detection.

Whilst waiting for the other two to join him, Tom had already run through the probable scenario of his demise in his mind. The proton beams would travel along low magnetic permeability stainless steel tubes for the majority of their 27-kilometre journey around the Collider and, as such, present little risk to life. However, at the four points where the two opposing beams impacted, the composition of the tubes would change to Beryllium, a metal chosen for its transparency, to radiation.

The detectors here would monitor the aftermath of the collisions and map the radiation fields generated by the sub-atomic particles. The detectors themselves were surrounded by reinforced concrete seven metres thick to prevent any radiation leakage. Deiter would, most likely, remotely manoeuvre the train along the tunnel to one of these detectors. Once the train was in position, he would fire up the Collider and it would then be only a matter of milliseconds before the fallout took its toll, the equivalent of six atomic bombs exploding in a space no bigger than a church hall. Death would be instantaneous – no pain, no cognitive awareness, no memory.

'If you can, try and think of this as your final experiment,' Deiter continued, walking down the line of captives, strung up like carcasses of beef in an abattoir. 'We have never been able to assess the aftermath of the Collider on the human body; your contributions will be invaluable.' He looked each one of his colleagues in the eye and seemed to feed off their distress. 'I'd just like to say that it's been a pleasure working with you all. I wouldn't have been able to achieve my objectives without you.' With that, he turned his back on them and descended the metal ladder.

'You're insane!' Serena screamed after him. However, the only response she received was the retreating sound of leather on metal.

***

It had taken Gervaux a lot longer than normal to reach the main entrance to the complex; the road blocks that he had set up to trap the fugitives were causing massive delays on all routes. Twice they had to use their blue lights and sirens to jump to the head of the queues. It also didn't help that the roads from the police station to CERN were covered with impacted snow and, although Lavelle was an expert driver, they were held up in several sections by less experienced motorists.

Gervaux jumped out of the car and made his way over to the two officers that were guarding the gate. 'Where's the Chief Security Officer?' The inspector had phoned ahead and requested that he meet him onsite.

'Keeping warm in his office,' the younger of the two replied, gesturing to the small, innocuous-looking concrete hut with his eyes.

Gervaux marched over to the building, closely followed by his sergeant, and rapped on the door. After several seconds it opened, revealing the rather sleepy features of the head of security.

'Not disturbing you, are we?' Lavelle asked sarcastically.

The Chief Security Officer, ignoring the jibe, turned his attention to Gervaux. 'More security videos?' he asked with a pained expression.

'No,' replied the Inspector. 'I want to do another search of the disused building and service tunnels leading to the Collider.'

'I'm afraid that won't be possible,' replied the security officer. 'Well, not until this afternoon, anyway.'

'Why's that?' the sergeant asked, his irritation evident.

'Because we're testing the Collider this morning, and protocol dictates that no personnel are allowed below ground during its operation.'

'But that doesn't stop us searching the unoccupied office building,' Lavelle retorted.

'Be my guest,' replied the officer. 'I've got some paperwork I need to catch up on, so I'll give you a ring when I receive the all-clear from the control room.' With that, he stepped back into the warmth of his office and closed the door on the two policemen.

***

'What are we going to do?' The defiance and composure that Serena had exhibited in front of Deiter was now slipping and Tom could detect a note of desperation in her voice. He had spent the last thirty minutes trying to loosen his ties, which had resulted in his wrists becoming bloodied and raw, but there was no give.

'Can you swing your legs up and hit the emergency stop button on the front of the train?' asked Frederick. 'It may give us a bit more time.' He had also been trying to free himself, but soon realised the task was futile.

'I could if I was a Russian gymnast,' replied Serena sarcastically.

'Perhaps we can shake it off its rails. On the count of three we should…'

Tom's suggestion was interrupted by the gentle hum of the motor starting up in the carriage above Frederick's head, followed by a jolt as the wheels engaged the track. Serena let out a scream as her body was jerked forward, the sound echoing down the tunnel in front of them. Another jolt, another scream, but this time the wheels above their heads continued turning, advancing the carriages and pulling its payload towards the end of the gantry. Serena had to walk on the balls of her feet in order to prevent herself from being dragged along. The end of the platform was fast approaching. Three feet… two feet… one foot.

'Tom, what do I do?' Serena cried over her shoulder.

'Try to stay calm,' was Tom's only advice.

She was now at the edge of the gantry, resisting the final leap off. She looked down and could see the floor of the tunnel some ten metres below. The train above them carried on its inexorable journey, unfazed by its free-loading cargo.

'*Tom!*' Serena's shoes could grip the metal grid of the platform no longer and she was yanked off. She swung out, her arms stretched straight by the full weight of her body, the plastic handcuffs biting into the flesh of her wrists. Her body twisted, her legs kicked and then she was still. Tom thought that she had passed out; but then, over the sound of the motor, he heard an almost animalistic whimper coming from her direction.

'Serena? You alright?' This time, he could make out her gentle, child-like sobs. He tugged at his restraints, but the pain was excruciating. He could see Frederick in front of him. He was shuffling along, keeping pace with the train. It was almost as if he'd resigned himself to his fate.

When it was his turn for the platform to run out on him, he didn't falter; stepping over the edge, he allowed his weight to be transferred to his bindings. His body went limp and he let out a low moan.

Tom had never been one to pray; but he told himself that, if he was ever going to start, now would be a good time.

***

Gervaux, Lavelle and one of the four-man dog team had assembled in the disused building's underground car park. The dog, a pitch-black Labrador Retriever with liquid brown eyes, could sense the tension in the air and was anxious to get on with its work. It had been given the scent of its quarry from clothes retrieved from Tom's apartment. Gervaux was well aware that the trail may have already gone cold. Out in the open, the human scent would dissipate within a few hours; but, in the enclosed spaces of the offices, he was more hopeful that the scent would linger longer.

He pressed the button to summon the elevator, which seemed to take an inordinate amount of time to arrive. Finally, the doors opened and immediately the dog became more agitated, straining at its leash, barking excitedly and sniffing the air. The handler gave it some slack and it headed directly into the lift, tail wagging.

'Looks like he's picked up a trail,' the handler said, stating the obvious.

They followed the dog into the lift and pressed the button for the first floor. During the few seconds it took for the lift to stop, the handler had unleashed the Labrador. As the doors opened, all three waited with baited breath to see what its reaction would be. The dog darted out into the office, its nose inches from the ground. It did a full sweep of the empty space and quickly returned to its master. It was obvious from the dog's body language that its prey hadn't been here.

They repeated the procedure on the second and third floors with similar results. On the way back down to the basement, Gervaux queried the handler. 'What do you make of that?'

'It's bizarre,' he replied. 'From the dog's reaction, it was obvious there was a very strong scent when the lift doors first opened, and I would have expected him to pick it up on at least one of the floors. The only way I can explain it is that our guy must have got in the lift, changed his mind and got out again.'

'Is it possible the scent is strongest in the lift because it's in such a confined space?'

'Yes, but I've never seen him react so positively to a trail and then just lose it.'

Gervaux inspected the stainless steel panels that made up the interior of the lift, first visually and then with his hands.

'What are you looking for? A secret trap door?' Lavelle scoffed.

The elevator came to an abrupt stop. The dog and its handler got out. Lavelle positioned his body to stop the doors closing again, whilst the inspector carried on with his investigation.

'How long would you say it took us to get from the third floor down to here?' Gervaux asked, scrutinising the button panel.

'Five, maybe six seconds,' Lavelle replied, unsure where this was going.

'And how long did it take for the lift to arrive when we first got here?'

The truth was that Lavelle hadn't been paying much attention. 'Longer?' he ventured.

'A lot longer,' Gervaux corrected.

Still baffled by what his boss was intimating, Lavelle fell silent, trying to join the dots in his head. Then it struck him. His face lit up and, like an excited schoolboy trying to impress his teacher, he blurted out the answer. 'You think there may be another level above the third floor that we haven't been able to get access to.'

Gervaux shook his head in exasperation. 'Don't you think we'd be able to see that from the outside of the building?'

Crestfallen, Lavelle turned to the dog handler, who was trying, and almost succeeding, to supress a laugh.

'I want detailed plans and drawings of the entire complex, above and below ground,' Gervaux ordered.

Lavelle passed on the command to the only person he could. 'You heard the Inspector. Don't just stand there sniggering. Go get the drawings.'

***

Tom was less than three feet away from the edge of the platform when his prayers were answered. At first, he thought he had imagined the voice, like some divine intervention. But, as the words were repeated, he became aware of a presence behind him.

'Sahib? Professor Sahib?'

He strained to look over his shoulder to see the svelte-like frame of Ajay climbing over the top of the metal ladder.

'Ajay! How..? What..? It doesn't matter – we haven't got much time. I need you to stop this thing. There's a red button on the end of this carriage. Press it!'

Ajay ran over and stretched up to the emergency stop button. However, even at his full height, he was a foot too short.

'I can't,' he called out. 'It's too high up.'

'Okay,' said Tom. 'You need to get on my shoulders and then you should be able to hit it. But hurry!'

There was less than two feet before the floor ran out. Ajay scrambled onto Tom's back and, with the agility of a chimpanzee, climbed onto his shoulders. He reached out, but he was at the wrong angle; he was too far forward to be able to stretch around the end of the carriage to press the button.

The extra weight on Tom made the bindings on his wrists cut deeper into his flesh, making him wince, perspiration spontaneously forming on his top lip. But then, just as suddenly the pain subsided, the pressure forcing him downwards was relieved. He looked up to see that Ajay had climbed onto the rail and was edging himself backwards.

Tom was now on the brink of being pulled off the platform. He strained to keep his footing, but his smooth-soled shoes couldn't get a purchase on the metal floor.

'Now, Ajay!' Tom cried.

Ajay leapt off the rail towards his target. He knew that he would only have the one chance. Fortunately, the movement was choreographed to perfection – he hit the button dead centre and the train came to a shuddering halt. He had been concentrating so much on his objective that he hadn't contemplated his landing, and he struck the gantry with a resounding thud, knocking the wind out of him.

Tom balanced over the edge at a forty-five degree angle; the heels of his shoes were the only part connecting him to the platform. He tried to look back to see what had caused the commotion, but couldn't crane his neck far enough to see.

'Ajay? Are you alright?' No answer. He tried again. 'Ajay, are you hurt?' This time he heard movement, followed by a rasping sound as Ajay tried to catch his breath.

'I'm… fine,' Ajay gasped, still trying to suck in enough air to fill his lungs.

'Thank God.' Tom let out a sigh of relief. 'Can you get to my bindings?'

Ajay got unsteadily to his feet and made his way over to Tom.

'Climb over me and onto the rail again,' Tom instructed. He braced himself against the inevitable pain as Ajay clambered on his back and then onto his shoulders before leveraging himself up onto the track, with less deftness than before. Tom gritted his teeth, knowing that the agony would soon pass.

'Can you bite through the ties?'

'No need, Sahib. I have a penknife.' Ajay reached into his pocket and produced his trusty Swiss army knife. He selected the sawing tool and went to work. The lightweight plastic handcuffs were no match for the sharpened teeth of the blade; within two strokes, one was completely cut through. The sudden release caught Tom off-guard, forcing him to lean against the remaining tie to stop himself toppling over.

'Give me a second to get my balance,' he shouted up to Ajay, who was poised to slice through the second thin plastic cuff. 'Okay, but slowly this time.'

Tom tried to anticipate the breaking point, shifting all his weight onto his heels. It still caught him out when the band snapped, but he had judged it right and he toppled backwards, landing safely, if not a little undignified, on his rear.

'Sorry, Sahib,' Ajay shouted down at him.

With no time to waste, Tom sprang to his feet and dusted himself off. He eyed the carriage above his head that he had been shackled to and judged that, if he could just jump high enough, he should be able to cling onto it and use it to haul himself onto the rail.

He bent his knees and launched himself upwards. His fingers caught the upper edge of the wagon and he held on. Using his upper body strength, he slowly pulled himself up. At times like these, which weren't that often, he wished he had his brother's physique. His arms strained to lift the dead weight, his face flushed under the exertion and veins protruded, throbbing at his temples, but he was determined not to give up. With a final gargantuan effort, he hauled his torso onto the carriage and let his legs dangle over the edge, out of breath and exhausted.

Ajay grabbed him by the arm and gently coaxed him onto the rail. They sat side by side for a moment whilst Tom recuperated. 'Thanks, Ajay. You may have just saved our lives,' he managed to say between pants.

***

'According to the plans, the lift shaft descends to a corridor, which leads to a large room.' Gervaux pointed out the features on the drawings, which were laid out on the floor of the first floor office in the disused building.

They had taken refuge there from the biting cold of the car park whilst waiting for the dog handler to return. Despite being indoors, Gervaux's breath fogged as he spoke. 'How can we get access to that room?' He was directing his comment at the Chief Security Officer, whose curiosity had overridden his desire to stay in the warmth of his office.

'I have no idea. I didn't even know that room existed.'

'Well, the lift obviously goes to it,' Gervaux replied sharply, irked by the Security Officer's lack of cooperation. 'How long will it take to get a lift engineer on-site?'

'The company that installed the lift are based in Lucerne. Normally it would take them three hours to get here. But, with the snow and the road blocks, I'd say you're looking at closer to five.'

'In five hours they could have tunnelled their way out the other side,' Gervaux said morosely.

Regretting the decision to leave the comfort of his office, the head of security decided to return. He made up an excuse that he had to get back to alert the office staff that there was going to be a possible breach of protocol by allowing the policemen officers to go underground when an experiment was running, and left them to it.

'Moron,' Gervaux muttered as the lift doors closed behind the Officer.

'There is an alternative,' Lavelle proffered.

The inspector shot him a weary glance.

'We could always ask one of the technical experts here. We're surrounded by boffins and eggheads. Surely, if they are capable of building a machine to discover the origins of the universe, cracking a lift code should be a piece of cake to them.'

'Brilliant, Lavelle! Get onto it straight away.' Gervaux's rare praise for his sergeant went some way towards making up for his previous faux pas.

***

Tom and Ajay crawled along the track to reach Frederick. While Tom supported his weight, Ajay cut the ties. They then both dragged the scientist's debilitated body onto the rail. Frederick seemed to be in a critical condition. At first, Tom feared for his life. However, as the bindings were cut and they hauled him up, he let out a low, guttural moan. It took him a few seconds to come round. He was initially unaware of his surroundings; but, when he saw Ajay, his eyes lit up. He reached up feebly and touched his face to make sure he wasn't dreaming.

'Ajay, where have you been?' he croaked.

'Here. I didn't know where else to go. Deiter threatened to kill me, but I knew as long as I stayed on the complex Shiva would protect me.'

Frederick rested his hand on his son's shoulder and looked earnestly into his eyes. 'I'm afraid Shiva has failed you… and so have I.'

'How have you survived for the past two days? What have you been eating and drinking?' Tom asked.

'Mary, from the canteen, smuggled some food out for me,' replied Ajay. 'I met her after work, behind the kitchens, when everybody had gone home. I think she took pity on me when she caught me rummaging through the bins.'

'Well, thank God for Mary, and thank God you were around to save us,' said Tom. He meant it sincerely, despite being an atheist.

'I saw Deiter and those guards pushing Serena along the corridor,' continued Ajay. 'So I followed them here. Then I discovered you and my father tied up, so I waited in the shadows for an opportunity to rescue you.'

'We're not out of the woods yet,' replied Tom. 'Let's get Frederick back to the gantry and then save Serena.'

***

They were all gathered safely on the platform. It had taken Tom and Ajay fifteen minutes to free their colleagues. Frederick had recovered enough to stand on his own two feet, albeit with the support of Ajay to lean on. Serena seemed to have fared better and, apart from some deep welts where the ties had dug in, she was back to her normal, indefatigable self.

'Do you think Deiter will be aware we've escaped?' she asked.

'I think there's a pretty good chance of it.' Tom pointed up to the last carriage, the one Deiter had selected to carry him to his death. 'Watch!' Tom walked to the far side of the gantry. The pan-tilt zoom surveillance camera followed his every move. He turned around and walked back – again, the camera tracked his path. Tom gave it a friendly wave before addressing the group. 'Which means we'd better get the hell out of here before Deiter's henchmen get back.'

They made their way down the metal ladder as quickly as they could. However, it was obvious, even before they reached the last rung, that Frederick was slowing them down, despite Ajay's assistance. Altruistically, he was the first to voice what they already knew.

'You'd have more of a chance without me,' he said. 'You three go ahead. Perhaps I can lead them off in a different direction and give you a few minutes head start.'

'I'm not leaving without you,' Ajay stated adamantly.

'Please, Ajay,' Frederick implored. 'Your mother needs you. How will she be able to carry the groceries in, if neither of us are around to help her?' He smiled weakly.

Ajay's eyes welled up and his bottom lip began to quiver. 'We can both get out of here and help her together.' His response didn't carry much conviction.

The sound of gunfire caught everybody by surprise, echoing off the walls of the vast tunnel behind them. They turned in unison to see the two goons tearing towards them in a golf buggy, the muzzle flashes clearly visible from the automatic weapon. Although they were some distance away, the bullets were winging off the metal fixings all around them. It was obvious the shooters were going for quantity over quality, hopeful of hitting their targets through shear firepower rather than any accurately-placed shots.

'Go!' shouted Frederick over the sounds of the machine gun fire. 'You need to escape. Millions of lives are depending on you.'

Tom and Serena turned and sprinted away from their pursuers, bullets ricocheting around them. Fifty metres further on, Tom spotted another two figures approaching them from the opposite direction, effectively cutting off their escape route. He pulled Serena off to his left and into a small service shaft that ran adjacent to the main tunnel. He knew that the reprieve from the barrage would only be temporary, but the narrowness of this passage meant that their assailants would have to abandon their vehicle and follow them on foot, psychologically levelling the playing field, if only slightly. In reality, they would still have four, fully-armed mercenaries chasing them, intent on their annihilation.

Ajay's eyes darted from his father to the approaching vehicle, to the fleeing fugitives and then back to his father, trying to make up his mind what to do.

'Please Ajay, save yourself,' Frederick pleaded.

Suddenly, he seemed to have made a decision. His body stiffened and he grabbed his father firmly underneath one arm, pulling him in the direction of the other two. The golf buggy was less than two hundred metres from them and closing fast. They needed to cover the distance to the service tunnel before the gunmen found their range. The problem now was that they had to cross open ground, *the killing zone* as the militia imaginatively label it. Spurts from the automatic weapons were immediately followed by the sound of bullets whizzing around them, like lightning followed by a crack of thunder when a storm's directly overhead.

They had less than ten metres to go when Ajay stumbled forward. However, instead of instinctively stretching out his arms to break his fall, he hit the ground, chin first and lay still. Frederick's momentum meant that he had to backtrack to where his son lay. He knelt down beside Ajay, suddenly unaware of everything else going on around him. Grabbing him by the shoulder, he rolled him onto his back. There was a deep gash on his chin, which was bleeding profusely; rivulets of blood ran down his neck and onto his shirt, mixing with the spreading crimson patch, emanating from a small black hole in his chest.

CHAPTER 32

Lavelle had been right. It had taken no time at all for one of the technicians to work out that the elevator was, indeed, capable of descent from the ground floor. He had taken off the control panel and by-passed the key activation using a simple wire connection.

Gervaux had just called in a forensics team to comb the large, windowless room for DNA samples, when they heard the faint, but distinct, sound of an automatic weapon being discharged. The two officers instinctively drew their standard issue 9mm SIG-Sauer P226 semi-automatic pistols from their shoulder holsters and made their way out of the room and across the corridor.

The inspector cautiously opened the door, his pistol raised in front of him. Lavelle was at his shoulder adopting a similar stance. The muffled sound of the gunfire instantly became clearer, but was still remote. Crouching low to present as small a target as possible, they ran down the tunnel towards the firefight, hugging the wall for cover.

As the chatter from the machine gun reached an almost deafening pitch, amplified by the acoustics of the tunnel, Gervaux could make out the shape of a man and woman running towards them. However, before he had time to shout out for them to stop, they veered off into a side tunnel. Behind them he could see two other people heading in his direction and, further beyond, a golf buggy closing the gap. One of the runners seemed to fall, but didn't get up. His partner stopped and went back to attend to him.

Intuition and training had given Gervaux the ability to read the dynamics of a situation within a split second. He instinctively assessed that the immediate threat was coming from the golf buggy and opened fire, aiming at its tyres. Lavelle, who was now standing by his side, followed his boss's lead, hitting the front right wheel with his first volley and making the cart skid to a screeching halt. The two men quickly decamped from their vehicle and took cover behind it, returning fire.

Finding themselves exposed, the two officers ran for the safety of the service tunnel they had seen the man and woman disappear into. Once there, they checked their weapons for ammunition. Each had a spare clip, but they knew they were no match for their adversary's arsenal. It was time for negotiation.

'Police! Put your weapons down and come out with your hands up,' Gervaux yelled.

He received a quick burst of automatic fire in response.

It was time to up the ante. 'Reinforcements are already on their way. If you give yourself up now, it will go in your favour.'

Another burst, but this time it was followed by the sound of retreating footsteps.

'Last chance!' Gervaux shouted. 'Hand over your weapons.'

Silence.

Gervaux gingerly poked his head out of their refuge. He could see the two gunmen had abandoned their position and were running flat-out in the opposite direction.

'Shouldn't we go after them?' Lavelle enquired.

'Not with these pea-shooters,' replied Gervaux, indicating to his weapon. 'Call in reinforcements. Give them their descriptions and tell them they are armed and extremely dangerous.'

Whilst his sergeant was on the radio, the inspector made his way over to Frederick and the crumpled form on the floor, expecting the worst. He was surprised to see that the boy was still breathing – shallow breaths, but alive all the same. He bent down next to Frederick to inspect the wound. The small hole in his chest was still seeping blood. He slid his hand underneath the boy's back but couldn't feel any wetness.

'You need to put pressure over the bullet hole to stem the bleeding,' he told Frederick. 'Here, use my handkerchief and press down firmly.'

Frederick did as he was instructed. 'Will he live?' Frederick's eyes searched the inspector's, imploring him to give him the right answer.

'I'm no doctor,' replied Gervaux, 'but I have seen enough bullet wounds to say that he must have caught a ricochet. If it had been a direct hit from an automatic rifle, there would be an exit wound the size of a grapefruit and he wouldn't be breathing at all.' He paused to take another look at the boy. 'He's still got the bullet in him; but if it's missed his vital organs and we can get him to the hospital soon, then there's a good chance he'll survive.'

Frederick's relief was palpable. His shoulders shook as fat, wet tears ran down his face. However, he still maintained the constant pressure on his son's wound, determined to keep him alive.

'Get an air ambulance here, immediately,' Gervaux called over to his sergeant.

***

Deiter was watching his plans unravel on the CCTV cameras in the Chief Security Guard's office, who was seated next to him, his eyes glazed, staring lifelessly at the monitor. A single trickle of blood ran down his face from the third eye drilled into his forehead by Deiter's bullet. The back of his head was a different story. His hair was matted with blood and brain tissue as the projectile had exited and embedded itself in the wall opposite, making a splatter pattern a psychiatrist would be proud of. Deiter had already interpreted it as an eagle in full flight bearing down on a small animal, possibly a rabbit or a cat.

Everything had seemed to be going so well. He had seen the Chief Security Officer leaving his hut, on the way back to the control room with his two henchmen, so he had not terminated him there and then, as was the original plan. He sent one of his men into the security office to monitor the progress of his passenger train, while he went to the main building to initialise the Collider start-up procedure. He was halfway through the sequence when the guard ran in to tell him that the prisoners were escaping. He immediately dispatched both men to put a stop to it, while he went to the security office to orchestrate proceedings via a two-way radio.

Expecting to find it empty, he was surprised to see the Chief Security Officer in his seat, eyes glued to the monitor, watching the drama unfold. He was about to alert his team when he noticed Deiter in the doorway attaching a suppressor to his handgun. Without a word, Deiter closed the door behind him, sat down next to the petrified man, put the muzzle to his forehead and pulled the trigger. Then, after deciphering the ink blot image on the wall behind him, he calmly returned his gaze to the screen.

His frustration at seeing Ajay rescuing Tom and then the others had turned to a seething rage by the time his men had reached the scene. *Why hadn't he killed the little bastard when he'd had the chance?* What was even more annoying was the fact that these highly-trained killers, who he'd paid a small fortune for, wouldn't win a prize in a duck shoot at a fairground let alone hit a moving target. He watched helplessly as Tom and Serena escaped down a service tunnel. Then Ajay hit the floor and he almost jumped out of his seat with excitement. Unfortunately, his elation was short-lived as he noticed the two policemen returning fire.

'Kill them! Kill them!' he shouted into the radio-mic. But, to his disgust, instead of putting up a fight, his two operatives high-tailed it back down the tunnel.

He slumped back in his chair, deflated. But then he realised that, although Tom and Serena were still on the loose, he could track them using the face recognition software installed in the CCTV cameras. He leant forward and flicked through the screens, picking the two of them up as they headed back to the accommodation block. *Surely they weren't going to hide in there?*

The cameras tracked them entering their rooms, only to exit seconds later. *Obviously they'd gone to retrieve something. Morantz's file, maybe?* But Deiter couldn't see any evidence that either of them were carrying it. He watched as they surreptitiously made their way through the complex, checking each corridor before making their moves. The CCTV screens in the security office changed as they left one surveillance zone and into the range of another camera.

'Where are you going?' Deiter said out loud to himself. He checked the plan of the facility on the wall against their movements. They seemed to be heading for the visitor centre. *But why? It didn't make any sense.* He checked the map again. *No, not the visitor centre – the private airstrip behind it.*

***

The detour to their rooms to collect their passports was a necessary risk. Although private air travel affords its passengers a greater degree of flexibility and less red tape, documents would still need to be checked and verified by the receiving airport on arrival. New York's Long Island MacArthur Airport was no different.

Although still some two hundred miles and three hours by car from MIT, Tom felt like he was going home and, with it, came a sense of security. They had chosen the regional airport over JFK, LaGuardia or Newark for two specific reasons. Firstly, Tom was unsure whether the manhunt Deiter had alluded to extended to international boundaries. If it did, they would have a better chance of avoiding detection through a smaller provincial airport where officials tended to be more parochial.

Secondly, it was the nearest airport to their destination and time was of the essence. The Relativistic Heavy Ion Collider (RHIC) was located at Brookhaven National Laboratory in Upton, less than twenty-five miles away from the airport.

The RHIC was the only other particle collider in existence and, although smaller than its Swiss counterpart, the electromagnetic fields generated during its operation still made it the world's second largest man-made magnet.

During their incarceration, Tom, Frederick and Serena had theorised that, if the butterfly effect of the LHC had instigated the polar reversal in the first place, then, hypothetically speaking, if a similar force were generated in an opposing geographical area, then the resultant reaction could slow down the polar progression enough to give the Earth time to adjust to its new environment, lessening the destructive phenomena they had witnessed over the last few days. Stopping the polar reversal itself was impossible; it would be like a swimmer trying to halt a cruise liner in mid-voyage. However, by using the RHIC as a tugboat to pull the Earth's magnetic core the other way, then, in theory…

That's all it was, though. A theory, Tom thought to himself. He went over their masterplan again as he reclined in the black leather seat in the French-built Dassault Falcon. *But what options did they have left*? He had to rely on his scientific doctrine in the hope that it bore fruit.

He looked across the aisle to the seat opposite him, where Serena was curled up in a tight ball, like a cat asleep in front of an open fire. They had cleaned and dressed each other's wounds using the rudimentary first aid kit on board and now sported matching crepe bandages, which could pass as sweatbands at a quick glance. Tom noticed Serena's shoulders shuddering; she was either sobbing or having a bad dream. Either was understandable given what they had just been through. He tried to reassure her.

'It's alright, we're safe now,' he said, but there was no answer.

He picked up the in-flight satellite phone and placed a call. Towards the end of the conversation, he realised he was slurring his words through exhaustion. He hadn't had a good night's sleep since leaving American soil and, with the adrenalin-fuelled activities over the past couple of days, he was totally spent. The last thoughts he had before drifting off were of Frederick and Ajay and he did something he seemed to be making a habit of recently – said a silent prayer for them.

***

'Welcome to the United States of America,' came the pilot's voice over the intercom, stirring the two passengers from their deep slumber. 'Please put your seatbelts on and return your chairs to an upright position as we will be landing shortly. Thank you.'

Tom awoke, disoriented. He cleared the sleep from his eyes and took in the plush features of the private jet: polished walnut trim, finest Italian calf leather seats and thick-pile carpet.

When they had discussed their plan back in the Bunker, Tom expressed his concern that its success was dependent on them getting out of the country and that they would probably be arrested as soon as they stepped foot in either Geneva or Zurich airport. Frederick pointed out that, as Director General of CERN, he had at his disposal the two Dassault Falcons, one of the few perks of the job. They could file a flight plan under an alias and explain the mix-up as a clerical error once they were on American soil. Their US passports should help expedite the repatriation.

'Morning,' said Serena, stretching her arms over her head to wake herself up.

'Is it?' Tom replied groggily.

'Well, not strictly speaking,' she replied, yawning. 'My watch says it's eleven o'clock in the evening, but then you Americans are a bit backward. Six hours, to be precise. So that would be… five o'clock Eastern Daylight Time.'

'Don't you class yourself as a US citizen?'

'Only when it suits.'

'You do hold an American passport, though, don't you?' A note of anxiety edged into Tom's voice.

'It's a little bit late to be asking those sorts of questions, Mr Halligan,' Serena replied. 'We're about to touch down in the good ol' US of A.' To placate him, she reached into her breast pocket and produced the navy blue booklet emblazoned with the bald eagle coat of arms.

'You had me worried for a minute, there.'

She smiled impishly. 'You're so easy to wind up.'

Tom was looking out of the window as the surprisingly large terminal building of MacArthur Airport came into view. It had recently undergone an expansion programme thanks to the patronage of Southwest Airlines.

'Will there still be somebody at the facility by the time we get there?' It was Serena's turn to be anxious.

'I phoned ahead and spoke to Charles,' replied Tom. 'He's keeping a full team on stand-by, so we can fire up the collider as soon as we get there.'

'Charles?'

'Charles Brannigan. He's the Research Director at the Brookhaven National Laboratory. I did some work there for my dissertation when I was a mere student at MIT. Nice chap, you'll get on well with him. He's sending a car to pick us up.'

The wheels of the Falcon kissed the runway, before landing with a resounding thud. The tyres screeched on the tarmac and the noise inside the cabin increased as the airbrakes were applied. They taxied off to the right of the main glass and steel structure, where the charter flights gates were, towards an apron, pock-marked by other private jets. A Marshaller guided them into a slot in front of a low-rise building before indicating to the pilot to cut the engines.

Once stationary, the door to the cockpit opened and out stepped the co-pilot, dressed in his crisp white short-sleeved shirt and neatly-pressed black trousers. He looked as fresh and alert as he had when they'd boarded some eight hours earlier.

'I trust you had a pleasant flight, Herr Direktor?'

Tom was a little taken aback by the moniker. 'Er… yes, thank you. I must admit, I was so beat I slept most of the way,' he said rather awkwardly, feeling the need to justify why he hadn't stayed awake to appreciate their flying skills.

'Do you want us to wait here for you, or should we return to Geneva?' asked the co-pilot.

Tom, unsure how long they would have to spend at Brookhaven, told him to return to CERN and he would call when they needed picking up. He was getting to like the extravagance of personal air travel. *How could he ever go back to the cattle market of scheduled flights?*

The co-pilot pulled a lever and the cabin door opened with a hiss, the steps automatically unfolding onto the apron. He directed them to the nondescript single-storey edifice, which doubled as the arrival and departure hall for executive passengers, and bid them a safe onward journey.

Tom's nerves were frayed as he stepped through the sliding doors into the brightly-lit building, holding onto Serena's hand for comfort and reassurance. *How on Earth had he gotten into such a position?* Prior to taking up the role at CERN, the most trouble he'd been in with the authorities was a speeding ticket and a verbal warning for marijuana possession when he was a teenager. Now, suddenly, he was a fugitive from the Swiss police, an escapee from a homicidal maniac and possibly about to be arrested for entering his own country illegally.

They made their way over to the immigration booths and joined the smallest queue. Tom peered around the only person in front of him to look at the official stamping the passports. He was a prematurely grey-haired man in his early fifties, with a lean face, steely-blue eyes and hooked nose. Tom was trying to work out whether he'd chosen the right person by comparing him to the other immigration officers, when the man in front of him moved forward. Tom resigned himself to his fate; changing lanes now would immediately draw attention to himself and arouse suspicion.

He squeezed Serena's hand tighter. She seemed to be keeping her composure better than he was; her expression hadn't changed since leaving the plane, and she appeared relaxed and confident. He made a mental note to himself never to take her on at poker.

'Next.' The official beckoned for Tom to come forward.

Tom handed his passport through the letterbox window, his hand trembling ever so slightly. The officer didn't seem to notice. He turned to the photograph page, checking it against Tom's physical features. Satisfied with the match, he scanned the barcode, which brought up Tom's biometrics and travel data. He tapped away on the computer keyboard, then read the results on the screen.

'Which flight did you come in on, Sir?'

'Private jet from CERN, Switzerland.'

Tom's response elicited another flurry of typing, after which the Customs officer checked his screen again.

'Sir, I have the manifest from that flight and your name doesn't appear to be on it. Were you travelling with a Professor Morantz and a Miss Serena Mayer?'

'Yes... erm... I mean, no... I mean yes,' replied Tom, perplexed. 'I was flying with Miss Mayer, but not Professor Morantz. He died and I took his place... I don't mean on the aeroplane. Although I did take his place on the plane, he just didn't die on it. He died at work, but I wasn't there when it happened... I just took over from him. So the person who booked the flight must have booked it before he died, but then I came along and she probably forgot to change the name... Does that make sense?'

The official just stared at Tom. A trickle of sweat ran down the centre of his back. He was convinced that, any second now, the man behind the bullet-proof screen would call out for reinforcements and Tom would be surrounded by armed security guards, who would drag him off to some windowless interrogation room.

However, without another word, the officer raised his hand and stamped the passport before handing it back through keyhole window to Tom. He reached to take it, but the official held onto it.

'Sir, next time, get your paperwork in order before you fly,' he said curtly. 'Otherwise, you may be refused entry.'

Tom pulled a little harder, managing to wrest the passport from the other man's grip. 'Sorry, of course I will. And thank you.'

He had to pace himself leaving the booth. He didn't want to seem too eager, but he did need to get away as quickly as possible in case the immigration officer changed his mind. What he actually wanted to do was run as fast as his legs would carry him. Having exercised immense self-control, he waited around the corner for Serena to join him.

A few minutes later she sauntered up to him. 'Well, that was easy enough.'

'Easy for you to say,' he replied. 'I must have lost two stone and aged ten years in the last fifteen minutes. Come on, let's get out of here.'

Still on edge, he grabbed Serena by the arm and hurried her past the baggage collection hall, through the 'Nothing to declare' channel and out onto the arrivals concourse, where he spotted a familiar face. Being met at the airport reminded him of the first time he'd seen Ajay. *How long ago was that?* Less than a week, but it seemed like a lifetime to Tom. He made his way over to a rather rotund man who was still scanning the crowd of arriving passengers.

'Looking for somebody in particular?' he asked the man.

The man's annoyance at having his concentration broken by a total stranger was evident on his face. He turned to the interloper, intending to give him a piece of his mind. In an instant, the frown vanished and his features were transformed by a huge grin as he recognised his young friend.

'Tom, ya wee bastard! You'll give an old man a heart attack, sneaking up on him like that,' he admonished in a thick Scottish accent, before throwing his arms around Tom in a massive bear hug.

The two men embraced, rocking backwards and forwards, oblivious to anybody else around them. Eventually, the older man pushed Tom to arm's length to inspect him. 'Ya have ne changed a bit. How long has it been? Seven, eight years?'

'More like ten and you always was a liar.'

'Well, maybe you're a wee bit skinnier, then, if I'm going to be honest.'

'That's more than I can say about you,' Tom replied patting the older man's paunch.

Serena, feeling a little awkward about being side-lined for so long, cleared her throat.

Tom broke away from the other man and straightened his clothes. 'Sorry. Jed, this is Serena Mayer. Serena, this is my good friend

Professor Jed Campbell. Although, I have to say, he's not your stereotypical academic.'

Serena stepped forward and proffered her hand. Jed held it in both of his. 'It's a pleasure to meet you, Miss Mayer,' he said politely.

'Please, call me Serena.'

Without letting go of her hand, he turned to Tom. 'Is she ya girlfriend?'

'Jed! You always were as subtle as a brick,' Tom chided.

'And he always had a good eye for the ladies,' Jed countered, turning his attention back to Serena.

Serena's crepe bandage had slipped slightly, revealing an angry red welt. Jed turned her hand over to inspect her wrist. 'Kinky. You two into that S & M, are ya?'

'Sorry?' Tom replied, baffled by the comment.

'Ya know, bondage and all that.'

Tom realised what he was alluding to. 'No, no,' he said quickly. 'Quite the opposite. It's a long story.'

'Aye, that's what you say!' Jed winked in Tom's direction. 'Whatever floats ya boat. Ya know me… I'm not one to judge… Did I tell ya about that time I was in Bangkok?'

Tom shook his head slowly. 'Maybe later. We'd better be going before you say something that will really embarrass me.'

'No suitcases?' Jed observed.

'No, we had to leave in rather a hurry,' Tom replied without going into too much detail.

'Well, if you need anything, anything at all, just let me know,' Jed volunteered obligingly.

Tom considered asking for a change of clothes and some toiletries, but settled for his more immediate needs. 'A sandwich and a coffee would be good. Can we grab one on the way?'

'Aye, you look as though you need fattening up, and I know just the place,' Jed replied, linking arms with them both to lead them out of the airport.

CHAPTER 33

On the way to Brookhaven, they made a brief pit stop at a 24-hour diner cum watering hole named *Stars 'N' Bars* where, Tom and Serena had been reliably informed, they served the best Jambalaya this side of the Mississippi, not to mention the best Mojito outside of Mexico. Cherie, their waitress, wearing a little too much foundation and lipstick for her age, seemed to know Jed well. From their flirtatious banter, it was obvious to Tom that his old friend had spent more than a few nights sampling the delights on offer, which probably included Cherie.

Jed himself was no oil painting. Now in his mid-fifties the once tall, broad-shouldered, lithe frame had turned flabby thanks to years of over-indulgence. The broken nose he'd received as a young firebrand in his native city of Glasgow hadn't quite set right, giving him the appearance of an ex-boxer. His unfashionably long, strawberry-blond hair, tied back in a ponytail, was starting to recede and turn grey.

But there was something about him that seemed to attract the opposite sex. Perhaps it was the rebel in him, still evident behind his watery blue eyes, or his free spirit which, mistakenly, drove women to think that they could be the one to tame him. Many had tried, all had failed.

Tom couldn't recall a day he'd seen Jed wearing anything other than his battered brown leather bomber jacket, jeans and sneakers, regardless of occasion or the weather outside. Today was no exception.

They had first met when Tom came to Brookhaven to conduct research for his doctorate and Jed was head of the physics department. Despite the age difference, they had bonded immediately, mainly due to Jed's youthful outlook on life rather than any maturity on Tom's part. For over two years they were inseparable, both socially and academically, and it was in no small part thanks to Jed, and despite the alcohol-fuelled nights, that Tom graduated *summa cum laude*, the highest distinction achievable at MIT.

'Remember that time in Tijuana, when I saved ya sorry arse?' Jed was about to recant one of his favourite anecdotes, one that Tom had heard a thousand times and never failed to embarrass him.

'Jed, I don't think we've got time for this,' he replied. 'We'd better get going.'

'What's the rush? Trying to save the world?'

Tom caught Serena's eye. 'As a matter of fact…'

'Aye, well, that can wait, laddie.' He cut Tom off mid-sentence before turning to Serena. 'Ya see, wee Tom here had just bought this clapped-out Beetle, so we decided to go on a road trip over the border into Mexico.'

'There was nothing wrong with that car,' Tom interrupted indignantly and resigned himself to the fact that he'd have to hear the story one more time.

'Aye, apart from the three times it broke down on the way there and four on the way back. Anyways, we eventually get over the border. On our way to Tijuana, we spot these two young lasses hitchhiking. Well, being the gents that we are, we stop and give them a lift. Turns out they live there. When we get to the town, they want to show their appreciation and offer to buy us a drink in the local cantina. Being parched from the dusty road, we kindly accept their offer. To cut a long story short, after several large *cervezas*, poor Tom here is feeling a little the worse for wear and asks the bartender if they have any rooms available so he can sleep it off. Luckily, they had two left so I take one and Tom has the other.'

Tom gave Serena an embarrassed smile and raised his eyes skywards, as there was no hope of stopping Jed now.

'By this stage,' continued Jed, 'the poor wee lamb can hardly walk, so one of the girls helps him up the stairs. She must have been tired herself because she didn't come back down, leaving me in the bar to entertain the other young lady – out of politeness, of course. After about an hour or so, me and the gal are getting on famously, hitting the tequila, when suddenly in barges this middle-aged, fat, sweaty bloke carrying a shotgun and dashes upstairs. He kicks open the door to Tom's room and disappears inside.'

'Oh no!' said Serena, obviously enjoying the story.

'Well,' said Jed, 'I can't speak the lingo, but I can tell straight away from the raised voices that this guy's not too pleased. So I excuse myself from the young lady and go to find out what all the commotion is about. I can hear through the door that Tom and his new friend have found the intrusion a little distressing, to say the least. She's rambling on in Spanish, he's wailing like a banshee, while the only word I can make out is *Papa.* By now I've sussed out that Tom may need a little help, so I kick open the door, not realising that the fat bloke's behind it. He goes sprawling and the shotgun goes off, taking half the ceiling down with it. Well, ya can imagine the look on everybody's face.' Jed let out a huge belly laugh and took a sip or two of his drink.

'Anyway, thinking we've probably outstayed our welcome, I grab Tom by the arm and yank him out of bed, only to discover he's stark-bollock naked – excuse ma French. Our boy here had the good sense to take his clothes off before going to sleep, but he's thrown them all around the room. I grab a couple of items I can see and we run like hell before the fat bloke realises he's got another shot left in the barrel.

'Halfway back to the crossing, Tom's in the passenger seat struggling to put on his jeans, only to realise they're five sizes too small for him. I must have picked the wee lass's up by mistake! Ya should have seen the looks we got from the immigration officials when we tried to explain our predicament. Can ye imagine what they must have thought: an older man driving a half-naked young boy over the border from Mexico in a beaten-up VW Beetle. I'm surprised they let us back in at all.'

'Did you hear from the girl again?' Serena asked Tom.

'Just the once,' he replied meekly. 'It turned out that she was the Mayor's daughter. Her father, the one with the shotgun, swore that if he ever saw me again he would *"hunt me down like a rabid dog and have me castrated"*. I think those were her exact words. Funnily enough, I've never had the urge to go to Mexico again.'

Jed barked out a laugh and slapped Tom on the back. 'C'mon, wee man, we can't sit around here gassing all day. I need to get you back to Brookhaven so ya can save the world.'

CHAPTER 34

On the short journey to the laboratory, Tom gave Jed a potted version of the events leading up to their arrival.

'Sounds like a right nutter, this Deiter,' Jed commented when Tom had finished.

'That's putting it mildly,' Tom replied.

'So, let me get this straight. You think by using the RHIC as a bloody big magnet we can pull the Earth's electromagnetic field back into line?'

'Succinctly put, as ever, Jed,' replied Tom. 'But no, I don't think we'll achieve equilibrium, just a slowing down of the Polar reversal.'

'And if ya cockamamie theory doesn't work?'

Tom shook his head slowly. 'Best case scenario: we ride out the effects of the reversal. Worst case: we bring on another Ice Age.'

Jed gave a low whistle. 'Let's feckin hope it works, then.'

***

They arrived at the security entrance to the complex just as dusk was descending. The purple mist of nightfall enshrouded the definable shapes of the buildings around them. It was cold; the sun setting in a cloudless sky belied the crispness of the evening air. Jed handed over his pass to the gatekeeper, whose breath fogged as he gave it a cursory inspection before giving it back. Tom and Serena presented their passports. The guard checked their ID against the visitors' log and ticked off their names. The barrier rose, allowing them through.

Like CERN's sprawling campus, the site of the RHIC covered the area of a small town, having been built on a former US Army base. It had its own police station, fire department and postal code. Funded primarily by the US Department of Energy, Brookhaven National Laboratory was designed as a multipurpose research institution covering a number of scientific disciplines from physics to medicine. Over three thousand scientists, engineers and support staff made Brookhaven one of the largest scientific establishments in the world.

As they drove down the main arterial road, Tom's memories of the halcyon days of his youth came flooding back. He had lived onsite, where there was a real sense of community connected by a shared purpose: to unravel the mysteries of the Universe, from the Nano to the cosmic scale. Anything was possible and he was going to be the one that pioneered it. As he looked out of the passenger window at the silhouettes of the trees lining the road sweeping by, it saddened him to think that age and, with it, so-called wisdom, had tempered the intrepid explorer within him. He needed to rewind the clock and tap into that indomitable spirit now if he were going to succeed.

They pulled up outside the main building and made their way to the reception area for visitors. There, they had to re-present their passports before being issued with badges that would allow them to proceed through the sliding doors and into the inner sanctum.

Jed led them down a long corridor, flanked on either side by the closed doors of darkened offices, towards a room at the far end, where they could see light seeping out from under the bottom. It was identified by the brass nameplate screwed onto the wall as the Research Director's. Jed knocked resoundingly and, without waiting for a response, opened the door and showed his two charges in.

A well-groomed, stately gentleman was just leveraging himself out of his high-backed leather chair when Tom and Serena entered. He continued with the movement, but accompanied it with a broad smile as he recognised one of the newcomers.

'Tom, good to see you again,' he exclaimed, covering the distance between them in a few strides.

The two men shook hands warmly. Tom noticed that the preceding years hadn't been too kind to Charles. He remembered him as a stalwart man with the vitality and vigour of someone half his age. The weak, almost effeminate, handshake was that of a fragile old man, whose features were gaunt, his eyes dulled and sunken by age. The hairline had receded to his crown and deep furrows ploughed across his forehead, linking the liver spots at his temples. Despite the ravages of time, it was obvious that he still cared about his appearance. The dark blue suit was perfectly tailored to his frame, not something that could easily be achieved off-the-peg. The silk tie with its geometric pattern and pale blue shirt complemented the made-to-measure apparel, perfectly.

'Charles,' said Tom, 'I'd like to introduce you to Serena Mayer.'

'It's a pleasure to meet you, my dear.' The elderly gentleman's bony fingers reached out to take her hand. 'Come, please sit down. You must be exhausted after your long journey.' He led her to one of the two chairs opposite his and beckoned for Tom to take the other.

Jed, who was still standing in the doorway, shouted across the room. 'If you don't need me anymore boss, I'll get cracking on firing up the beast.' With that, he left without waiting for an answer.

'Damned fine physicist, bloody awful employee,' Charles remarked as his office door slammed shut. 'So, why don't you start at the beginning and tell me what all this is about,' he said, turning his attention back to his guests.

For over an hour Tom told him everything – everything that was, apart from Shiva's role in trying to stop the Collider discovering the God Particle. For some reason he couldn't explain, he felt protective over the organisation, as though he'd been let into a confidence that he couldn't betray. He concluded by summarising what he hoped to achieve by firing up the RHIC.

Charles listened intently, without interruption, his fingers steepled contemplatively underneath his chin. Once Tom had finished, Charles leant back in his chair, as if to digest the information. After what seemed like an eternity, he broke the silence.

'When you phoned me on your way here, I took the liberty of contacting some colleagues in NASA and pulled in a couple of favours. You know they have a facility here, don't you?'

Tom did. 'Yes, the NASA Space Radiation Lab.'

Charles addressed Serena, who was looking blank. 'We have a programme running that can identify the possible risks to astronauts associated with prolonged space travel. To study the effects of space radiation we use beams that can simulate cosmic rays.'

'Sounds dangerous,' she replied. 'Remind me not to volunteer as a guinea pig.'

'Quite,' Charles turned back to Tom. 'I asked them to run a simple algorithm to track magnetic north against true north, over time. As you're aware, they're not the same point – magnetic north tends to move around a bit.' He adjusted the angle of the laptop on his desk so they could see the image. It showed a global map of the earth dissected by a straight red line with various points marked on it. 'In 2001, magnetic north was determined by the Geological Survey of Canada to lie near Ellesmere Island in northern Canada. In 2009, whilst still within the Canadian Arctic territory, it was moving toward Russia at between thirty-four and thirty-seven miles per year. Last year, the pole moved just beyond the Canadian Arctic territorial claim.'

He pressed a button on the keyboard and the image changed to a similar map but, on this one, the red line had dog-legged. 'This is in real time. As of now, magnetic north is hovering somewhere over Greenland, travelling south at a rate of seventeen miles an *hour*. That means that, within the next thirty days, it will reach the South Pole.'

Tom and Serena stared at the screen, aghast. It was obvious to them that the directional change could only have been caused by the collider. In the bottom left quadrant of the display was a scrolling table with three columns. Tom read the headings: Time, Speed, Acceleration. The first column measured second intervals, the next, the actual speed of the field, while the third had a series of red numbers in it.

'Does that indicate that the field is accelerating?' Tom pointed to the last column on the screen.

'Unfortunately, yes. They change to green if the field decelerates. Since I've been monitoring it they've always been red. When I said that within the next thirty days the field will have reached the South Pole, I should have pointed out that that was at its current speed. If it carries on accelerating the way it has been, there's no telling how long it will take.'

'Can't they extrapolate the data?' Serena queried.

'Yes, but the acceleration isn't constant,' replied Charles. 'It varies by the second. The only thing we can say for certain is that the speed of the magnetic field is increasing, but by how much is anybody's guess.'

The phone rang on Charles's desk. 'Excuse me,' he said, apologising to Tom for the interruption, and picked up the receiver. He listened to the voice on the other and then responded. 'Good, send him straight in,' he said, before putting the phone back in its cradle. 'There's somebody I'd like you to meet.'

Tom and Serena turned in their chairs to see the door opening and the menacing figure of Deiter strolling in.

CHAPTER 35

Tom's jaw dropped, his face a picture of incredulity as a thousand questions flooded his brain.

'But... but how did you know we were here?' was all he could say.

Deiter strode across the room and positioned himself behind Tom and Serena, casually resting his hands on the back of each of their chairs. Serena cowered in her seat at the close proximity of the man who had tried to kill her. Tom was more defiant; he made to stand up, but was forced back down by a firm grip on his shoulder.

'I wouldn't do anything stupid.' Deiter inclined his head in the direction of Charles, who had retrieved a handgun from the top drawer of his desk and was now levelling it in their direction, his hand trembling slightly as he aimed it from one to the other.

'To answer your question,' continued Deiter, 'I followed you to the airfield and checked your flight plan. You didn't need to be a genius to work out why you were heading to MacArthur Airport. It's not exactly a main tourist destination. So I simply commandeered the other jet, and here I am. I phoned Charles when I'd landed, who confirmed that you were on your way.'

Tom's face was ashen. He turned to his old mentor. 'I don't understand, Charles. Why are you doing this? I explained what happened at CERN. You should be pointing that gun at him, not us.'

'Deiter said that you'd try to blame him,' replied Charles. 'So I checked with the Swiss police, who confirmed you're suspects in a murder enquiry, as well as being wanted for industrial sabotage. Did you really think you could just waltz in here and blow our collider up as well? If it wasn't for Deiter and the fact that I knew you as a student, I'd have called the police and had you arrested at the gate. But he pleaded with me to give you a chance to explain yourselves. You owe him a debt of gratitude that you're not in police custody right now, being deported back to Switzerland to face charges – which, if there isn't a rational explanation for your actions, is exactly where you will be going.'

Tom's mind was working overtime. He knew he would only have the one chance to convince Charles of their innocence, and it was obvious that Deiter had the upper hand with regards to the incidents at CERN. He scanned the room for inspiration.

'You have five seconds, then I'm calling the police,' Charles warned.

Tom's eyes rested on a solid brass statuette of an Indian deity on the bookshelf and took a gamble. 'Deiter's telling the truth,' he began. 'I planted the explosives at CERN, but you have to believe me when I say it was a regrettable accident that those people got killed. They were just in the wrong place at the wrong time.'

'Tom, what are you saying?'

He turned to Serena. Seeing the shocked expression on her face, he tried to sooth her by telling her that they could trust Charles with the truth, but it didn't appease her agitation.

'And why would you want to destroy the collider?' Charles enquired, his mood softening.

'Not destroy, just to stop it from discovering the God Particle.'

'Why would you want to do that?'

'For the same reasons you do… I also work for SHIVA.'

Charles lowered the gun, placing it on the desk in front of him. 'How did you know?'

'Two things, really,' replied Tom. 'Something Frederick Volker said to me when we first met. He said that you sent me your regards, so I presumed you were either discussing my suitability for the position at CERN or my role in SHIVA. The ornament confirmed the latter.' He indicated to the bookshelf on which sat a statue of Shiva in mid-dance.

'I always was a bit of a sentimentalist,' said Charles. 'I picked it up whilst on vacation in India. How is the old dog, by the way?'

'I think Deiter was the last to see him. Why don't you ask him?'

All eyes turned to Deiter, who stood impassively staring at the gun on Charles's desk. With no answer forthcoming, Tom went on to explain how they had only recently discovered that the collider was responsible for instigating a shift in the Earth's polarity, reiterating that the only way to alter such a paradigm shift was by creating an opposing force using the RHIC, hence the reason for their trip. At no point did Tom make any reference to Deiter's involvement in the whole scenario.

Charles looked from Tom to Serena as if trying to make up his mind. 'Well, you'll have to make your peace with the Swiss authorities,' he said. 'But, as far as the other matter is concerned, it doesn't look as though we've got a second to waste. I'll call Professor Campbell to see if he's ready for us.' He picked up the phone and dialled Jed's extension.

With the agility of a gazelle leaping from the jaws of a lion, Deiter sprang forward and snatched up the gun, pointing it at Charles. 'Put the phone down,' he ordered.

'You wouldn't dare,' Charles remonstrated.

Without missing a beat, Deiter shot the Director through the forehead. His body toppled forward, his head hit the desk and a pool of blood formed that expanded across its surface. The fingers of his left hand twitched and then were still, while his other hand held the phone in a death grip.

Serena shrieked and instinctively recoiled from the gruesome sight.

Tom watched Deiter as he made his way around to Charles's side of the desk, the gun levelled directly at his head. Deiter pried the phone out of the dead man's hand and replaced it in the receiver. Then he picked it up again and dialled zero for the reception.

'Sir, are you alright?' The voice on the other end of the line sounded agitated. 'We thought we heard a gunshot.'

'This is Dr Weiss. Quickly, call the police!' He disconnected the call and threw the phone down on the desk. 'I would estimate we've got about five minutes before the boys in blue come to the rescue.'

'Why did you have to shoot him?' Tom found his voice.

'He'd served his purpose. I just wanted him to keep you talking until I arrived. Besides, he's more useful to me dead than alive.'

'What do you mean?'

'Let me tell you how this is going to play out,' replied Deiter, smiling. 'You escape from the police in Switzerland and make your way here. I follow you, intending to alert the authorities of your final destination, but by the time I've landed you've already cleared customs. Realising that you're probably going to Brookhaven, in an attempt to destroy the RHIC, as you did the collider at CERN, I phoned Charles to warn him. My call to him will be logged at the switchboard, for verification purposes. When I arrive, I find that you've managed to relieve Charles of his own weapon and are holding him hostage. Charles makes a lunge for the gun and you shoot him dead. I manage to make a call to alert the authorities before you have time to stop me. You then make your way over to the door to lock it.'

Deiter acted out the plot, making his way across the room to turn the key in the lock, the gun never wavering from its two targets. 'Seeing an opportunity, I grab Serena and use her as a human shield. You take a shot, but miss.' He raised his hand and discharged the weapon, the bullet embedding itself in the wall to the left of the window behind Charles's desk. 'You fire again but, unfortunately, this time you hit Serena, fatally wounding her. Distracted by your aberration, I charge towards you. You manage to shoot another round, missing me by a whisper.' Deiter raised the gun again and put a shot through the window. Glass exploded into the room, showering Charles's lifeless body with shards. 'I throw myself on you and we struggle. The gun goes off again, but this time it is you that is killed. Then the police arrive.' He nodded to himself. 'Perfect.' A self-satisfied grin broke across his face as he assimilated the details of his game plan. 'Okay everybody, let's get into position.'

Tom and Serena sat deathly still, transfixed by the depth of insanity to which this person had sunk.

'I said move!' Deiter bellowed.

Both flinched, but neither complied. It was like asking a condemned man to put his own noose around his neck. Deiter marched over to Serena and dragged her out of her seat, the gun pressed firmly to her temple. He stood her behind the slumped body of Charles and between the two bullet holes he'd just made. He checked the angle to the door. Satisfied, he went back for Tom.

'I'm not going along with your absurd plan,' Tom said obstinately, planting himself firmly in his seat. 'You're going to kill us anyway, so why should I help you?'

'Fine, I'll kill you where you sit. It makes no difference to me.' Deiter pointed the barrel at Tom's head.

'Won't that screw up your well-rehearsed pantomime?'

Deiter thought about it for a moment. 'You're right.' He turned the gun around and brought the butt of it crashing down onto Tom's head, opening up a two-inch gash at his hairline.

Serena screamed and made to go to his aid, but Deiter held her back.

Blood gushed out of the wound on Tom's head, streamed into his eye and ran down the side of his face.

'I'll think of a way of incorporating *that* into my scenario, when you've gone,' he said, hauling Tom's dazed frame out of the chair and depositing him on the floor by the entrance to the room.

Deiter backed up to the door to inspect the crime scene and to ensure that all his players were in position. Happy with the result, he aimed the gun at Serena's face and pulled the trigger. Her head jerked to one side, blood splattered against the wall and she hit the floor like a sack of potatoes. Tom's outcry at seeing the motionless body on the floor was drowned out by the sound of the blast echoing around the room.

CHAPTER 36

The exact millisecond the bullet was about to leave the gun barrel, Deiter's arm had been involuntarily nudged up and to the left by the door crashing into his back. It was only a fraction of an inch but, over the distance the bullet had to travel, it was enough to save Serena's life.

Jed burst through the doorway, his mind taking a snapshot of the carnage before him. He saw Serena lying immobile underneath the shattered window, blood splatters on the wall, his boss, Charles, slumped over his desk, more blood, his friend on the floor in front of him, half his face covered in blood, a man hunched over him holding a smoking gun...

He launched himself forward, but the figure had regained its composure. Straightening its posture, it turned towards him, firing indiscriminately. Jed had decided that a rugby tackle would be his best option and the bullets flew innocuously over his head, lodging somewhere in the wall behind him.

He caught Deiter just above the calves, his knees buckled under the weight, bringing them both crashing heavily down to the floor next to Tom. The gun went clattering across the room.

Deiter managed to free one of his legs from the grip and lashed out, the heel of his shoe connecting with Jed's jaw. His head snapped back but he clung on, clawing his way up Deiter's torso. Another kick, this time aimed at Jed's face. It landed on the bridge of his nose, fracturing it. Blood flowed from his nostrils. Momentarily stunned, he loosened his hold on Deiter's leg, who scrambled towards the gun.

Tom tried to clear the fog that was clouding his head; he could see that Jed was no match for his opponent's superior physical fitness and knew they had to join forces if they were going to overpower him. He willed himself to stand, but the connection between his brain and his leg muscles was impaired. He staggered to his feet but was unable to keep his balance, instead wheeling drunkenly in the opposite direction that he wanted to go. He managed to make it to the desk and held on to steady himself.

Deiter knew that if he could just get to the gun he would be able to regain control of the situation. Dislodging his assailant with his second kick gave him the opportunity he needed. He could see where the gun had landed some twenty feet to his left and belly-crawled towards it. His breathing was laboured, having been winded by the impact of the tackle, but his focus remained resolutely on the weapon.

Less than two feet away, he felt a vice-like grip around his ankle. He lunged for the firearm but he was inches short, the gap widening as Jed dragged him back away from it. He twisted his body over, trying to break loose, but Jed held firm, drawing him in like a fisherman reeling in his catch. He kicked out with his free leg but failed to connect with anything solid.

The force of the blow to Jed's nose had made him see stars, but he quickly recovered his cognitive powers when he realised his adversary had broken free and was making for the gun. He shook his head to clear his thoughts further, the blood from his nose dripping liberally onto the floor. He half crawled, half slithered after the retreating form, knowing that if he didn't manage to catch up in time it would be the last thing he ever did.

He was gaining, but he could tell it wasn't going to be enough to prevent the other person reaching his objective. Risking everything, Jed got unsteadily to his feet and pounced at the flailing legs, managing to latch onto an ankle. His rival squirmed underneath his grasp like an alligator performing a death-roll, but Jed had no intention of letting go. He pulled him away from the revolver and, having studied his opponent's form, was ready for him when he lashed out with his foot, dodging the kicks with ease. He drove his fist hard into the other man's groin, promptly stopping the thrashing limb and replacing it with a low, guttural moan, followed by a whimper.

Tom pulled himself upright using the desk as a crutch; Charles's blood was now spilling over the edge. He looked beyond the body to the window where Serena lay, expecting the worst. He could see where the bullet had grazed her forehead; it looked bad, but not bad enough to be life-threatening.

He manoeuvred around the desk, almost slipping on a congealed puddle on the floor. Still a little shaky on his feet, his mind had started to clear. Kneeling down next to her, he felt for a pulse. He hadn't realised until that point that he had been holding his breath and exhaled at the relief of feeling the faint rhythmic beat on his fingertips indicating that life was coursing through her veins. Her breathing was shallow, but steady. He inspected the crease above her eye more closely; it didn't appear to be that deep and had stopped bleeding. A commotion on the other side of the room drew his attention back to the immediate threat. Unsure of who had the upper hand, he looked around for a weapon. His eyes rested on a familiar object and he gingerly made his way over towards it.

Deiter knew that he was at a disadvantage. One leg was incapacitated and he was lying on his back, like a turtle with its underbelly exposed. He was vulnerable to any attack that his advisory wanted to deliver, so it came as no surprise when he felt the searing pain in his groin; he had half expected it and, as such, had mentally prepared for it. But, to catch his opponent off-guard, he needed to make him think he had delivered a killer blow. The moan that elicited from the punch was genuine, but the whimper after it was pure theatre.

As he continued the charade, he could feel the grip on his ankle slacken and the weight transfer to both legs as the person sat astride him. Timing was the key; if he made his move too soon the other person would be in a position to counter it. He waited, eyes screwed up as if in agony, hands clutching his crotch, moaning softly to himself. He could feel the hot breath on his chin as the victor leant over to inspect his kill.

Now! He launched himself into a sitting position using the weight on his legs as leverage. His forehead connected with the already shattered cartilage that was once a nose, obliterating it. This time it was his opponent's turn to cry out. As his hands flew up to protect what was left, Deiter pushed him backward, toppling the weight off his legs.

He was on his feet in an instant, delivering a barrage of kicks to his adversary's head and torso, like a man possessed. Even when the person stopped moving, he carried on remorselessly. It was only when he himself was exhausted that he relented. He quickly retrieved the gun from where it lay and walked back to the vanquished form on the floor. He pointed it at the bloody mess of a face and cocked the trigger, hesitating only because he caught a glimpse of something out of the corner of his eye.

Tom had worked his way around the perimeter of the room using the walls to prop him up, like a novice at an ice rink. He was relieved to see his friend had the situation under control. Jed was sitting on top of Deiter, who was crying like a baby, his manhood apparently being the object of his anguish. He was about to call out to his friend, when Deiter suddenly sprang up, delivering a crushing blow to Jed's nose with his forehead.

He edged his way closer as his friend was being pummelled on the ground. He thought about calling out for Deiter to stop, but he knew that that would only put the focus on him and he was in no position to defend himself. If he was going to have any chance of saving them, he would have to disarm Deiter once and for all. He was in the shadow of the corner of the room when Deiter went to pick up the gun. Tom had the disturbing feeling from the frenzied look in the man's eyes that he wouldn't have been noticed, even if he had stood next to him. His blood was up and he only had one thing on his mind.

He saw Deiter raise his arm and prime the weapon, the gun pointing directly at Jed's head. He was under no illusion that if he didn't act now his friend would be dead in less than a second. He left the shadows and moved stealthily behind Deiter, raising the object in his hand high above his head as he did so. Deiter half turned as if sensing him coming, but it was too late; Tom brought the statue of Shiva the Destroyer crashing down onto the back of his head.

CHAPTER 37

'Looks like I saved ya sorry arse, again.' Jed had regained consciousness and was being stretchered out of the room on a gurney to a waiting ambulance.

'We both owe you our lives,' Tom replied, walking by his side. 'How did you know to come in *all guns blazing?*'

Jed winced at the pain in his ribs as he tried to laugh. 'When Charles rang me, the call connected so I heard the shot. I have to admit, my first thought was to get the hell out of Dodge as fast as I could and then phone the police.'

'Well, I'm sure as hell glad you didn't.'

The police had arrived, as Deiter predicted, within five minutes of being called. They, in turn, had alerted the medics on the complex who were able to stabilise the injured before ferrying them to the local hospital in the only ambulance they had available. Serena, who they deemed the most seriously hurt, was the first to go, followed by Deiter accompanied by two deputies, and then Jed, who insisted he'd been in worse fights.

'Out on the piss on a Saturday night, in Glasgow,' he'd said, apparently referring to when he was younger. Tom didn't doubt this.

One look at the state of the room had convinced the on-site police officer that it was way out of his league and had called in reinforcements from the Suffolk County Sheriff's Department. They arrived en masse; clearly, nothing as juicy as this had happened in their jurisdiction for a very long time, if at all.

Statements were taken from those able to give them – which, as the only two still conscious at the scene of the crime, meant principally Tom and Jed. Receptionists and security guards were interviewed; however, as they'd had only limited contact with those involved, they were only able to confirm arrival times and calls transferred.

A forensic team was duly called in to dust for fingerprints and to take DNA samples. The murder weapon was 'bagged and tagged', as one of the Sherriff's Deputies put it, along with the statuette. Photographs were taken of everything from every conceivable angle, including Charles's body. He was the last of the whole shooting match to leave the office, his journey to the hospital being considered not as urgent as the others.

The Sheriff in charge of the investigation was in his late fifties. Having completed twenty-four of his twenty-five years in service, he was looking forward to retiring next year. He was a rather rotund man with a snow-white thatch and matching facial hair, making him look like Colonel Sanders on a diet of too much of his own Southern fried recipe.

Sheriff Pete Watkins told Tom that he was obliged to call in the FBI, as was de rigueur in murder cases involving a foreign national. However, he would postpone the call until after he'd had a chance to interview the prime suspect – and, given the condition Deiter was in, that could be several days away. Tom suspected the Sheriff had his own agenda for not wanting to involve the FBI, possibly because he wanted to have the case sewn-up by the time the suits arrived, or he didn't appreciate external agencies trampling on his turf. Either way, it suited Tom, as the last thing *he* needed was anybody making the connection back to the Swiss authorities.

'How's Serena?' Jed asked.

'The medics say she's stable,' replied Tom. 'But they won't know for sure if there's any brain damage until she regains consciousness.'

'You must have really pissed that guy off back at CERN?'

'I gave you the condensed version on the way here. Why don't I save the rest of it until you're feeling better, then I'll tell you all about it over a couple of beers?'

'A couple? Ya wee shite, I think I deserve the barrel.'

Tom laughed, despite the excruciating pain in his head. 'You've got it, big man. The whole barrel.'

They had arrived at the waiting ambulance. Its blue strobe lights melded with those from the dozen or so police cars in the car park, illuminating the buildings and the faces of the crowd that had gathered out of curiosity in a monochromatic light show. The two orderlies collapsed the gurney's framework, lifted Jed onto the ambulance and then expanded it again, ensuring the wheels were locked in place. Tom clambered in afterwards, taking a seat on the chair opposite.

***

Despite Jed's protestations, they were rushed through to A & E, where they received immediate attention. The buzz going around the hospital was that a crazed gunman had gone berserk at the lab up the road, killing one and injuring at least three others. They weren't that far off the mark.

Tom received six stitches to his head wound, had an X-ray, which was clear, and had to stay in overnight for observation.

Jed had X-rays followed by a CT scan. Miraculously, all his vital organs were undamaged, apart from his liver, which was in poor shape; however, *that* was put down to years of self-abuse rather than anything he'd sustained in the fight. He had severe bruising to his arms, legs and torso, two black eyes, as well as several fractures to his nose, in addition to three cracked ribs which, the doctor informed him, should heal by themselves in six to eight weeks.

The nose was a different matter; it would require extensive rhinoplasty surgery to rebuild and straighten it. However, he was assured that, over time, they would be able to give him his old profile back. He was also advised to stay in overnight for observation; but, as soon as his ribs were taped up, he took one look in the mirror, tweaked his nose into some form of shape and discharged himself.

***

Tom had been allocated a gown and a bed in a private room, but he was desperate to see how Serena was. He had ascertained from his nurse that she had regained consciousness. The brain scans showed no significant damage, but she had mild concussion.

He threw back the covers and made his way to the door. He was still a little woozy and his head hurt like hell; it felt like the worst morning hangover of his life without having had the enjoyment of getting it the night before. As he made his way down the corridor, he noticed two docile deputies, lounging on either side of a closed door. Their alertness piqued when they saw him approaching.

'Shouldn't you be resting, Professor Halligan?' the younger of the two enquired, rising out of his seat and moving to block the door they were guarding.

'I'm just checking on my friend. Do you know where she is?'

'Miss Mayer? She's in the room at the end, but I heard the doctors saying she shouldn't be disturbed.'

'I'm sure they wouldn't mind if I just popped my head in.'

He continued on his way before they had a chance to object. It was an alien feeling to him, being uncomfortable around the police. He half expected one of them to say, *'Hey, aren't you wanted by Interpol?'*

He stopped outside Serena's door and knocked softly. Hearing no reply, he went in. She was propped up in bed, bolstered by some over-sized pillows. Her eyes were closed. A catheter ran from her arm into a transparent bag containing a clear fluid, suspended above her head. On the index finger of her left hand was a clip connected by wires to a heart rate monitor. As Tom approached the bed, he could see the visual representation of her heart beating on the screen. He was mesmerised by the green line pulsating its steady rhythm.

'Will I live?' Serena asked groggily, opening her eyes when she heard Tom approach her.

Tom smiled, leant over and kissed the bandage on her forehead, being careful to avoid the site where the bullet had struck. 'My prognosis is that you'll live to a ripe old age, but you certainly had us all worried for a while.'

She reached up and tenderly touched the dressing above Tom's eye. 'And you?'

'A few stitches and a scar that I'll be able to bore the pants off explaining how I got it to anybody stupid enough to ask.'

She paused for a moment, trying to organise her thoughts. 'What about Deiter?'

He told her how Jed had burst into the office and tackled him to the ground, effectively saving their lives. How Jed and Deiter had fought over the gun and how he had managed to sneak up and knock Deiter out.

Her face clouded as the memories slotted into place. 'Poor Charles,' she said almost to herself.

'Deiter's under armed arrest. It looks like he won't be going anywhere for a very long time,' Tom replied, in an effort to comfort her, but her melancholy persisted. 'What's with the drip?' he said, to change the subject.

'Painkillers, antibiotics and saline solution,' she replied faintly. 'Apparently, I'm dehydrated.'

'Any idea how long they're going to keep you in?' He was trying to keep her mind off the images of Charles slumped over his desk, which he knew must be haunting her, as it did him.

'The doctors were a bit vague, but they said they wanted to keep me awake overnight so they could monitor my concussion. Any suggestions on how I can do that?'

'A few, but none that would be appropriate, given your condition.'

'Try me.' Her hand reached out and gently stroked his cheek. He bent forward and kissed her full on the lips.

Just then, the door suddenly flew open and in pitched the deputy he'd spoken to earlier, his right hand brandishing his gun, his left clutching at a patch of blood that was spreading across his abdomen. Tom could see the hilt of a scalpel poking out through his fingers.

'Stay in your room,' the man managed to gasp. 'I've called for support.'

'What's happened?' Tom asked, alarmed. But before the deputy had a chance to reply, Tom already knew the answer.

'He's escaped...'

CHAPTER 38

Jed had made his way directly from the hospital to his favourite drinking hole, where he knew he'd get the type of solace he was looking for.

'What the hell happened to you?' was the greeting he'd received from Cherie as he walked into the bar. 'You look like you've been hit by a truck.'

'Ya should see the state of the other fellah,' was his response.

He was already on his fourth pint of Steel Reserve High Gravity Lager, when Cherie shouted across the bar to him that he had a phone call from a colleague who wouldn't give his name. Puzzled, he reluctantly left his drink and slid off the stool, wincing at the pain, the anaesthetic qualities of the lager not yet having worked their magic. In the ten years he'd been coming to Stars 'N' Bars, not once had he divulged his recreational whereabouts to anyone, not least the people he worked with. He made his way over to the waitress, who was impatiently holding the phone out for him.

'Aye,' he said into the phone, annoyed that he'd had to leave the second love of his life on the bar getting warm.

'Jed? It's Tom.' A note of urgency was evident in his voice.

'Tom, ya wee shite. How did ya know I was here?'

'Trust me, Jed. It wasn't difficult to work out. Sorry I didn't give the barmaid my name, I'm getting a little paranoid in my old age.'

Tom then told him how Deiter had stabbed one of the deputies before disarming the other one. He'd then taken a doctor hostage with the deputy's gun and used him as a human shield whilst he made his escape, shooting him dead once they were off the hospital premises.

'The Sheriff's adamant that he's going to flee the country,' he continued. 'He says in his experience *that's what they always do*. Probably head to Canada first before boarding a flight to Europe. He's deployed most of his men to search for him between here and the border.'

'Let me guess,' replied Jed. 'You're not so convinced.'

'No,' Tom said resignedly. 'Knowing Deiter, he's going to head for Brookhaven and try to destroy the collider. It's the only way he can stop us from slowing down the field. Can you meet me at the facility? We need to get the collider up and running before Deiter has a chance of sabotaging it.'

Jed looked longingly across the bar at his pint. 'Aye, she'll jest have to wait for me,' he replied, as if to himself. 'I'll see ya there in two shakes of a lamb's tale.'

***

Jed was already in the control room by the time Tom arrived, having made a detour via Charles's office. He got an eerie feeling crossing the police barricade tape and seeing the room where he could quite easily have lost his life. He didn't want to spend any more time there than was necessary; so, being as there were no police guards present, he hastily retrieved the laptop from the desk, tucked it under his arm and scurried out of the door.

The distinct lack of police presence around the campus worried him. He had tried again to convince the Sheriff of Deiter's mission, but had been condescendingly put in his place by the insularity of the officer.

'Stick to what you know best, son, and I'll do the same,' the Sheriff had said. He had conceded to increase the frequency of patrol cars passing the facility, but that was as far as it went.

'How's Serena?' Jed asked, as the two men sat side by side.

'She's fine. They're keeping her in overnight for observation.'

'Any more luck with Deputy Dawg?'

'If I'm right about Deiter,' replied Tom, 'we're pretty much on our own.'

'We'd better get this show on the road then,' said Jed, turning to face the computer screen in front of him. 'I managed to get the beams calibrated and aligned this afternoon before our run-in with Doctor Death. So all we have to do is start up the primary particle accelerators, wait until they're up to speed, then release the beams.'

Tom knew from his time at CERN that it took at least twenty technicians to run a full experiment, but that was mainly down to the four monitoring stations equispaced around the ring, each of which had to have its own team to ensure their equipment was functioning properly and to analyse the results. All Tom was interested in was running the collider to its maximum potential for as long as possible to generate the strongest magnetic field it was capable of producing. *That* would normally require at least four people to ensure safety limits were being adhered to; today however, they would have to manage with just the two of them.

'How long do you think we'll be able to run the collider for?' Tom enquired.

'The thermal shields are effective for about ten hours,' replied Jed. 'After that, the collider reaches critical temperature and the system automatically shuts down, dumping the beam's energy.'

Whilst Jed went through the initialisation sequence, Tom powered up the laptop he had retrieved from Charles's office. He found the programme he was looking for – aptly named *'Armageddon'*, presumably by some smart alec at NASA, and opened it up. The red line that they had seen earlier had continued its steady progression south, but had increased its speed; it was now travelling at thirty miles per hour. Tom did a quick mental calculation: seventeen days until total polar reversal. He checked the figures in the last column; over the last twenty-four hours, there had been a continuous acceleration.

'Primary particle accelerators activated,' said Jed.

The notification drew Tom's attention back to the schematics Jed was studying on the screen in front of him.

'Seventy… eighty… ninety… one hundred per cent. Primary accelerators at maximum capacity. Releasing the beams now.'

Jed keyed in an instruction on the console and the image changed from a diagram of the collider to a series of scrolling numbers. 'That's odd.'

Tom could tell by the intensity on Jed's face that something wasn't quite right. 'What is it?'

Jed pointed to a column of figures that were increasing in value. 'That's the temperature generated by the collider. I wouldn't have expected to see anything like those values until nearer the end of the run.' He pressed some more buttons on the keyboard and the screen changed again, this time to a line-graph showing an upward trend. 'Looks like we've got a wee gremlin in the system.'

'What's happened?' Tom's concern was apparent in his voice.

'Somebody, mentioning no names, seems to have manually deactivated the thermal shields.'

'How's that possible?'

'There are override panels dotted around the length of the tunnel. Maintenance use them all the time whenever they're working on a section. I should have checked they were fully operational before releasing the beam. That's the protocol. Sorry.'

Tom was at odds with Jed's calm demeanour. 'What are we going to do about it?'

'Nothing,' replied Jed. 'Without the heat shields, the system will reach critical temperature in a matter of minutes and the failsafe will kick in. Then we'll have to find out which panel that bastard has pressed and reactivate it. It's an inconvenience and a waste of our time, but nothing more. The problem is, if he keeps doing it we'll never be able to operate the collider long enough to generate a magnetic field. We'll have to find him. Why don't you call our friendly local Sheriff and ask him to send his boys round?'

Tom placed the call and told the Sheriff what had just occurred. At first he was sceptical, but eventually agreed to send in a posse to search the tunnel for any signs of Deiter. When Tom had finished, he put the phone down and turned to his friend. Jed's face was ashen.

'Houston, we may have a problem.'

CHAPTER 39

The core temperature had already reached the point at which an automatic shut-down should have occurred and was still rising.

'Why hasn't the fail-safe triggered?' Tom asked anxiously.

'Ya cunning bastard,' Jed said to himself and then looked at Tom. 'Looks like our wee gremlin has also been buggering around with the fast kicker magnets.'

Tom recognised the terms, but couldn't place their significance.

'They redirect the beam into the dumping tunnel,' Jed explained.

Tom remembered from his days as a student: the beams themselves are made up of two hundred and eighty trillion protons squeezed into a stream much thinner than a human hair. Each hair-thin beam of protons that races around the collider contains as much energy as an express train going at over two hundred kilometres an hour. During any one cycle, there would be thousands of these, smashing head-long into each other. When it is time to shut the machine down, that energy, which is so concentrated that it could liquefy anything directly in its path, must be safely disposed of.

The fast kicker magnets deflect the beam into a straight, six hundred metres long, tunnel that runs at a tangent to the collider. Like throwing the points on a rail track, it directs the beam from its circular path into a siding. Once inside the tunnel, other magnets cause the beam to spread vertically and horizontally so that, when it hits the dump, its destructive energy is dissipated over a larger area. At the end of the tunnel is a cylinder of graphite composite, eight metres long and one metre in diameter, encased in steel and concrete, which is designed to absorb the beam's energy. The beams smash into their target with the sound of one hundred and fifty kilograms of TNT exploding.

'So, what happens now?' Tom asked.

'If we can't dump the beam, then the system won't shut down,' Jed replied.

'And if that happens?'

'The temperature within the core continues to rise, until... boom! We create our own personal black hole, right here on Long Island.'

'So what do you suggest?'

'We need to realign the magnets so we can dump the beam. But somebody needs to stay here to monitor the system.'

'Okay, you stay here and I'll sort out the magnets,' Tom volunteered.

'No way, wee man,' replied Jed. 'That nutter's still on the loose. I'll have more of a chance against him than you.'

'Look,' said Tom beginning to lose patience, 'we could debate this all night, but the fact is we're running out of time...' As if on cue, an alarm bell sounded. 'You know the system better than I do, so you should stay,' Tom shouted over the top of the ringing.

Seeing the logic in Tom's argument, Jed reluctantly agreed and fished the electronic pass key out of his pocket.

'The magnets are located at the entrance to the dump tunnel, Sector 4H,' Jed shouted in reply. 'You'll need to gain access to the tunnel via the inspection chamber. Once you're in, set the computer coordinates to thirty degrees, then get the hell out. You'll have three minutes before the system resets and dumps the beam – and, believe me, you won't want to be on that station when the train passes through.'

'Got it, 4H,' Tom replied. He took the pass from Jed and headed for the door.

'And watch out for that feckin nutter,' Jed shouted after him, but he had already gone.

***

He made his way cautiously into the service tunnel that ran concentric to the collider, his faculties on high alert. If Deiter had any sense, he would have set the collider to self-destruct, then escape to the border as the Sheriff predicted. But Tom knew that Deiter wasn't the sensible type; his obsession to stop them slowing the polar reversal down overrode any cognitive reasoning.

He climbed into one of the golf carts used by the maintenance crew and set off in the direction of the dump tunnel. He had a vague recollection from his student days at the complex where it was located, but the signage was so clear it didn't take him long to find it.

The vacuousness of the deserted service tunnel belied the crisis that was unfolding in the accelerator ring just feet away from him. The alarm bells had been silenced, but he knew that that was no indication of a catastrophe being averted; they had probably just got on Jed's nerves.

Through the reinforced concrete and steel walls, Tom could hear the beams circulating at almost the speed of light, completing over twelve thousand laps every second. It sounded like a cross between an angry nest of hornets and a light aircraft taking off.

He parked up at the spur that doglegged out of the main structure. The proliferation of warning signs confirmed that he was in the right place: Danger, Radiation Risk, High Temperature, Electromagnetic Radiation, Wear Protective Clothing. The last one made him smile: Mind your head.

His hearing was tuned in to detect any sound that would indicate he wasn't alone; but, apart from the drone of the beams, his sensors didn't pick anything else up. *Perhaps he had misjudged Deiter? Perhaps he had valued his own life above the satisfaction of personally overseeing his plans come to fruition, after all?*

Tom retrieved the pass key from his pocket and swiped it in the electronic lock; it was similar to the ones used by most hotels to allow guests access to their rooms. The red light remained on, unblinking. He tried again. Nothing. He was about to try a third time when he noticed the panel on the front of the lock was cracked. He pulled at it and it came off in his hand, revealing a circuit board underneath. A wire had been hastily attached from one part of it to another with chewing gum. He removed the makeshift modification, replaced the cover and tried again. The light flicked from red to green, followed by a resounding clunk as the door unlocked.

He stepped over the threshold and found himself in a small, brightly-lit chamber. The fast kicker magnets that diverted the beam were located in the collider ring itself, which was separated from the ante-room, in which Tom stood, by a set of steel doors two feet thick. A similar pair of doors was located to his right, which would simultaneously open to allow the passage of the beam into the dump tunnel.

In the centre of the room was a metallic silver podium, similar to the lecterns Tom had used onstage when addressing a large group of students or visiting dignitaries in one of the auditoriums back at MIT. On top of it sat a control panel and screen.

He made his way over to it. Initially, his heart sank when he noticed the bullet holes that peppered the screen; but, as he got closer, his despondency faded. Behind the spider-web of cracks emanating from the holes he could see a faint image, disjointed as it was, where the schematics of the collider ring and dump tunnel could still be made out.

Sweat peppering his top lip, he keyed in the word *'elevation'* as an instruction and the screen changed to display a set of figures; the elevation of the fast kicker magnets was set to zero degrees. He let out a sigh of relief; everything seemed to be functioning properly. A few more keystrokes and he had changed the angle to thirty degrees as instructed by Jed.

Pressing the *'enter'* key took him to another set of instructions: *'operate, Y or N'*. His finger trembled as he pressed the affirmative key. Immediately, he heard the distinct hum of an electric motor starting up, above the sound of the beams. The screen changed yet again to a diagram depicting the magnets being tilted to the programmed angle. It took several seconds to complete the procedure, after which the screen changed a final time to show a digital clock, its luminous green digits counting down from one hundred and eighty in second intervals: his three-minute warning to evacuate the chamber.

He hastily turned to leave, but his passage out of the room was blocked by a figure standing in the doorway – Deiter. The gun he'd taken from the deputy at the hospital was pointed directly at Tom's chest. He had been so engrossed in trying to get the magnets to operate that he hadn't heard him sneak up. Tom wondered how long he'd been standing there. His intuition had been right the first time; Deiter was going to see this through to the bitter end, even if it meant he would lose his own life in the process.

'I have to admire your tenacity, Professor Halligan,' he said. 'But it takes a better man to realise when his actions are futile.'

It was obvious to Tom that Deiter believed he'd disabled the control panel permanently.

'I've finally reached that conclusion,' replied Tom. 'Looks like you've won.'

The gloating expression on Deiter's face said it all. 'No hard feelings, I hope?'

Tom looked at the gun in Deiter's grip, trying to judge whether he could surmount the three-foot gap between them and disarm him before he had a chance to discharge the weapon. It was possibly suicidal; but then again, what option did he have left? He glanced back at the display; its numbers indicated that a third of the time had already been used up.

Deiter noticed the gesture and looked past Tom's shoulder. 'What have you done?' he bellowed. 'Move away from the controls.' Deiter waved the gun in the direction he wanted Tom to go.

That was all the distraction Tom needed. He closed the distance between them in a single stride and lunged for the gun. Gripping Deiter's wrist, he pushed his arm upwards so the muzzle pointed innocuously at the ceiling and held on. Deiter reacted by trying to bring it down so he could get a clear shot at Tom. The two men's strengths were equally matched as they strained, while the gun's aim was balanced somewhere between each of their objectives, just above Tom's head.

As Deiter reached up with his other hand to reinforce his grip, he exposed his flank. Tom wasted no time in delivering a well-trained body blow to Deiter's ribs. The air was forced out of Deiter's lungs and he slackened his hold on the gun, giving the advantage to Tom.

But Deiter wasn't playing by the Queensbury Rules; he took a step back and launched a kick in the direction of Tom's groin. The foot landed at the top of Tom's thigh, missing his vital parts by inches. However, the force of the blow knocked him off-balance and he went careering into the podium in the centre of the room, dropping the gun in the process.

Deiter made a move for it, but Tom quickly regained his composure and landed an uppercut on his opponent's jaw as he bent down to pick up the gun. Deiter reeled backwards. However, as Tom made for the gun, Deiter kicked out, his foot failing to make contact but forcing Tom to take a step back, empty-handed.

They circled the weapon, their eyes locked, never wavering, like two male lions fighting over a kill. Deiter broke rank and darted for the gun, but Tom sprang forward and hit him on the shoulder before he had a chance to grab it. Closer now, they traded blows, each giving as good as he got. Deiter's nose was bloodied and the stitched cut above Tom's eye had opened up.

Exhausted, their punches were becoming less effective. Tom threw a right cross at Deiter, who blocked it easily and parried it with a jab to Tom's stomach. Winded, Tom let down his guard. Deiter seized the opportunity and went for Tom's throat, clasping both hands around his neck. He tried to squeeze the life out of him, but Tom still had some reserves left.

Reaching up, he clawed at Deiter's face, managing to hook his fingers in the fleshy part at the corner of his mouth. He pulled down with as much strength as he had left, ripping a tear an inch long in the other man's cheek. Crying out in agony, Deiter released his strangle-hold and took a step back, blood gushing freely from his extended smile. Tom took a second to catch his breath as Deiter tried to stem the flow.

They were about to go for round two when the siren went, distracting them both. The huge, stainless steel doors behind and to the left of Deiter started to open. Tom, being the closest to the exit, made a run for it, while Deiter went for the weapon. He picked up the gun and aimed it at the centre of Tom's back. His fingers tightened around the trigger, but he was unable to drop the hammer as a beam of super-charged energy bore through his torso, cauterising the blood vessels instantaneously and leaving a perfectly formed hole the size of a grapefruit.

As Tom made it to the doorway, the stench of burning flesh caught in his throat making him look back at Deiter, who was staring with incredulity at the void in his chest. Tom wanted to avert his eyes, but he was transfixed. As Deiter sank to his knees, the beam travelled up his back towards his head, vaporising skin and bone. Tom already knew that the image, so vividly emblazoned in his mind, would haunt him for the rest of his life.

CHAPTER 40

It was just after two in the morning when the Sherriff's posse arrived to search the tunnels. Tom explained to them what had just taken place. With a successful beam dump and system shut-down, a Coroner was called who pronounced Deiter dead at the scene – a surprise to no one, given the horrific injuries. What was left of his decapitated body was taken away and deposited at the County morgue.

Tom had made use of the extra man-power to search for the override panel that Deiter had tripped, to deactivate the thermal shields. By 4 am, the officers had found the breaker, reset it and then decamped to their homes for a well-deserved rest, leaving Jed and Tom alone in the control room to restart the collider.

The effects of the adrenalin rush that Tom had experienced during the fight were wearing off, leaving him tired and drained. What was more, he could feel the site of every punch and kick where Deiter had struck his body over the last twenty-four hours. He had patched himself up as best he could using a first aid box and a mirror in the washroom, but his face looked as though it had gone ten rounds with Mike Tyson. The cut above his eye would need re-stitching; however, for the time being, it would have to make do with a temporary dressing held in place with sticking plasters.

'Ya look like shite. Are ya sure ya can carry on?' Jed asked, troubled by his friend's appearance.

'I'm fine,' replied Tom. 'Besides, I don't think I've got much choice. Somebody has to make sure you don't overlook anything this time.' Tom was referring to Jed's oversight at not checking whether the thermal shields were activated the last time they ran the collider.

'Bollocks!' was Jed's only response.

'Now boys, play nicely!'

They both turned in their chairs at the sound of Serena's voice.

'Serena, what are you doing here? Have they discharged you?' Tom got up to give her his seat.

'Not exactly,' she replied. 'I discharged myself. I overheard the nurses talking about the fugitive who had murdered their doctor – they said he'd been cornered here. Apparently, there'd been a shootout and he'd been killed. So I came to see if you two were alright and if you needed any help. And, by the look of your face, Tom, it's a good job I did.'

'You could have just phoned,' Tom said reproachfully, concerned for her well-being.

'And would you have told me the truth?' Serena gave him a knowing look.

'Well... probably not,' Tom had to admit.

'So, now I'm here, what do you want me to do?' The determination in her voice put an end to any thoughts Tom may have had about persuading her to go back to the hospital.

Acquiescing, Tom grabbed a spare chair and pulled it up to join the other two. 'Okay, Jed and I will operate the collider, while you monitor any changes in direction or speed of magnetic north. We're looking for a decrease in acceleration.' He pointed to the last column of figures displayed in the table on the laptop. 'If you see an increase, let us know immediately and we'll shut the system down.'

'Then what do we do?' Serena asked.

'Pray and head for higher ground. Ideally where there are no volcanoes,' he smiled ruefully. 'But I'm sure *that* won't be necessary,' he added optimistically, in an attempt to bolster everybody's spirits, but neither of his two colleagues were convinced.

***

Four hours into the collider's operation and they were gradually joined by a stream of technicians just starting their day. Word was going around the complex about what they were trying to achieve, drawing a small crowd that formed in a semi-circle behind the three seated individuals. Within the hour the room was packed, spilling out into the corridors, the latecomers being informed of any changes by the people who could see the gigantic image on the wall, projected from Serena's laptop. Jed had had to set up the connection in response to the 'How's it going?' question invariably asked by new arrivals.

The simple answer was that it wasn't going anywhere. The collider was running at its maximum capacity within the safety parameters dictated by the thermal shields, but it didn't seem to be having an effect on the geomagnetic field, which was still accelerating in a southerly direction.

'Jed, we need more power,' Tom instructed.

'I'm giving it all she's got, Captain,' Jed replied in a strong, virtually indecipherable Scottish accent.

'Sorry?' Tom said, a little taken aback.

'Ah, you're obviously not a Trekkie,' Jed responded, rather embarrassed.

'*Trekkie?*'

'*Star Trek*,' Jed clarified.

'Sorry, I've never watched it.'

'Feck me, you call yourself a man of science and you've never seen *Star Trek*!' Jed tut-tutted whilst shaking his head.

'…and the power?' Tom prompted.

'If I increase the power, the system will reach critical temperature sooner and will shut down prematurely,' Jed explained.

'It might be worth the risk. A short, intense blast of electromagnetic radiation might have more of an effect than a sustained weaker field.'

'Aye, Aye Captain,' replied Jed. 'Switching to warp speed.'

'More *Star Trek*?' Tom ventured.

Jed just smiled and turned back to the control panel, keying in a new set of instructions which increased the speed of the beams circulating the collider. He flicked to a new screen that showed a corresponding rise in the core temperature. He split the screen and had the two sets of figures running side by side. He raised the power further. An increase in beam velocity was followed by an incremental rise in temperature.

'At this speed, I reckon we've got fifteen minutes before the failsafe kicks in and the system shuts down,' Jed advised.

'Any change in the field's acceleration?' Tom asked Serena.

'No, it's still the same.'

'Can you increase the power anymore?'

'Marginally, but the running time will be reduced,' Jed replied.

'Do it!' Tom directed.

As Jed returned his attention to the control panel, Tom looked up at the image from the laptop projected onto the wall in front of him, willing the red line to slow down.

'Five minutes to shut-down,' Jed announced.

The red line seemed stationary, but the scrolling numeric values indicated otherwise. It was still accelerating.

'Four minutes,' Jed continued.

Still no change.

'Three minutes.'

Tom studied the acceleration figures in the last column of the table. *Had he discerned a slight variance?*

'Two minutes.'

Yes, it was definitely there. He stood up to get a better view; his focus never wavered, shutting out everything around him apart from the scrolling figures on the wall.

'One minute.'

The values were diminishing. It still meant the field was accelerating, but not by as much.

'Thirty seconds.'

The figures continued to fall towards zero. Someone at the back of the room shouted out that it was stopping; he was silenced by a hundred pairs of eyes turning in his direction, willing him to be quiet, as if his outburst would change the outcome.

'Ten seconds.'

And then the first green value appeared on the screen, signifying that the field was actually slowing down, followed by another and then another.

'Beam dump initiated.'

Tom stood staring at the wall in front of him, transfixed by the scrolling green numbers. He couldn't believe what he was seeing. *Had it worked? Had they really managed to slow the geomagnetic field down?*

The spontaneous cheer from the crowd filling his ears seemed to be all the confirmation he needed, as the room erupted in a jubilant uproar, bringing him back to his senses. Serena was ecstatic by his side, jumping up and down with a huge grin on her face. She flung her arms around his neck and continued her jig. Jed, not prone to outbursts of emotion, was similarly animated; he had grabbed the nearest person to him, an elderly woman with thick glasses and a tight bob, and was swinging her off her feet. She seemed to be enjoying it. He put her down and went over to Tom, slapping him on the back.

'You did it, wee man. You bloody well did it!'

'*We* did it,' Tom corrected. '*We* did it.'

EPILOGUE

'When did the doctors say he'll be allowed to go home?'

Tom and Serena were standing on one side of Ajay's bed. Frederick, looking suddenly older than his years, was on the other. The patient had lost interest in the conversation and had tuned into a comedy programme on the TV.

'In a few more days,' Frederick replied. 'The bullet lodged in his rib cage. He was lucky it was a ricochet and didn't have the full force to penetrate his lungs. Otherwise, we may be looking at a different scenario.'

It had been two weeks since Tom, Jed and Serena had fired up the collider at Brookhaven, effectively stopping magnetic north's transition south. It had localised just off the coast of Greenland, which meant that most of Northern Europe would have to navigate using a compass pointing to magnetic west, whilst those in Canada had magnetic east as a guide. The rest of the world would just have to rely on Satellite Navigation and GPS for their bearings, which was no great hardship to anybody apart from a few million boy scouts.

The natural disasters had all but petered out. There were a few rumblings from some active volcanoes, but nothing that would make the headlines.

Flying back into Geneva, Tom and Serena had expected a welcoming committee consisting of Interpol, the local police and even the Swiss Army; but, as they passed through customs into the arrivals hall, the only person waiting for them was Frederick. He had explained, on the way to the hospital to see Ajay, that Gervaux and Lavelle had cornered Deiter's henchmen, who had then given themselves up without a fight. What was more, once they had started to talk they couldn't shut them up; they spilled the beans on all Deiter's activities. By the end of their confessions, they had implicated their boss in the death of Professor Morantz, the explosion that killed the maintenance workers and the attempted murder of Frederick, Ajay, Serena and Tom.

Liaising with Sherriff Watkins, in Suffolk County, Gervaux had concluded the case, dropping all charges pertaining to everyone apart from Dr Deiter Weiss and his mercenaries.

'So, the Inspector believed Deiter's thugs when they told him that he was responsible for everything?' Tom asked.

Frederick gave him a sly look. 'I'd already had a word with the Police Commissioner.'

'You know him well?' Tom queried.

Frederick gave a short laugh. 'Let's just say SHIVA has many fingers in many pies, to borrow one of your expressions.'

Tom knew not to push the topic any further, so changed the subject. 'So what are you going to do now, Frederick?'

'That all really depends on you, Tom. What are *your* plans?' the older man countered.

'As of an hour ago, the only plans I was making were to stay out of prison, so I haven't really had much of a chance to think about it. But I will say that I have been offered a position at Brookhaven – Charles's old job.'

'Do you think you'll take it?' Frederick pushed.

'Probably,' Tom conceded. 'I don't think the Swiss air is all that good for me.'

Tom could see Frederick looking at Serena. He realised he'd been a bit tactless, as he hadn't discussed any of this with her. He didn't see the point if he was going to spend the next thirty years in a Swiss gaol. He turned to her now.

'I will, of course, need someone to manage all the statistical data that we generate from any new projects I instigate.'

'Ha!' she said in mock indignation. 'Make it a directorship and I may just think about it.'

Their banter was interrupted by Ajay, who had sat bolt upright and appeared to be having a fit.

'Sh… Sh… Sh…' was all he could manage.

They followed his eyes to the TV screen to see a news bulletin breaking. The reporter was broadcasting live from Yellowstone National Park. In the background was what looked like a huge domed mountain, several hundred feet high and at least a mile in diameter. As the footage switched to an aerial view from a circling helicopter, the top of it exploded, throwing millions of tonnes of rock and ash into the air, in an incandescent display of force. The picture went black, transmission lost.

'Sh… Shiva,' Ajay finally managed to say.

The End

Printed in Great Britain
by Amazon.co.uk, Ltd.,
Marston Gate.